THE DEVIL IN
HER HEART

THE DEVIL IN HER HEART

Copyright © 2014 by Lauren Parks

Published by
> **Blue Starling Publishing,** LLC
> 303 Shaftesbury LN, Summerville SC 29485
> BluestarlingpublishingLLC@gmail.com

Cover design by Lauren Parks.

ISBN: 978-0-692-28916-7

To my incredible husband, Fields

To my amazing editor, Chris English

To my wonderful friend, Vanessa Kerns

*I wouldn't have been able to finish
this book without your support.*

To my incredible husband, Fields

To my amazing editor, Chris English

To my wonderful friend, Vanessa Kerns

*I wouldn't have been able to finish
this book without your support.*

THE DEVIL IN HER HEART

Elle Charles

BLUE STARLING PUBLISHING, LLC

"I love you as certain dark things are to be loved, in secret, between the shadow and the soul."
- Pablo Neruda

Deep down, I had always believed that there were supernatural things in the world. I'm not a religious person, but now that I'm thinking about it, I wish I were. But would God have even accepted an abomination like me if I asked? Surely not. There must not be a place in heaven for demons and monsters.

In the beginning it had been so much fun, realizing I was different. Isn't it ingrained in us as children to want to be supernatural or have magical powers? For me, it wasn't just a childish daydream anymore. It was reality, but it wasn't very pretty.

All I could see were bodies hanging, seeming to go on for miles and miles. And blood. So much blood. I covered my face, trying not to see the bodies hanging before me. Someone was screaming...and I realized it was me.

One

I stifled an exasperated sigh when we pulled up into a gravel parking lot off Highway 17.

"I'm so excited!" one of my sister's friends, Maggie I think her name was, practically screamed in my ear. "And a little nervous," she added sheepishly.

"This lady better not tell me that me and Scott are going to divorce in a year, or I'll seriously be pissed!" my sister said dramatically, turning in her seat so she could look at her friends in the back, all while holding her bachelorette crown in place.

Jessie is technically my half sister, but I never call her that. It seems wrong to refer to her as my half sister as though I consider her less than the real thing. I never liked telling people anyway, because the follow-up question is always, "Well, who's your dad, then?" Since I don't know who my father is and neither does my mom, that conversation always ends in awkward silence. When I was born, Bruce, my mother's on-and-off boyfriend, was there, ready to assume the responsibility of dad even though I wasn't his. They each recall the story a little differently, but one thing Bruce and my mom can completely agree on when it comes to their early years is that when I was born, everything changed. When Bruce held me for the first time in that hospital in Charleston, South Carolina, eyes brimming with tears, my mom knew that he was the one for her. No one else would ever compare. I whole-heartedly agree with that. Even though I am a little curious about my birth father, Bruce has always been and will always be my dad. Cara Marie Hansen, they named me.

They got married a couple months after my birth and a year later, my sister Jessie was born. Oh, what can I say about Jessie? Jessie is beautiful. She has a lot of my mom in her: blue eyes, soft features, and admired by everyone around her. Then she has Bruce's easily tanned skin, which further accentuates the paleness of her highlighted hair and blueness of her eyes. Through high school she was on top of her class, head cheerleader, and Miss Popularity. She did everything right by my parents as if it were just natural to her. She worked at Bruce's concrete company as a secretary, something I've never been interested in doing, while also attending nursing school. Now she has a career and she's getting married. So, she's basically perfect. Very, very different from me.

I, on the other hand, have never really felt beautiful, especially next to her and hell, even next to my mom! The only physical trait I've inherited that resembles either of them is light blond hair, which I usually keep at shoulder length. I didn't get my mother's oval face or soft features, but more of a square face and dramatic features. My eyes are a little too far apart to be standard pretty, and they are black. Not brown, but black. My skin is blindingly pale, and I get burned so easily I was thought to be allergic to sunlight. I'm not, but I might as well be. And living in a sunny town where human interaction revolves around going to the beach and going boating has made my social life even less existent. But what I hate most about my looks is my height. I'm six feet and skinny as a beanpole. I don't have poise and grace like some leggy girls. No, I'm just awkward and tall. I still cringe remembering middle school, where I was the tallest kid in my class, even taller than the boys. I didn't seem to develop like the other girls, but just kept on growing taller! So, there was no shortage of ammo for bullies to throw at me growing up. I don't like to complain, but it is a little depressing always being in your sister's shadow. If you can be in your sister's shadow when you're a head taller than she, that is.

I do have good things to say about myself, though. I am gifted musically, enough so that I've been able to play almost every instrument I've picked up since I was a child. Despite my family believing I was a musical child prodigy, no one besides them has ever recognized my talent. For example, I was in marching band and entered competitions with my high school, but though our school always placed high, I was one of the few to not get a music scholarship. It's not that I'm looking for everyone to pat me on the back, by any means; I just want to feel like I have a place in the world. I don't want to be my sister or have everyone's admiration. I guess I just want to know what it's like *not* being invisible.

But all things considered, I have a lot to be grateful for. I have an apartment in the city that would be enviable to most my age, which I pay for by waitressing and bartending, and I have a wonderful family. I consider my sister Jessie to be my best friend, though lately we haven't spent much time together, because she met Scott, her soon-to-be-husband. But she's happy and I'm not resentful… except for the fact that I was suckered into being the designated driver, AKA babysitter, for her bachelorette party.

"Oh, this lady is amazing! I'm sure she will say that

you and Scott will be together forever, just like we all know you will!" gushed another one of Jessie's friends. I rolled my eyes. Even though I agreed their relationship would last, I couldn't take much more booze-fueled babbling. It was almost three o' clock in the morning, and we had been out at the bars all night. Still, the torture continued and we had one last stop: a "Psychic Vision Center" in the straight-up ghetto of Charleston. *Yippee!*

I couldn't help but let out a tired sigh when we parked at our last destination. Well, our last destination before I'd be taking them all home. *Ugh, kill me.* "Here we are, girls." I had meant to sound happy or excited, but it came out as a grumble.

They all squealed, a wordless sound that pierced my ears, and hurried out of the car, practically stumbling over each other. A red neon sign in the shape of a hand hung above the small building with "Lady Sage's Psychic Readings" under it. As dark as the windows were, I would have assumed the place was closed, but for another neon sign in the window that flashed *open*. I vaguely remembered that the building had been a chiropractor's office a few years back.

"This lady is so amazing," said Michelle, the one who had dragged us here. "She told me I was about to have a new, like, change in my life and I totally got the job I wanted."

"Oh my god, that is *crazy*," said another one of Jessie's friends, a short blond that had introduced herself as Alyssa.

They all clutched each other and hobbled on their high heels as they walked toward the building, my sister adjusting the plastic crown on her head for the millionth time that night, and I resisted the urge to groan as I followed.

When we walked in, the smell of incense overwhelmed my nose and a little bell rang above our heads, singing our arrival. There was no overhead lighting, but the room was lit with countless candles flickering in every possible space, making me wonder if that was a serious fire hazard.

"Hello, my children!" A woman sang from where she

sat behind the counter, surrounded by candles. She was a heavier-set woman with a large amount of frizzy, brown hair with very visible grays throughout it. When she came around the counter, I was surprised to see that she hadn't been sitting at all; she was just very short. She looked the part of a psychic in a puffy white shirt, a cloth belt tied underneath her large breasts, and a billowing crushed velvet skirt. All she needed was a purple cloth headband and maybe some gold coins jingling from her belt and she would be the perfect gypsy psychic reader.

"I am Lady Sage, and I will be your psychic guide this evening," she said in a sing song voice, with a dramatic sweep of her hand. "Are you ladies the Hansen party?"

"Yes, yes, that's us. I'm Jessie Hansen," my sister blurted out, her words slightly jumbled together with both drunkenness and excitement.

Lady Sage gracefully kept her smile in place, though I noticed it faltered just a bit.

"Would you like us to pay now, or would you like us to wait till the end?" I chimed in.

"Payments first, my children, please," she said, beaming at me, and I think she could tell that I, at least, wasn't drunk.

"Four, all separate!" said Michelle, the one who had been here before.

Lady Sage's eyes rolled over each one of us for a second. "Not five?" There were five of us, after all.

"No," Jessie said, rolling her eyes. "My sister *doesn't want a reading*." The last part she said very uncivilly.

"I am fine," I said quickly. *Just get me into my bed, please*, I thought.

"Are you sure?" Lady Sage asked.

"I'm OK," I said. If all else fails, use different wording. I didn't believe in psychic mumbo jumbo, but maybe under different circumstances I would have been curious enough to get a reading. As it was, I was sober and tired, and more interested in sleep than anything else.

"All right," she said, shrugging. "Miss Hansen, the

lovely bride to be, will you step into this room..." She gestured to an open door to the right. "The others, you may sit in the chairs behind you, or feel free to go into the room on your left for some items for sale."

I followed Jessie's friends into the room of "items for sale," while Jessie went into the room with Lady Sage. The room that had once been clean and had a chiropractor's table now appeared to have been long neglected, giving it a totally different feel. The vibes the room gave off were those of a disorganized room in someone's house that you weren't supposed to be in. *Trespassing*, it almost felt like.

One floor lamp bathed the room with a yellow glow. I think it was the only actual electric light in the entire place. A sign on a nearby stand looked like it belonged at a fast food restaurant, but instead of saying "Line starts here," it said "You steal it, and you take bad luck." I huffed at that. That didn't actually deter anyone from stealing, did it? Two tables took up most of the room, stacked with books and random little trinkets. There were books claiming to be spell books, little jars of spices and herbs, and a lot of other things that seemed to have no specific order to their placement. I finally got bored looking through the books and sat in the candle-lit, thickly incensed lobby. Jessie's friends chattered to each other, flipping through magazines, completely ignoring me, which was fine. Each took her turn with the psychic and came back out with a little story of what Lady Sage had said.

"She said Scott and I will last," Jessie said happily. "I knew she would."

"She said I'm gonna marry rich," said Maggie, the first friend.

"I totally get the feeling that she is the real deal," Jessie said.

"I know!" said Maggie, and they squeezed each other's hands and made an excited squeal. I rolled my eyes to myself.

"Cara!" said Michelle. "It's your turn!"

"I didn't pay, remember?" I sounded grumpy even to my own ears.

"Too bad, she says she'll give you a reading for free!"
she said, ushering me up out of my seat. "You're going!" They
all gave a drunken cheer.

I opened my mouth to protest, but my sister pushed
on the small of my back toward the open door. "Go ahead
and just do it! There is nothing to be afraid of!" But her
warning tone said, *Don't insult the lady.*

"I'm not afraid!" I said, but I knew there was no
reason to argue at this point. Better not to express my true
feelings. *I'm sick of all of you and I want to go home.* Lady
Sage stepped to the side to let me through the door, and I
was very aware of how much I towered over her as I walked
into the room.

The other rooms had been small, but this room was
tiny and I wondered if it had been a walk-in closet in its
former life. There was just enough room for two people to
maneuver around a small table and two chairs, but she had
managed to stuff lit candles in almost every other space. I
suddenly felt anxious, and I chalked it up to being in such a
tiny room that could be engulfed in flames at any given
moment.

"I know you don't believe, Cara Marie Hansen," she
said, shutting the door behind us. Light flickered and cast a
strange, ugly shadow on her face when she looked back at
me. "Almost no one believes when they come. But that will
change."

How did she know my full name? I wondered. *Had
the girl that had set up our appointment given our names?* It
wouldn't be too hard to find in this day in age, especially in a
small town like this, but I guessed she would reply with
superstitious crap if I asked, so I said nothing.

"Please, sit," she said, motioning to the farthest
chair from the door. I tried not to sigh and stepped around an
arrangement of lit candles on the floor to sit in the chair she
had indicated. When I sat I noticed the display she had laid on
the table: a stack of cards, along with an honest-to-god
crystal ball. I don't know why, but I had to stop myself from
barking out a laugh at seeing the crystal ball, maybe because

I'd always assumed they were just something fabricated by Hollywood. She sat across from me, her short, stocky body almost completely blockading the entrance. Her thick arms on each side almost touched the walls; brown and gray hair cascaded around her.

No wonder she sits closest to the door; she can't fit around the table! I thought, then felt a little bad for thinking it. I was being cranky.

She picked up her stack of oversized cards and started shuffling them, staring into my face. The laughter inside me quickly died away and was replaced with discomfort at her intrusive gaze. Something about her gave me the willies. "First I will assess your personality and past as I can see it. Then we will go on to your future," she said as she placed cards on the table, face down.

"Okay," I answered.

When she set the remainder of the deck aside there were eight cards spread out between us, four in a straight line with two above them and two beneath them. She flipped over the middle two cards and I was awed at the beautiful detailed pictures on them. They were hand painted with gold details here and there, one of them a lady with a flower crown and the other one a hand holding a sword. "Your center cards represent your personality traits that are currently the strongest or most prominent. These sometimes change depending on what you're learning about yourself or going through at the time. Your center cards are the Ace of Swords and the Empress," she said, touching each card. "The Ace of Swords, like all cards, could be interpreted many different ways, but based on my first impressions and intuitive thoughts, I believe this means you are a brave person. Even though you may not feel like you are brave, I see you being a person who continuously sticks out her neck for other people."

That didn't seem right. I'd like to *think* it was right.

"The Empress represents creativity in a lot of cases," she continued. "I'm seeing that you are a creative person, but more specifically, musically inclined. I see you playing instruments constantly. All types of instruments."

I was taken aback, and I know my eyebrows shot up in surprise. When she looked up at my face, she smiled, my look of shock confirming her assumptions.

"Your outer cards indicate traits that are more deeply ingrained and not likely to change," she said, flipping two cards, each on opposite ends of the spread. "These are the Queen of Wands reversed and the Knight of Swords. I'm seeing that you are a woman who is driven by a desire to be helpful and kind toward others, especially your family. I believe you are very passionate about your family. You are fairly upbeat and cheerful, though not overly so."

I snorted at that. I certainly wasn't overly cheerful and upbeat tonight!

"Are you ready to go to your past?" she asked.

"Sure," I said, smiling. I was starting to enjoy this card reading. I was liking my cards, and I hoped she was right about me.

She flipped the two cards closest to me. The first card she flipped had a drawing of what looked to be eight sticks. The second card showed a dark, cloaked figure with his head bent down, as if sad, with five cups. Three cups were spilled before him and two were upright and whole behind him. Of course I knew nothing about tarot cards, but the character looking dark and depressed bent over the spilled cups looked like a bad card to have.

"Your cards representing the past are the Eight of Wands and Five of Cups. When the Eight of Wands appears, nothing seems to be moving ahead in your life. This card indicates that you have been frustrated and tired of waiting for a long time. I see you putting yourself out there and never getting anything back in return. You don't have much of a love life to speak of, and I don't see that you have many friends, for that matter..." I flinched at that piece of hurtful truth. How could she possibly know that? Did something about the look of me give her that impression and she'd made a lucky guess? Or was she really somehow getting a glimpse of my past?

"This other card," she continued, pointing to the dark figure bent over his spilled cups, "the Five of Cups implies that you've been too focused on the negative instead of the positive. I believe that you view yourself in a bad light, like you are not pretty or good enough for people. I see you trying to live up to the expectations of your parents, and you feel that you'll never succeed at that. I'm glad to see that this card is in your past and not your future. I can see you've been struggling for a long time, but I encourage you to try to leave those negative feelings behind you."

I nodded at her, trying to listen, but still a little distracted by the very plain card with eight sticks, wondering how it could have possibly indicated that I didn't have much of a love life to speak of. Surely my sister or one of her friends had told her?

"Let's go to your future cards, shall we?" she said, turning the last two cards closest to her. I stiffened involuntarily at the sight of the last two cards. Death and the Devil, they read. The Death card had a skeleton in knight's armor riding a horse. People prayed before him, for mercy I suppose, and people lay dead on the ground underneath his horse. The Devil card showed the devil, obviously, but with two naked demon-like humans chained to his seat beneath him, one male and one female. Before I could even think of what I was doing, I leaned away from the cards as if they might burn me, letting discomfort show plainly on my face.

"Oh!" she said, sounding surprised until she collected herself. "Don't be afraid of the Death card. The Death card usually means transformation or a new beginning, and looking at your past, a new beginning is what we'd want to see." Her words were as soothing as milk and honey, but the slight pucker between her brows seemed like a warning.

"The Devil card..." she paused for a moment, tapping a finger to her lip while thinking. "The Devil card is another card that isn't as ominous as it may seem. A lot of times it means internal struggle or trickery. I'm seeing..." She was quiet again, but the look on her face showed her confusion, and the way she looked down at the card, I wondered if she was seeing things that I couldn't see. Hell, she'd figured out I'd never had a boyfriend from eight sticks!

She moved the finger that had been over her lips to gently trace the shape of the devil on the card, and I watched her in expectant silence. Without warning, she jerked in her chair and her head snapped backwards at a painful-looking speed. I jumped out of pure surprise, and I caught a glimpse of white where her eyes rolled into the back of her skull. I stared at her in horrified amazement and before I could ask what was happening, her head fell back forward, her eyes meeting mine. They looked too large, bulging out of her head with too much white visible. I could almost see my reflection in those too-wide, fearful eyes. Her breath came out in heavy gasps.

"Are you okay?" I asked, reaching a hand out as if to comfort her or steady her, but not completely closing the distance. She looked as if she'd just seen a ghost—or like she was still seeing one!

Her voice came out as a whispered hiss. "A darkness...a darkness approaches you. He is very close. *Coming.*" The candles that surrounded us seemed to dim and I could see nothing but her shadowed face in the sudden darkness. The hair on the back of my neck stood and threatened to jump off my body, and I thought if she was trying to scare me, she was doing a damn good job.

"I'd like to stop now," I said, and my voice came out in a low squeak.

"A demonic presence straight from hell itself!" she continued, her dark eyes boring into mine. She looked like a demon herself in that moment as shadows distorted the look of disgust on her round face. Her eyes focused more, and I realized she was aiming the look of disgust toward me... But why?

"You!" she yelled and jumped up into a standing position, flinging her chair back and toppling over some candles. Luckily the excess wax spread along the floor and extinguished the flames on impact. I was surprised at how fast she could move. "You're one of them!" she breathed.

I wanted to ask "One of what?" but my fear and shock overwhelmed my curiosity. *This lady is clearly insane*, I decided, wanting to believe that instead of believing that she had seen something horrible in my future. I suddenly wanted to be far, far away from this room. My insides felt as cold as ice.

"Are we done?" I was glad my voice had recovered and I didn't sound like a cowering girl this time.

There was a moment of silence before she said, very calmly, "Yes."

She seemed recovered, her face a smooth mask that showed no hint of her outburst just a few seconds before. But her hands were shaking, even as she adjusted her skirt, and I wasn't fooled. Something had scared her, and I was too stunned and frightened, myself, to ask what.

Suddenly her voice sounded cheerful. "Expect a new change and maybe some internal struggles in your near future! Nothing to worry about!" she said to me, but as she quickly swept from the room I knew she had said it for everyone else's benefit, not mine. "Good night, everyone! I hope you ladies had a wonderful evening," she continued in her sing-song voice, wasting no time opening the front door and holding it open for us to exit through.

I walked out first, passing the other girls as they glanced up at me from their seats with expectant smiles on their faces, psychic magazines in hand. I couldn't help but notice in my peripheral vision that Lady Sage cringed back from me when I walked past her. I caught a few confused glances from the other girls just before I stepped out onto the porch into the muggy July heat. I could hear my sister and friends scrambling up out of their seats and murmuring their thanks as I waited, staring out toward the empty highway. How had she known I'd never had much of a love life? How had she known I played a lot of instruments? Those two predictions were so strangely accurate that someone before me must have told her them. Maybe I could brush her reading aside, but I'd never forget the look in her wide eyes when she had whispered, "A darkness approaches you. He is very close. Coming." I shivered involuntarily, though the air was uncomfortably thick and warm around me like an unwanted blanket.

When they were all out, surrounding me and whispering amongst themselves, the door slammed and one of the girls jumped and made a surprised yip. I heard, more than saw, the *Open* neon sign in the window flicker and die as the plug was pulled.

"Wow, what was all that about?" asked one of Jessie's friends; I wasn't sure who.

"I feel like we just got kicked out of there," muttered Jessie. "Did that seem a little rude to you guys?" Good, someone else had noticed, and they all seemed a little less drunk.

I started walking toward the car, leading the way. "We definitely did just get kicked out of there," I agreed, then instantly regretted saying it.

My sister and her friend Maggie almost ran to catch up with me in their high heels while the others lagged behind. "What happened?" Jessie asked.

I ignored her question and asked one of my own. "Jessie, did you tell her I had never had a boyfriend?"

"No!" she exclaimed, almost missing a step, then walked more quickly to catch up to me. "I never said a thing about you!"

"She knew things," I said, giving her a hard look.

"She knew things about all of us," Jessie said defensively.

"What was she yelling about?" Maggie interjected, sounding a little too interested for my liking. "It got really quiet in there and all of the sudden it sounded like she yelled and there was a loud bang." Of course they would have heard Lady Sage yell and the chair falling, knocking over candles when she had jumped up. But I didn't want to explain.

"Nothing," I lied as I unlocked the doors to my sister's Toyota 4Runner and slipped into the driver's seat.

Jessie wouldn't let up. "Something happened in there," she said, sliding into the passenger seat next to me.

"Tell me, Cara!"

I sighed loudly to buy myself more time. If I told them how weird she had acted and that apparently some dark presence was going to come into my life, I'd never hear the end of it. Every time I saw them, it would be "Have you experienced the dark presence yet?" That wouldn't be ideal, considering I wanted to forget about it. I wanted to forget about the fear I had felt when I was in that room.

"The noise was me," I said suddenly. "I thought I saw a bug."

"You thought you saw a bug?" Jessie repeated with barefaced skepticism. I could feel her stare as I checked the mirrors for something else to look at, so my eyes wouldn't give away my lie.

"Yes, just a bug," I said, flashing her the most innocent smile I could muster.

Everyone piled in the car then, their voices low and thick with sleepiness. I glanced back to make sure they were all wearing their seatbelts before I pulled out of the gravel parking lot. Jessie looked away finally, and though she didn't believe my bug excuse, I think she was too tired to care.

As I pulled out of the parking spot, I felt the weight of someone's gaze on me and I took one last glance at the building. There was a finger pulling down on one of the blinds, just separating them enough for someone to peek an eye through and stare as we left. Another shiver escaped me and I drove away.

Two

The next morning I woke up on my parents' couch, sun streaming through the windows and lighting up the room. I haven't lived at my parents for a few years now and my room has been converted into Bruce's office, so here I was. The night before, we had left the psychic place so late that I hadn't wanted to drive home after dropping Jessie off.

I glanced up at the clock hanging on the wall. *Three thirty*. I rolled myself off of the couch, almost not believing the time.

"Hey, sweetheart," my mom chirped, and if my reflexes hadn't been so slow from grogginess, I would have jumped. "You've slept the whole day away!" Her blond hair was styled and her makeup had been carefully applied, not too much and not too little. Seriously, she's a total MILF. She walked past the couch and started flipping through a notebook, which I think was her "wedding organizer" she had made for my sister's wedding.

"Hi, Mom," I grumbled, feeling very aware of my disheveledness. "You should have woken me up earlier. I could have helped you with some of the wedding stuff."

"Honestly, there's nothing you could have done at this point. Well, I could have had you help me take the flowers to your aunt's, but I know you had a long night."

"Okay, well, I gotta get going." I tried to run my hands through my shoulder-length, sleep-tousled hair and was stopped by a few knots.

"You working tonight?" she asked as she laid her notepad on the kitchen counter and started scribbling down something.

"Yeah, at five."

"You don't have much time!" she said, turning back to me. "How was last night?"

"Awful," I said, walking into the bathroom just off the living room, leaving the door open.

"What, you don't like babysitting a bunch of drunk people?" she joked, somewhat yelling so I could hear her from the bathroom.

"No," I called back, turning on the sink and splashing some water on my face, then wiping it dry with a clean hand towel. "And that psychic place was bogus. The lady was such a..." the first word that came to my head was *bitch*, but I wouldn't say that in front of my mom. I know better. "Jerk," I finished.

She came up to the bathroom door and leaned on the doorframe. "Really? It wasn't fun? Your sister loved it!"

With the hand towel, I tried to remove the mascara that had fallen underneath my eyes, without much luck. "The lady tried to be all dramatic, playing the role of a perfect psychic with everyone else, especially for Jessie. But with me she just acted...weird."

"She didn't tell you you're about to meet the man of your dreams?" she teased. My mom had an irritating way of hinting that I needed to find a man to marry or at least date, but I was pretty used to it by now. Most parents hate when their children date, but I think my lack of dating was starting to worry her.

"Ha, you wish!" I said, dropping the towel in the sink and going past her to the kitchen, trying to make an escape.

"Oh, Cara," she sighed, not bothering to deny it.

I quickly tried to change the subject. "Apparently, I'm going to meet a dark presence or a demon in my near future—or something like that." I knew instantly that saying that was a mistake and I mentally kicked myself. A couple seconds of complete silence passed between us.

"Well, that's kind of scary. What if it's true?" The teasing tone was gone and she was all seriousness now.

"Mom," I said, going to the fridge for something to take and shooting her a look over the fridge door. "Not likely." I found some blueberry yogurt and a spoon, ready to make my exit.

She stopped in front of the kitchen passageway, casually blocking my way out. "Now, Cara…" she started. *Oh god, here it comes*, I thought. I squeezed by her, quickly kissed her forehead, and headed for the front door. She was on my heels immediately, trying to tell me some superstitious nonsense about evil spirits existing in the world according to *blah blah blah!*

My parents aren't active church-goers, but my grandparents on my mother's side were devout Christians, so because of whatever they filled her head with, my mother occasionally explodes into religious rants. If I didn't want to tell Jessie, I really didn't want to tell my mom, but it was too late now. She would start mulling over my ridiculous psychic reading, and I would never hear the end of it. *Damnit.*

"Don't worry about it, seriously! Bye, Mom! See you tomorrow morning."

"I am *talking* to you!" she said, irritation evident in her voice.

"Don't worry about any of that stuff. That lady was bat crazy! If I don't hurry up, I'm going to be late for work, Mom!"

She sighed. "Well, have a good day at work and be safe tonight."

"Thanks, Mom!" I said, and she shut the front door behind me. I hopped into my old white Honda Accord, started the engine, and put it in reverse when my mom came out the front door and started frantically waving.

I debated about just leaving, but thought better of it. I was possibly going to have to skip my shower before work and I really didn't want to do that. I rolled the window down and she came walking up to the car.

"Why don't you spend the night here tonight." It wasn't a question.

"Mom, the devil is not going to come after me," I said, my tone a little more disrespectful than I had intended.

"No, not because of that!" The look on her face showed that she was not amused. "I want you to get up bright and early and help me and your sister do the very last preparations and setting up for the wedding." That's right. My baby sister was going to be getting married tomorrow! I could hardly believe it was already happening.

"Okay, Mom, I guess I can do that. Now I've really got to go!"

"Okay, okay, just be safe tonight!"

I rolled up the window, put the AC on full blast, and almost peeled out of the driveway. I just had enough time to drive to my downtown apartment, take a shower and do a hurried version of my hair and makeup routine, which is pretty minimal to begin with.

Downtown Charleston is a unique place, where a lot of the buildings date back to the 18th, 17th, and even the 16th century. It's known for its rich history, well-preserved architecture, and its acclaimed restaurant community. All year round, horse and carriage rides go through the city, making it feel that you've really stepped back in time. Well, except when you look at the people: a mix of well-dressed yuppies, tennis-shoe wearing tourists, and tattooed twenty-somethings.

I live on King Street, probably the most well-known

of the streets downtown. It has all those old houses and buildings dating back to previous centuries, but they've been filled with good restaurants and big name stores. At night, the restaurants close or turn into bars and nightclubs, and most often my sister is dragging me out to them. On Sundays people play music on the sidewalks, and every once in awhile someone will sit on the window ledge of a second-floor apartment and play the guitar for the people below. There is a farmers' market just down the block from me in the park, and sometimes I go and buy fresh fruit. It's a wonderful little town.

My apartment is a small two bedroom above a pizza parlor—my former place of work, actually, until I had to find a better paying job. The almost doubling in apartment costs at the beginning of the year gave me two options: find another apartment or get a higher-paying job. I love, love, love my apartment with its large window overlooking the busy street. My only qualm about my apartment is my roommate, Amber, who lives with me about eight months out of the year. She's a student at College of Charleston, but when she isn't going to school, she lives with her family in Michigan. I don't have any reason to not like her, but for reasons I cannot fathom, she seems to hate me. I try to be clean and respect her privacy, but every time we're forced to be near each other, I can see her aversion to me. The only thing I can think of is, she must not approve of my lifestyle. I don't think of myself as an excessive partier by any means, but I go out drinking with Jessie one night almost every weekend. From what I've gathered about Amber, she hates alcohol, but has never tried it. She stays inside and studies most nights, and I assume she's only happy if I'm not in the apartment.

Anyway, when at the beginning of the year I had to quit my job at Simon's Pizza, I found another job within walking distance of my apartment. Angel Oak, one of the best steak restaurants and definitely one of the more expensive in the area, hired me as a server by day and bartender by night. I don't love waitressing, but it pays the bills and I'd rather be self-reliant than work at my stepdad's concrete company.

As I hurriedly walked to Angel Oak that evening in the stifling summer heat, I was distracted. It started off like any normal night at Angel Oak. There was a large dinner crowd, as was the usual for a Saturday, but by ten o' clock it had died down. While half of the staff left for the night, I went from waitressing to bartending, but before I started working the bar, I went to take a quick bathroom break. I looked myself over in the bathroom mirror and sighed with disapproval at my appearance. I was wearing my work uniform: black shorts, black socks, black Nikes, and my white collared shirt with the Angel Oak restaurant logo on the breast. When I had bent over a table to clean it at some point during the evening, I had leaned into some mustard. I've already learned that mustard stains do not come out under any circumstances, so I would be buying a new shirt. After re-doing my ponytail that had fallen loose and washing my hands, I left the bathroom and headed straight for the bar.

"We might actually get some fucking customers, if the drink prices weren't so high," Liz said grudgingly, wiping the bar with a clean rag. Liz was the only waitress/bartender that I considered somewhat of a friend. We never really hung out outside of work, but we were buddy-buddy at the restaurant. Besides me, no one else liked her, even our manager, but she never got fired. I'm sure it had nothing to do with her work ethic and everything to do with her uncle owning the restaurant. Most of why the other waitresses don't like her is because she is gorgeous. She is tall, just a couple inches shorter than me, but she has this gracefulness and bone-deep sexiness that I definitely don't possess. Her hair is always the first thing you notice, almost waist length and raven black. Her second feature you notice is her eyes. They are big and gray and not in the stormy, muddy gray that some people have...they are crystal gray, bright and almost shocking amid her otherwise dark features. Her only physical flaw that I've ever noticed, and that's because I've heard the other waitresses laugh about it, is the small bump on her nose. But I think it's cute and damnit, you can't be absolutely perfect!

She is grumpy, antisocial, and just plain bitchy. But I like her.

"Yes, twenty-three dollars is a little steep for a martini," I muttered. Usually, I try to change the subject when she complains about the restaurant or at least try to word things carefully. No sense in getting myself fired just because she can't.

Liz had gone to get something from the back and I was putting away some wine glasses behind the bar when I perceived a customer at the corner of my eye. All I noticed from first glance was that he dressed nicely and had shoulder length, dark hair. I stopped what I was doing and I went to serve him.

"Hi, what can I get you...?" I said, my words faltering a little bit as he met my eyes. His eyes were a shocking shade of red, but as I stared at them, something else seemed odd about them. His pupils were in the shape of rectangles and made sideways slits across the reds of his eyes. I struggled to process what I was seeing, but I finally came to the conclusion that he wore red, goat-slitted contacts. They were the most unsettling contacts I'd ever seen.

"I'll have the dirty bloody Mary," he said, flashing a smile at me. I blinked and glanced away, realizing that I had been staring and too intensely.

"All right, coming right up," I said, putting my uneasiness aside as I tried to sound polite. As I made the drink, I couldn't resist glancing back up to get another look at him. He was looking down at a menu, and I could see a flash of red as his eyes darted around the page. As I stared, I wondered, *Is it Halloween already?* No, it was July, I reminded myself.

When I placed the drink in front of him and he glanced back up me, I couldn't resist asking, "So, what's up with the crazy contacts?"

He froze. "W-what?" he stammered. It was hard to read his expression with those inhuman eyes staring back at me, but I think he was shocked.

"Your goat-like contacts," I said, stupefied.

"You...you can see my eyes?" He stammered again.

"Yeees," I said, slowly, staring at him dubiously. Was he serious? He looked as alarmed as I was at first seeing them, but that didn't make any sense. Did he literally not know he was wearing them? Was that even possible? He looked down suddenly and took the olive out of his drink, popping it quickly into his mouth.

"Yes, they're *contacts*...," he said while chewing, drawling out "contacts" in a strange way that I didn't understand.

I had thought my follow up question would ask if he was going to a costume party or why he was wearing them, but now it seemed irrelevant. He looked so disturbed and uncomfortable, I felt almost guilty for asking about them. "I hope you like your drink," I said. "Let me know if I can get you anything else."

"Thank you," he said, keeping his gaze down, and it seemed that he was looking at anything except me.

I went back to restocking the bar for a minute and when I looked up, he was gone and his drink was empty. I hadn't even given him his check, but he had left cash that more than covered it.

"Oh my god, that guy was so good looking." Liz was suddenly right at my shoulder. "You know I don't swoon much over men, but *my god*..." It's true, I had never heard her remark on any man's looks. I had wondered if she was interested in guys at all. Or the human race, for that matter.

"You really thought he was good looking?" I asked, wrinkling my nose.

"Uh, yeah, didn't you?" she asked, sweeping her hair in a way that somehow emanated sexuality.

"Well, I had a hard time not being creeped out by his eyes."

"What, they were pretty! I have no idea what color they were, but I just know they were gorgeous."

"He had red contacts in and they were super creepy," I said, making a face at her. Were we talking about the same guy?

She looked puzzled. "They were something light, but they didn't look like red to me. I thought they were blue or green, maybe."

"I don't know how you missed it," I said. "They were like crazy, fire-engine red."

After a moment of us scrutinizing each other, she shrugged. "Oh, well, whatever," she said, waving her hand as if to clear the air, dismissing my words. "He was serious eye candy. Too bad he was here for like five seconds... I can't say I blame him. He probably saw how expensive his drink was and ran."

I gave a half hearted laugh and got back to work.

Fortunately for my under-rested body, yet not so fortunate for my wallet, my manager let me off a few hours early. Regardless of how it would affect my pay, Jessie's wedding was going to require a lot of last minute tasks, and I was thankful for the extra hours I would get to sleep. As I walked the few blocks from work to the parking structure near my apartment, I cursed myself for not having parked in the employee parking lot. It wasn't just walking through the uncomfortable heat and humidity, though that always bothered me. Something else made me irritated and made the hair on the back of my neck stand at attention. It was a safe area on this side of downtown and there were a lot of passersby, yet for reasons I couldn't understand, I felt unsafe. I glanced around me every ten paces, peeking in every dark doorway and potential hiding place as I walked. I felt uneasy the whole drive to my parents' and even as I crawled onto their couch to go to sleep, the feeling stayed with me. I closed my eyes, wishing sleep to come, but still feeling uncomfortable as if feeling the weight of someone's eyes roaming along my skin. Finally, the feeling faded and my pretending to sleep became the real thing.

Three

My sister's wedding turned out beautifully. It was huge, extravagant, and it would probably take ten years for my parents to pay off. It didn't make any sense to me, or to Bruce for that matter, to have such a ridiculous wedding. But Jessie said it was perfect, and I couldn't argue that.

The few days following it were business as usual. I worked Monday and Tuesday, was off Wednesday, then went back to work on Thursday night.

"That guy was here again last night," Liz said, as she tied a little knot at the bottom of her collared shirt so it hung tight and showed a little strip of flesh.

"What guy?" I asked as I slid my purse underneath the bar.

"The gorgeous one. He was here for like three hours by himself. Not a very talkative guy…"

Oh, that guy, I thought, remembering a very unsettling pair of red goat-slitted eyes. "Oh, really?" I said, mostly out of politeness rather than real interest.

"I tried to strike up conversation with him several times. Even flirt with him a bit. I'm pretty sure he's gay."

Just because he doesn't hit on you, doesn't mean he's gay, I thought, but I knew better than to say that aloud. Truthfully, when men looked at the two of us bartending, they went straight for Liz with their tongues lolling out of their mouths and didn't take a second glance toward me. She was a horrible waitress, to say the very least. Even so, she had repeat costumers and a handful of steady admirers that seemed to frequent the bar with only the intention to woo her.

"I don't know if he's gay," I said, doubtfully. Very strange, yes. Gay, no.

"All the hot ones are either married or gay," she said, sighing wistfully.

"I'll have to take your word for it. I've never had a boyfriend."

Liz almost dropped the glass she was putting up behind the bar. She whirled around and looked at me. "What? How could you have never had a boyfriend?"

I shrugged. No one had shown real interest in me. My mom had gone through a phase a couple years ago where she constantly tried to make me over. She'd taken me to get spray tanned, replaced all my bras with push-up padded bras, bought me skimpy dresses, taken me to get my hair done, makeup done, *everything*. She had tried to turn me into a life-size Barbie, but it never seemed to make a difference. I never got hit on, and no one ever asked me out. I still try to look decent, don't get me wrong, but I try to look good to make myself feel good and not for anyone else at this point.

"You probably get asked out all of the time. You're pretty!" she said.

I wrinkled my nose and made a face that showed I didn't agree.

"Why haven't you ever dated anyone?" she pressed.

Ugh, was she going to make me say it? "I don't know," I said after a few seconds. "No one has ever shown real interest in me. Whenever I'm with my sister, they go straight for her. Whenever I'm here, they go straight for you! Or Beth, or Tracy," I said, naming other waitresses. I really didn't feel comfortable talking about this.

"Well, I'm sure you've been hit on and you're just too oblivious to see it."

I wished that were the case. "No one really interests me anyway," I said truthfully.

"Well, I'm going to take you out," she said. "You're off tomorrow, right?"

"Yes," I said, not liking where this was going. I didn't want to suffer the humiliation of going out for the sake of trying to get hit on *again*. I'd long accepted that it wasn't going to happen, or like my mom would say to try to cheer herself up, "It's just not the right time." I liked going out just for the sake of enjoying myself.

"We are going to meet at my house, get all gussied up, and go out. Do you like dancing?"

"I love dancing," I admitted. I loved music and anything to do with it, more than the average person.

"Well then, we are going to go out and dance and have a good time!" she said. "And we will mingle," she added and did a little wiggle with her eyebrows.

I laughed. "Okay, okay, it'll be fun."

"It'll be so much fun," she said.

I glanced over my shoulder and suddenly noticed *the guy*. Though he looked different than I remembered, he definitely had to be the same guy as a few nights before.

"Hi, I'm sorry, I didn't see you. What can I get you?" I asked.

His eyes were covered with dark shades, so I could absorb all his other features that I couldn't believe I had missed before. His black hair hung in loose waves around his shoulders, and it looked like it might be silky soft if you ran your fingers through it. His lips were fuller than average, and they were positively sultry. Despite the pouty lips and long hair, he was obviously male with a perfectly squared jaw line and broad shoulders. I felt as if I were looking into a chest-achingly gorgeous ad for sunglasses. I didn't usually want to stare so appreciatively at a man, but he was worth some dirty thoughts and ogling.

"No problem," he said, smiling, and even with his eyes hidden, I could tell it was a genuine smile. "I guess I'll get what I got last time. A dirty bl..."

"Dirty bloody Mary, right?" I finished with him and his smile broadened. I turned and started making It.

"So you ladies are going out tomorrow night, huh? I'm new to town, so where's a good place to go?" Oh god, he had been listening. I hoped that he hadn't heard our whole conversation.

"Not here," Liz said, leaning on the bar toward him. "Except to see the prettiest bartenders."

He seemed to glance at her, smile still intact, but then turned back to me as I served him his drink.

"Where do you like to go?" he asked me.
Liz stiffened and drew away when she realized she had been dismissed. At the corner of my eye I could see her going back to stocking the bar.

"Um..." I stammered. Wearing suit pants, a green collared button up, and what looked to be a Rolex watch on his left wrist, he didn't look like he'd want to go to the places I'd like to go. I liked to go to crowded, trashy places toward the less-nice side of town where I could dance to loud music or stand on the sidelines and blend in. I hated going to fancy wine bars where everyone just kind of stares at each other and listens to jazz. "Well, what kind of place are you looking for?"

"I like going to places where there's a lot of energy and good music," he said, sounding boyish in his enthusiasm. "Big crowded bars or dance clubs. I don't know, I guess it varies. Just as long as there is good energy."

I laughed. I couldn't help but find it humorous that he had picked the bar with the dim-lit romantic lighting, classical music, and almost no people in sight.

"What's so funny?" He asked, a light teasing in his voice.

"I'm sorry, I just think its funny that you picked the bar that least fits that description," I giggled. Shit, I actually giggled. What was happening to me?

"Yes, I did, didn't I?" He laughed too. "This isn't my kind of bar, but it does have *the* prettiest bartender."

For a split second, I thought he meant Liz, but as we stared at each other I knew otherwise. I awkwardly froze into place, unsure what to do with my hands suddenly. I felt as if my brain stopped producing coherent thoughts and before I could collect myself, our exchange became awkward.

"I'm sorry, I shouldn't have said that," he said, looking down and shaking his head a little bit, seeming to laugh at himself.

"No!" I said, trying to salvage the situation. "Thank you, you are very nice. I'm just not used to being called pretty, I guess. Thank you." I tried to smile and look warm.

The short, carefree moment we had had between us was over. It seemed that in a blink of an eye, everything had changed. His easy posture became rigid and I could almost sense the air around us change, becoming heavier. His playful smile was transformed into a tight line, and I could see the hollow of his cheeks as he clenched and unclenched his jaw. He sighed suddenly, but it sounded like a frustrated sound through clenched teeth. For the life of me, I couldn't figure out what had caused this sudden mood change. Was he mad at himself for flirting with me? Had I offended him? Nothing that had just happened should have caused a reaction like this in someone.

He pushed his untouched drink forward. "Know what, I'm in the mood for something else. Can you make my next drink Dom Pérignon?" He said it like it was supposed to sound: French.

"Yes, of course. Not a lot of people order that, but I think we do have some in the back." I was babbling. I had no idea where that was even kept, so instead of looking all over the place, I decided to go directly to my manager in his office.

As I went, I shook my head, trying to figure out what had just happened. For the first time in my life, a handsome guy compliments me on my appearance, and I freeze up and ruin it. I must have offended him, somehow.

"Where is the Dom Pérignon?" I practically barked at Harrison.

He looked up from his computer, seeming to perk up at just the thought of a customer ordering one of the most expensive champagnes. "There are two bottles in the wine fridge. You've probably seen them a million times."

"Oh, thanks," I mumbled, kind of embarrassed, and headed back to the bar. I almost didn't want to go back, afraid that I'd do something wrong. *Again.*

"It took me a minute to find it," I said, smiling at him as I tore the foil from the pretty champagne bottle. I noticed that his lips slightly moved like he was saying something underneath his breath... or maybe I imagined it? I didn't have time to question it, because when I looked back down to pop the cork, I saw blood pooling on the tip of my index finger. "Oh!" I said in surprise. I had cut my finger taking off the foil. "I'm sorry," I said, before I could think of anything else to say, stepping away to grab a paper towel.

"Are you okay?" he asked, leaning over the bar with genuine concern in his voice.

Liz was graceful enough for once to step in and help pop the cork and pour him a glass without being asked or complaining.

"Yes, I'm fine, just a little cut," I said, taking a piece of paper towel and holding it to my finger. Ugh, it wasn't like me to be so clumsy when it came to working the bar. This was embarrassing.

"I actually think I have a bandage," he said, going in his pockets. "Here, will you let me put it on you?" He suddenly was holding a little Band-Aid out to me.

It seemed like a strange request and I felt unprofessional letting a patron put a Band-Aid on me. At the same time I felt unprofessional by objecting. Hell, could it get any worse?

"Okay," I said uncertainly, coming back to the edge of the bar and showing him my index finger. He placed a Band-Aid on it and wrapped the sticky strip around my fingernail. He only barely touched me, but when I pulled away I could feel an electric current going from my finger to, well, down south.

He smiled at me.
"Enjoy your champagne," I said, smiling back. As silly as it sounded, I didn't want to say the name of the champagne in case I butchered it. I went to the bar's POS system and after a minute found Dom Pérignon. When it rang up for $60 dollars for a glass, I just stared at the screen for a moment, at first thinking I had rung up a bottle. But no, you could buy the bottle for $200. *Whoa Nelly!*

A group of four people came in suddenly, all talking at once, their voices loud. Drunk people. But *rich*, drunk people from the looks of designer clothes and shiny jewelry, so they had my manager's stamp of approval. One thing I didn't like about this job was that I was supposed to turn away people that didn't meet a certain dress code after the dinner hours. A steady stream of people came in after the drunk quartet and I was glad to have work to do to distract me. Slow nights were long nights and honestly, I didn't want a chance to further embarrass myself.

Long-haired-sunglasses moved from a middle seat at the bar to one in the corner so the party of people could group together. He sat silently, ordered one more glass of champagne, paid, and left.

The next morning I woke up slowly, or should I say the next afternoon. I never wake up in the mornings unless forced. Working at a bar will do that to you.

One of my first thoughts was Long-haired-sunglasses at the bar. Oh, he had been gorgeous. I hoped he would come back, though I cursed myself for even thinking it. He had called me "the prettiest bartender," hadn't he? It was okay to think dreamy thoughts of him, right? It didn't matter. I couldn't help myself.

I looked at my finger as if to make sure that it hadn't been a dream. The Band-Aid was gone, but the small cut was there. I looked around, running my hands around me, trying to find the missing Band-Aid. Where had it gone? *Oh well,* I thought. *It'll turn up when I get out of bed.* I snuggled in my sheets, allowing myself to think about him a little longer.

When I finally got out of bed, spots flashed in front of my eyes and I braced myself not to fall from dizziness. I stood there for a second, willing my head to clear, but the spots didn't leave. I blinked slowly a few times. There were two small red spots in my vision. They weren't blurry blind spots as I had first thought, but just two tiny areas of my eyesight that were tinted red.

"What the hell?" I muttered to myself.

I walked slowly out of my bedroom to where the small dining area and kitchen were. The only thing that separates the kitchen from the dining space is a counter. The spots were slightly unsettling to me, but they didn't seem like an immediate hazard. At least I could walk around the room without falling down. I went to the front door where I had dropped my purse the previous night and fished out my cell phone, speed-dialing my mom.

"Hey, honey."

"Hey, Mom," I said. "Something is going on with my eyes—"

"Something's going on with your eyes?" she interrupted. "What do you mean?"

"Well, I can see okay, but there are two red dots in my vision. I was just wondering if I could get the number to your eye doctor." I was walking past the bathroom, holding the phone to one ear, when I caught a glimpse of myself in the mirror. Something in my reflection looked strange, and I froze. I walked into the bathroom to get a better look, turned on the light, and took a closer look at myself in the mirror. The closer I got to the mirror, the more the red dots seemed to get to the middle of my face. But if I backed up at just the right spot, the red spots hovered over to where my eyes were in the mirror. At that spot, my eyes looked like they were glowing fire engine red.

The memory of red sideways slitted eyes flooded back up and I suddenly felt sick to my stomach. My mom was babbling, and I hadn't heard a word she was saying.

"Mom, do you think I can get an eye doctor's appointment *today*?" I interrupted her. I had a sinking feeling that this was something an eye doctor couldn't take care of, but I should see one before I let myself officially freak out.

"Maybe," she said slowly, sounding suspicious. "I'll give you the number and you can find out." When she gave me the number, I barked out a goodbye and got off the phone faster than was polite.

I stared at my evil twin in the mirror for a moment, wondering what this meant. *What had that Lady Sage said last Friday? That I would meet a demonic presence from hell?* Did she mean a literal demon, or did that just mean an evil person? I wanted to call her or go to her place to try to get more information, but she had almost kicked me out and said I was "one of them." Had she predicted that this would happen, whatever was happening to my eyesight? Was I becoming what that man at the bar was, whatever he was? I thought about the goat-slitted eyes and shuddered. I finally had to look away from the mirror, because the sight was too unsettling. For some reason I thought that when I looked away, the red dots would stay in the mirror, but they followed my gaze with every move.

Four

A few hours later I came out of the eye doctor's with a stamp of perfect eye health. *Sure.*

As I slid into my little car, I tossed the receipt and an eye-care pamphlet into the backseat and let out a sigh. I had been able to get an eye appointment almost immediately on James Island, a town in the Charleston County. It had been a different eye doctor than my family usually used, but what mattered is that he could see me quickly. He hadn't been able to detect anything, but he had recommended a neuro-ophthalmologist that could give me further testing if the "issue persisted." I hadn't expected him to find anything, but I had hoped he would. It would be a relief to hear that it was just something normal. A stigmatism, a retinal disorder—*I don't know!* Something with an easy explanation.

I thought about canceling with Liz, but then thought better of it. Sitting by myself alone and mulling this over with nothing to distract me seemed like a bad idea. I would go out and try to enjoy myself.

I went back to my apartment, gathered a few dresses and low-heeled shoes and threw them in an overnight bag. I never wore high-heels, because there was no sense in making myself taller than absolutely *everyone* else.

Liz also lived on King Street, a mile away from me toward the even nicer side of downtown. King Street is a very long street, going from one side of downtown to the other. On one end there are the million-dollar homes and a park overlooking the Charleston Harbor. On the other end are low income houses, strip clubs, and warehouses. That is not where you want to be walking come nightfall. I live about a mile from the Harbor where the nice houses come to an end and the line of shops, restaurants, and apartments starts.

I could walk to Liz's house, but only if I wanted to arrive dripping with sweat. It was about 90 degrees outside with about enough humidity to swim through. Not ideal weather to walk a mile in. I parked on what the locals call *the Battery*, the street running along the Harbor, and walked the block up to her house.

All of the houses had beautiful and interesting architecture on this side of the street, but when I came across her house, my mouth fell open. I had partially expected her house to be one of the very few in that neighborhood that was broken up into apartments or looked slightly shabby with a violation notice taped to the front door. This house was *not* one of those houses. It was a three-story white house, skinny across the front, but extending quite a ways back. Houses on this street are generally really skinny, because in the 1700s, your taxes were based on how wide the front of your house was along the street. Though it had that old-Charleston charm with its familiar architecture, flower boxes bursting with flowers in the lower windows, and a gas light fixture above the front door, the house looked newly updated and maybe newly painted. I took the step up to the door and opened it, knowing it would open up onto a long porch alongside the house before I saw it. The porch looked like a perfect place to lounge if it were a cooler day. A cute little iron table with a glass top, along with two matching iron chairs, sat in the far corner. A vase full of yellow daises decorated the table, along with an overflowing ashtray of cigarettes. If I'd had any doubts that I had come to the right place, the overflowing ashtray squashed them.

From the porch I could see her small, manicured yard and a black Cadillac sedan in the driveway. I knocked on the front door as I stared admiringly at the shiny, black car and wondered whose it was. It looked expensive, but so was this house.

Only a couple seconds passed before Liz was at the door. "Hello," she said, smiling for just a second before her face smoothed out into a serious mask. She never holds a smile for long, I realized.

"Hi," I said, adjusting my bag over my shoulder.

"Come in," she said, walking away and leaving me standing at the front door. I quickly followed her inside and shut the door behind me. In front of me was a flight of stairs going to the second floor. Liz took off without another word into a short hallway to my left that appeared to open up into a room, but I couldn't resist taking a quick peek in the open doorway to my right. It was a beautiful living room like a spread from *Homes and Gardens* magazine. Both the dark wood flooring and the red brick fireplace looked old and might've been original features of the house. The modern white and gray furniture didn't exactly match the older elements of the room, but it somehow meshed perfectly. A large framed black and white photo of Liz hung above the fireplace. She appeared to be topless, her back to the camera, peering over her shoulder with a intense look in her bright eyes, dark hair flowing down her back. The photo reminded me of one of those National Geographic photos; a naked young woman with eyes so penetrating they seemed to see you right through the photo. It was a stunning picture, but it was an interesting choice of decoration for the first room you'd see in the house.

"Come over here in the kitchen!" she yelled, her

voice traveling down the hallway with an echo. I followed in that direction and came into an open kitchen. The color scheme matched the living room, all white, besides the dark wood flooring and some silver touches here and there. Along the back wall were a fridge, counters, and cabinets; nearby stood a marble top island counter, grey and silver designs throughout it. On the opposite side of the room, underneath the front windows with a view of the street, sat a small breakfast nook.

"Wow, this place is amazing," I said.

Liz had a cigarette to her lips and a lighter in her hand. "Thank you," she said, the cigarette muffling her words as she lit it. "You can set your stuff anywhere for now," she said, blowing smoke.

I set my bag against the wall and slid into the breakfast nook. "So who do you live here with?" I asked.

"Myself." She leaned over the island counter, cocking an eyebrow, and seemed to judge the look on my face.

"This place is all yours?" I gasped, hardly able to believe it. This house was probably worth three million dollars, at least.

"Yes. It's mine. You look like you're gonna shit yourself." Leave it to Liz to be graceful.

"Sorry, I just can't believe you can afford something like this. I'm struggling to share an apartment with another person! I wouldn't expect someone our age to be able to live somewhere like this."

"Well, I'm older than you. I'm twenty-nine. But yeah, I think I am one of the youngest, if not *the* youngest, owners here."

She wasn't even a renter, but an *owner*! "Wow," I said again. "How could you afford this?" I realized a little too late that saying that might be rude.

She held the cigarette with only her lips as she grabbed an opened bottle of red wine from the counter and snatched two wine glasses that hung upside down on one of those under-the-cabinet wine glass holders. "Well, I didn't earn it by working at Angel Oak," she said, though that was a given. She took the cigarette out of her mouth and held it to the side as she poured the wine. She moved around like the lovely lead in her own '60s film, somehow managing to make smoking look sexy. "It's really a long story." She pushed one glass toward me and I sat up to retrieve it. We faced each other from opposite sides of the island counter.

I wanted to ask her to tell me, but she seemed uneasy and I didn't want to scare her off the subject. "If it's too private, you don't have to tell me," I said, reassuringly. Always best not to act too eager when someone's about to tell you a secret. I took a sip of my wine and made an appreciative *mmm* sound. It was just the right combination of sweet and dry that I preferred.

"Well, I used to model…"

"Yeah, I saw the picture in the living room! It's gorgeous."

"Thank you," she said, smiling for a moment. "Yeah, so I used to model and I got married to a photographer. I feel like it sounds a little creepy when I tell the story, like he was some skeezeball photographer that made me his pet project, but that's kind of how it started." She seemed to not know how to continue for a moment and glanced over her shoulder. At first, I thought she might be trying to hide an onset of tears. Then I realized she was looking back at a white picture frame standing up by the sink.

"Is that him?" I asked.

She reached behind her and brought the picture to where I could see it, standing it up on the island counter. She nodded and smiled, but it wasn't a happy smile. "I had been in modeling for a couple years, but I hadn't gotten very far in the industry. I was in the LA fashion week and had a few little odd jobs here and there, but nothing big. When I was eighteen I finally got a job with my first big line, and my photographer was *Jason Black*." She made his name come out like a sad sigh. "He was older than me. He was twenty-seven and I was only eighteen when we met—so there was a nine year gap there—but I was instantly in love." She took her cigarette and stubbed it out onto an ashtray that she had pulled from some hiding spot behind the counter. "His name was just becoming well known in the industry, and he was hired for this big line and that big line. I was his muse, he would tell me, and we took tons of pictures all over the world. I started getting more runway, more designer lines, and we just kind of followed each other around the world, back and forth. It was mostly me going where he went, but yeah, point is we both had a lot of work and it was exciting."

I was leaning into the picture as she talked. It was a picture of the two of them with a city landscape behind them that was unfamiliar to me. "Wow, he's really handsome." And that was the truth. He looked American Indian with golden brown skin and long black hair. He looked like he was used to smiling and being in the sun by the looks of the little crow's feet by his eyes, but they were handsome and distinguishing. She had much shorter hair in the picture, just past chin length, but otherwise looked the same. Her current hair looked a lot like his had, and I wondered if that was coincidence.

She looked into her glass and smiled wistfully. "We got married almost immediately after meeting," she continued. "He was on his way home from the airport when he got in an accident. The police came to my door and just like that, it was all over." She took a few more swigs and drained her glass. "We had just celebrated our seven year wedding anniversary, and I was suddenly a widow at twenty-five years old."

"Oh my god, I'm so sorry. That's just awful." Lame, I know, but I couldn't think of anything better to say.

"Yeah, it was really awful," she agreed. "We had decent money and he had a great life insurance policy, so when he passed I was financially set. I'm okay now, sort of, but I was a wreck for a long time. I still feel like I'm just going through the motions to get through life."

"I bet," I said, frowning. My romance-less twenty-three years of existence suddenly seemed a lot less depressing. They say it's better to have loved and lost than never to have loved at all, but in this case, whoever said that was wrong. All the mean things other waitresses at Angel Oak said about Liz suddenly crossed my mind, and that made me glad we were hanging out now. Perhaps I wasn't the only one that needed a friend.

"Yeah," she sighed, pouring herself another glass. "But that's not even the end of it."

"Tell me," I said, letting all my curiosity show.

"I..." she seemed to not know how to continue for a second. "I started getting into drugs." She paused, as if attempting to judge my reaction. When she was satisfied with my non-judgmental expression, she continued. "After Jason died, I continued to work, because I didn't know what else to do with myself. As you probably know, there is a lot of pressure to do drugs in the modeling industry. I'm glad that Jason was so smart with money and put it into a trust fund, or else I would have spent it all. After he was gone, I just didn't care about anything anymore. I got really into cocaine for awhile before I moved up to heroin. A year after he died, my parents and my brother came up to New York, where I was living, and convinced me to go to rehab. I went to rehab in North Carolina for a few months and then went home with them. They're here in Charleston, so I stayed with them for awhile and eventually moved out and bought this place," she said, looking at the ceiling and surroundings like she was coming back to the present. "Now I work at Angel Oak to take up time and distract myself. As I'm sure you know, my uncle owns the restaurant, and I think my parents convinced him to hire me. Pretty sure he's regretting that now!" She let out a half-hearted laugh.

"Oh, I'm sure he's not," I said, trying to reassure her.

She gave me a knowing look. "Don't try to be so nice; you know it's true. No one likes me there, except you. I need a new job, because I really can't stand that place. I really need to be doing something I *like* to do."

I nodded, understanding. "Angel Oak is definitely not my life's calling."

"Too bad no one will hire me to smoke cigarettes

and drink wine." We laughed and Liz poured more wine in our glasses. I was going to be drunk, but we wouldn't have to drive anywhere if we didn't want to, so it was all right.

"We should start getting ready," I said. *Before this wine hits me and I give myself clown makeup*, I thought. It wouldn't be the first time.

"All right, let's go upstairs. Bring your stuff up." She started walking out of the kitchen and made a jerk of her head to signal me to follow. I held the wine glass in one hand and scooped up my night bag in the other. The old floorboards creaked and groaned as we walked through the hall and up the stairs. The first room she led me into was a huge bedroom with a large bay window overlooking the street. The walls were black, which I would have thought was a bad color to paint a room because it could make the space look small, but this room couldn't have that problem. She had a king size bed with a large, intricate frame, all white except for gold detailed pillows. An extravagant gold mirror took up a good portion of wall space and a large flat screen TV took up another. Everything was in shades of black, white, or gold and though it was luxurious, it didn't look particularly inviting or comfortable. It somehow seemed unlived in, perfectly clean except for a pile of clothes lying on the bed. There were no family photos, no personal jewelry hanging, or anything homey you might expect to see.

"Your house is beautiful," I admitted.

"Thanks, I had an interior decorator help me."

I still had a hard time believing Liz could afford this house and these expensive furniture pieces. She never had even hinted that she had money, but I suppose if you have money, you may not want people to know. I had no personal experience with that.

"I wanted to see if you wanted any of these dresses," Liz said, going to her bed and laying some of the clothes out so I could see them. From what I could tell, they were from expensive designer clothing lines. "I have gained a few pounds since my recovery and I can't fit in them."

If she had gained a few pounds, then she must have

needed to, because she was slim. Not thin and shapeless like a rail as I am, but thin and with curves where you want them. I traced the beading on a gorgeous red dress that I was instantly drawn to, admiring the details. The nude colored fabric at the top was very sheer to give the effect of bare back and shoulders. Red lace flowers were expertly placed to cover what needed to be covered, concealing more flesh as it went down to where it ended at knee-length. I had no idea where I could wear it and I doubted I could pull it off, but it was the most beautiful dress I'd ever seen. I wanted to tell her that I couldn't accept it, that it looked too expensive, but I wanted it.

The other two dresses looked expensive, one black and covered in sequins and the other similar to the first, except green and much shorter with a slimmer fit. If the red one was revealing, the green one was scandalous.

"These look so expensive. Are you sure?" I asked, nearly holding my breath.

"Please take them. I really won't wear them again," she said. "I will have to go through my closet and see if I find anything else I can't fit into."

"Thanks for thinking of me," I said, folding and laying the dresses next to my overnight duffel bag as gently as possible.

"Of course," she said, shrugging. "Now if you want to put your makeup on, the bathroom has the best lighting." She pushed open a door attached to her bedroom and revealed a bathroom as extravagant as the bedroom. The first thing my eyes were drawn to was a white claw foot bathtub with a gold spout and hot and cold nozzles. There was a small gold and crystal chandelier, a gold mirror, and a white marble washstand with gray swirls in it, also with a gold spout and nozzles. It wasn't a huge bathroom, but it was lovely. The only thing that stood out of place was a big, purple cosmetic bag by the sink.

"We will have to squeeze next to each other. Hope you don't mind."

"Of course not. Your bathroom is actually about the

size of my bedroom," I admitted sheepishly.

"Really?" she exclaimed, eyebrows raised.

I nodded and retrieved my own cosmetic bag as she rummaged through hers. As I applied my makeup, Liz concentrated more on consuming red wine. She put on some makeup, though: mascara, powder, and a dab of lip gloss. She's one of the few girls that only needs the most minimal makeup to look perfect. I, on the other hand, put on purple eye shadow, which I've been told brightens up brown eyes. Sure, I don't really have brown eyes, but black, but I guess that's close enough. Also, concealer on the recently darkened circles under my eyes, mascara, lip gloss, bronzer, and a little bit of blush to give me some color. I frowned at my reflection, realizing I'd put on a little too much blush.

"So that good looking guy that's been showing up at the bar seems to like you," she said nonchalantly.

"Dude!" I exclaimed, and as that came out of my mouth, I knew I was beginning to feel the wine. "I have a crazy story to tell you." As I rubbed my cheeks to get rid of the excess blush, I proceeded to tell her about Lady Sage's warning, the red dots in my eyesight, and my fears about the whole bit being part of her prediction. By the end, Liz was staring wide-eyed at me.

"Whoa, that's a crazy story," she admitted. "And you think this guy that's been showing up at the bar could be the demonic presence that psychic lady was talking about?"

"I don't know," I confessed. "As crazy as it sounds, I think so."

"I don't know about demonic presences, but he is gorgeous enough to be the devil himself," she said, tossing her hair over her shoulder and running a brush through it. "You know you gotta call this psychic lady, right?"

"I do?" I asked doubtfully. Though I had thought of calling her myself, the thought of actually doing it did not appeal to me. "No, I don't think so," I said decidedly.

"Uh, yeah, you do!" she said, pointing her brush at my reflection in the mirror. "What you're telling me is just too strange not to try to figure out. You have to have another reading."

"Yeeeaaah..." I said in way that meant *no*. "But that lady doesn't like me."

"Maybe she doesn't, who knows," Liz shrugged. "But you have some questions that need answering. And what's the harm in just calling? Worst thing she can say is no, she won't see you."

"True," I admitted, considering it.

"What's the place called again?" she asked, exchanging her brush for her cell phone.

"Sage's Psychic Center, or something," I said, assuming she was looking up reviews or pictures of the building.

"Got the number!" she exclaimed after a moment, shoving the phone at my face. A loud ring came from the phone, notifying me that she had already dialed the number and it was on speaker.

"Why did you do that?" I hissed.

"Come on, you have to!" she urged.

"Lady Sage's Psychic Readings, this is Tansy, how may I help you?" said a very bored female voice.

"Hi, uh," I started. "I came about a week ago with a bachelorette party. My reading seems to have been accurate, and I just want to know if I can get another appointment..." I let my words trail off.

Silence for a moment. "Is your name Cara Hansen?" The voice suddenly had a lilt of excitement to it.

Liz and I met each other's wide eyes. "Uh, y-yes, it is," I stammered.

"Lady Sage said you would be calling back. If you don't mind, I would like to take your appointment."

She had said I would call back? I hadn't even planned on calling and if it weren't for Liz, I probably never would have. "Well, I would really like to get an appointment with her, no offense. I feel like it might be counterproductive going to someone else after I feel like her reading was accurate."

Silence for a second. "To be perfectly honest, Cara, Lady Sage has given me strict orders not to let you come back here or make an appointment with you. I'm only doing this because I am personally interested in your, er, situation. If you don't want to make an appointment with me, you're on your own."

I paused, considering this. Maybe I wanted to deal with this on my own. Or ignore it and try to forget about it? I liked that idea.

"Okay, when's a good time?" Liz piped in and I tried to swat her away. She belted out a laugh and dodged my hand.

"It'll have to be on one of her nights off," the feminine voice answered. "How about tomorrow at 10 o' clock PM?"

"I'll be working," I said shortly.

"I'll take your shift, I'll take your shift!" Liz whispered, just about jumping up and down with excitement.

"Never mind, I can come," I mumbled, shooting Liz an exasperated look.

"Good. And just so you know, Cara, I may not be able to predict your future or use flashy cards, but I have gifts of my own. I think what you're going through is more of my expertise."

I wanted to ask her what her expertise was, but before I could say anything, she said, "See you at your appointment. I'll be looking forward to your arrival." *Click*.

"I'm starting to really believe that something weird *is* happening to you," Liz said, taking back her phone. "I kind of want to see if someone else will take your shift tomorrow. Would you let me go with you if I can get someone else to cover it?"

"Yeah, I guess," I grumbled. "If I'm going to be subjected to this torture, you should have to suffer with me."

Suddenly a text message sound rang out and Liz tapped at her phone's screen. She pushed her phone in front of my face again and I caught her strange, wide-eyed expression before focusing on the text. "Oh yeah, and please come alone," I read.

The next morning I woke up on Liz's large white bed. At first I couldn't put the pieces together. I only vaguely remembered the cab picking us back up after the club. I had drunk way too much, and Liz had drunk a lot more. I glanced over and saw her, head and one arm sticking out from underneath the blankets. She was still passed out.

It had been a really fun night. We had taken a cab ten blocks away to SINergy, one of the newer nightclubs downtown. Fortunately for me, Liz had forgotten that she had dragged me out to get hit on by guys, and for a few hours I had forgotten all of my worries. Maybe it was the alcohol or the flashing lights at the dance club, but I forgot about the red pinpricks in my vision. Now they were back in full force.

I caught a whiff of cigarette stench on my hair and made a face. I didn't smoke, but Liz had smoked all around me and I reeked of it. I really needed a shower. I rolled out of bed, gathered my things together, and left the house. The sun was more painfully bright than usual and I checked the time. One o' clock. Before I walked away I took one last glance up at the house, and my mouth dropped open again. A lone window I hadn't noticed before made the house look like it might even be four stories, unless it was an attic window. Above the long porch going alongside the house was an equally long balcony. Some kind of vine with yellow flowers snaked up from behind the house and clung to the balcony's ledges. *Gorgeous,* I thought.

As I walked to my car, I felt very conscious of my unkempt appearance in my oversized t-shirt, cotton shorts, and head topped with a slept in-bun. When I got home, I took a hot shower and washed the stale cigarette stench out of my hair; then clad in a towel, I went to my bedroom to throw on something to wear. My room was unbearably hot with the sun shining through the windows onto the wooden floor. The building was so old and poorly insulated that the air conditioning found a way to escape, making it a furnace in the summer. I slid into a pair of jean cut-off shorts and a thin, black tank top. Normally I'd be going to work in a few hours, but with Liz taking my shift I had half the day to kill. Turning back toward my bedroom, I realized I didn't know what to do with myself. It was Saturday and sometimes I'd go to the farmer's market, but it was too late in the day for that. Jessie was still on her honeymoon for one more day, so I couldn't invite her to do anything. If I watched a movie or read a book, the red pin pricks in my vision would distract me and I didn't want to think about what they could mean. *Were they getting brighter or was the effect somehow induced by my hangover?* I wondered.

I grabbed my guitar for something to distract me and settled on the bed. With the guitar laying against my stomach, I closed my eyes, my fingertips knowing where every string and fret was. The only sound in the room was the whirring of the fan that's only purpose seemed to be to move the hot air around. When I started playing, my strums filled the room, making the space feel less empty and lonely. It had been a little while since I had played, but as I did, I felt that familiar feeling of peace and wholeness. That is, until I noticed the red pin-pricks. I could have sworn they hadn't been visible when I'd had my eyes closed before, but there they were, bright against the dimness behind my eyelids. They looked like two eyes peering at me in the dark, and with that thought came the almost itchy sensation on my skin that I was being watched. I paused, my fingers freezing in place, the music dying out. The sensation that someone was in the room and close by was so strong that I almost expected to feel someone's breath on my face. If I opened my eyes, I felt certain that someone would be hovering right above me.

I forced my eyes open and looked up at the cracked, painted ceiling. Nothing was there except the two inescapable red dots in my vision and the feeling that I was being watched.

I felt nervous excitement fill me as I drove to Lady Sage's Psychic Center. As I drove, I suddenly realized I was biting my nails and quickly yanked my hand away from my teeth. I had naturally strong fingernails that I kept long, even, and neatly painted—that being one of the few things I liked about my appearance—and I hadn't chewed on them in a very long time. I wouldn't let myself start now.

When I walked inside, the harsh fluorescent lights that buzzed overhead were strangely comforting. Though candles are usually nice and relaxing, the way Lady Sage had nearly stacked them on top of each other was not soothing to me. I wasn't in the mood tonight for spookiness and theatrics. I just wanted to hear the truth behind Lady Sage's reading and nothing more.

"Hello," the girl behind the counter said as she pulled her gaze from a computer screen. She was a tiny little girl with dramatically-cut, black hair in a sort of Cleopatra-style, cut just above her shoulders with blunt bangs that stopped in the middle of her forehead. She wore heavy black eyeliner, a black T-shirt that said "zombie" in a pink font I recognized as the Barbie logo, and a black hoop septum piercing. I couldn't be sure of her age, but I would have guessed she was younger than me, yet too old to be in high school.

"Hi, I'm Cara," I said, smiling.

"I'm Tansy. Glad you could come," she replied, coming around the desk to meet me. I thought she was going in for a handshake, but I was surprised when she came in for a hug instead. I had to stoop to hug her back and I felt extremely awkward as I did, not being accustomed to hugging complete strangers. She gave me a couple pats on the back before she drew away.

Tansy's short stature was where any similarities between her and Lady Sage stopped. She must have been under five feet, because even wearing black platform boots with more straps than a straitjacket, she was still about a foot shorter than me. Her arms were covered in black tattoos, and though I don't know much about tattoos, to me they looked like amateur work done in someone's basement. I couldn't exactly pick out what any of them were from first glance, but they appeared to be script and symbols in a different language. She was fair skinned and had large, doe-like blue eyes. I couldn't decide if her dark makeup accentuated or decreased her beauty, making those doe-like eyes stand out as much as they did. All things considered, I thought she might be a very pretty, dainty girl if her look had been more natural. I got the impression that she was one of those small girls who wouldn't appreciate being called cute, but no matter how tough they tried to make themselves, you still couldn't help but think: *cute*.

"Sorry, I just feel like I already know you, because Lady Sage told me so much about you," she said excitedly. "You look different than I imagined."

I didn't know what to think about that and I self-consciously looked down. "Why would Lady Sage tell you so much about me?" I asked, bemused.

"Honestly, we don't get a lot of interesting people

coming in here," she admitted. "All of our readings are very boring past, present, and future readings. Lady Sage is especially adamant about keeping things quick and to the point. So for her to tell me that someone was unique and the reading didn't go as she planned, I knew something was up. She didn't tell me so much about you, as I tried to get information out of her."

I opened my mouth to ask more, but Tansy waved her little hand as if to dismiss any further questions. "Let's get started!" she exclaimed, motioning me into the small closet-like room that Lady Sage had done her readings in. I went into the room, like she asked, and sat in the same chair as before. With the illumination of one naked light bulb above our heads, I realized that without a doubt it was an ordinary closet stuffed with a zillion unlit candles, no longer mystical.

"Wait, hold on," she said and left the room. I wasn't sure, but it sounded like she locked the front door.

"I do things a lot differently than Lady Sage," she said, coming back and taking her seat. She pulled out a small notepad and pen from her pocket and set them on the table before flipping to a blank page. "For one thing, I don't do any bullshit. Lady Sage might have used your full name for example?" she asked, absentmindedly fiddling with her pen.

"Yes, she did," I admitted.

"You won't believe how many people that make appointments here, post about it on one of the social media sites and tag their friends in it. All Lady Sage has to do is look up the person who made the appointment and *bam!* From that point, you can find everyone coming to the session and find a lot of things about them from there. It's so easy, it's almost criminal."

I gaped at her, showing my surprise. I had originally come with no expectation of any of it being real, yes, but I wouldn't have dreamed that Lady Sage would perform a background check on me. I could see now how she would have figured out my lack of a love life and my background with music. There were a few social sites where I had a profile, and I made a mental note to set those profiles to private when I got home.

"I feel like she practices more on how to be a scam artist than actually practice her craft," she continued, tucking a few dyed black strands of hair behind her ear, revealing a row of silver hoop earrings. "But she isn't totally fake, in her defense. She does have a natural ability to read people's personalities, and she sometimes gets visions that are crazy accurate."

"Now as for me," she went on. "I am a witch. I am a spiritual person and practice my craft daily, and that is where my ability comes from. I can't read futures so much as I can help guide people's futures. I can give good luck charms and lift hexes and things like that. I can speak to the spirits, too, but they don't tell me people's futures per se. They might tell me something currently going on with you that might impel me to give you advice, but they don't tell me your future. My understanding is that they don't want you to know your future." It sounded like it was a practiced speech and she had said it a million times. Then she added in a hushed tone, "I can also do some less than acceptable stuff, but I don't practice dark arts, I just study it. Lady Sage doesn't approve of a lot of my techniques. She doesn't seem to like me doing any kind of spells or charms."

"So even in the psychic world, psychics judge other psychics?" I asked lightly. Even though I didn't believe in what she was saying, more specifically the talking-to-spirits bit and her being a witch, I found myself wanting her to like me.

"Ridiculous, right?" She beamed at me. "I guess no matter who you are, you're never free from judgment. Okay, let's get down to business. Tell me what Lady Sage told you. I don't think she told me everything, so I just want to get a clear picture of what happened."

"Okay," I started. "From what I remember, she said that I am musically inclined, which is true. She also knew that I'd never had a love life or a lot of friends..." I hated admitting it, but it was also true.

She made a curious *hmm* sound and scribbled something on her blank page. "What is your real name,

Cara?"

"My real name?" I asked, confused by the change of subject.

"Lady Sage told me your name is Cara Hansen, but that's not the name I'm getting. The spirits are giving me another name..." She started writing again, a look of pure concentration on her face as she wrote.

I shook my head. "Cara is my real name," I said, wondering at such a strange question.

She looked up from her scribbled piece of paper to look directly in my eyes. "I have this name," she said, turning her small notepad toward me so I could see it.

Carus Carminis, it read.

Goosebumps erupted on my legs and arms as I recognized the name. "I... I had almost forgotten about that," I stammered. "That was the original name my mom put on my birth certificate. She told me she didn't know what possessed her to name me that, except maybe the systemic painkillers she was given in labor. My name was supposed to be Ashley Marie, but after seeing Carus Carminis on my birth certificate, she decided to rename me Cara Marie a couple weeks after my birth." I was almost babbling at that point, but I was so taken aback.

"Wow, *I'm* even shocked a little bit. I wonder why that was important for me to know," she said, then shivered.

"That is so weird," I breathed, still in shock. I believed in her now. I wasn't sure what kind of abilities she had, but she definitely had something. No one should have known that, unless they knew my parents personally or did *very* extensive research on me—more than just social networking sites.

"Very weird," she agreed, though she didn't seem nearly as shook up as I was. "What else do you remember from the session?" she continued.

I shook my head again, trying to clear my mind. "Everything seemed accurate and kind of fun until she read the cards that supposedly told my future. The death card and the devil card..."

"Yes and that's probably when she saw that you didn't have a visible aura," Tansy said, nodding.

I stared at her blankly, not sure what she meant by that.

She stared back for a moment, then blinked those big doe eyes at me. "You know—an aura?"

I shook my head again.

"It's the electromagnetic energy surrounding your body. Every living thing has one, or is supposed to have one, but not many people can see them. Depending on a person's type of soul, whether they have a sensitive or a selfish soul, or whatever, it projects different colors. It's almost like a soul fingerprint. Lady Sage told me that she couldn't see your aura, which surprised her, because she's never *not* been able to read someone's aura before. That's what was so interesting about you."

"So, what does that mean—that she couldn't see mine?" I asked.

"I personally can't see them, so I only know what I've heard on that subject," she said slowly, as if preparing me for what she would say next. "But Lady Sage thinks that you don't have a soul."

I froze still, not daring to breathe as I tried to absorb this information. I had a soul. I had a personality, feelings, a conscience—you had to have those to have a soul, *right?*

"I don't believe that, though," Tansy said, waving her pen around as she talked. "I think you may have some special abilities, maybe one of those being to shield your aura from others. I've never heard of it, but hey, weirder things have happened."

Me, have special abilities like shielding my soul? I tried to make sense of that. Though I liked that idea better than not having a soul, they both sounded crazy.

"Okay, sorry, I interrupted... what else did Lady Sage tell you? Did she say anything about the death and devil card?" Tansy asked.

"Um, she got all weird. Her head snapped back and her eyes rolled in the back of her head for a moment," I said, trying to remember what I'd been trying to forget for the past week.

She flipped a page in her notebook so that she had a blank page ready. "So she had a vision," Tansy confirmed, an excited edge to her voice and gleam in her eyes. She seemed to hold onto my every word, gripping the blank notepad in front of her.

"I guess so," I shrugged. "Then she said I was going to be approached by a demonic presence or a demon and that he was near." *Coming,* she had said, her wide, panicked eyes staring at me. My blood went cold in my veins at the memory. I especially didn't like talking about it while being back in this closet-like room where it had happened.

"Have you come into contact with anyone new lately that stands out to you?" she asked, eyes intent on mine.

"Yes," I said immediately, thinking of the red-eyed man at the bar. "I think I know exactly who she saw in her vision. Or *what* she saw, or whatever." I almost surprised myself that I was freely talking about this. I didn't want to even tell my family of the weird things that I thought were happening, because any sane person would think I was going crazy. *I* thought I was going crazy! I wanted to stop myself from admitting these thoughts to this stranger, because part of me was trying to rationalize the strange things that had been happening. When I had been drunk with Liz, it had been easy to admit to my bizarre fears, but when I was sober and talking to a stranger, not so much.

"Tell me what you saw," she said, scribbling down in her note pad.

Might as well tell her everything, I thought, *or there was no point in coming here at all.* I sighed in defeat. "I work in a bar and this man sat down and he had red eyes with these weird slitted pupils that go sideways. They were sort of like a goat's, but not taking up the entire eye like a goat's do. Half human, half goat-like I guess..."

Her writing became more furious.

"...The next time I saw him, a few days later, he wore sunglasses."

"Were both of these instances at night?" she asked, her eyes still down on her notepad as she furiously drew on the page.

I thought about that for a second. "Yes, the only two times I saw him were at night. Is that important?"

"In this case, yes. Anything else happen?"

"Well, I don't know if this is relevant, but yesterday morning there were red dots in my vision, and they're still there. This started happening the next morning after I last saw him. I went to the eye doctor yesterday and they couldn't tell me anything."

She finally stopped scribbling and looked up at me. It looked like she had written a few sentences, drawn a pair of eyes, and scrawled one word over and over again. I couldn't exactly tell what it said.

"I have his name," she said, and that confused me.

"You've met him?" I asked incredulously.

"No, I haven't met him, but I'm almost positive that this is his name." She showed me her notes again. "Caymnaburus" was written over and over on the bottom of the page.

"How do you know that is his name, then?" I asked.

"Just like I knew your name. Spirits move me into writing things sometimes. Only when I concentrate do I get little snippets of things, and I try to write them down before I can forget them. I can't explain, but this is getting off subject." She started shaking her head. "I also keep on seeing a black cloud of smoke. This is usually the image the spirits give me for a curse. What I think has happened is you've been cursed by this demonic being with the red goat eyes."

"Cursed?" I asked. I suddenly felt my pulse pounding inside my head.

"It's okay, relax," she said, evidently sensing my panic. "A curse doesn't necessarily mean what people think it means. It doesn't mean anything bad is going to happen to you like a barren womb or a course of bad luck. Charms, incantations, and curses are all different forms of spells. A charm or incantation generally means it's been made up of plants or use of words, but a curse means that it has been made with blood magic. Bad, evil magic. It may not be anything too bad as far as the curse goes, but it's not from a friendly source."

Not at all comforting, I thought.

"He would have had to come in contact with your blood. Did you wake up with a cut the morning you started seeing the dots in your eyes?"

The memory of cutting myself on the Dom Pérignon foil flooded back to me. "No, but I cut myself at the bar that night on a piece of foil. He gave me a Band-Aid."

"Oh man," she groaned, lightly slapping her hand over her eyes. "And let me guess, the Band-Aid was gone the next morning."

"How'd you know?" I asked, surprised.

She sighed and moved her hand away from her face, big blue eyes staring intently. "Let me tell you about demons, Cara. They are the worst things you can come in contact in this world or the next. They can read your greatest fears and use them against you. They can watch you by day and they can prowl this world in any kind of form they wish by night. They can take a part of themselves and give it to you—in this instance, the Band-Aid. But he disappears out of existence at daybreak and the Band-Aid, along with your blood on it, went with him. Poof!" She flung her hands in the air. "Gone."

I stared at her for a moment, not sure how to proceed. "What do I do?" I finally asked, and it came out as a whisper.

"First we have to lift this curse, whatever it is. It could be something as innocent as keeping tabs on you out of curiosity. I bet he could sense that you were different, couldn't see your aura, maybe, and wanted to figure out why," she said, then seemed to remember something. "Did you ask him about his eyes?"

"Yes," I answered. "He seemed shocked, like he didn't know his eyes were red at first."

"Because he definitely has a disguise he has conjured up, and that probably included some kind of pretty eye color.

For some reason you could see his real eyes. I don't know how that is possible, because I've seen a demon once and I don't think even I could see anything that it didn't want me to see." She looked as if she saw something that wasn't in the room and suddenly shook her head and waved her pen around as if she were swatting it away. "Anyway, we are going to have to lift this curse, whatever it is. Even if it's not causing you any current danger, being in a demon's radar is never a good thing. We may have to do it somewhere else, though. This is not an appropriate place for lifting curses. I'd get my ass handed to me if Lady Sage caught me lifting curses in here."

As if on cue, we heard the sound of someone unlocking and opening the front door. The little bell above the door jingled. "Tansy! Why is the front door locked and the open sign off?" someone called out. I was pretty sure it was Lady Sage and the look in Tansy's suddenly wide blue eyes showed her alarm.

Suddenly Lady Sage looked inside the door frame and there was a moment of stunned silence. She looked startled as she caught sight of me, but her expression quickly flashed into anger. Tansy looked like she had already accepted whatever was going to happen, still facing me, and not bothering to turn in Lady Sage's direction.

"Tansy," Lady Sage whispered, as if she did more than whisper she would scream. "What is she doing here?" There was another painful moment of silence, the tension so thick you could slice it up and fry it. When Lady Sage realized Tansy wasn't going to respond, her eyes flicked back to me. "Please leave. And never come back." I was surprised at how she said it, so calmly, like she was saying something entirely different. I didn't move for a second, and not because I was trying to be uncooperative. I was scared shitless of her!

"Please leave and never come back!" she screamed. I flinched, then stood up kind of nervously as she moved away from the door to let me move past her.

Suddenly Tansy snapped out of her frozen state and jerked her head. "I'm just trying to help!" she yelled.

"Tansy, you went against *exactly* what I asked of you. I don't think you can possibly come up with a good excuse this time. I've had enough! You're fired."

I walked out of the building and froze on the front porch, wondering if I should leave or not. I knew I should at least shut the door behind me, but I didn't.

"Get your stuff and go." A lot of the anger had left Lady Sage's voice, and I could hear a lot of clambering around as Tansy packed her stuff.

I caught a glimpse of Lady Sage walking around with what looked to be a smoldering stick in one hand and a feather in the other, waving smoke around. "I cleanse this room of impurities, evil spirits, and anything that does not support the good energy of this place of business," she was saying over and over, and I wondered if it was her intention to have me hear. I decided to wait by my car, suddenly aware of how very unwelcome I was. A few minutes later, I saw Tansy come out onto the porch, illuminated by the light coming from inside, a cardboard box in her arms.

"You're insane, you know that?" she yelled into the doorway. I didn't hear if Lady Sage replied, but the door slammed shut in her face.

Tansy walked to me slowly, looking down into her box and kicking pieces of gravel with her black boots. She finally looked up when she got close.

"I'm sorry I got you fired," I said before she could say anything. I guess I hadn't really gotten her fired, but I did feel somewhat responsible.

"It was a long time coming," she said, sighing. "I might be able to get a job at one of the other psychic places in town. I have some connections."

"I'll still pay you for our session."

"You don't have to pay me. That wasn't much of a session."

"But I want to," I insisted, going through my bag to get to my wallet.

"No, no, pay me at the next session if you want," she said and I stopped digging through my purse. "We should meet as soon as possible so we can get this curse lifted."

"Okay, when should we do it?" I asked, thinking of my work schedule.

She chewed on her lip, considering it. "Probably at night. The full moon is coming up in a few days, so that'll probably be helpful."

Thinking she was making a joke, I laughed, but when she only stared with a very serious expression, I cleared my throat. "Okay. Well, I work tomorrow morning, but I'm off at night."

"The full moon is the night after that, and I'm going to need a little bit of time to get all the things I need. How about then?"

"Monday?" I clarified. "I have to work that night till two thirty. Is three o' clock AM too late?" Ugh, that was too late for me, but hell! If I was going to do this, I wanted to get it done and over with as soon as possible.

"Monday night—or Tuesday morning, I should say— is good. Sorry, I'm just not up for anything after this shit," she said, jerking her head toward her now former place of work.

"Yeah, I understand."

"All right. Well, let me give you my number and you can call me Monday to get my address," she said. "And if anything else happens, you can call me." She gave me her number and I saved it in my phone. "Well, see you then," she said, walking away, heading toward the back of the building, where I'm guessing she parked her car.

"Bye!" I said.

"Oh!" she turned suddenly, facing me again, gravel crunching beneath her boots. "Do you own a blessed cross?"

"A blessed cross?" For the life of me, I couldn't handle the subject change.

"I read in a very reliable book that a cross or crucifix that's been prayed over can protect you," she answered.

"I don't have one," I answered. "But my mom has a cross necklace. Could I have her pray over that?"

"If she is a believer, yes, do that as soon as possible. And a silver cross is preferable, or so I've read."

"I'm actually allergic to silver..." I let the words hang. As soon as I said it, I had a passing thought. My allergy to silver suddenly seemed more strange than it ever had before, though I couldn't really figure out why. It had always been a little strange, because the allergy was rare, but everyone has weird facts about themselves, right? Some person may have one foot significantly larger than the other or have the urge to sneeze every time they eat chocolate, but that doesn't mean anything significant. Something nagged at me like an itch wanting to be scratched, but I dismissed the feeling.

Tansy seemed to have an idea of her own, because her eyes got a little too wide, but I dismissed that as well. "Non silver may work just as well. Also, lay salt underneath your doors and windows," she said.

"Just the ones leading outside?" I asked.

"Just the ones leading outside," she confirmed. "Goodnight, Cara. See you Monday night," she said, her voice sounding oddly shaken.

I locked the doors immediately after jumping in my little white Honda and drove off the lot. My mind raced with thoughts, and before I realized what I was doing, I was taking a right to go to my parents' instead of going straight toward downtown. I cursed, then took a deep breath and allowed myself to feel relieved about the change in direction. I would feel much safer if I stayed the night at my parents'. Also, I could snag a cross and have my mom pray over it. That was going to be a strange conversation, but I'd cross that bridge when and if I came to it.

After a moment, I started thinking about all the worrisome things Tansy had said and I started trembling. As I drove down a dark street, I imagined the red-eyed man appearing in the road to get me and thankfully, nothing like that happened. I chuckled to myself, thinking maybe I watched too many movies, but anxiety quickly set in again. My heart was beating so hard, I felt like it might explode out of my chest. I didn't feel safe, even with my car doors locked, and when I finally parked in my parent's driveway, it took all my courage to not sprint toward the front door. As soon as I walked in the door and shut it behind me, I sighed, feeling instant relief.

"Hey, Carebear," my step-father said, calling me by my childhood nickname. He heaved himself up from the couch to give me a squeeze and a kiss on my forehead.

"Hi, Dad," I said, my voice coming out a little breathy.

"Didn't expect you coming home tonight," he said.

"I know, I..." I started.

"Cara!" my mother exclaimed from the kitchen. "Do you want a grilled cheese sandwich?" she asked, holding up a plate and setting it down at the bar.

"I thought that was for me!" Bruce said, only slightly teasing.

"I'll make you another one," she said, waving a hand at him in a dismissive gesture and then aiming a smile at me.

He went back to the couch, eyes focused on the TV in a sudden trance. By the familiar sounds, I knew he was watching football, and I couldn't believe that he had gotten up from the couch to give me a hug and kiss while it was on. "Good to have you here, Cara, it really is," he said, eyes still glued on the game. I smiled.

I was kind of surprised they hadn't asked me why I'd come. It wasn't like me to show up before bed time unannounced, but they acted as if it were a common occurrence. "You guys are going crazy now that both of your children have flown the coop," I accused, pretty much bounding toward my grilled cheese sandwich. I felt so much safer at home, like I could forget all the madness of the week.

"Yeah, well, your dad is going crazy," my mom admitted, pointing at him with her spatula as she made another sandwich. I stuffed some grilled cheese in my mouth, watching her from my bar stool.

"Whatever she says, you cannot move back in!" Bruce yelled to us over the TV.

"You can move back in if you want to," my mom whispered, smiling.

"It's okay, I don't want to move back in, Mom," I whispered back, not able to help my own smile.

She forced her mouth into a frown to say she was pouting, but I wasn't fooled. "How did your appointment go? You never told me."

My psychic appointment? I stiffened before I realized she was talking about my eye-doctor's appointment the day before. Either way, it all revolved around the same subject that I just couldn't get away from. I hoped the anxiety I had been feeling earlier and was suddenly feeling again didn't show plain on my face. "Well, um," I started, then took another bite of my grilled cheese to give me some time to come up with something. I held up one finger, motioning her to wait a minute. "They thought it might have something to do with my sensitivity toward sunlight. They told me I need to get a really good pair of UV protection sunglasses," I said finally. The lie was so good, I surprised even myself. At first, I didn't think she was going to buy it, due to my obvious attempt at buying time, but if she second-guessed me, it didn't show.

"Do you have money for nice sunglasses?" she asked, grabbing a plate from the cupboard and dumping Bruce's sandwich onto it.

It suddenly occurred to me that she might try to buy me expensive sunglasses on the count of my lie. "Yeah, I do," I said, letting the lies pile on. I didn't have a couple hundred dollars to get nice sunglasses lying around, but I would scrape up money for them if it stopped her from buying them. I really hated lying, but in this instance, I was convinced it was better than telling the truth. I was worried enough for myself without my mom getting involved. I could only imagine what she would do if I told her everything. Try to have an exorcism performed on me? *Please, no, thank you.*

My mom is really weird when it comes to religion. I

feel like she's tried to convince us that she's not Christian and she doesn't want anything to do with church—except the occasional holiday—but I don't buy it. I think she doesn't *want* to believe, because when she grew up, she felt she was forced to believe. "In our house, we will serve the Lord," was my grandfather's quote when he was alive. I think because it was forced down her throat before she had a chance to make up her own mind, she still rebels against it. I think she does believe in God though, whether she says so or not. Whenever some crisis happens, she turns to prayer and when she wants to give advice, it seems to come straight from the Bible. As much as I hated lying, it was the price I had to pay to keep the peace...and not a church service.

"This isn't something to be taken lightly, Cara. You need your eyesight. If you can't pay for your own sunglasses, let me know."

"Thanks Mom, but I got this," I assured her.

"Okay, if you say so," she said, putting the used pan in the sink to soak. "Now I'm going to go to bed." As she went to give Bruce his sandwich and kiss him goodnight, I contemplated asking for a cross necklace. Though I didn't want to ask for fear of more questions I'd have to lie through, if I was going to do it, there'd be no better time than now. When she turned to say goodnight to me, I spat out, "Mom, before you go to bed, can I borrow one of your cross necklaces?"

She suddenly looked suspicious. "Why do you want to borrow a cross necklace?" she asked. *Ah, mother, you know me all too well.*

I laughed a little. "It's silly, but I feel like maybe it will comfort me and help me from having bad dreams." Another lie.

"Oh, no, are you having bad dreams again?" she asked, looking suddenly sympathetic. I had had frequent night terrors throughout my childhood, so bad that I couldn't spend the night at other peoples' houses. I never knew what had spiked the dreams, because as far as I could remember, I had never had anything traumatic happen to me that they might've stemmed from. Nevertheless, I used to wake up screaming bloody murder and when one of my parents came into my room, I'd tell them about a "snake man" on the ceiling. I hardly remembered the actual dreams now, only the feeling of terror and what my parents relayed to me. Though I don't remember much of the actual dreams, I've since developed a severe fear of snakes.

I shrugged, not wanting to open my mouth to say another lie.

"Well, that's not silly at all," she said, all suspicion leaving and a hint of a smile playing on her lips like she was proud I was turning to God in a crisis. "Let me go get one. I think I have a cheap nickel one that you can have that Aunt Bonnie gave to me."

Usually a little silver pendant won't irritate my skin too badly, but a silver chain necklace or earrings that are constantly on the skin leave chafed red marks or welts. My mom never forgets about my allergy and only buys me really cheap costume jewelry, or gold on special occasions, which I appreciate about her.

I sat there for a moment finishing my sandwich and when I went to put my dish in the dishwasher, my mom reappeared. "Here you go," she said, placing the necklace around my neck. It was a very plain metal cross and chain, decorated with fake turquoise beads. "There's no reason to worry about any bad dreams. You're safe." She put her arms around my shoulders and squeezed.

"I know, Mom," I said, leaning back into her hug. "But just in case, will you say a little prayer over my cross?"

She let me go and spun me around to face her so she could look at me suspiciously again. She had that look that said, "Who are you and what have you done with my daughter?" But she did as I asked without question. "Lord God, please protect Cara tonight and every night. Keep her safe and keep your loving arms around her. Amen." She hugged me again, and I hugged her back. "There's really nothing to be afraid of."

"I know there isn't," I said. But I was lying again.

There might be something to be afraid of.

She released me, said her goodnight to Bruce again, and went to their bedroom. I waited till she closed the door behind her and Bruce's eyes were back on the game to grab salt from the cupboard. I poured a large amount of it into a measuring cup and looked at the back of Bruce's head, frowning to myself. I could take a cup of salt and spread it heavily underneath the door and windows of Jessie's room, but I couldn't possibly do it to every door and window in the entire house. Not without my parents wondering what I was doing.

I hoped the salt ritual wouldn't keep me safe and leave them as some sort of targets. I tried to push those thoughts out of my mind. If Tansy was right and he was just curious about me, he probably didn't want to do me or my family any harm. *Just a curious demon. Totally harmless*, I thought. *Right.*

As soon as I woke up on Monday, I got Tansy's address by way of text message and began counting down the hours till I would see her. Her home was about thirty minutes away in Johns Island, which was outside my realm of familiarity, but I'd manage.

Angel Oak was very crowded that night, and the first few hours I hardly had a moment where I wasn't running between tables, which I was grateful for. When the dinner crowd started dwindling away around eight-forty, I suddenly realized the sun had set. It hadn't really occurred to me that *he* could be coming tonight, but as soon as I thought it, I saw him. And he was sitting in my section. I froze for a moment, staring at the back of his head while he gave the appearance of casually looking over the menu. Just a regular customer, here to get some food and drink. *Suuure.*

I contemplated giving my table to someone else, but when I looked around, there were no other waitresses in sight. Just my luck. I took a deep, shaky breath and walked to his table. He looked up and smiled at me as I approached, sunglasses pushed high on the bridge of his nose to hide his eyes. He was wearing a dark blue collared shirt rolled up over his forearms, which were perfectly muscled, I couldn't help but notice. When some people are pale, you can see all their veins, hairs, and blemishes, but he didn't have any imperfections to speak of and the dark blue of his shirt accentuated the milky paleness of his skin. His curly hair looked soft and those full lips looked absolutely kissable. My heart started beating fast in my chest, and it wasn't just because I was afraid of what he might be. He looked even more perfect than I remembered. I found myself wishing that he would take off his stupid sunglasses. *Then again*, I thought, *I probably don't want that*.

"Hello, what can I get you?" I asked, trying to sound like my normal cheerful self, the way I usually talked to customers.

"Hello again. I think I'm going to get a dirty bloody Mary, like usual." At least it wasn't the Dom Pérignon, I guess.

"All right, coming right up," I said, twirling on my heel to put the order in with the bartender.

"Hold on," he said, reaching out and touching my wrist. I jerked my hand back as if I'd been stung, not able to stop my reaction. I glanced around the restaurant to see if anyone had noticed my dramatic behavior, and surprisingly, no one was paying any attention to us. To me, it seemed that everyone should notice this guy and sense his otherworldliness. The small patch of skin on my wrist where he had touched me tingled, and my whole body seemed to focus on that one spot. *Tingle* was maybe too mild of a word. It almost felt like I had touched a live wire and could still feel the effects. I thought it wasn't just the feeling you get when someone attractive touches you. Not that I know much about that, but it felt like something much more. A flashing neon sign in my head blinked, *Danger! Danger!* "Is something wrong?" he asked.

"No," I lied quickly, thinking that was an odd question to ask your waitress. Then again, nothing about our interaction since he'd started coming here had been normal for a waitress and patron.

"You're afraid of me," he said. It wasn't a question, but there was a hint of surprise and maybe accusation in his voice. I wondered if he really could read my fears upon sight like Tansy had said. "Why?" he asked.

"I'm not afraid of you," I said, and tried to smile convincingly, but the sudden high pitch of my voice gave me away.

"Well, good. My name is Caymn, by the way." He was trying to be friendly and probably ease some of my tension, but it wasn't working.

"Caymn," I repeated, logging it into my brain for storage or maybe for lack of anything else to say. Suddenly, I realized that it most definitely had to be the shortened version of Caymnaburus, the name Tansy had given him. My mouth suddenly felt dry.

"What's your name?" he prodded. I realized I must be looking at him strangely.

"Cara," I said, my voice cracking a little bit.

"Cara," he said, repeating my name as I had done. "That's funny—our names are kind of similar. Caymn and Cara."

That was true, but I didn't remark on it, too distracted with the sound of our names together—like a couple. A moment passed where we just stared at each other, me probably looking like a deer in headlights and him looking puzzled, though it was hard to read his expression with sunglasses on. "I'll get you your dirty bloody Mary," I said when I was finally able to pull myself out of my stupid inner-monologue.

"Fine," he said, flinging his hands up and making an exasperated sound like he was giving up making small talk with me. *Good*, I thought. *Please give up.*

As I asked the bartender on duty for a dirty bloody Mary, Hannah, the hostess on the clock, slid casually next to me. "Hey, girl," she said, giving me a mischievous grin and huddling in close as if we were long-time buddies. We weren't.

"Hello, Hannah," I said warily.

"So, who's that guy?" she asked, turning her head to stare at Long-haired-sunglasses across the restaurant.

I shrugged. "I don't really know him."

"He seemed to know you! He asked to sit in your section," she said, eyes still glued to the back of his head in obvious lust.

That didn't completely surprise me. Though I couldn't come up with a logical reason why he would be interested in me, he apparently was. According to Tansy, I was different, but since no one was ever interested in me, I dubbed him Weirdest Dude Ever.

"He's so hot," Hannah went on, running her fingers through her hair. "I wonder why he wanted to sit in your section," she said incredulously.

I didn't miss the insult there, though she seemed oblivious to it. When my bloody Mary was set in front of me, I smiled at the bartender and walked off without another word to Hannah. As I set the drink down in front of Long-haired-sunglasses, I tried to smile. I was doing my best not to be openly rude, no matter how much discomfort I felt around him.

"Cara, I have a question," he said. The sound of my name coming out of his mouth made my stomach flip flop. I wasn't sure what scared me more: him knowing my name or that I liked how he said it. I didn't say anything, not trusting my voice. "Are you good friends with Elizabeth?" The question was so unexpected, it caught me off guard.

"Liz?" I asked.

"Yes, *Liz-z-z*." he answered, strangely dragging her name out.

I considered Liz to be one of my only friends, but I contemplated what I should tell him. He evidently had some weird interest in me, so I wondered if my next words would steer his interest toward her. Did I want him to be interested in Liz? No. And not only because it seemed his interest could be hazardous to one's health. If I was honest, I felt a little twinge of jealousy. Not sure what to do, I decided to downplay our friendship. "No, we're not really friends. We just chat while we're at work sometimes." After I said it, I thought I should have just told him it was none of his F-ing business and to butt out.

"Oh," he said, not offering an explanation. I felt so uneasy being near him that I didn't want to ask for one and risk causing the conversation to go on even longer.

"Anything else I can get you?" I chirped with false cheerfulness.

"No," he said dismissively, looking at his drink as if in deep thought. "Thank you."

He ordered another drink later on and asked for his check, but that was the last we conversed that night. When I went to pick up his change, I caught a glimpse of him walking out of the restaurant and onto the street. I stared maybe a little longer than I needed to, but I had almost expected him to vanish into thin air. I opened the check holder and collected the cash. He had left me a twenty-dollar tip, which was generous. I wondered if the money would disappear out of existence the next morning like the Band-Aid had. *Not like I need one more piece of evidence against him*, I thought.

Seven

I growled with exasperation at myself as I hopped into the driver's seat of my little white Honda. Why would he have asked about Liz? I could think of one good reason: she's beautiful. Way prettier than me. I hated that Caymn had asked about her and I hated myself for hating it. I should have been more worried for her, but my jealousy was getting the better of me.

I turned the key in the ignition, the engine puttering to life, and before I put the car in reverse I checked my cell phone. *A missed call from Liz.* We had worked opposite schedules these past two days, which I realized was how our shifts normally worked for Sunday and Monday, but I hadn't noticed it till then. I decided I'd call her the next day, since it was almost three in the morning. I had to pay close attention to the directions to Tansy's house, anyway.

The first fifteen minutes of the drive were easy, but when I got out to Johns Island, the rural roads had hardly any street lights and darkness hugged closely around the windows of my car. I hunched over the steering wheel, trying not to miss any turns. Large oak trees hung over the winding road, looming dangerously close to my car as I whizzed by.

I almost missed her driveway, but at the last moment caught sight of a sign with reflective letters reading "McGee," a marker that Tansy had told me about. With a sharp right turn and the scary sound of my tires skidding on loose gravel, I was on her driveway. The driveway turned out to be a dirt road going through trees, and for a whole long minute of driving down it, I wondered if I had accidentally made the wrong turn. Finally it opened up and I saw a little house. It was hard to see details in the dark, but it appeared to be a small one story in multiple shades of brown brick and wood paneling. Tansy sat on the front porch, smoking a cigarette and curled over her knees like it was cold, which it certainly wasn't.

I parked behind an old station wagon with too many stickers on the back. There was a cluster of stickers on the back window showing a little family of stick figures: a mom, a daughter, and two cats, each either carrying a wand or wearing a witch's hat. There was a "My other car is a broom" sticker as well as others about preserving nature and animal rights.

When she walked up to my car window as I stepped out, it was hard not to feel insanely tall next to her, her head hardly reaching my chest area. At a passing glance, you could easily mistake her for a child. She looked a lot different from last time without a drop of makeup and her short bangs pulled back with a clip. She had dressed a lot more relaxed in checkered sneakers, gray sweats that went to the knee, and a faded black cami with no bra. Her face was pretty and she looked like a dainty, china doll, the way I imagined she would without all that black makeup and 6-inch boots. No matter how pretty and normal her clothes and makeup, though, she would always stand out in any crowd with her arms and lower legs covered in tattoos that looked almost like a kid's sloppy handwriting. I noticed that the tattoos on her right arm were noticeably neater and better than the chicken scrawl on her left arm. And even if she covered up the tattoos, the bull-like nose piercing on her delicate face would make you do a double take.

"Is it okay that I parked here?" I asked.

"Yeah, that's fine," she whispered. "We have to be quiet when we go through the house, okay? My mom's sleeping."

"Okay," I whispered back.

We walked up the tiny porch and I noticed the wreath on the front door was a pentagram, a star made out of twigs in the center of an otherwise simple-looking wreath. The first room was a small living room with a green and brown color scheme, the only light coming from the TV which was on low volume. Though her family seemed to be lower income, someone kept the house clean and smelling nice, like herbs and flowers. A little white and brown cat lay on the back of the green couch, staring at us as we walked through, its eyes catching the light off the TV. She motioned me through the living room, through a kitchen/dining room that was too dark to pick out a color scheme, and through a glass door to the backyard.

A few brick steps descended from the back door into the backyard, if you could call the tiny space a yard. The small amount of earth between the house and the trees was filled with flowers and plants. Down the middle was a dirt path, which led straight into the woods.

"This way," she said and I followed her down the path.

"Into the woods?" I hissed, not liking this. Hell, I didn't like going into the woods in the day time, let alone at night trying to lift curses.

"Yeah, it's not far, don't worry. We'll be able to talk more freely when we get to the circle." I wondered what she meant by the circle, but decided not to ask. I'd find out soon enough. I sighed as I made the first step into the woods, unsuccessfully trying to release my unease.

We hadn't walked far at all when something made me look behind us and I was surprised to see a pair of cat eyes, eerily catching the moonlight. "Someone's following us," I said.

"Who?" I wasn't looking at Tansy, but I could hear the surprise in her voice and I would've bet she'd jumped. She was nervous too and that wasn't at all comforting. "Oh, that's Herman," she said and sighed with obvious relief.

"Your cat?" I asked as Herman came up. I held my hand out and he pressed his head into my palm, coaxing me to pet him. He was kind of an ugly cat, in a cute sort of way. He was black with a very thin face, pointed snout, very slanted greenish-yellow eyes, and disproportionately large ears. The more I looked at him, the more I decided he had the ugliest cat face I'd ever seen.

"No, he just kind of comes and goes. He's been coming around here since, geez, it's been almost ten years now."

I ran my hand along him a few times, then stood so we could continue down the path. He went along ahead of us like he knew where we were going, and I idly thought he looked like a younger cat with his shiny black coat, much younger than ten years. Not like I know much about cats, but it was a passing thought.

"Strangely, I've been seeing Herman since I saw a demon when I was eleven. I like to think that he is my little guardian, protecting me. Is that silly?"

"No, that's not silly." Of course a cat wasn't protecting her, but who was I to burst her bubble?

"Do you want to know how I first came to see a demon?" she asked. She looked at me and I could hardly see her face, but I thought she looked vulnerable. Insecure, maybe. She peered at me as if to judge the look on my face.

I didn't really want to talk about demons more than we had to, at least not here, in the woods and in the dark. This was a horrible place to do whatever it was we were doing, I was sure of it, and I wondered why I had agreed to it.

"Yeah, tell me," I said, politeness ruling over.

She was right, we didn't have to go far, just far enough so that we were hidden from view of her house in the trees. The dirt path ended at a large, beautiful circular patio made from white stones and lined with whitewashed brick. The only light came from a fire pit with a dying fire in the center of the circle and the full moon, hidden behind trees. First thing Tansy did was put a log and a handful of pine straw in the fire pit to boost the flames. It looked like an amazing place to tell ghost stories and huddle by the fire with s'mores, but without any chairs or other furniture that you'd expect to see. Besides the fire pit in the middle, there was only a small table with objects I could only guess were things to start a fire. Besides that, the large slab was pretty barren. Herman sat as far as he could from the fire while still being on the patio, tail twitching back and forth, watching us with those slanted, yellow-green eyes.

Tansy poked at the fire and began her story. "When I was eleven, me and my old best friend went with my mother to one of her coven meetings at this old woman's house. We got bored during the meeting and ended up peeking in a few of the rooms that were open. There was this bookcase in her house with the most books on spells and magic that I'd ever seen, and we found this book... it was this huge red leather-bound book with demons all over it." As she talked, she motioned with her free hand, poking at the fire with her other. "Of course, we were instantly intrigued by it. My friend ended up stealing it and hid it in her backpack. I told her not to, but she wouldn't listen to me." The way she told it, I could tell it still infuriated her. "That night she spent the night over, and she talked me into doing an incantation from the book. We ended up calling a demon into my bedroom! Fortunately, I had convinced her to take the extra time to cast a circle for it to come into, so we were sort of protected. It was a woman, or a man making himself like a woman, however they do it, I don't know. She was naked, except for being covered in rats, which is my worst fear. She even made her hair to look like long, wriggling rat-tails." Tansy shuddered.

"It's an irrational fear, especially because I'm a witch and I believe in being connected with nature, but I'm deathly afraid of rats."

"So what happened?" I urged. I was interested now, even though the story caused me to get goosebumps even in the summer heat.

"She warned me that if I ever called her again, she would kill me. She was very…" She stopped prodding at the fire and looked at me. "Descriptive." I could tell it had been a traumatic experience by the haunted look in her eyes.

"That's terrifying," I said. "What happened to the book?"

"I still have it," she shrugged. "I thought about burning it after that experience, but I had a strong urge not to. I also didn't want to tell my mom that my friend had stolen it and I hadn't told on her. Time just kept going on, and I never had the guts to tell her. You're actually the only person I've told about that."

I stared into the flames for a moment, watching them lick over the wood. We were quiet for a while.

"Let's get started," she finally said. She walked over to a spot between the fire pit and the small table and pointed to her feet. "Why don't you stand over here." She stepped aside, moving closer to the table so I could move to the spot she'd pointed out. As I walked closer to the thing, I realized it wasn't a table on the edge of the circle at all, but an altar made from one large stone slab with bricks underneath it, supporting its weight. On it was an animal skull with small antlers, probably a young deer, along with a small statue of a woman, a double-edged dagger, chalices, candles, crystals, and a few other little things.

"Okay, so I'm going to cast a circle around us. It's a common ritual that I've done before. It basically makes a circle of protection around you, so that you can do your magic in a safe place, free from bad entities. I think if you're in it, it will cast any bad entities and curses from you," she said. "Just in case it doesn't, I'll have you do a cleansing ritual."

"O-okay," I said, my voice shaking a little nervously.

If the obvious tension in her shoulders told me anything, she was nervous, too. "Most witches believe that if you simply don't believe in a curse, you don't give it power. I do believe that to an *extent*, but I think if it's a curse from an actual demon, there is power to it whether you believe or not. Most witches don't believe in demons either, but I think you and I both have reason to."

I had no idea what to do with my arms suddenly, and I hugged them against myself. "Two weeks ago I didn't believe in them," I whispered.

She nodded. "So just stand there and don't move or talk until I say, all right? I don't want to get distracted and have to start over."

She grabbed a little bell from the altar and jingled it three times. A silence fell over the woods; I hadn't even noticed there were sounds until there was an absence of them. She took a match from a matchbox, struck it, and lit two of the candles on the altar, one on the right, one on the left. "Goddess and god, be here with me and guide me." She started lifting things from the altar up in the air and chanted, asking for blessings from "the goddess" and "the god." She then grabbed the double-edged dagger off the altar, kissed the blade, pointed it toward the woods, and walked around the edge of the circle, chanting:

"In this place, a circle round,
I consecrate this sacred ground,
With golden light, this place surround,
O power here, contain and bound."

She repeated the chant and her walk around the circle three times, then lay the dagger back down. She started walking around the circle once more and stopped a quarter of the way. She bent over and for the first time I noticed three other candles around the circle, all in opposite corners of the altar. Well, circles don't have corners, but you know what I mean. She bent to light a candle, stood, then chanted,

"The guardians of the East, I call upon you
to consecrate this circle with the element of air.

Be welcomed and honored,
and may you guide me with your presence."

She lit another candle and then another, welcoming fire in the south, and water in the west, and then lit the large candle on the altar and chanted for earth in the north.

As soon as the circle was closed, I knew it, and not just because the red spots in my eyes disappeared. Somehow I knew that if I went to the edge of the circle and extended my hands, I would touch something solid. It should have made me claustrophobic, but instead I felt something else. It was something that I had never felt before, like a sense that I never knew I had, almost a looseness or stretchiness in my skin. I had been trapped in a tight, constricting shell my whole life and I hadn't known it existed until now that it seemed to be gone. I almost felt like I could extend myself, feeling the fire and the stone—no, *tasting* the fire and stone. Tasting the cleansing energy within the fire. Tasting the remnants of magic and the energies of the people who had stood on the stone before me. I was trying to figure out all of what I was feeling when Tansy screamed and latched onto my arm, fingernails digging into my skin. There was pure fear in that scream, but I was feeling too many things to think clearly. I looked at her and then followed her eyes into the woods.

I saw someone then, but it took a few long seconds for my brain to register what I was seeing. Just a few yards outside our circle loomed a man—or what had the body shape of a man—holding onto a tree, only touching it with his fingertips and balls of his feet. No human could possibly hold onto a tree like that. He was sickeningly skinny with saggy, pale pinkish skin. His eyes were red, but they weren't goat eyes or like any eyes I'd ever seen. They were completely red and the only thing that hinted at where his gaze aimed was a ring that caught the light from the fire. He had no ears and absolutely no hair on his naked body, making him look like a mix between human and a naked mole rat.

"Taaaaannnsssssyyyy," he said, drawing her name out, twisting his neck to an impossible angle. His voice was surprisingly deep, not just in tone, but as if there were power behind it. The very sound felt like scratching fingernails inside my head and I could swear I heard the high-pitched screeching of frightened rats. I didn't have to be afraid of rats to have fear knot up my stomach. Tansy put her face into my body and made involuntary noises, her whole tiny body shaking.

He laughed, loud and deep, and the sound painfully reverberated in the back of my skull. His teeth were rat-like, too long for his face and grotesquely yellow and brown.

"Don't be afraid, Tansy," I whispered, trying to sound brave. "He can't touch us." I thought less of myself for it, but I was silently grateful that his eyes were on her and not me.

"Tansy, you have done a very naughty thing," he continued, waving a long-nailed finger at us. "You will have to pay the price. A very high price, at that."

"What did she do? Why is there a price?" I yelled at him.

He ignored me. "Do you even know what you've undone, little witch?" he asked her, leaping down the tree. Like a cat, he fell perfectly on his feet. He walked closer to the circle and Tansy moved back, pushing me closer to the fire in the center. I could feel the heat on my skin, uncomfortably close. She was frantically shaking her head like she could shake the image of him away. When I glanced down, I saw that even Herman had moved to stand behind us, trying to get out of the demon's line of vision. "You've undone a more complicated curse than you can ever imagine, one that requires enough blood to drown an ox in." As he stomped around the circle, as if searching for a weak spot, he wore a disturbing expression that I couldn't distinguish between anger and derangement. "Ten curses in one!"

Who was this? Why had I been cursed with ten curses in one? I couldn't imagine why anyone would want to curse me at all! I was just a very uninteresting girl raised in an uninteresting place!

He continued to stare down the frightened little girl next to me and opened his mouth of too many teeth again. "I could take you home and you could be my familiar for the extent of your miserable life, little witch. I really could do that, you know. It's about time for a new one."

What the hell is a familiar? I wondered. Tansy made another noise that sounded like a whimper.

"But I won't do that, little witch. Not to you. You know what I'm really going to do to you?" He hovered close to the circle, hands suddenly moving along it. *Oh god, please tell me he couldn't break the circle.* "I will tear you in two and spill every drop of your blood into my new curse. I must remake it, you see. If your little body doesn't hold enough blood for me, I'll finish it with your loved ones. Your..." He paused, squinting toward the direction of the house. "Mother."

"Caymnaburus," Tansy finally spoke, the threat toward her mother helping her to gather enough anger, and through that, strength. She stomped toward the altar, and I saw him suddenly disappear. She screamed when he reappeared right before her, close enough to grab her if it weren't for the protective circle. She managed to grab whatever she needed from the altar, the task bringing her only inches from him, and retreated to the center next to me. He had moved so fast, it created the illusion that he had disappeared and reappeared. She extended her arm toward him, holding the small knife she'd used to make the circle that I now know as an *athame*. "I banish you back to whence you came, the goddess as my protector, the saving light, and your ultimate bane!"

He laughed again, long and deep. The very sound crashed into my head like a lightning bolt and we both wobbled on our feet. "You... can't... banish... me... without... my... name," he said, forming every word so slowly and deliberately like he didn't have to worry about how much time it took. It was very inhuman. "Very curious that you think I'm Caymnaburus. Very curious." He cocked his bald head to the side, implying his curiousness.

For the first time, he looked at me, and my stomach threatened to jump out of my body. "I am someone else, but you already knew that, didn't you, Carus?"

Did he call me Cara or Carus? The thought occurred to me, but it was a fleeting thought. His question seemed more important. I had known that he wasn't Caymnaburus, hadn't I? Whoever this was, he evidently knew me enough to put curses over me, but I didn't know him at all. I knew he wasn't Caymn, at the very least. "Yes," I whispered, knowing that my voice would tremble if I spoke aloud. His eyes caught the light from the fire, red light shining eerily when I met his gaze. The hair on the back of my neck was standing up at attention. When I looked down at Herman, curled around my feet, so was his.

"Do you know who I am?" he prodded.

"No," I answered truthfully, glancing back up and regretting it.

He laughed again, more uproariously than ever. Tansy smacked her hands against her ears and held them, falling to her knees. I covered my ears too and cowered from the noise. Suddenly he seemed to change, his pale, saggy body becoming darker and hard-muscled. It wasn't like molding clay morphing into a different shape, but like sand was coming from nowhere and adding pieces to his body. Horns sprouted, and his skin darkened till he was so black, it seemed that even the light was afraid to touch him. His red eyes brightened into yellow, and black vertically-slit pupils swam up from within. *Snake eyes*, I realized in horror. My heart pounded in my chest and into my head so fast and loud that the laugh that still boomed was drowned out. My hands went from my ears to hold myself around my stomach. Fear wrenched my gut so hard, I thought I might throw up. I had been afraid of snakes for as long as I could remember, and here the snake man of my nightmares stood before me, impossibly black and horrible. I had the urge to run and run forever, but I was frozen in place, immobile with complete, overwhelming fear. He saw the horror on my face and laughed even louder. When I finally thought my ears would start bleeding, he disappeared. He seemed to cave in on himself and was gone, but not before I heard a little hiss inside my ears and felt a flick of snake tongue that wasn't there. I pulled my shoulders up to protect my ears and I swatted at where little snakes should be, but my hands batted against empty air.

I hadn't even known I was crying, but suddenly I could hear my own sobs. I had a horrible headache and a deafening ringing in my ears, but I could hardly care about that. Seeing snakes had given me a panic attack once before, but this was so much worse. I couldn't even remember what the snake man had looked like, but he had plucked the fear from deep within my brain and dished it out to me. How could you go against something like this? How could you ever feel safe?

For the first time, I wondered if snakes were really what I was afraid of. The very sight of them had always crippled me with fear, but had I been a baby in my crib with the snake man casting curses over my head? Could it have been a demon that I had always been afraid of? The thought occurred to me, then was gone, as if my brain couldn't handle what it was that I might have forgotten. That door was slammed shut as quickly as it had been opened and I stopped thinking about it.

Tansy and I stood there for a long time without saying a word, trying to steady our breathing. The woods went back to making noises: an opossum shuffling across the path between us and the house, and birds singing the sun's soon-arrival. Even Herman stirred and went toward the house. As soon as he stepped off the bricks, the circle broke, and I felt it sort of pop and fall. I thought it was lucky that he hadn't gotten scared and broken the circle too early. Then again, I would bet that animals felt and saw things like protective circles even better than we did.

"Okay, let's get out of here," I said.

"Hell no, we are not breaking the circle." Tansy grabbed onto my arm tightly, forcing me to stay where I was.

I blinked at her. She hadn't felt the circle fall? I'd have to tell her that animals could break the circle, but it didn't seem like the right time. I had a feeling she would start frantically making another circle if I did. Though having another circle around me was tempting, I thought the demon was gone by now and we were as safe as we were going to be. At least for this night.

"We only have about an hour to sunrise," she muttered, glancing toward the sky.

I sighed but didn't argue. I decided to sit down and after a few minutes, Tansy sat as well. A while passed where we didn't speak, but finally I asked, "What's a familiar?"

"A witch's familiar is an animal that can assist a witch in her powers. We can draw energy or power through our animals. It benefits both witch and animal, because the animal has a longer and healthier lifespan. I've only read about demons having familiars. *Human familiars.*" The last part she whispered as if it were too horrible of a thought to say aloud, and maybe it was. It certainly didn't sound pleasant.

"Is Herman your familiar?" I asked.

She laughed, but it wasn't a happy laugh. "No, I tried for a long time. I can't draw power through him. I guess he's just too wild. My cat you saw inside, Kiki, is my familiar." She looked at me and I looked back. Though the fire had died, we could see each other well enough. We weren't able to see the sun directly, but it was rising.

"You look different," she said, studying me through squinted blue eyes.

"I feel different," I admitted. I felt an energy that I'd never felt before, prickling over my skin. "How do I look different?"

"I have no idea what's different, that's what's weird. Somehow it's like I'm seeing you for the first time."

Strangely, I felt like I was alive for the first time.

Tansy chewed on her lip for a moment, before adding, "Don't take this the wrong way, but you look...pretty."

"How could I take that wrong?"

She shrugged and stood up, dusting off her sweat pants before walking off the round patio toward her house.

"Where are you going?" I called after her.

"Lady Sage was right, Cara!" she said, not turning back. "I had no idea what I was getting into." I followed after her until I realized she was going back inside her house. She opened the sliding glass door, but instead of walking through, she whirled around. "Do you think you're evil, Cara?"

The question surprised me. "Do *you* think I'm evil?" I asked back.

She chewed on her lower lip again, staring at me. "No, I don't think you're evil. But something's not right with you."

I frowned. Feeling the crawling within my skin, like electricity looking for an exit, I knew something was wrong with me. Maybe not wrong, exactly, but not normal. There was a demon out there that had put multiple curses on me for reasons that I couldn't fathom. But there *had* to be a reason. And if his threats weren't idle, he would be back to make the curses again. But why? I wanted to be afraid for myself. I wanted to scream and have a full-blown meltdown, because it seemed like the right thing to do. It seemed like Tansy was on the verge of a meltdown herself, but I felt fine. At least for the moment. Maybe the night's events had been too much for my mind and body to process and I was going into shock. All I could feel was numb... and the warm buzzing inside.

She just shook her head and closed the sliding glass door behind her, rudely cutting off our conversation. I couldn't exactly blame her after our very frightening night together and I had nothing left to say anyway, except sorry for getting her into this mess. I had only met her twice and I had gotten her fired from her job and been the reason for her having one of the most terrifying nights of her life. Then again, it had also been the most terrifying night of *my* life, and removing curses had been *her* idea. She also hadn't had to invite me back to the psychic place in the first place. Maybe it wasn't either of our faults. No matter whose fault it was though, I really doubted she would be contacting me again.

I sighed, suddenly feeling my lack of sleep, and

walked around the house to my car. After I fell into the driver's seat and started my engine, I angled the rearview mirror toward my face to inspect myself. I looked exactly the same, if a little more tired than usual. Definitely not more pretty.

I was driving toward my apartment when I suddenly felt ravenously hungry. It was probably due to so much adrenaline having coursed through me and then having nothing left. I wasn't sleepy, exactly. Too shocked from the night's events to be sleepy, but I was drained. I pulled into a McDonald's just a few miles from Tansy's house and went through the drive-thru. While there, I counted my cash, then counted again. I was twenty dollars short of what I had counted the night before. If that was right, I'd either dropped a twenty somewhere or Caymn's money hadn't been real. I wondered if his soft-looking black hair was real—or those pouty lips. I shook my head, trying to clear my head of him. I got two breakfast sandwiches and a huge black coffee and continued to my apartment, eating and thinking as I drove.

I thought that I should've asked Tansy if I could borrow her demon book. She might've said no, but it would've been worth a try. I didn't want to think it, but the thought kept coming, *what if I'm a demon?* Well, a half-demon. It seemed insane, but after my past week, who knew what could be possible! And Lady Sage had said I was one of them. I had always been a little different and I'd never fit in well, but I figured most people experienced feeling like misfits at times, except maybe Jessie. Maybe being "one of them" would explain why my eyes were black, I had an aversion to the sun, and I was allergic to silver. Jessie had always joked that I was a vampire. Now that I thought about it, in all the movies there was always that one person who would call the vampire "a *demon from hell*" or something along those lines. Maybe there was some truth in that. I didn't believe necessarily in vampires—though I guess who knew at this point—but what if demons had been discovered in real life forms centuries ago? What if that's where a lot of the myths about vampires and other monsters came from? I wondered if demons drank blood. The thought made my sandwich lose its taste as I chewed, and I put the rest of it back in the bag. Drinking blood was not something I wanted to do. Maybe demons didn't drink blood at all, or maybe I hadn't gotten that trait. "Or maybe I'm not even a demon *at all*!" I yelled aloud. I sighed and glanced out my window, suddenly catching the eye of an older woman staring at me from one car over. We were at a stop light and she'd obviously heard me—or at least saw that I was yelling to myself. I stifled the urge to stick my tongue out at her and went back to my thoughts, grumbling in frustration. I wasn't sure what I could believe. When I tried to tell myself there couldn't be such a thing as half human, half demon, my thoughts went back to that creature I'd seen just a few hours before. I didn't know why he had cursed me, but if I was something different, something labeled as "other," then maybe delving into this identity would answer some questions.

And Tansy had said I looked different. Had one of the curses been that I would appear different to anyone who looked at me? Was that why I'd never been hit on before? Did I look ugly, or was everyone just compelled to not give me a second glance?

I'd have to ask Tansy about that book. I needed to know more.

#

That evening when I awoke, I was almost late for my shift. I only had enough time to throw on my Angel Oak uniform, tie my hair back, and almost run to the restaurant. When I arrived, two minutes late for my shift, I was dripping with sweat. As I was clocking in I noticed Beth, a bleach-blond waitress, staring at me with a strange open-mouthed expression.

"Hi, Beth," I said, smiling at her.

"Hi," she answered reluctantly. The restaurant was crowded and I didn't have enough time to ask why she was staring, so I hurried off to serve my tables. All my customers treated me normally that night, some of them friendly and personable and others not so much. Still, I thought it odd when some of them did a double-take at me.

When I went to take a quick bathroom break an hour

into my shift, I heard Harrison, the head manager, talking on the phone in his office. "...Elizabeth hasn't shown up for her shift tonight. I know she's your niece, but I've about had it with that woman...."

I came to a screeching halt. From just a few feet past Harrison's office door, I could no longer hear what he was saying, but my sudden avalanche of thoughts kept me frozen. She had called me the previous night, but I hadn't called her back, assuming that I'd see her at work today. I'd been so busy, I hadn't even noticed when she hadn't shown up. It was a common occurrence for her to show up late for her shifts, but not by a whole hour. *Had something happened to her?* I shook myself out of my thoughts and continued toward the bathroom, silently praying that everything was okay.

Toward the end of my shift that night, when the dinner crowd finally died down and I was stationed at the bar, I made a quick call to Liz. When I got her voicemail, I hung up and hurriedly wrote her a text message.

Liz, where are you? Whenever you get this, call me and let me know you're okay.

"Hey." I jerked in surprise and stuffed my phone in my waitressing apron when I heard Harrison's voice come from right behind me.

"Sorry, I was just trying to make sure that Liz is okay," I mumbled, glancing over my shoulder at him.

"It's okay," he murmured. Suddenly I felt his hands on me, rubbing my arms from shoulder to elbow. I stiffened, my skin prickling at his unfamiliar touch, and I wondered what the hell he was doing. "I didn't mean to startle you."

I instinctively squirmed away from him and when I turned, I didn't understand the unfamiliar expression on his face. His hazy eyes were half-lidded and his lips were slightly parted. Finally, I realized I had seen this look a million times, but never directed at me. *Bedroom eyes.* The other waitresses had complained about Harrison before, that he was a big flirt and a pest, but I had never seen it for myself. I generally try not to make judgments based on what other people say, and honestly, I assumed they had vastly over dramatized it. But this was wildly inappropriate.

"Why don't you go home, sweetheart. I'll take over," he said, casually running his hand through his thick, unmanageable brown hair.

Sweetheart? I thought. *Ew.* I mumbled a *thanks* and left, too stunned by his strange behavior to know how to react.

On my walk home, I followed a little close behind some young college students, not wanting to be completely by myself as I walked on the dimly-lit street. I replayed the awkward exchange between Harrison and me in my mind, wondering what had come over him. Then I remembered the double-takes from my customers and the way Beth had nearly gaped at me. *What was coming over everyone?* I wondered.

A couple guys walked down the sidewalk toward me, one wearing dark sunglasses, and not able to stop myself, I jerked away from them. *Was he a demon? Was he Caymn?* The thought of Caymn made my heart beat a little faster. In an instant they were walking past me and I wasn't sure, but I thought their eyes followed me. Maybe it was just the stupid look on my face. *Had to be just another idiot wearing sunglasses at night,* I decided. My nerves were really getting the better of me. I glanced back to see if the guy with sunglasses was still looking at me, but he and his friend kept on walking, chatting amongst themselves.

Had anyone else been wearing sunglasses in the restaurant? I couldn't remember. I wondered if Caymn could have been there the whole night, unbeknownst to me, spying in some other form. I felt another wave of anxiety and huddled in closer to the small crowd in front of me. A young couple glanced over their shoulders to give me a questioning look, but I didn't care enough to move back. Luckily my apartment was close, and they unintentionally walked me to the building. I walked through the green door off the street and bounded up the iron stairs, taking on three at a time. I pulled my keys out of my waitressing apron and after I fumbled for the right one, I was able to get the door unlocked in record time. I flicked the light switch on in the hallway and sighed heavily, vastly relieved to have bright lights. I padded into the kitchen, taking my apron off and setting it down on my way. As I undid my hair and slipped my shoes off, I contemplated pouring myself a glass of wine. Then I decided coffee would be better if I wanted to keep my head clear, and better yet, it would help me stay up till sunrise.

I knew I shouldn't let my fears take over my life and affect me this way, but I couldn't help myself. How could I sleep peacefully when demons wanted to put curses on me, especially at night when they were supposedly more powerful? As I went to retrieve my coffee grinds from the freezer, I realized I was chewing on my fingernails again and stopped. When I studied them, I saw that they were already severely chewed like I had been gnawing on them for days, and maybe I had. I sighed, wondering if I should just give into my old habit, and poured the coffee grinds into a fresh filter.

I watched the coffee drip into the pot for awhile, my thoughts eventually wandering to Liz again. I suddenly decided to call her and after a few rings, I got her voicemail. "Hey Liz, just seeing if everything is okay. I'm feeling kind of like a psychotic boyfriend right now, but I'm a little worried that you didn't show up for work. I have a lot to tell you. Bye." I hung up. I wasn't sure if I was going to tell her everything, but maybe that would give her some incentive to call me back. If she got the message, I was almost positive that she'd take the bait. When the coffee maker started hissing and making its last hoorah, I realized I was chewing on my nails again and I growled at myself in frustration. With sudden purpose, I opened my pantry and grabbed a box of sea salt. I was going to cover the entire apartment in the stuff if there was any chance it'd stop a demon from entering. An uneasy feeling that I just couldn't shake was starting in the pit of my stomach.

The next day I awoke with a start and grabbed for

my alarm clock. 5:14 PM, it read. "Shit!" I said, scrambling out of bed. As soon as I said that, I realized it was Wednesday, my day off. I sighed and slumped back onto the covers. I was waking up later and later every day, but I'd never woken up *this* late. I'd have to start setting my alarm clock for four.

I found my phone buried in my bed and saw a missed call. I hoped it was from Liz, but no. I sighed again. It was from my mom. I listened to her voicemail message. "Hey honey, making sure you're still up for dinner tonight with the family. We're meeting at Kendall's at seven, in case you forgot. If I don't hear from you, I'll assume you'll be there."

I *had* forgotten. I deleted the message and moseyed out of bed for the second time. I had plenty of time to get ready, so I decided I'd try to look nice. Kendall's was an old house made into a nice restaurant and one of the Hansen family's favorite dinner spots when Mom felt like splurging. It wasn't near as expensive as Angel Oak, but I thought the food was better. I guess if you love steak and don't work there, you might love Angel Oak, but I love Southern food from Kendall's. Give me the country fried stuff any day.

I combed through my closet a few minutes before choosing a navy blue tube top dress that was tight around the top and fell loosely a few inches above the knee. It would keep me cool in this unbearable heat, but was still appropriate for a family dinner. I tucked away the cheap cross in my purse for safekeeping and replaced it with some of my favorite jewelry: gold earrings with small, round sapphire stones that I had gotten for my birthday a few years ago and a thin gold bracelet. I took time on my hair, using a curling iron to produce tight curls going from roots to ends. Even though I held every curl for almost a minute, my hair doesn't hold a curl well, and my tresses ended up being soft and loose by the time I was done. I sprayed the loose curls with hair spray and prayed that they wouldn't be straight and flat by the time I got to the restaurant. I didn't apply a lot of makeup, but what I did put on was carefully applied; concealer over those ever-darkening circles, bronzer and mascara as always, and a dab of clear lip-gloss. I looked myself over in the mirror and gave myself an approving nod. I didn't look half bad. I grabbed my purse and after staring between a pair of comfy black flip-flips and a pair of low-heeled pumps, I finally slipped on the flip-flops and headed out the front door.

Kendall's is tucked away on Queen Street just a few blocks from my apartment. If it weren't for the sign at the front reading "Kendall's" with their lunch and dinner hours below it, you would assume it was just another old house. It's painted a pale cornflower blue with a white doorframe, white window frames, and a white balcony with a black door and shutters. Old gas lamps are bolted on each side of the front door, and small flames wave back and forth inside glass. As I walked up its walkway, taking in the beautiful house, I smiled and remembered why I loved Charleston. I wouldn't say I'm very well-traveled, but I've traveled enough to appreciate its exceptional charm.

"Cara!" I turned to see my sister and her new husband, Scott, coming up the walkway, holding hands. She was dressed in a pink flower-printed dress, tall nude heels, and wore her hair in a neat pony-tail. Scott is one of those fraternity boys from a family with old money, who wears things like salmon colored shirts and pastel pants with embroidered whales on them. He's nice enough, don't get me wrong, but sometimes I wonder what drew Jessie to him. On this particular evening he looked decently normal in dress slacks, a blue button-up shirt, and a navy tie with his hair parted off center. He's kind of cute in the very clean-cut Southern kind of way, which really isn't my type. I had always thought my type was more of the rugged outdoorsy type— well, until I had met Caymn. I mentally shook myself, trying to rid my brain of him, but my attempts were hopeless.

Jessie let go of Scott's hand to hurry up the steps and give me a hug, her clacking high heels making it a humorously slow process. "I've missed you so much!" she said, embracing me. I squeezed her back, realizing how much I had missed her, too. I missed my best friend. I couldn't wait to get some alone time so we could talk. So much had happened in the past week and a half, and I needed my sister to confide in. If anyone would know how to help me or get my mind straight, Jessie would. When we pulled back, she grabbed my hand. "You look so beautiful!" she exclaimed.

I looked down at myself, smoothing my dress though it didn't need it. "Thank you," I said. "Not sure why."

"Doesn't she look beautiful, Scott?" Jessie asked.

I glanced at Scott and noticed he was staring at me strangely, lips slightly parted. "You look very nice, Cara," he finally said. I caught his eyes and he let them drift lower, making me think he was taking me all in with appreciation. I was so caught off guard with that look, especially it being from Scott, that I hoped I'd imagined it.

"She looks more than nice," Jessie said, smiling at me and unaware of her ogling husband behind her. "Cara, you look more beautiful than I've ever seen you." That was the third time she had said *beautiful*.

"Um, thank you," I said again, not comfortable with this sudden attention.

My parents came walking up the street then, smiling at one another and all but glowing in their admiration of each other. I smiled and waved at them with my free hand.

"Seriously, what has changed about you?" Jessie persisted, tugging my hand to get my attention. She narrowed her eyes at me, searching my face. She was relentless.

"I honestly don't know," I answered. It was the truth. Though I was pretty sure nothing physically had changed, something *had* changed. The only thing that I could figure was that maybe the curses had altered how people had previously seen me.

"Hello, darlings!" my mom said, walking up the walkway.

Bruce came up behind her, his hands on each of her shoulders. "What are we waiting for?" he belted out. "Let's go inside! I'm starving."

Jessie dropped my hand and I was free to open the door. A hostess stood at the front, smiling. "Five?" she asked cheerfully.

"Yes, and we have a reservation," my mom said. "The Hansens."

"All right, come this way," she said. Kendall's was set up very differently from most restaurants, considering it had been a house. Instead of knocking down the walls and making a large dining room like in a typical restaurant, the owners kept it as it was built so that most often you'd have your own private room. We were brought to a rectangular table in a back room, large enough to seat six but with one of the chairs missing. The hostess told us our waitress would be with us shortly and hurried off to her post.

"Cara, you look pretty," my mom said, sitting next to me at the table.

"Thanks Mom, so do you!"

"No, but you look like you're glowing! Tell me, is there a dashing young man that's come into your life?" She had a mischievous grin on her face.

I thought of a particularly handsome man that I'd met recently, but then I frowned at the thought. "A dashing young man? What century are we in, Mom?"

"Ooh, but you didn't say no..." she teased.

"Do I have to, Mom?" I all but snarled. "No! There is no man in my life!" I surprised myself at my own ferocity, not sure where this outburst of anger was coming from. Maybe it was the constant badgering. Maybe it was the stress building up. Or maybe it was that I had instantly thought of Caymn. There could never be a relationship with him, and I was mad at myself for even thinking about him in a romantic way. Everyone was staring at me, I quickly realized. I took a deep breath, trying to release my anger. "I'm sorry, Mom," I murmured. "I'm just stressed out lately."

"Are you having those dreams again?" Jessie asked casually. Mom and she had had a discussion about me, no doubt.

"Yes," I sighed. "Something like that. I've been having a weird week. I don't know what's wrong with me." I looked down at my menu.

"It's okay," my mom said quietly. The way she said it so timidly made me feel a little stab of guilt, but then I caught myself. No, I was so tired of her making me feel guilty for not having a boyfriend. It wasn't fair. "Well, are your eyes better at least?" she asked.

"What's wrong with your eyes?" Jessie asked before I could answer.

"I've been seeing spots in my vision and yes, they are better," I said. "Gone, actually. So that's been good, at least."

"So what else has been going on?" Jessie asked, resting her elbow on the table and laying her chin in her hand, giving me her full attention. I glanced up to see Bruce and Scott already ignoring us and talking about the menu. My mother's attention was still on me.

"Okay, this sounds crazy, but I think a waitress at Angel Oak might have been kidnapped." I hadn't even realized that I had considered it a possibility until it was suddenly out of my mouth.

"Kidnapped?" Mom almost yelled in surprise.

"Mom, shhh!" I said. Bruce glanced toward us again before Scott brought him back into their conversation about the menu. I'm not sure why, but I didn't want to make this a family discussion. I continued, speaking softly. "This girl at my work, Liz, may have been kidnapped."

"How do you know?" Jessie asked, and I didn't miss the skepticism in her voice.

"I don't know for sure. But this strange guy at the bar, who has only come a few times, asked about her two nights ago. Then last night she didn't show up for her shift."

"Oh my gosh," my mom said. "Have you called the police?"

"Wait," Jessie said, raising her hand in a gesture that said, *Stop.* "Is she that waitress you've told me about that always shows up late and never gets fired?" Jessie asked.

"Well, yeah," I admitted.

"Mom, this girl probably didn't get kidnapped," Jessie said, then looked back at me. "From what you've told me about her in the past, I'll bet she just blew off her shift." I didn't like how she instantly dismissed me, like I was always overdramatic or something. I wanted to believe she was right and Liz hadn't been kidnapped—after all, it was the most logical answer—but nothing that had happened in the past week and a half had been logical. It occurred to me for the first time that Jessie might not believe me if I told her what had happened while she had been on her honeymoon. The thought made me feel...I don't know, sad?

"Hell, maybe she ran off with that guy you said has been coming in!" Jessie added, shrugging a shoulder.

I found myself clenching my teeth tightly together and tried to release my sudden anger with an exhale. *I will not let that bother me, because I have no reason to,* I told myself.

"If she doesn't show up at her next shift, maybe you should talk to the police," suggested Mom. "Or at least try to find out what happened to her."

"Yeah," I muttered.

Suddenly, a waitress walked in, pen and notepad in hand. "Hi, what can I get y'all to drink?" Jessie, Scott, and I ordered wine. Bruce ordered a beer and my mom stuck with water, as she always does. We also ordered a plate of fried green tomatoes to share. *Mhmm.*

Bruce and Scott chatted about football for awhile, Jessie gushed about the honeymoon, and my mom listened and asked questions at the appropriate times. I sat back quietly, sipping my wine, deep in thought. The waitress took our dinner order, poured me another glass of wine, and brought the food. Most of the dinner went on without me contributing in the conversation.

"Carebear, you seem different," Mom said, bringing me out of my thoughts. The waitress appeared over my shoulder and Jessie asked her to pour us more wine before I could stop her.

"I do?" I asked with little interest in my voice.

"Yes, what's different?" she asked.

Well, I don't know, Mom. I am starting to think my father could have been a demon and maybe I'm turning into one, but besides that, I don't know! I tried to imagine my mom around my age and wondered what my father might have looked like to her. Had he been as beautiful as Caymn? A thought occurred to me...*what if Caymn was my father? Was that possible?*

"Cara?" Mom asked. I realized my face was twisted up in a grimace. I quickly feigned a smile. "I don't know what's different, Mom."

"I asked her the same thing. Something *is* different," Jessie accused, looking at me too intently as she took a sip of her wine.

"You remind me of your father a little bit," my mom said suddenly. This I hadn't expected. She had never said anything like that before.

"Really?" I asked. I was strangely a little happy to hear it.

"Your father felt so influential. He had such a strong presence, so strong that I could feel his energy before I even laid eyes on him. It was nothing like I'd ever experienced from another person," she said, eyes unfocused before she shot a wary glance toward her husband, as if she were double-crossing my stepfather just by mentioning my birth father's existence. This was probably the reason I, too, was so uncomfortable talking about it with anyone outside the family. It seemed like a dirty secret, even now. I could see as well as feel her sudden mood change, and I thought she might be regretting having brought him up. "I didn't learn much about him, but I remember that."

Her saying that only strengthened my conjecture that my father was a demon. Maybe my mom was more intuitive than I gave her credit for. "So you feel that way around me now?" I asked. "This...energy?"

"As I'm looking at you, I sense it. I can't even explain what it is exactly," she said. I must have looked concerned, because she patted my hand and reassuringly said, "Don't worry, honey, I think it's a good thing." But I wasn't as sure.

Bruce had paid the waitress at that point and suddenly he and Scott were standing up, ending our conversation. I took a few last sips of my wine before standing and collecting my purse. The room spun slightly and I thought to myself that I might have drunk too much.

"Scott, would you mind if I stayed out with Cara for a little bit?" Jessie said, then turned to me. "Maybe we could go get another glass of wine?"

I started to object, but Scott cut me off. "How would you get home?" he asked her.

"We could take you home, Scott," Mom said. "And you could leave the car with Jessie."

"Yeah!" Jessie agreed and grabbed my arm. "That works."

I was very conscious of the sun setting outside. If I stayed out much longer I might have to walk back to my apartment alone in the dark again and I preferred to not do that. Not until I had some things sorted out. Not until I was sure I was safe out there.

"Jessie, I'm really tired," I said, feigning a yawn.

"It's not even eight thirty!" she said. "We'll make it quick, anyway."

As we walked to leave, Bruce warned Jessie not to drink too much and drive and that there was no shame in calling a cab. When we were outside everyone started saying their goodbyes, everyone but my mom ignoring me. She gave me a parting squeeze, and then everyone was walking away.

"Okay, let's go." Jessie tugged my arm toward King Street as everyone else walked to the parking garage across the street.

"Where are we going?" I asked.

"I don't know. Let's go to Enoteca! It's close."

I groaned. Enoteca was a fancy little wine bar that was owned by Frank Long, the owner of Angel Oak *and* also my boss. For once I was dressed nicely enough to get through the door, but I didn't want to go there. Jessie let go of my arm, but ignored my protest and we walked a few minutes in silence. I kept my eyes on the sidewalk, willing myself not to trip over any loose stones or cracks.

"So what's happened to you since I've been gone?"

The way she said it sounded off. She was asking me about my appearance again, not wanting to know what I'd been up to.

"What do you mean?" I asked.

"Um, I'm not sure," she said, voice oozing with sarcasm. "My big sister suddenly looks and acts completely different—"

"I don't look completely different," I objected.

"Fine," she said, still sarcastic. "You don't look *completely* different, but you are different. That's not the point! You're hiding something from me."

"I am not!" I said. She was right, I was hiding something from her, but she wouldn't believe me if I told her. More than anything, I didn't want to give in, because I didn't like her attitude.

"Tell me," she said, stopping me in the middle of the sidewalk, forcing other pedestrians to maneuver around us. "Did you get some kind of minor plastic surgery? Botox? Microdermabrasion treatments?"

"What?" I said, glancing around to make sure no one was hearing us. "That's insane!"

"Is it?" she challenged. "What's crazy is my sister has done something to appearance and won't tell me what!"

"If something is so different about me, then you should be able to tell what it is, right? You tell me! What is actually different about me?" Like her, I wanted to know what was different. I really wanted to know what everyone was seeing that I apparently couldn't.

She studied me—no, glared at me. "I don't know, you tell me!" she crossed her arms over her chest.

This was ridiculous. I'm not sure if it was the wine or not, but suddenly I felt angry. No, *furious*. "I've wanted to be in your shoes our whole lives, Jessie!" I yelled, my body beginning to tremble. In only a second's time, everything I had suppressed bubbled up to the surface; all the cute boys chasing her, all the teachers that praised her, and all the friends that surrounded her. All while everyone in the world seemed to pass me by without a second glance. "I've always wanted to look more like you! I've wanted to be your height, have your tan skin! I would have killed to have your eyes!" I hadn't meant for it to come out in a scream, but I suddenly couldn't control my voice. I glared at her and I felt heat in my face as tears threatened to spill.

She stared at me, open mouthed. "Cara?" she finally said, her voice faltering. Her tone and expression didn't fit the context.

"What?" I spat.

"Your eyes..."

"What about them?" I snapped.

"They're blue," she whispered.

Blue? What was she talking about? Jessie started digging through her purse, not taking her eyes off my face. She pulled out a little compact case, opened it, and shoved it at me. She did all of this without taking her eyes off me. I grabbed it and looked at myself in the little mirror. *No, it couldn't be.* I angled my face toward a street lamp. The bright blue eyes I saw in the mirror didn't fit. They looked identical to my sister's, but on my face they seemed alien. The image didn't bring me some sort of joy that you might think since I was someone who had always wanted blue eyes. It was an alarming sight.

"What..." I didn't have words.

"You were yelling at me and they just, just..." Jessie was at a loss for words as well. A moment passed and finally she exclaimed, "They just turned blue!"

I almost couldn't stop staring at myself. I noticed another group of people walking around us on the sidewalk, and it brought me away from the mirror, finally.

"I want to go home," I said, suddenly aware that we were acting like two crazy, drunk people in the middle of the sidewalk, yelling and carrying on. She nodded, probably having come to the same conclusion. Without saying another word, we made a beeline for my apartment, jaywalking across the street when there was a break in the line of cars. She didn't say anything until I was unlocking my apartment door. "What is happening, Cara?"

"I really don't know," I answered truthfully.

"Look at me," she said and I looked at her as the door swung open.

"Your eyes are back to normal," she said.

I walked into the apartment first, dropping my purse by the door as I went. The following thuds indicated that she also dropped her purse before shutting the door behind her. I headed for the bathroom mirror, not letting myself be slowed down for anything. When I met the mirror, I saw the face and eyes I was familiar with.

"That was crazy," Jessie whispered as she slid up behind me. "How is that possible?"

"I don't know," I answered.

"You don't even sound like you're weirded out by this!" she exclaimed, flinging her arms up.

I was "weirded out" by it, but I think my wine buzz dulled my ability to react. "I just said 'I want your eyes' and I had them?" I asked.

"That's what you said. And as you said it, your eyes just, just…" She was at a loss for words again.

"I want your eyes," I said to the mirror, trying to will myself into having blue eyes again. A moment went by and nothing happened.

"You were a little bit more angry," she told me.

"I want your eyes!" I screamed at my reflection. I half expected the mirror to shatter like it did in the movies, but nothing happened.

I looked at Jessie in the mirror. *She's so pale*, I thought. *Like she's seen a ghost.* For a moment I wondered why that was, my brain working sluggishly in my state of intoxication. It finally occurred to me that she was frightened. Maybe even frightened of me! If I told her that demons were real and they were walking, talking beings among us, would she believe me? I really had no real way of convincing her. If I actually could convince her, would the knowledge benefit her in any way? No. If anything, it might make her life more disastrous, like mine! At the very least, she would see the world in a new light that I wish I didn't see it in. She already couldn't handle what was going on, and she knew nothing.

No, I couldn't tell her. Jessie wasn't ready for this new part of my life.

"Jessie, I'm sorry, but I think we should call it a night."

"How can you want to call it a night after that? Don't you want to figure this out?" she asked.

"I do," I admitted. "But I want to do it alone." There was hurt in her eyes, but I ignored that look as I motioned a hand toward the open door, signaling her to leave. Her face twisted up into an ugly expression and she stomped out, slamming the bathroom door behind her. I didn't hear anything for a few minutes, but stared at myself in the mirror, willing something to happen. Finally, I heard the front door slam shut.

I suddenly burst out crying. I'm not normally an emotional person, at least not often, and the sudden onset of tears actually surprised me. I collapsed against the wall, covering my face to sob into my hands. I ended up on the floor, my whole body racking with my sobs. I wasn't sure if it was the alcohol, but I had never cried so hard in my life. *What is happening to me?*

"I'm the one who can't handle it," I said to myself when finally I couldn't cry anymore, my voice thick with emotion. "I'm the one."

Nine

A week went by without an event, but that didn't make it an average week. I spent even more time alone than normal, Liz not having come back to work and Jessie never calling to hang out. I knew I should've called and apologize to Jessie. I didn't want us to not be talking to each other, but I also had no idea how to tell her what was going on, so I put it off.

On Wednesday, I woke up and left my apartment, starting the day off by walking to the corner store to get some snacks, for lack of anything else to do. In my groggy state, I passed the store without realizing it. When I finally looked around and realized where I was, I made an aggravated sound aloud, but kept walking.

Since I'm walking this way, I'll see if Liz is home. I knew that she wouldn't be home, but a tiny part of me hoped. I almost hoped that she was hiding out and boozing on wine, because at least then I would know she was safe. Hell, I'd even have been be a little relieved if she'd relapsed on drugs if that meant she hadn't been kidnapped.

I called her as I started getting close. This time it didn't even ring and went straight to voicemail, followed by a computerized voice saying, *this mailbox is full.* I was disconnected before I could even hang up. When I looked up from my phone, I saw her house and that someone was walking out, a dark-haired woman in grubby clothes, struggling a little to carry a large vacuum down the three steps.

"Hey, excuse me!" I said, quickening my pace.

The vacuum clattered down the stairs and she set it right side up on the sidewalk. When she turned her face to me she smiled politely. She was a pretty, older woman probably in her fifties, with tan skin and dark brown hair pulled into a loose ponytail.

"I'm one of Liz's friends. Is she home?"

Her brow furrowed and she frowned. "No, she isn't in," she said simply.

"Well, have you seen her?" I pressed.

She sighed and looked toward the harbor. "It's not really my business and I shouldn't give out information about her, but…" She met my eyes again, concern showing plain on her face. "I don't see her most times I come, so normally I wouldn't think anything of it, but she usually leaves a check for me. I cleaned anyway, because I have been cleaning for her family for a long time."

That was a little bit more information than was appropriate, but I dismissed the inappropriateness, as the information was to my advantage. "Maybe she forgot?" I offered.

"Maybe." She rolled the vacuum to her green minivan with maid service stickers on it while she talked. "But the strangest part is, I don't think anything's been touched since last week. Her bed was still made and *that's* definitely a first." I helped her pick up the vacuum and set it in the back, and she closed the hatch over it. "Thank you," she said.

"You're welcome," I said and smiled weakly.

She went to get into her car. "Know what I think?" she said, turning back to me.

"No, what?" I asked.

"She's probably just staying with her family this week. That's a good family, the Long family. They stick together."

I nodded and kept my smile in place as best as I could. Maybe Liz was spending the week with her family. Another thought occurred to me: *maybe she* had *relapsed and gone to rehab*. When you go to rehab, you give up your phone and you lose all contact with the outside world, except your close family. Maybe that's what Liz had called me about before she had so suddenly vanished. I sighed loudly, feeling some of my tension release. That had to be what had happened. "You're probably right," I said, finding it easy to sound reassuring. "Well, goodbye."

"Goodbye," she said and got into her car, shutting the door as I started walking again. I walked past the last few houses on the street, past the small park to where King Street came to an end at Murray Street (or the Charleston Battery, if you're a local). This area overlooking the Charleston Harbor was bustling with tourists, who unknowingly always came when the weather was the worst: the summer. Too hot and muggy to enjoy the sights, that's for sure. I leaned over the railing, looking into the water a few feet below. The sun was getting low, not too low where I would want to be safe at my apartment, but low enough for it to get in my eyes when I looked toward the harbor. The sun was also hot on my skin, almost painful, and I knew I'd have to run to the shade soon or I'd be sunburned tomorrow.

I sighed loudly, feeling like I couldn't escape this worry I was holding onto. Liz had gone missing right after *he* had asked about her. Even if the most logical and likely scenario was that Liz had gone back to rehab, it wouldn't be right to try to just hope that that was the case and not look into it. Maybe I could contact her family somehow. If she wasn't at rehab, then what would I do?

The sudden ringing coming from my bag stopped my thoughts and I fished my cell phone out. *Tansy*, the screen read.

"Hello?"

"Cara," Tansy's voice came through. "It's me, Tansy."

"I know," I answered. "What's up?"

"Oh, okay, right. Um, would you like to come over for dinner tonight?" When I didn't answer right away, she added, "It's kind of important."

An hour later, and just before the sun set, I was knocking on the door of Tansy's little brown house. I stared at the green door while I waited, my eyes fixed on the wreath with the star in the center made out of sticks. A pentagram. I associated the pentagram with Satanism or evil, and I was curious why they had it on their door and what it meant to them.

Tansy opened the door and was heavily made up in black eyeliner and lipstick like she had been when I'd first met her. She was wearing a faded black shirt and purple jeans with not-so-expertly added studs and doodles drawn on them. I immediately noticed that she was sporting a new, crusty looking tattoo on the right side of her neck. It was a small symbol, which looked to me like the trinity symbol with an added ring around it. A Celtic trinity knot, I believe it's called? If she hadn't been looking straight at me, I might not have seen it through her almost shoulder-length cropped hair.

"Hey, come in," she said, opening the door wider.

"Is that a new tattoo?" I asked, walking inside.

Tansy shut the door behind me and lightly touched her neck as if she had forgotten it was there. "Yeah, it is. I gave it to myself last week. It's the Wiccan symbol for protection." Her inexpertly drawn tattoos suddenly made sense, especially the way those on one arm looked sloppier than those on the other.

"Wow, I feel like that would be so painful—tattooing yourself."

"I'm used to it," she said with a shrug.

"I don't have any tattoos, because I couldn't imagine picking anything that I'd want on my skin forever," I said.

"Well, I don't tattoo myself for the sake of making art, like some people do," she said, rubbing her arms absentmindedly. "Almost all my tattoos have to do with life lessons that I want to remember, some of them spells that I want to have on a moment's notice. I guess in my own way, it's art; the story and lessons of Tansy McGee." I had noticed that there were hardly any designs, mostly just writing. She was like a walking, talking journal! I had the urge to lift her arm and look more closely at the words, but that might be inappropriate. If she were taller and more at my eye-level, they would have been easier to make out. And some, I was sure, had to be in a different language. No one's handwriting was just that sloppy. "My dad hates my tattoos. My mom doesn't much like them either, but I think she likes the idea of me writing things I learn. I think she prefers me to write them on paper though—I guess we'll wait for my mom in the kitchen," she added, leading me toward the kitchen.

Now that the lights were on inside the house, I could see that even though the McGee family wasn't rich, they weren't as poor as I had originally thought. They definitely spent their money differently than most. The couch was worn and on the verge of cracking with old age and heavy usage, for example. The living room was altogether simple and gave the impression that they were low-income, but the kitchen was nothing short of extravagant and appeared to have been remodeled within the last few years.

The kitchen and dining room were a conjoined space, the kitchen on the right and the dining area on the left. The far right wall had whitewashed brick that reminded me of the stone circle in the backyard. The walls were off-white, but most everything else, the wood floor and cabinets, were rich brown in color. On the wall above the stove, a quote had been expertly painted: *"An it harm none, do what ye will."* I felt like I had seen that quote before, but I couldn't recall where.

One large copper pot sat on the stove, steaming and filling the room with a delicious smell. It smelled spicy and sweet and my stomach grumbled.

The table and chairs at the dining area were brown, which matched the off white and brown tones in the kitchen. Against the wall on the far left was a large shelf like you'd see for separating mail. In every small slot was a little jar, at least a hundred of them, all containing spices, herbs, and dried flowers. If it was a spice rack, it was the craziest one I'd ever seen!

"Wow, your mom must be very into cooking," I guessed, looking at all the spices and herbs.

"You can kind of say that. But it's not just food she likes to cook," Tansy said. I stared at her, and seeing my empty expression, she added, "She also cooks spells."

"Oh," I said, not sure of what else to say. This whole witch and spell thing was still something I was a little unsure about. Growing up with my on-and-off religious mother, I'd heard that people who believed they were witches were either crazy or worshipped the devil. Though I believed in demons, recently more than ever, real witches were harder to swallow.

"A witch doesn't exactly fly on a broomstick or make love potions," a voice said as if reading my mind. "Most witches' spells are spiritual, sort of like prayer."

I turned to see who I guessed was Tansy's mother, though she looked like she might be her hippie older sister. She was very short, like Tansy, no taller than five feet. Her strawberry blond hair was put in a simple half-up do, the hair around her face pulled out of the way, while the rest trailed down her back. The blue maxi dress she wore had flow-y sleeves and showed the barest hint of bare feet underneath. Her features were pixy-like, and her blue eyes were surprisingly warm. Only the barest hint of wrinkles around her eyes and mouth hinted that she was older. I could easily picture this woman tending to the garden outside or even dancing around a fire in the moonlight. I knew instantly that there was something different about her, my brain somehow registering her as *other*.

"I'm Tansy's mother, Darlene," she said extending her arm for a shake. I put my hand in hers and her shake was surprisingly firm for such a small hand.

"Hi, Ms. Darlene, I am Cara."

"I know who you are," she said. "I would have recognized you in a crowd of faces... and you can just call me Darlene! Ms. Darlene makes me sound so old."

I blinked at her. *She would recognize me in a crowd of faces?* That was odd. "Okay, *Darlene*," I said, trying to leave out the *Ms.*, though it almost pained me to do so. Calling someone's mom by just her first name is frowned upon in the South, especially in my household.

"It's a pleasure to meet you, Cara," she said and went toward the pot on the stove to give it a stir. "I hope you like chili."

"I love chili," I answered.

"It's vegetarian," Tansy piped in. "We are strict vegetarians. But I think you'll still like it. It's my favorite."

"It's called Apple Autumn Chili," Ms. Darlene said. "It tastes a lot like regular chili, but sweeter and with slivers of green apple."

I made an approving *mmm* sound.

"Mom, you probably don't remember what regular chili tastes like," Tansy said and they laughed together. I smiled. You could see the love and warmth between them, something you don't always get to witness between mother and daughter. Though the house and the McGee family were obviously different than my own, it felt nice to be there. The whole house exuded a vibe of warmth and happiness.

Darlene scooped the chili into three green bowls for us and we all sat at the dinner table, eating and making small talk about the summer heat and gardening. When I was the first one to finish my bowl, Darlene set her spoon down and sighed. "Cara, we invited you over for more than just chili," she said. "Tansy told me everything. Your little rendezvous in the woods..."

I glanced at Tansy, who was suddenly shoveling chili in her mouth at an alarming rate.

"And your experience with the *shadow*," Darlene continued, emphasizing the one word while returning her gaze to Tansy.

I figured what she meant, but I wanted to make sure. "What's a shadow?" I asked, looking from one to the other. "I mean, I know what a shadow is, but..."

"I don't mean the shadow you leave on the ground," she said. "I am talking about evil spirits. Tansy knows about shadows, and I was simply a little disappointed that she referred to them as demons." I could feel a sudden tension in the room, like we were stirring up a past argument.

"Well, the book had horned, red figures, Mom. Don't get mad if that was what I assumed," Tansy said, glancing up at her mom while hovering over her empty chili bowl.

"If you don't mind me asking, what's the difference?" I asked.

Ms. Darlene looked like she wanted to say something to Tansy, but with some effort, she tore her eyes away from Tansy to look at me. "A demon is from the Christian religion. We don't believe in the Christian God, Jesus, or Satan. Therefore, we don't believe demons exist. You see, *shadows* are the bad entities that roam the earth," she explained, putting a lot of emphasis on that one word again.

Tomato, Tomata, I wanted to say, but I thought better about saying it aloud. The way Darlene kept looking at Tansy, that wasn't a can of worms I wanted to open.

"I'm only a little disappointed in Tansy, because she should know this. I guess this is my fault for not informing her, but demons don't exist. Shadows exist. That is why we make a book of shadows, to record our séances and spells that fight against them. *That is what you stole from my friend, Amaryllis. Her book of shadows.*" The last part was aimed at Tansy and held a biting edge.

"I didn't steal it, Mom. Becca did!" Tansy said, dropping her spoon into her empty bowl.

"Right, your friend stole it. Still, you should have come to me."

Tansy made an exasperated groan. We were definitely digging up a previous argument, and I felt slightly awkward. I vaguely wondered why I had been invited and what this had to do with me.

Again, as if reading my mind, Darlene said, "I'll tell you why I've asked you here."

Tansy stood and started collecting the dirty bowls and spoons. I started to help, grabbing the cups, but Darlene stopped me. "Let Tansy do that," she said, touching my hand lightly. Her touch was gentle and soothing, a mother's touch, but I sensed something else. Like maybe behind this little pixy-like woman, there was something stronger. I let the cups go and Tansy scooped them up, awkwardly juggling them and the bowls.

"I've asked you to come here, because I had a dream about you last night—"

"*You* had a dream about *me*," I said to clarify.

"Yes, I had what I believe is a premonition. I saw you and another girl. A girl with beautiful, long black hair—"

"Liz!" I exclaimed, my eyes widening to the size of saucers. I hadn't mentioned Liz to Tansy, had I? I was almost sure that I hadn't.

"Yes, I saw you two together in a whole different world. A city in some other dimension or something—I'm not sure. It's a world of black and neon, which was the strangest and most vivid thing I've ever dreamed. I saw you being drawn to someone—someone calling out to you—and I believe it is going to be a trap. When the voice sings to you and draws you in, you must stop yourself. Does this make sense to you?"

"Not really," I murmured. Being in some alternate universe with Liz? No, it didn't make sense at all.

"I felt a glimpse of the power, and it will be hard to resist, achingly strong, but you must say no and turn away. Or you and hundreds, maybe thousands, of others will be lost," she continued, staring off at nothing. She looked at me again and added, "I was hoping you'd be able to shed some light on this."

"The only thing that sounds familiar is Liz," I said, shrugging my shoulders. Darlene scrutinized me with her blue eyes and when I looked at Tansy, who was leaning on the counter by the kitchen sink, she had a similar expression. They were waiting for me to say something, I think, but I had no enlightening words. I wasn't sure what any of this meant!

"I went to Tansy's room as soon as I awoke this morning to tell her my dream," Darlene continued, "and she had pulled her bed to the middle of the room and had a large ring of salt around it. I knew then that something was wrong."

"I had to tell her everything," Tansy broke in. "Our curse-lifting in the woods and the...shadow."

"And as soon as I told Tansy my premonition, she knew it was you," said Darlene.

"Blond hair and black eyes is not a combination you see every day," Tansy added sheepishly. I knew that to be true. I hadn't met anyone else my whole life with blond hair and black eyes.

"This is hard for me to take in," I said. *And believe,* I thought. "I'm not sure where to go from here."

"Let's go through the book of shadows that belonged to Amaryllis. Come with me to my safe room," Darlene said, standing and motioning me to follow her into a hallway off the dining room.

"Okay," I said uncertainly.

#

I stood and followed her into the…it wasn't exactly a hallway, because a hallway suggests a long passageway. No, this was a small middle area between three rooms, two of which were most likely bedrooms.

When Miss Darlene opened the door to the "safe room," as she called it, something spilled out and surrounded me. It wasn't wind or a certain smell, but a feeling. The only thing I can compare it to is like feeling a light bulb that has just been turned off and feeling lingering energy and warmth. It didn't feel evil, nor did it feel good, but it was definitely something.

Magic, I thought.

I walked into the darkness, the energy that surrounded me giving me some sense of security. Whether it was a false sense of security or not, I did not know. With every step I felt it thicken like smoke around a burning fire. A lot of magic happened in this room, or so I was guessing. I closed my eyes for a brief moment, reveling in the feeling that hugged me and brushed my skin. When I closed my eyes, I could almost see a yellow cloud around us and where the cloud was absent. I could see where objects were— something large against the far wall in particular. A piano, maybe. I could see Darlene's shape in the smoke as well, like a shadow in the fog. There was something special about this room and her. And maybe I was special, too, if I could see what I was seeing in my mind's eye.

"*Accendo!*" she suddenly said, the strange word sounding like a command, and I opened my eyes.

Fire. Suddenly there was just fire in the darkness. The tiny angelic woman twirled around the room, waving one free hand, finger pointed. And as she waved her hand, flames ignited on candles. It happened so fast, like the dark room was suddenly dancing with candlelight, but I saw that she had lit them with only her one word and pointed finger. She looked at me, triumph in her eyes. She was making a believer out of me, and she knew it.

Now that I could see the room lit by fifty candles or more, I could see, rather than just feel, that this was an area they poured a lot of time and energy into. It was nothing like Lady Sage's chiropractor's office turned psychic den. No, this place looked and felt authentic. In a few seconds I took it all in. The windowless walls were painted dark green and a line of candles circled the entire room on one, endless shelf. The shiny wood floor had an expertly designed pentagram in darker wood in the middle of it. I could only imagine what the floor guys' faces might have looked like when they'd been asked for a pentagram. It looked too nice for Tansy and Darlene to have done it by themselves, but you never know— someone in their family could have been a carpenter, for all I knew.

An altar, not a piano, filled the wall opposite the door. It appeared to be a table, on top of a table, on top of another table, all covered with rich purple and gold fabric like a large satin cake. Ever tier was covered in candles, wine bottles with candles on them, small statues, crystals, a couple deer skulls, and dried flowers. Three green pillows with gold tassels lay on the floor in front of the altar so someone, or both of them and an extra person, could pray. Or spell cast? Either way, the sight was strangely beautiful. The room was pretty open; only one other corner was occupied with a large cast iron bowl that suspiciously looked like a witch's cauldron and a stack of books.

"How did you do that?" I asked, my voice coming out low and breathy.

I heard Tansy enter the room behind me. "She did her candle lighting thing?"

"Is it a trick?" I asked.

"No, not a trick. At least, not like a magician's trick," Darlene said as she started for the stack of books. "It's just a handy little invocation my mother passed to me and her mother before her. You don't come through a line of witches without learning a few things."

Tansy walked past me to stand near her mother. "I'm learning some things, slowly but surely," she said, and closed her thumb and forefinger around a candle's flame to squelch its light. "*Accendo*," she whispered while tapping the wick with one finger, and the flame returned. "But I'm not very good with invocation spells."

"It takes time," Darlene said as she picked up the top book on the stack. It was a huge, red leather book and she had to use both hands to lift it. She and Tansy both sat on the wood floor on the pentagram design, Tansy signaling me to sit with them by patting the floor next to her. I sat down as Darlene set the book before us. The front cover showed an obscene image of naked people and demons—or, um, *shadows*. It felt strange and kind of wrong somehow, sitting in a circle on a pentagram floor as we read a book of shadows. I could only imagine what my mother would say if she could see me now.

Darlene opened the book and the first page read, *Book of Shadows*. "You can see that she hand-wrote this," she said, lightly brushing the page with her fingers.

"No way," I said, leaning forward, not believing these expertly written words could have been hand written. The font was perfect, but as I looked very closely I could just barely see the dents the pen had made in the paper. "Wow."

"She had a very steady hand," Darlene said, and I thought that was a huge understatement. It was so beautifully written and the pages looked like a magical book from a fairy tale. They didn't match the very crude front cover. Though the book looked like it should be magical, I felt no magic behind it. Just a beautifully written, yet creepy journal.

"Are you sure Amaryllis won't mind us reading her book of shadows?" Tansy asked.

"Usually, I'd say yes, but in this case I don't think she'll mind."

"Why not?" Tansy and I chimed in unison, then gave each other half-hearted smiles at our timing.

"Because she's dead," Darlene said simply.

My breath hitched in my throat and Tansy gasped.

"Well, that's what I believe, anyway. She's been missing for about six years," Darlene added.

Tansy found her voice first. "How come you never told me?" she asked.

"I never thought it concerned you, and it wasn't like all of the sudden she disappeared out of our lives. I had stopped going to those coven meetings years prior to her disappearance. When one day I tried to contact her, I was told that she had been missing for awhile."

There was a moment of stunned silence. When Darlene decided that we weren't going to interrupt again, she continued, "When I met Amaryllis, we were both about thirty years old. She was a very talented and experienced white witch, but she confided in me that she hadn't always been white. Way before she was a part of our small coven, when she was a child, she grew up in a black magic practicing cult in a small Floridian town. They had done horrible things to her like raping her through adolescence, performing animal sacrifices, and the way she told me about it, I had the impression that they had done human sacrifices as well. When she was sixteen, she finally escaped them and eventually found herself here.

"The police investigated the cult when she disappeared, but came to a dead end when they learned that all of those people had either died or gone missing as well. Some of my old coven members believe that the cult fanatics caught up to Amaryllis and killed her. But I believe something much bigger and greater caught up to her—all of those black magic practitioners. By associating with black magic practice and sacrifices, I believe you make yourself susceptible to being snatched up by the darkest of the shadows."

A shiver ran down my spine and I stifled an urge to squirm.

"This also had to have happened to your friend, Liz," Darlene said, glancing at me.

I was so startled by Liz's name coming up that I froze. "What?" I asked, stupidly.

"Your friend, Liz," Darlene said again. "She's missing, isn't she?"

"Well, maybe not missing," I said, not wanting to truly believe it, even when it came from someone else's mouth. But how had she known about Liz in the first place? "Okay, maybe she is missing. I'm not sure. How do you know this?"

"She most certainly *is* missing," Darlene said, no hint of doubt on her face. "In my premonition, I learned that this is the tenth day that her soul has been missing. When someone's soul is missing, I would assume she were dead, but I know she's not. She's not dead, but she's not here either."

Not here? What did that even mean? I shook my head, not sure what to make of this. "How do you know this?" I asked again.

"Both Tansy and I know things sometimes," Darlene said, meeting eyes with her daughter.

Tansy nodded at her mom. "I told her that the spirits

sometimes speak to me—to us."

They looked at me and I didn't know what to say. This was crazy talk, wasn't it? Talking to spirits and Liz's soul being missing from this world? It sounded ridiculous! Then again, Darlene knew that Liz was missing and I hadn't told her that I'd even suspected it. I hadn't even told either of them that she existed! If Liz was missing, I had a good idea of who had taken her. I had thought it to myself, but hearing it come from someone else didn't make me feel any less crazy. It made me wonder if we were all crazy!

As absurd as this woman's ideas were, I couldn't dismiss some of the things I'd seen in the past month. Snippets of memory paraded through my mind: the look of horror on Lady Sage's face, those black and red unsettling eyes in the bar, and the ugly creature in the woods. As much as I wanted to forget them, these visions would haunt me, forever changing my outlook on the world.

"What do I need to do?" I asked, strangely feeling more confident in these strangers than I would have thought possible.

Darlene started flipping pages and I glimpsed perfectly hand-written text and dark-looking drawings.

"We are going to get you to where you need to go. Not tonight, but eventually. I think I've found a spell in here that'll get you into this alternate dimension, but I'm going to have to translate the elements and incantations into English. Amaryllis wrote most of her book of shadows in Latin, probably for safety reasons. I know a lot of Latin words, but she was fluent. I believe she called this other world *Barathrum* or *Limbus*, so I need to find that page."

"Barathrum," I whispered, trying to save the names to my memory. "Limbus."

"Ah, here is a page that interested me," she said, stopping at a page that read, "Warnings." She started to read the page aloud, "*ONE. Do not drop or leave traces of blood behind. Blood will give the shadow the ability to curse you from a distance. It can give a shadow or any dark magic practitioner power over you and make you susceptible to possession. Any blood spilt should be burned."*

I couldn't help but laugh aloud at my naivety. Tansy snorted simultaneously. Both of us knew I had unconsciously given Caymnaburus my blood a couple weeks before. As I thought about it, I realized that meant two demons probably had traces of my blood, if the demon in the woods had put curses over me.

"What?" Darlene piped.

Tansy answered before I could. "At least one already has her blood, probably two." Obviously she had come to the same realization, and I slumped, already feeling defeated.

Darlene pursed her lips as she looked at me. "Well, I guess we can't do anything about that, then. We just have to hope you won't come in contact with them when you're in Barathrum." She sighed and started flipping pages. "I guess we will skip over the warnings for now. After all, they didn't really save Amaryllis, and she wrote them."

That wasn't comforting, and I felt the beginnings of uneasiness. Was I about to make myself available to demons? Was I opening myself up to being another captured person with no way of getting home? Maybe I was already available to them, if they were casting curses on me, and I had no desire to make it worse.

Other questions came unbidden. How had I been able to see Caymnaburus's eye color like I had? How had my own eyes turned blue? How had I felt Tansy's circle fall when she hadn't? Who was that shadow in the woods, and why had he put curses on me?

"Could I be a half de—uh, shadow?" I asked, my voice coming out lower than I had intended it to.

Darlene touched my arm with her hand, trying to be comforting. "Oh, honey, why would you think *that*?"

I met Tansy's knowing eyes. "I'm allergic to silver, I'm just about allergic to sunlight, and my eyes are black."

"And isn't silver the metal that represents purity?" Tansy added. I had never heard that before, and I couldn't stop myself from feeling even more certain.

Darlene started. "That doesn't mean anything..." I

didn't miss the uncertainty in her voice as she let the words hang.

I shook my head. "When Tansy lifted those curses from me, my whole life has changed. People see me differently—"

"That's true, she looks different," Tansy piped in.

"I sense things that I've never been able to sense before," I continued. "And last week, my eyes changed color."

"Your eyes changed color?" Tansy asked, leaning back and looking surprised. Darlene didn't move, but her expression made her look just as startled.

"Yes," I said, looking between both of their surprised faces. "I was angry at my sister and somehow we got on the subject of me basically being jealous of her appearance and when I yelled at her that I'd always wanted her eyes, they turned blue...they looked identical to hers."

"Mom, shadows can change their appearance, right?" Tansy added. I nodded, agreeing.

Darlene pursed her lips again for a moment, thinking it over. "Shadows are spiritual beings. They can't..." Her words trailed off.

"That thing in the woods seemed to be much more than just a spiritual being," Tansy said.

"If they can kidnap you, doesn't that mean they are not just ghostly beings, but real-life beings that can touch you and..." I didn't want to finish, pushing the thoughts of my mother with one of those creatures out of my mind. That's what they were, creatures. Was it possible for humans and demons to procreate, if the demon could change himself into a human form?

"I don't think it's possible, but...I just don't know."

"Doesn't she seem different than most people, Mom? Can't you sense something?" Tansy went on.

"I sense something different, but I just think that Cara has some gifts of her own, like maybe some psychic ability or some special intuitiveness."

"It's more than that, Mom," Tansy said.

Darlene evidently wanted to change the subject.

"What I know is both of you have much to learn. Cara, if you want to know how to protect yourself from shadows and not live in fear of the night, we should start having meetings twice a week."

"Okay," I answered without a moment's hesitation.

She apparently thought I needed more convincing. "I believe that you are a strong, young girl, and you have the ability to save your friend and a lot of other trapped souls. I believe I was meant to prepare you and help you do this. Will you meet with us?"

I wasn't sure if I could do whatever she thought I was going to do in this premonition of hers, but I really wanted to know how to make protective circles. If I could better protect myself from Caymnaburus, or any shadows for that matter, I'd be resting a lot easier.

"Yes, I'll do it."

Eleven

The next afternoon at 4:30, I woke up to my wailing alarm clock and groaned. I had had an especially hard time getting to sleep the previous night. Talking with Darlene and Tansy hadn't answered many questions, just stirred up new ones, and they had swarmed around my head relentlessly.

I slipped into my work outfit and tied my hair into a ponytail, not bothering with makeup. Foregoing makeup was something I didn't frequently do, but it wasn't my intention to impress anyone that day. I didn't want to do anything except go back to sleep, and I shot a longing look at my bed before I left. As I walked to work, feeling disheveled and very conscious of the humidity that very quickly made my forehead bead with sweat, two young men caught my attention. They were just two regular guys in their mid-twenties, not particularly handsome or nicely dressed. It wasn't the look of them that necessarily caught my attention, but their muttering as I walked passed.

"Damn girl, you are beautiful," one said, and I caught his gaze as he shamelessly stared.

The other one pretended to be struck into stillness, looking at me with wide eyes as if he couldn't believe how beautiful I was. It was silly, and I wondered if they were mocking me, because this had never happened to me before. I couldn't help my shy smile as heat rose into my cheeks and I muttered an embarrassed, "Thanks."

"Seriously, you are be-YU-tiful!" he called after me when I was a few buildings past them.

I blushed harder and when I walked into work, I was beaming. What was coming over everyone? Whatever it was, I couldn't help but like it. I went to clock in and as soon as I walked into the back office, I was confronted by Harrison. "You're not wearing any makeup today," he commented.

My smile faltered and I avoided his gaze as I punched my time card. "Yep," I answered, noncommittally.

"You look nice," he said. When I peeked over my shoulder at him, I noticed his stare that almost seemed hungry. I didn't like that look on his face one bit. Maybe I didn't like what was coming over everyone after all.

"Thanks," I muttered, trying to sound polite without giving him the wrong idea. Before he could say anything else, I retreated into the hallway and headed for the bar. As I stocked the bar, Tracy, a brunette waitress with a cute Southern drawl, came to chat with me.

"Did you hear?" she asked.

"Hear what?" I asked back.

"Liz has gone missing!" she exclaimed, then lowered her voice when a few customers glanced our way. "Two detectives came in asking questions. And there is a rumor going around that she might have relapsed on drugs!"

I froze, too stunned to reply. So it was true. Liz *was* missing. I could no longer hope that she was in rehab and that Darlene was just a crazy witch-lady.

Tracy seemed to like my surprise, enjoying the fact

that she was the one to deliver a little tidbit of gossip, and mistaking me for one of the other snobby waitresses. "I knew she was an alcoholic, but I had no idea she was a drug addict. I can't say I'm surprised," she went on.

This wasn't harmless gossip, and I was *not* another snobby waitress. I wanted to grab her neck and shake her, but of course, I wouldn't do that. Instead, I gripped the bottle I had been about to put in the wine fridge a little too tightly. "Go away, Tracy," I said flatly.

Her mouth fell open a little and she stared stupidly at me. I had never stood up to her or any of the other waitresses before, no matter how much trash they talked, but she had crossed the line.

"I said, *go away.*" I spoke the last between clenched teeth and found myself gripping the bottle even tighter.

Her jaw suddenly clamped shut and she twirled on her heel. She went hurriedly to tell another waitress my bad reaction, no doubt, but I didn't care. I continued to stock the bar without giving her another glance. As I put the bottle in the wine fridge, I noticed a crack in the bottle going from top to bottom. *Did I do that?* I thought, before I shook my head and laughed at myself for even thinking it. Regardless of how the crack had happened, I decided the wine might not be safe for consumption and put it aside.

When everything was stocked and cleaned two times over, I rested an elbow on the bar top with my chin on my hand. My good mood was dead and gone. I was tired from lack of sleep and already over being here. I wondered where Liz was, and against my will, I imagined her being chained in a dark cell. I tried to wipe that image from my mind and hoped that she was somewhere safe.

My eyes focused on a young customer making a beeline toward me, and I hadn't realized I had even been looking toward him till he was only a few feet away. He looked like he might be under the legal drinking age and I sighed heavily, not looking forward to this interaction.

"Hi, can I see your ID?" I said before he could spout a drink order at me.

"Well, I'm not here for a drink," he said, giving me a weak smile. If a smile could look dead tired, that's the smile he gave me. Probably the same smile I had that day. "But I wanted to see if I could ask you a few questions about my sister, Elizabeth Black."

This was Liz's brother? I stopped to give him a good once-over. His hair was dirty blond and cut short, and his eyes were innocently wide and brown. Though young and baby-faced, he was very handsome. Besides being uncommonly good looking, I could see no similarities between him and Liz. I also noticed the tiredness in his eyes and stance. He looked exhausted, like he was trying to make normal expressions and gestures, but hardly able to manage it. A young person his age shouldn't act like that, but I guess if your sister were missing, you would.

"Yeah, I know your sister," I said, then quickly added. "She's a friend of mine."

He seemed to perk up at that, not in actual happiness, but in anticipation. "Well, have you seen her?" he asked.

"Not in over a week," I said, frowning. I wanted to tell him more, but what could I tell him? All I had were suspicions and out loud, they sounded crazy.

He slid into a stool and put his face in his hands, elbows resting on the bar. I thought he might be about to cry, but when he wiped his face with his hands and looked up, he revealed his red, tearless face. "Look," he said, looking straight into my eyes. "I know you probably know about Liz's alcohol problem—" then he huffed, "and her drug problem, but I do not believe she would just run away without telling me. My parents, maybe, but if she could, I think she would tell me if she was leaving town."

I nodded, but kept eye contact, though it was hard to look at the raw sadness in his eyes. He must be wondering if she had been kidnapped, as I was wondering the same thing.

"She even called me in the middle of the night," he continued. "But I just thought I'd call her back in the morning.

I just feel like, if only I had picked up, maybe she would still be here—I don't even know why I'm telling you this," he said, shrugging and finally looking away.

"She called me too," I said, then wondered if I should have admitted that. "It was while I was working on Monday night."

"Me too!" he exclaimed, then slumped lower in despair. "She called me at like—" he glanced through his phone for a moment. "One thirty-two in the morning."

I scrolled through my call list as well. "She called me at one twenty-nine." We met each other's wide eyes.

"Did she leave a message?" he asked.

I shook my head sadly.

"Me neither!" he said, sounding exasperated. "Why wouldn't she have left a voicemail? If something was wrong, why wouldn't she tell anyone?"

Because she knew she was about to leave, but she didn't know how to say goodbye or explain where she was going? I guessed. If she was calling people, she must've known she was leaving. Had Caymnaburus let her call her friends and family before he took her away?

"I just hate that the police seem to think she must have just gone on a drug spree and skipped town. They think there is a possibility someone *might* have kidnapped her, but they don't seem very worried about it."

"Hey," I said, and with some effort he met my eyes again. "I don't think she skipped town to go on a drug spree, and I'm going to do *everything* in my power to find her," I said. I was glad I could say that with complete honesty even if I didn't want to tell him all my thoughts about her disappearance.

One corner of his mouth perked in a slight smile. "Thank you," he said quietly. I smiled weakly back, and I felt a sort of kinship between us then.

A young couple parked themselves at the bar, just a couple seats from him, and I asked him if he would hold on a moment while I served them.

Liz's brother nodded and waited patiently while I got

the drink order of the couple, who found it hard to keep their eyes off each other. I served them their drinks as quickly as I could and went back to the young boy with wide, brown eyes. I noticed that though they weren't the same color as Liz's, the shape of their eyes was similar.

"My name is Henry," he said quietly.

"I'm Cara," I said and we awkwardly shook hands over the bar. I stood there for another moment, running through the past couple weeks in my mind and trying to decide if there was anything I could tell him. There wasn't.

"Okay," he said suddenly. "If you can call me if you hear anything, I'd appreciate that." After scribbling a number on a napkin, he smiled weakly and was gone.

The following couple of weeks I practiced magic with Darlene and Tansy in all my spare time.

Darlene explained to me that magic came from the energy of the earth, and with much practice, you could bring the energy into yourself. She had a few names for this energy: the life force, cosmic energy, but she most frequently called it the *universal force*. I imagined that bringing the universal force into yourself was like pulling on a thread of energy from the ground and bringing into your chest, winding it in an already existing ball of yarn inside yourself. Once you were able to collect the energy from the earth and combine it with your own energy, the next step was to hold it. If you didn't hold it, the energy could unwind itself out of you as quickly as you brought it in. Magic could be done simply by bringing in the universal force and willing things to be so, like lighting candles, shutting doors, and more. If you didn't hold onto the universal force, you could still use magic, but your magic would be more or less unpredictable. Darlene had stressed that practicing unpredictable magic was not something you wanted to do. Maybe instead of lighting a candle or shutting a door, you'd set the whole room on fire or slam the door right off its hinges.

Darlene said that it had taken her many, many years to become one with the deities through rituals and through that to become in tune with the overall life force. With all her practice, she had learned how to wind the force into herself and hold it. Tansy had learned to wind it into herself and hold it, also, but she said she couldn't seem to bring enough energy into herself yet, which was why her abilities were still just a fraction of her mother's.

When I first collected the universal force into myself and held it, which I imagined was like closing a door with my ball of energy safely inside myself, and lit a candle with the point of my finger, Darlene and Tansy had been in shock. Tansy had just about exploded into cheers and praised my natural ability, but her mother seemed more than a little uneasy. I couldn't be sure, but I think she was afraid of me being able to collect energy without doing rituals or praising the deities.

I realized that the universal force manifested itself as the familiar buzzing sensation through my body and that I had been in tune with it the moment the curses had been lifted. I explained that to Darlene, who was obviously relieved to hear this.

"I believe when you were very young, the universal force was cut off from you with a curse. Now that you know the absence of it, you can identify it that much easier," Darlene explained. "Even that being said, I think you are especially in tune."

"That makes sense," I admitted. "But why would someone want to put that curse on me?" The very thought of the demon in the woods sent shivers down my spine, and I heard rats screeching in my head. I was forever going to be scared of rats now.

"I don't truly know, but my best guess is someone, maybe that shadow in particular, was trying to hide you. You were blocked from your own abilities and the life force, and in turn it blocked you from most people's notice. You said that people seem to see you differently now that the curses are lifted. Maybe being completely separated from the universal force almost shields you from people's notice. Like maybe they can physically see you, but not physically feel you. It probably has made people you've come in contact with feel disconnected from you and in a way, see you differently. I wish I had met you before the curses had been lifted, because then I'd have a better idea of what it was like."

"I see and feel her completely differently," Tansy told her mother, then looked toward me. "Before, you felt strangely absent. When I looked at you, it was like I could see you staring back at me, but I couldn't feel your gaze. You were like an empty vessel. Not really, but that's what you felt like. Now, I can feel your energy stronger than I can feel most other people. It's polar opposite."

I used to accidentally scare people all the time, I suddenly remembered. Walking in line at a restaurant, I would startle the person in front of me when they turned and saw me there. No one seemed to notice me until I was in their face. It made me angry that someone would put a curse on me that had changed my life so much. I tried to tell myself that it was over now and I should just be relieved. I could be normal now, except maybe even better! I was learning how to do magic. Who would have thought my life would go from so boring to so exciting?

"Hmm, very interesting," Darlene said. They were both staring hard at me and I caved into myself a little bit at their ogling. "The beauty people are suddenly seeing in you must be the beautiful, pure light that shines out. The very existence of life," Darlene explained.

"Though you are really pretty anyway," Tansy added with a smile.

I smiled back. Is it strange that I believed all of it, except the very last part?

Twelve

The following Saturday evening, I took some time to clean and organize my bedroom. Darlene had given me a lot of her old witch ceremonial tools that she didn't have need for anymore or had replaced. Some of the stuff I wasn't sure I was going to use, like a small altar set with everything I needed for an in-home altar, including a small table just slightly bigger than a step stool with a pentagram carved on the top. I thought it was nice gesture to give it to me, but I couldn't see myself using it. As much as she was trying to convert me into the Wicca religion, I wasn't planning on doing rituals to the god and goddess on my own. I did them when Darlene was teaching me circles, but I found it unnecessary and tiresome. She would tell me that I needed to become one with the deities so that they could protect me from being tempted by shadows, but I felt like my will to be a good person and to use my magic for good was enough. And though I believed the Wiccan way was a good way to live, preserving nature and harming none, I didn't have any proof the deities existed. After all, I didn't worship them, but I still could use the universal force. Regardless of all that, I set the altar up in my room, shoving it to the right of my TV so that if my door was open, no one would see it from the hallway, particularly my roommate when she came back from summer vacation.

Some of the other tools Darlene had given me I was looking forward to using. She had given me a scrying mirror, which is made of darkly-tinted glass in which you can sometimes see spiritual visions, similar to a crystal ball. Previously I had laughed at the idea of seeing visions in a crystal ball, but I was seeing things differently now that I had been spending so much time with Darlene and Tansy. The little black, almost opaque, square piece of glass she gave me was eight-by-eight inches and came with a little stand. I probably wouldn't be able to see anything in it, but I wasn't going to knock it until I'd tried it. Even though I prohibited myself to have lingering thoughts about it, I believe a small part of me hoped I might find out who my birth father was by using the square of dark glass.

Darlene had also given me a couple of books of very simple and traditional spells, a necklace that held an empty glass vial with a tiny cork in it that could hold an elixir, and a pack of black chalk for drawing circles. I stashed the box of black chalk in the drawer of my bedside table, but put one piece inside a pocket in my purse for emergency use. Magical circles could be made in a hurry without the rituals and without a physical marker like chalk or candles, but making circles with your mind can be unpredictable magic practice. The last thing you want to do is trap yourself in a circle with just the thing or person you're trying to protect yourself from. Or make a circle so small that you accidentally break it too early by touching it.

According to Darlene, salt could also be used to create a protective circle and was very commonly used to protect you while you made spells. In fact, it's considered cleansing and is used in most all spells. But Tansy had told it to me wrong. Salt underneath the doors and windows could possibly slow a shadow in its most solid form from entering my house, unless I for some reason invited it in. It could stop Caymn if he tried to enter in his solid form, but since it wasn't a complete circle or closed shape, it wouldn't stop him from coming through the walls. It also wouldn't deter any shadows from simply appearing or peeking in in their spectral form. It terrified me that I wouldn't be able to stop anything from coming in and seeing into my apartment, but Darlene assured me that I would be able to sense it coming before it came, since I seemed to have more intuitiveness than most. If shadows did start appearing, Darlene was teaching me how to make them leave. I was still scared of sleeping at night, but I found some comfort in having more knowledge and feeling like I was a little prepared.

I had more to organize in my bedroom than just what Darlene had given me. I had also bought a bunch of candles at Wally World that she had said I would need for my magic in the future. Most of them were just small white, tea-light candles, because apparently you shouldn't use the same candle twice for a spell. But I also bought colored ones that she had said I needed to close a circle the ritualistic way, though I doubted I would use them. As far as I could tell, my circles weren't any stronger when I did them the ritualistic way. But just in case my mentor asked, I bought the four different colored candles for the different elements: green for earth, yellow for air, red for fire, and blue for water.

I glanced at the clock by my bed. Seven o' clock. Generally I would be at work at seven on a Saturday, but I had switched shifts with another waitress so I could go to my little cousin's violin recital later that night. I gently placed most of the candles in a half-empty junk drawer of my dresser and went to my closet. I knew exactly what I wanted to wear.

I finally had an occasion fancy enough to wear one of the beautiful, designer dresses Liz had given me. I picked the red one, which was my ultimate favorite. The fabric was so sheer on top, you could hardly tell where the neckline began and where it met my skin. At a quick glance it almost looked like the dress didn't start till my waist, except for some expertly placed clusters of red flowers that were woven in the fabric, covering some of my stomach, my breasts, and a little bit of shoulder. There were little red, shiny beads on the lace flowers that gave the dress dimension and caught the light beautifully. It was borderline scandalous, but I didn't have the boobs to make it sleazy. It helped that it went to my knees and flared out in a full skirt instead of being skin-tight all the way down, or so I convinced myself.

I pulled my hair into a half pony tail like Darlene often did. Since my hair is only shoulder length, it doesn't have the same flow-y effect, but it kept my hair out of my face and didn't distract from the dress. I added some gold dangly earrings that I felt added to the whole glamorous effect. I hoped my parents wouldn't have a heart attack seeing me wearing something that showed so much skin.

As I pulled out some nude heels from my closet and started sliding my feet into them, I heard my cell phone ring out, notifying me of a text message. I shuffled toward the bed, trying to get my feet in the shoes as I went to grab my cell on my pillow. The text message read, *Do you have a hair from Liz's head? Either in a hair brush or an article of clothing...*

The message was from Darlene. She asked me the strangest, most off-the-wall questions sometimes. She also had a peculiar way of saying or asking things at the most convenient times, and it made me wonder how intuitive she really was. For example, she would ask if I would pick something up from a particular store just as I was about to pass it. Tansy was the same way too, now that I thought about it. Maybe there was something to this whole *becoming one with the deities* thing that I was dismissing.

The dress I wore was clean and free of any stray hairs, so I went back to my closet to inspect the other two dresses Liz had given me. Sure enough, the black dress she had given me had a long black hair woven in between sequins. I had almost mistaken it for a black string, but as soon as I found one hair, I noticed another one and massaged them both out of the fabric.

I texted back, *Found two hairs.*
Excellent! Bring them to our session tomorrow.

I put the two hairs in a baggy and slipped it in the pocket inside my purse next to my black chalk so that I wouldn't forget it. I hoped that this was what Darlene needed to locate Liz and that soon we could get this over with, whatever it was. At the same time, I never wanted to go into this world further from our own. I imagined it'd be filled with darkness, glowing red eyes peering at me, and clawed hands stretching out to grasp my ankles. How were my little magic tricks supposed to help me against the magic of demons? Maybe Darlene could use Liz's hair to bring her back and I wouldn't have to go anywhere. Doubtful, because nothing is ever that easy, but I let myself hope.

I slung my purse over my shoulder and headed toward the door. With a quick tug of the universal force and a few seconds of concentrating on holding it to myself, I was able to open the front door and close it behind me with a thought. I smiled to myself as I let the universal force escape, almost giddy enough to jump up and down. Every time I practiced it became easier, and I became much quicker at holding it. Finding the universal force was almost second nature to me and soon I would be able to hold it to myself just as easily as I found it. I still had to use my key to lock the door, though.

The violin recital was nice, though I hadn't been aware of how far away it was and missed part of it. It had almost taken me an hour due to the distance and a wreck on the interstate and when I finally walked down the aisle, my cousin was already playing her violin solo. A lot of eyes were on me as I made my way to my seat, and I silently cursed myself for not leaving earlier.

When I sat down next to my mom in an empty seat she'd saved for me, she glanced at me and smiled. That is, until her eyes caught my dress and she frowned. *Oops*, I thought, maybe the dress wasn't family-friendly after all. A few seats over, Jessie leaned forward to wave at me, and I smiled and waved back. Good. At least maybe now we were on good terms again.

After the recital ended, my parents, Jessie, Scott, and a few other family members chatted in our corner of the music hall. Everyone praised my cousin Lacey on her violin playing and chatted about how well she was doing in school. When she came out from the back stage area, I hugged her and told her that she had done a magnificent job. My mom and her mom, my Aunt Bonnie, decided we should go out as a family to a nearby Italian restaurant, so we headed out. When we walked outside to our cars, our parents walking ahead of us, Jessie and I hung back with Lacey. We slung our arms around her shoulders and when Jessie smiled at me, I felt relieved to have my sister back. I had missed our friendship. Maybe our stupid little argument a few weeks ago was just that. *Stupid.*

I stared down at my vodka tonic and stirred it with a tiny black straw as Jessie talked loudly in my ear over booming music. After our nice family dinner, Jessie had started begging me to go drinking downtown. I complained that I had the morning shift at the restaurant the next day, but Jessie argued that it was a waste to put on such a beautiful dress and not go out in it. This exchange was nothing new with us, her begging and me trying to abstain, and though I didn't really feel like going out, I was happy to have Jessie acting like her old self. And she was right about one thing: the dress was incredible.

"I don't mind if y'all go out," Scott added, not helping me. "I could meet up with a few of my buddies."

"See, even the married people want to go out!" Jessie said. She started to bounce up and down, seeing in my expression that she had already won.

"Fine, let's go," I said in defeat. So forty minutes later, SINergy was where we ended up. The club was in full force that Saturday night, people dancing and crowding around us at the bar.

Jessie had talked the whole way there and after we got our first drinks, she was still talking. Apparently marriage life was tougher than she'd imagined, and it was a big adjustment moving in with Scott. I couldn't exactly relate, but I could try to sympathize. I was getting slightly irritated that she hadn't even asked how I was or what was going on with me. I guess I should have been relieved, because I didn't know what to tell her, but after almost an hour of listening to her complain about her life, I was getting tired. As she talked, I found myself looking around the club, tuning her out. I caught sight of a guy with long black hair on the dance floor, and I craned my neck to get a better look, my heart suddenly beating faster in my chest. When I realized it wasn't a guy at all, but actually a girl in a dress too tiny for her body, I laughed at myself. I realized then that I had been looking for *him*. *Hoping to see him*. Why was I hoping to see him like a giddy schoolgirl with a crush? I should be hoping I'd never see him unless it was to strangle him. I wished more than anything that I could get him out of my head.

"See those guys across the bar?" Jessie said, and I glanced in the direction she looked in, glad for a new topic. Across the bar was a group of guys, decent looking, but not guys I would usually take a second glance at. That sounds mean, but I don't usually give second glances to most guys. I'm just not one of those people that's always on the prowl, scoping all the guys out. Maybe in high school I had been like that, but I had given up on being boy-crazy years ago. I have to admit, though, one of them stuck out to me and deserved a second glance. His head was shaved short in a buzz-cut and his skin was tanned like he spent a lot of time in the sun. He wore a cute green and black checkered button down shirt, and I could see a tattoo peeking out from underneath his shirt sleeve. He looked very casual and boyish, like he had just come from the beach or the park. I liked it better than how some of the other guys were dressing, in too-tight collared shirts and gelled hair. *Trying way too hard.* This guy's eyes were pretty, too, somehow looking bright and playful in the dim lighting. And they were aimed to make eye contact with me.

I glanced down at my drink, quickly avoiding his gaze. I took a sip of my drink to keep my hands occupied and hide the smile that was forming on my lips. "Yeah, I see 'em."

"Well, the cute one with the kind of shaved head..." she said, leaning in close to talk. "He is Maggie's older brother. I had a huge crush on him when we were in high school, but he went to another school. His name is Jonah."

"He's cute," I admitted, sneaking a look back toward the group across the bar. Jonah was gone, but all his friends were still there, laughing with each other, and some of them glanced our way. If I hadn't known better, I would've said they were talking about us. As I turned to look around the club to see where he'd gone, someone scooted up next to me. A man's voice came over the roaring music. "Hi, what's your name?"

I looked toward the person and jumped when I saw it was the guy from across the bar. He was grinning at me and extending his hand. I took it and smiled. "Hi, I'm Cara!" I yelled back, giving his hand a firm shake. His big hand was warm and dry around mine. I realized he was taller than me, even in my couple-inch heels, which is tall. I liked that a lot. He wasn't gorgeous or beautiful, the way you would describe Caymn, but he was *very cute*. Still too good-looking to be talking to me.

"I'm Jonah," he said, and he flashed his grin, his straight teeth very white against his tanned skin.

"Nice to meet you," I said, and we dropped hands. "I think I'm a little overdressed," I admitted, trying to keep the conversation rolling as best as possible. I suddenly felt nervous and awfully exposed in my revealing dress.

"I'm the one *under*dressed, I promise you. You look wonderful." I smiled at that and couldn't help but glance down at nothing as heat crept into my cheeks. He leaned in closer so we could hear each other better over the loud music. *Right.*

"I don't usually do this, but I wanted to come talk to the prettiest girl here."

"I'm not the prettiest girl here," I argued, not able to stop my broadening smile.

"Yes, you are," he said, looking around as if to make sure.

I looked with him. There were a lot of cute girls out, actually. I pointed one out by the dance floor. "I don't know, that girl with the blue dress is pretty hot."

"Eh, she's too short. I'd have to stoop down to talk to her," he said. I glanced back toward him and smiled shyly. I liked this game.

"What about her?" I asked, nodding toward a girl a few seats away from us at the bar.

"Which one?" he said, turning to look around. He pretended not to be able to see her, comically looking all over the place.

"You know, pink dress and brown hair," I said.

He whipped back around toward me when the girl saw that we were obviously talking about her. We hunched over our drinks and laughed with each other at being caught staring.

"I don't know, I prefer the red dress and blond hair."

I almost asked, "*Who?*" when I realized he was talking about me. I felt my cheeks heat up again and hoped I wasn't as red as my dress.

All of a sudden a drink slammed on the bar behind me, and I felt liquid splash a little on my shoulder and seep through the fabric of my dress. It wasn't a lot, but it got my attention. I turned to see my sister still sitting there, glaring at us with her hand tightly gripping a new drink. I had completely forgotten she was sitting there, and when I took in the new drink and the way her eyes seemed red and hazy, I knew she was drunk. And pissed off. *Oh geez.*

Before I could ask what her attitude was about, she grabbed my arm and yanked me. "Excuse me, but me and my sister need to have a girl chat." I was tempted to yank my arm back and tell her to stop, but I really didn't want to start a scene in front of this guy. Well, an even bigger scene.

"I'll be back shortly," I said, smiling at him, but now it was a tight smile.

Jessie made a noise in her throat that sounded suspiciously like a growl and I let her pull me away, nearly dragging me to the bathroom. I would not let her make me lose my temper in front of all these people, I told myself. When we were in the bathroom and the door swung shut, she faced me with a look that was pure hatred. "What are you doing out there? I told you I've had a crush on that guy forever!"

I stood back, shocked. "You're married!" was all I could think to say.

She huffed. "Yeah, I'm married, but that's against the sister code. You can't go for guys I've always liked!"

I felt my temper start to rise and I took a deep breath to calm myself. "First off, I did not go after *anyone*. He came to talk to me. And even if I did, you never dated him! The sister code doesn't apply for someone you've had a little crush on! I really hope this is just alcohol talking, because this is crazy."

"Are you calling me *crazy?!*" She all but screamed at me and I braced myself, starting to think she might launch herself at me. "I can't stand you anymore, Cara! I can't *fucking* stand you!"

I couldn't help but feel a little hurt. "What did I do that made everything change with us? You used to be my best friend," I said. I knew I shouldn't even try to talk to her, that there is no reasoning with a drunk person, but I couldn't help myself.

"Well, there's the key words, huh? *Used to be!* You're not the same anymore. *You've* changed! I hate this new..." she waved her hand in my general direction. "Version of you!"

I was finally starting to like myself instead of just forcing myself to be satisfied with what I had been stuck with.

I was finally happy, but she hated me for it? As much as I knew she was being childish and I shouldn't let her words said in drunkenness hurt me, they did. I believed she meant them.

She took off out of the bathroom, stomping out. As the door swung crazily back and forth, I thought about letting her go. Let her throw her hissy fit! I didn't deserve this. But I followed her. I had to. Though the club wasn't in an especially bad area, no girl should be walking around in the dark in a drunken stupor. Who knew where she'd end up? I walked out of the bathroom and tried to stay a good fifteen feet behind her as she pushed through people.

Suddenly, someone came up close beside me. "Cara!" It was Jonah.

I kept walking, though I slowed my pace for him. "Hey, I actually have to go…"

"Well can I get your number or something?" He scratched the back of his neck and stooped down as he walked with me, looking a little unsure of himself. Little did he know, this was the first time a guy had ever asked for my number. And here he was, nervous. It was very…attractive. Kind of charming.

"Sure, I'll give it to you," I said, elated.

"Great! Here's a pen." He handed me a pen and I clicked it open. I wondered if he didn't have a cell phone to input my number into or if he just wanted an excuse to touch me. Either way, it didn't matter. He gave me his forearm and I grabbed it to steady it. My fingers tingled where they touched him as I wrote my number.

Fortunately, I got Jessie into my car without any screaming or arguing. In fact, she didn't even talk to me as she fell into the passenger seat and slammed the door shut.

"Should I call Scott to pick you up?"

"Fine, yeah, call *Scott*," she said, spitting out his name in hatred. I wasn't sure if the hatred was aimed at me or him, but I called.

"You want me to pick her up *now*?" Scott complained when I tried to gently explain the situation. Now Scott was aggravating me. In my opinion he should be rushing to save her. "Yes, please pick her up."

"Fine," he grumbled. "I'll head that way in a few minutes."

"No, Scott, now!" I yelled. I was trying to avoid having another argument start between Jessie and me, but now Scott was getting on my last nerve.

There was silence on the phone for a moment, except for some chatting in the background.

"He's a fucking jerk!" Jessie screamed, leaning toward my phone. "He doesn't care about me!"

"You know what, Cara? Keep her!" Scott yelled through the phone. "I'm not coming anywhere!" And he hung up. I stared at the phone, shocked. Jessie started yelling more, as if Scott could still hear her. I started driving toward my apartment, not wanting to sit in a dark parking lot any longer.

"Stop it, Jessie! I'm taking you to my apartment."

"No, take me home! Take me home, take me home!" she demanded.

"No!" I shouted back. "I'm going to call dad to pick you up." She all but begged me not to call Bruce, but I had had enough. Let someone else deal with her that would be able to handle her. To my relief, Jessie didn't scream at me while I was on the phone with Bruce, even though I sat next to her, ratting her out. Even in her inebriated state, she knew better than to throw a screaming fit with Bruce listening in, and after some convincing on my part, he agreed to pick her up.

By some miracle we made it up and into my apartment without any more arguing, but it didn't last long. "Sit down on my bed till he gets here. We'll watch some TV," I suggested as we walked into my bedroom. She stared dejectedly around my room, until she caught sight of the pentagram table shoved between my TV and dresser drawers.

"What is that?" she asked, pointing to the table.

When I realized what she was looking at, I was at a loss of words. "I, uh…"

"Oh my god!" she exclaimed. "Have you become a Satanist?"

"What? No!" I tried to explain. "The right side up pentagram actually means the complete opposite of what you might think. It means protection, and the five points represent the elements and the spirit…" I realized she wasn't listening, but staring at something past me.

"Practical Spells for the Modernized Witch?" she said accusingly as she pointed to the books on my bed and started marching toward them. I tried to grab them before she could get to them, but she knocked them out of my hands and they clattered to the floor.

"The Book of Complete Witchcraft?" she said, reading another book's title before I snatched them away and shoved them underneath my pillow.

"A witch is not a Satanist! You have it all wrong!" I said, frustrated.

"Oh my god, wait till I tell Mom and dad! Do you think you're an actual witch?" There was laughter in her voice.

"No!" I said. "Please, Jessie, you know they won't understand!" Though my parents didn't actively go to church or read the Bible, they would absolutely not understand or want to understand. Bruce might not shun me for it, but my mom? Who knew?

"It all makes sense now," Jessie said, staring off distantly, then meeting my eyes with a look of shocked horror. "How everything about you has changed all of the sudden, the thing you did with your eyes…"

"You have it wrong, Jessie!" I said, my voice rising higher in warning.

"You are putting spells on yourself, aren't you? Oh, wait till Mom hears about this!" she said. "That you're a Satan-worshipping witch!" I could care less that she was drunk. That was a low blow and she knew it. And suddenly her lips twitched in a smile, as if I were her enemy and she'd finally found my one weakness.

"How dare you!" I screamed, wanting to slap that look off her face and finally losing the last bit of patience I had. "How dare you come to my house and threaten to tell our parents about what I'm doing. Look at yourself before you start pointing fingers at me!"

She suddenly looked scared, not angry or accusing, but flat out panicked. Her eyes showed too much white as she frantically ran for my bedroom door and clattered out of my apartment, glancing back once with terror showing plain on her face. First, I was confused, but then I noticed the buzzing against my skin and knew it wasn't just my anger that was making me shake. I was holding onto the universal force. I touched my face and for a moment I felt that my cheekbone was so sharp that it should cut out of my skin before it seemed to mold back to its normal, softer shape.

Thirteen

"Cara, are you paying attention?"

I jerked my head from where I stared emptily into the woods to face Darlene, who stood above me holding the large, red leather book with both hands. She looked annoyed, but I don't think it was wholly because of me. She was having trouble translating the last part of the locating spell: one ingredient. She hadn't been able to find the translation for the one Latin word anywhere.

We sat outside in the muggy August afternoon heat on the stone circle slab. Tansy and I sat on the white washed stones and Darlene paced around us with the large book in her hands. "Yes, sorry, I'm listening," I lied, wiping the beads of sweat forming on my forehead. I was stripped down to nothing but jean shorts and a sweat-soaked tank top that I had rolled up to reveal my stomach, hoping to get some kind of relief from the heat. My shoulder length hair clung to the back of my neck where sweat mixed with the SPF 80 I'd spread all over myself. The sun had finally hidden behind the trees, but the stones were still uncomfortably warm. I felt awful and looked worse. On top of being painfully hot, I was exhausted. The previous night with Jessie had been frustrating, work this morning had been agony, and I had no idea why we were outside in the heat.

"Where are the hairs?" Darlene asked, finally sitting in front of us and splaying the book in front of herself. Her purple dress pooled around her and her long strawberry-blond hair fell over her shoulder like a curtain. She looked beautiful and made me think that if she had pointed ears, she would be a wood nymph or a woodland fairy—some kind of magical thing from the woods. Tansy looked like a shorter-haired gothic version in a long black dress with slits going to her upper thighs and graphic design of three moons on her chest in different lunar phases. They both looked too comfortable in this heat.

"Cara, the hairs!"

I jumped and grabbed my purse that was lumped beside me. "Sorry, it's just so hot out here. I can't concentrate," I whined as I fumbled around for the baggy with two hairs.

"You spend too much of your time hiding out in the air conditioning!" Darlene snapped. "You should spend more time outdoors in nature! We're getting that now!"

I refrained from groaning aloud, but couldn't help frowning at her as I put one of the hairs gently in her palm. She grasped it with two fingers and inspected it.

"What if it's something like pig's blood or something?" Tansy offered, going back to the mystery ingredient.

I wrinkled my nose at the image of myself smeared in pig's blood. I did not want to go anywhere covered in pig's blood, let alone some scary alternate universe, but when I imagined Liz, possibly being tortured and locked up, I thought I could do it.

"I don't believe we need anything that harms another creature. I wouldn't have seen the premonition if that were the case, because we would never sacrifice anything for any reason."

"You don't have to sacrifice an animal to get pig's blood. You could get that from pork chops at the grocery store," I said. "Maybe it *is* some sort of blood."

Darlene looked at me very seriously. "I hope it's not."

We sat silent for a minute, not sure of how to proceed. We had been talking about this all week, all searching for answers separately, and not getting any closer to finding out what the ingredient was. Darlene had even gone as far as contacting a college professor of the Latin language, and even he hadn't known what the word meant. In fact, he said he didn't believe it was a word from the Latin language.

"And you don't think there's any way around this ingredient?" I said, though I knew the answer already. *We are going in circles.*

"There are two very similar spells in the book," Darlene said as she flipped from one page to another, both with sticky notes poking from the pages, which for some reason looked humorous to me. "One is for going to this Barathrum and another one is to locate an object, both containing this mystery ingredient. I believe if you mix the spells a certain way and have the ingredient smeared against your skin, you will be able to go into this further world and land right by the person that the focusing object belongs to, in this case the strand of hair. When we find out what this other ingredient is, we are going to smear it on your chest, you will hold onto the cosmic energy, and say these words..." Darlene flattened a piece of lined paper with her handwriting on it, the writing being an incantation from the two spells that she'd put together.

"*Ad abyssos de Barathrum, ego expectamus hanc mulierem, i accipere in tenebris, invenire hanc mulierem in Barathrum.*"

Without thinking, I was weaving the universal force within myself, and I absentmindedly twirled Liz's other hair around my forefinger. I repeated the words, practicing the pronunciation.

The moment I said the last word, my ears popped and I felt the air pressure change around me. I met eyes with Darlene, who looked surprised, and at the corner of my eye I could see Tansy making a similar expression. Almost as soon as I realized that they were feeling something too, I felt as if someone kicked me in the stomach and the air whooshed out of my lungs. Panic rose up in me and I wanted to scream. Next, my eyesight went and I was pushed into complete, utter darkness. I felt paralyzed, separated from my own physical body. The only things I could feel were the panic rising where my gut should have been and the sensation of being pulled at a thousand miles an hour by my aching lungs.

When I thought I might not be able to bear another second, the sensations slowed until everything seemed still. When my vision started to return, I blinked and tried to focus. I was standing right side up in a new place, and I wobbled on my suddenly weak legs. With my first deep breath of dry, hot air, I took in my surroundings. Everything in this world I saw was either in the shade of blood red or black shadow. Red buildings of all different styles and architecture surrounded me, each one more extravagant and ridiculous than the next, like palaces from foreign countries and lost wonders of the world. The dusty dirt road underneath my bare feet was red. The few people walking down the street wore different shades of red and black. Even I was red! I stared at my red-tinted hands for a moment, idly wondering where the hair had gone, before I realized I was standing in red lighting. When I looked up at the sun, if a sun was what it was, it shone bright in the blood-red sky like a crimson light bulb. It was the strangest sensation, appearing there—like stepping for the first time into a darkroom where photographs are developed, except on a much larger scale.

Noticing that other people were walking by, I took a few steps up the dirt road, trying to focus my eyes through the red thickness while trying to be inconspicuous. The street wasn't heavily populated, but the few people that were out didn't take a second glance at me, which was unexpected, because I looked very conspicuous in jean shorts, a tank top, and no shoes. They were dressed in long hooded cloaks with the hoods up over their heads, just glimpses of their faces showing. The faces I glanced at looked human and normal, besides a few of them being decorated with black designs that looked shocking, but somehow pretty in their placement. Tattoos, maybe? Though the people never glanced back at me, they seemed to make an effort to avoid getting too close to my path. I didn't know if they were demon or human, though I assumed they were human, but I avoided their paths as well.

I did feel someone's eyes on me though, their gaze boring into me and making the hair on the back of my neck stand. I glanced back and up at one of the buildings as I walked, and sure enough, two yellow eyes peered at me through an arched opening a few stories up. I didn't slow my pace but hunched slightly in on myself as I continued. As I turned back toward the path in front of me, I suddenly caught sight of a figure with black, swaying hair. If I hadn't had such a hard time focusing through the disorienting cloud of red, I would have noticed the girl with her hood brazenly draped over her shoulders immediately. I was relieved and amazed that the spell had worked and taken me straight to her, even without that secret ingredient! Who would have known?

But now she was getting away. *Liz!* I wanted to shout her name out, but the street was too strangely quiet. The only sounds I could hear were strange music playing far away, like a whining violin or guitar, and the shuffling of my feet in the sand. She was walking fast and I tried to quicken my pace to an almost run, hoping I wasn't going to draw any *more* unwanted attention to myself. I imagined a million eyes suddenly peering through windows above me, but I didn't dare look up to check.

I stifled a groan and slowed my pace as she walked straight into a large open building. As I got closer, the area became more congested and I realized it was an indoor marketplace. I took a deep breath, gathering my courage, and walked into the crowd of hooded cloaks. It was darker in this long indoor market, but still red, making it almost impossible for me to see. People were yelling at each other in English and at least one other language, which I was guessing was Latin.

"Lamb's blood! Get your blood of the innocent!" someone shouted, and it was the only thing in English that stuck out to me. I was tempted to look in the direction of the voice, but I trained my eyes on Liz to prevent myself from losing her. She stopped at a table with jewelry, all the pieces made from simple-looking metal strands holding small, smooth black stones of some kind. Or were they actually red stones? I couldn't tell.

She started struggling to communicate with the woman selling the jewelry, talking slowly and deliberately in another language. Without saying a word, I went to stand next to her, trying to get her attention without tipping off the other woman or anyone around me.

"Ah, *sanguinem innocentem*?" Liz was saying and pointing to a piece of jewelry when she turned her eyes toward me. She didn't have a drop of makeup on, but she could pull that look off better than anyone I knew. Her outfit looked like a monk's robe, but her dark hair and strikingly light-colored eyes were beautiful, even in the red lighting.

Her eyes suddenly widened. "Cara!" she said a little too loudly, and a few passersby glanced our way. I felt so self-conscious, being the only person in sight not wearing a robe. I got closer to her so we could whisper. The lady conveniently ignored us, shouting in Latin to the passersby to take a look at her product. "Oh my god, you're here! Who is your host?"

She took in what I was wearing, eyes getting larger, as I asked her, "What do you mean, 'host'?"

She grabbed my wrist a little too hard and without another word, she yanked me away from the table, taking me back the way we'd come. I didn't struggle, trusting that she knew better than me and relieved to be escaping the crowded marketplace.

"Cara, why aren't you wearing your blood robes? You should know only demons can go without blood robes," she hissed, glancing up to the tall buildings as if looking for eyes staring through the windows and arches. She put her arm around my shoulder, drawing me really close, maybe so we'd look like one person at a quick glance. Her cloak billowed around me, shielding me. I took a glance at her face and her eyes bulged, too much white visible.

"I don't have a robe," I replied. "Liz, I've come to take you back home."

"I don't want to go home," she said and I almost stopped, I was so surprised. Only her tight grip on me kept me walking.

"What do you mean, you don't want to go home?"

She stared back at me as we walked, our noses almost touching. It would have been uncomfortably close in different circumstances, but being where we were, it was comforting being so close to a human I was well-acquainted with.

"My former life was almost unlivable, Cara. I couldn't stand being alone before, but now I'm living a new, exciting life. My host is probably one of the best in the third city, and I'm one of the few human familiars that have gone outside at night."

I at least knew what a familiar was, thanks to Tansy. But former life? Third city? *What was she talking about?*

"What is a host?" I asked for the second time, deciding I'd ask one thing at a time.

"A host is a master of someone."

"So you're like a slave or a pet?" I hissed.

"Maybe some familiars are," she shrugged. "But I'm treated more like a favored servant."

"And you're okay with that?" I couldn't believe this. This didn't seem like the Liz I knew, who was the worst server at Angel Oak, who griped and complained almost every chance she got. How could this girl, of all people, enjoy being anyone's servant? I'd imagined I was going to have to save someone who was chained up and broken of spirit. Liz seemed cheerful as we walked down the street, if not a little concerned for me. It should have been the other way around!

"I have come to terms with it," she said. "Everything is so new and interesting. I'm not ready to leave."

"What about your parents? And your brother!"

She frowned, and our pace slowed. "Are they looking for me?" she asked quietly.

"Yes, you've been an official missing person for two weeks! Your brother came into the restaurant once when I was in, and the other waitresses have talked to your parents! They've put signs around town..." I let my words trail off as I watched her face. She looked a little sad, but not like my news really changed anything.

"Maybe I can have you deliver a note for me. I especially miss my little brother, Henry. It makes me sad that I might not ever see them again."

"I-I don't understand," I said, fumbling over my words, feeling at a loss.

"You don't understand, because you've never had a relationship and never been in love. Once you love something so much, everything and everyone else seem less important. You still love your family, but you can live without them," she said, her frown turning into a smile as she seemed to talk herself out of missing her family.

"You're in love?" I said too loudly, then lowered my voice, "Is it Caymn?"

"Caymnaburus?" she said, then laughed. "Oh god, no!" Then she couldn't seem to stop chuckling at the thought.

"Well, then who?" I asked, irritated that she was laughing at me.

"No one! I'm in love with this place. You must not have been here long at all if you don't know what I'm talking about. Everything is like taking drugs, giving into your greatest desires without regret in the morning. We have no reason for regret here! There are no consequences for your actions if you know the rules. I eat all I want and never gain weight. That's just one example."

"What, like you just don't get fat at all?" She was distracting me.

"There is a spell for everything. Our hosts don't want us to be fat. We are their servants, but to an extent they are ours and give us a lot of what we've always wanted. They don't want us whining and complaining when we both can have what we want. I am tired of resisting the things I want."

I was about to ask what it was that demons got out of their servants, because it must have been more than doing little errands, but suddenly we were walking through a door and the red thickness that clouded my vision waned. Due to either the troubling conversation or the red murkiness, I hadn't noticed where she had been taking me, but now she was shutting a door behind us and the red was forced out. She sighed loudly, obviously relieved.

"Oh my god, where are we?" I said, not sure if I should be relieved that we were off of the open streets or more scared that we could be near her master. A demon, for god's sake!

I noticed that she was much paler than before, most of her summer tan gone, but it didn't lessen her beauty. "Relax," she said, grabbing me by the shoulders and turning me away from the door and toward the room. A good way to describe the room's style was "gothic realm." There were no windows, no candles or lamps, but the room was somehow dimly illuminated. There were two black doors with intricate designs running through them, one that we had come from and one on the opposite side of the room. The design was a mix of modern and gothic, with everything in shades of grey, black, and some expertly placed silver here and there. It reminded me a little bit of the decorating style at Liz's Charleston house, but a little more gothic. "We are at my host's house. Like the couch? I actually picked out the color scheme," she said proudly, striding past me to run her hand along the black and grey couch.

"Your host is..." I was going to say, *"Caymnaburus, right?"* but the far door opened, the heavy door creaking on its hinges, stopping me short. I stared wide-eyed as Caymn walked through the door, gazing down at a large book in his hands. He had not touched the door; it had swung open for him.

"That was fast, Elizabeth. Were you able to find the..." He looked up and the moment he saw me, the book fell out of his open hand, tumbling to the ground. He looked gorgeous, even more than I remembered. His eyes weren't red or abnormal as before, but the most beautiful and astonishing shade of green. He was taller than I remembered and lean, not too skinny and not too muscle-y. He was wearing black fitted pants, a puffy white pirate-style shirt, and a green velvet coat with rich embroidered details that accentuated his broad shoulders and trim waist. It was a ridiculous outfit you might see on a runway in Paris or on a rich pirate. It should have been laughable, but he looked absolutely perfect. My heart jumped in my chest and I tried to chalk it up to fear or anger, but if I were honest, I felt neither of those things.

"You!" he said, surprised and accusatory. I jumped at the sound of his voice. It seemed to be a force more than a voice, loud and echoing, like it had power behind it. But the sound didn't feel like it rubbed uncomfortably across my skull like the voice of the demon in the woods had. Quite the opposite. That one word seemed to rub me in other places where it shouldn't, if you know what I mean.

Liz started talking cheerfully, maybe not understanding the gravity of the situation. Maybe she didn't understand how difficult it was for someone like me to get here, but Caymn must have known. "Look who I found wandering down the..." Liz started, voice faltering as we watched his face go from surprised to angry. *Furious*. His face turned into a scowl and the very shape seemed to get a little sharper as he started pacing back and forth.

"How did this happen?" he growled to himself. "She was not supposed to come here."

"What's wrong?" Liz asked.

Caymn's green eyes that met mine again burned with hatred as he began marching towards me. *Of course he would be angry*, I realized. I was trying to steal his slave from him. I was stunned into silence as I fumbled in my empty pockets for black chalk. Even if I'd had my black chalk on me, I knew it was too late to draw a circle. As he got closer, he extended his hands to grab me. My breath started coming in and out in panicked quickness, though I didn't know what he was going to do to me. I hardly noticed the altitude shift as he came for me, and suddenly I seemed to be kicked in the stomach by an invisible foot that sent me backward. My air whooshed out of my lungs and his hands had just barely grasped my arms when I was suddenly pushed backwards into darkness.

ℱourteen

When my body seemed to put itself back together, I found my eyes. I stared at the darkening blue sky above me as my hearing came back, first muffled noises, then voices filled with relief and triumph. I could sense Tansy dancing around, hearing the patter of her feet on stone and her voice going to and from, shouting praises to the goddess. I jumped slightly when I felt a pop as a circle broke around me. Then I was able to see Darlene bent over me, a happy smile on her face and tears of relief filling her eyes.

"We thought you were lost," her voice came softly, as if she were out of breath. "We have spent almost two hours doing spells. Thank the goddess, we finally got you back."

I could still feel where Caymn's fingertips had grasped my skin, and I rubbed my arms to wipe away the tingles. "How did you do it?" I said, my voice coming out weak. I was so tired, I could have passed out on the stone circle. I was relieved to be back, but I sensed that I was missing some bit of information. How had they been able to bring me back if they couldn't do it with Liz? However they'd done it, they had brought me back in the knick of time. I groaned as I struggled to sit upright.

There was silence for a second as Darlene helped me sit up. I noticed the large ring of salt around me, a perfect circle except for a small portion that had been wiped away, probably by Darlene when she'd come to lean over me. I looked at both pixie-like women, going back and forth between their faces, which had quickly gone from gleeful to...what? Guarded? Concerned?

"I don't want to scare you further. I don't know what you've gone through over there..." Darlene began.

"Tell me, Darlene," I grumbled, too tired for anything but straightforwardness.

"We tried every earth spell we could think of to get you back," Darlene said meekly, still dancing around whatever she didn't want to tell me.

"We had to try one last thing," Tansy said. "It was my idea. I decided we should try to summon you... like a dark magic practitioner would summon a shadow. We used the same summoning spell in the book that my friend and I used when we were eleven, except we changed the shadow's name to your name—the name that we talked about on the night we met. Carus Carminis."

Darlene peeked back at me from under her eyelashes, silently awaiting my reaction. I really focused then on the seven-foot wide circle of salt I was sitting in. I noticed the symbols drawn inside and outside the salt circle with white chalk, hardly noticeable at a first glance against the light-colored stones I sat on. I stifled a shiver and stood, wanting to get out of this circle.

"So what does that mean?" I asked.

"We don't exactly know," Tansy said. "But we did it as a last resort, and here you are..."

We were silent for a moment and I noticed Darlene's lips were tightly pressed together as she considered something. I could almost sense the flurry of thoughts around her, but I didn't much pay attention. I wasn't sure how this traveling into an alternate dimension worked, but I felt like I had been dragged for a trillion miles twice in one day. I was literally exhausted in both my body and soul.

"So what was the mysterious ingredient?" Tansy wondered aloud.

"The ingredient," Darlene whispered, eyes unfocused, "was the blood of a shadow."

"The blood of a shadow?" I said doubtfully. "We don't have that."

"We don't, but *you do,*" Darlene said as she focused her eyes on me. "I didn't think it was possible, but I believe it now," she whispered. "You are a half shadow."

After I told Darlene and Tansy everything that I had seen on the other side, they let me go home. It was finally nightfall when I got to my apartment and jumped in the shower, washing away all the sweat, sunscreen, and dust.

As I lathered my hair with shampoo, I heard a noise in the apartment that made me pause. It sounded as if heavy footsteps went from one side of the apartment to the other, going loudly past the bathroom door. Another thud a moment later told me that someone had opened and closed a kitchen cabinet. Someone was in my house!

Almost frozen with fear, I managed to pull the universal force into myself and even though I wasn't supposed to do it without a visual aid, I made a circle around me. The water coming from the showerhead bounced off my circle and splashed in all directions, shooting over the shower curtain and onto the floor, but I was too frightened to care.

Of course he would come for me, I thought to myself. I had gone into a demon's den, tried to steal his favored slave or whatever she was, and expected him to just leave me alone? Just let me go on with my life as usual? *How stupid was I?*

The noises ceased and after a moment of hesitation, I released the circle and rinsed the shampoo out of my hair. I could skip conditioner and the other amenities for a night. I padded across the wet wood floor and shrugged into my robe, the fleece sticking uncomfortably to my wet skin. I opened the bathroom door and peeked out. From what I could see, the kitchen and little dining area was empty. No one. But there was a cup filled with coffee on the small dining table that hadn't been there before. In fact, I'd never seen the little orange coffee mug in my life. *Do demons drink coffee?*

Movement happened suddenly to my left and I jumped, making a little embarrassing *eep!* I almost slammed the door shut, but I caught myself, realizing it was my roommate, Amber. She stared at me with her big brown eyes, startled as well. She was a lot shorter than me with tan, freckled skin and fresh highlights in her brown hair. Cute, bookworm-type girl.

I put my hand on my chest, trying to catch my breath. Good to know I could stand up for myself in the face of possible-danger, right? All I had done was scream, but I guess that was for the best. "What are you doing here?" I gasped.

"Uh, it's August seventeenth?" she said, sounding like I might possibly be the dumbest person in the world. "I came back yesterday. Tomorrow is the first day of school…"

Wait, so she had been here last night? How had I not known that? I guess in my tired state, I hadn't realized she had come back. Nothing had looked out of the ordinary. *Oh god, she probably heard mine and Jessie's argument*, I thought.

"You spilt salt all over the floor right in front of my door and I had to clean *that* up when I got home. *Then* you and your friend came in stomping around and shouting at one in the morning." She went to grab her mug and receded back into her room.

"I'm so sorry about that..." I said at empty air as she shut her bedroom door behind her. Wow, rude. She could at least *pretend* that she didn't hate me. I wondered if she had heard my sister call me a Satanist. With my luck, she'd probably caught every word.

As soon as I hit the pillow early that morning, I was asleep and dreaming of a world encased in red. It was our world, somehow overlapping with the further world, where demons crossed my path and other humans couldn't see them.

Though life went on as usual and I thankfully didn't run into any demons, this dream occurred every time I slept for the next few days. One night, though, when the red world flooded up, I thought, *Not this dream again.* As soon as I'd acknowledged and rejected the dream, I felt my bed beneath me. I was home and safe; my bedroom a red version of itself. Someone was calling my name, but it seemed to come from far away.

"Cara." Suddenly the voice was clear and it sent tingles along my skin, seeming to touch further, deeper into me where voices shouldn't touch. I knew it was him. I loved the sound of his voice, even if it was just the memory of it conjured up in my dreams. I turned in my bed and faced him. His eyes were green. Though everything else was red, he was pale cream, dark haired, and green-eyed. I thought he looked like an angel.

"What are you doing in my bedroom?" I asked him calmly.

"I have questions that need to be answered," he said, coming close in one smooth motion to kneel beside my bed. We were at eye-level then, and he was close enough to touch. Suddenly, I was reaching up to touch his face. And why not? It was my dream. Couldn't I at least touch him in my dreams? He widened his eyes at my touch, but he didn't stop me. His face was so smooth, no imperfections or even visible pores on his pale skin. He felt so real, and I could swear I even felt the electricity on my fingertips where our skin met. I wanted to touch those pouty lips of his, run my finger across his strong jaw line, and grab a handful of that dark hair. He caught my hand as it trailed from cheek to lips and held it, gently lowering it to the bed. He didn't let go right away, but wrapped his fingers around my hand. I relished the feeling of his touch.

He looked at our hands together and suddenly smiled. His smile was wonderful. "Cara, you need to pay attention to me. How is it that you came into the Barathrum?" His smile faded and he abruptly drew his hand away from mine. I frowned at him, not liking his sudden distance. "Cara," he pressed.

Oh, yeah, the question. Barathrum. "It was an accident. I did the spell wrong," I answered distractedly. Well, I hadn't done the incantation spell wrong, but I hadn't expected it to work, either.

"You did a spell," he said to himself, mulling it over. "So no one brought you?"

"No, I came by myself."

He sighed and closed his eyes. "So I was right. You are a nephion."

"What's a nephion?" I asked.

He opened his eyes again, green eyes suddenly looking too wide and frightened. He tried to look stern, though I still sensed his fear. He didn't answer my question. "Cara, you must never go back. There are lesser demons that spy on you here. If they become certain of what you are, you will be in serious danger. You must forget about everything that's happened in the last few months and live a normal life. Or else, you might die, or worse."

I grumbled childishly at him. "I can't forget about it."

"Why not?" he asked patiently.

"I can't forget about you," I said. "And I can't forget that you took my friend. I don't have many friends." That sounded stupid and I silently cursed myself.

"You lied about Elizabeth that last night I saw you at

the restaurant," he said, remembering. "Why did you lie and say she wasn't your friend?"

"I don't know. I didn't want you to pay attention to her. I was jealous."

"You were jealous?" he said, his lips curving into a smile. No, a grin. I didn't think it was possible, but a grin on his face made him even more handsome. It was almost unfair that a man should be that good looking. Then he shook his head and the smile was gone. "Cara, this is important. You must not go back into the Barathrum. You must promise me this."

I grabbed his hand back and he watched as I spun my pinky finger around his. "Pinky promise!" I exclaimed. I'm not sure why I did that, but I didn't regret it, because he laughed. It wasn't mocking, but sounded happy and carefree, which I suspected was rare for him. We were so close to each other now, our faces only a few inches apart. He seemed so real and I thought I could even smell him. Like campfire smoke and something that I could only identify as sweet. Some kind of fruit, maybe.

"I shouldn't kiss you," he said suddenly, eyes dropping to stare at my lips. Despite his words, he inched closer.

"Yes, you should," I whispered.

"I have more questions," he objected, turning his head to look away.

"No!" I said firmly, jerking him by his hand so that he was forced to be near me. "No questions!"

As soon as he looked back at me, the fight in him was lost and he closed the distance between us. Our lips met and his were surprisingly soft. The first few kisses were careful and gentle, light caresses of lips. Then his hands were around my body, pulling me into him, and I felt a feeling of pure bliss and excitement. He was suddenly on the bed with me, kissing me roughly, and I kissed him back. With every kiss, our hands moved on each other's bodies with a more feverish need. He grabbed my butt, pressing us against each other, and I gasped into his mouth.

I heard the sound of Amber's door slam, and all of a sudden I was alone. I looked around, almost expecting to see Caymn somewhere, but my sunlit bedroom was empty.

"Nooo," I grumbled loudly into my pillow, wishing the dream hadn't ended. I closed my eyes, willing myself to go back to sleep and fall back into the dream. I heard cabinets being slammed, the obtrusive sound of the coffee grinder, and I knew sleep was a lost cause. At least, until Amber left for school. I was angry enough to go on an *American Psycho*-style killing spree, but I decided Amber was worth sparing, seeing that she was making a fresh pot of coffee.

I rolled out of bed and went to the kitchen, exhausted after only a couple hours of sleep. I grabbed a coffee mug from the cupboard and didn't make eye contact, not wanting to face her after she had stomped out the night before.

"Did you make enough coffee for the both of us?" I asked, my voice coming out a little bit snappier than I intended.

"Don't you mean three of us?" she asked, biting right back at me.

I looked up at that. "Huh?" I was way too tired for this, whatever it was.

"Who's your sleepover buddy?" she said, tone thick with irritation. When I just stared at her blankly, she added, "The man that slept over last night?"

I stared at her, completely bewildered. "I-I didn't have anyone spend the night."

"Oh, okay!" she said, her voice oozing sarcasm.

"Really, you can go look for yourself! There is no one in my room!" I said, baffled we were arguing about this.

"*I shouldn't kiss you! But I want you to kiss me!*" she said, mimicking two voices talking back in forth. "I don't really appreciate you waking me up with your morning make-out sessions. It's disgusting. And don't pretend it was the TV, because I heard him say your name—like three times!"

As she stomped back into her bedroom, all I could do was stare after her.

ifteen

I canceled the day's session with Darlene with a vague text message. I didn't offer an explanation, but the truth was I was getting tired of supernatural shit—excuse my language. My strange dream with Caymn might have been just a dream, but I believed it was more. It had been so strangely vivid. If it had been some magic-induced dream, its purpose was to warn me, and that warning had been very clear. *Stay away from the further world or die...or worse.*

Whatever "worse" was. I'd probably be someone's slave for the rest of my natural life. And I definitely had no desire to die. Why should I risk myself any longer? Liz was happy, though it seemed to be in some deluded way. Who was I to force her to come back? And should I risk my life just so that I could do magic tricks? *No.* I was sad at the thought of giving up my newfound abilities, but some things you just shouldn't meddle with, and I was beginning to believe that magic was one of them. I had even gone as far as packing up all the things Darlene had given me: the books, the scrying mirror, the altar, everything. Everything was in a large kitchen trash bag, ready to go in my car and right back to Darlene's house.

My phone went off, notifying me of a text message. I guessed it was Darlene texting me back and I ignored it, sipping my afternoon coffee. I watched people on the street below through my bedroom window, shopping and doing whatever they were doing. It was mid-afternoon on Wednesday, my day off, and I was glad I didn't have anywhere to go for once. I could hide out all day in the comfort of my bedroom if I felt like it. I hadn't spent a day alone in my apartment since all this nonsense had started happening.

When my phone went off again, I grumbled and went to retrieve it. The first message had been from Darlene, asking if everything was okay. I didn't respond to it. *Later*, I thought. The other text message was from an unknown number. *Hi*, it read.

Who is this? I texted and sent.

Jonah, from the bar a couple nights ago. Sorry, I forgot you didn't have my number.

I smiled. We texted back and forth for a bit before he asked, *What are you doing for the rest of the day? Do you want to hang out?*

I thought about that for a moment. My first thoughts were about Caymn and I started to tell Jonah, "Thanks, but no thanks." Then I stopped myself. Why was Caymn even coming into the equation? It was because I had a stupid crush or something, but I needed to get over that. Plus, I didn't have plans anymore since I'd canceled with Darlene, and interaction with another human was probably just what I needed. A nice, normal person that had nothing to do with magic, demons, or anything that had happened to me this past month.

I'd love to hang out, I replied.

After finding out we both lived downtown, we decided to meet at Sweet Tooth's, a frozen yogurt place a couple of blocks away. Remembering how casually he had dressed at the nightclub a few nights prior, I tried to find something casual-but-cute in my closet. *You don't want to look like you tried too hard*, I told myself as I pushed past all the dresses. I settled for my favorite cut-off jean shorts, flip-flops, and one of my newer summer shirts, a flowy white tank top with a strip of lace at the bottom. I looked through my jewelry and picked a fake silver and turquoise ring that was one of my more recent buys.

Don't I have a necklace that matches? I thought, staring into my jewelry box. I remembered the cross necklace with turquoise beads that my mother had lent me, buried at the bottom of my purse. I recovered it, slipped it around my neck, and felt satisfied with how well it matched my ring. As I ran my fingers along the cross, I idly wondered if it held any protection for me. I had never asked Darlene about crosses, but I had an inkling of what she might say. She didn't hold very high regards for Christianity. Though I wasn't exactly sure what I believed, I personally didn't rule Christianity out. As I held the cross, I thought I could feel some good energy coming from it. Since the curses had been removed, my sense of energy had been changed or magnified. It was never too intense or overwhelming to handle; it was just that sometimes I sensed something "off" when entering a room or touching an object. I didn't pay too much attention to the feelings, because they most often didn't appear to have any significance.

After taking a quick glance at myself in the mirror, I didn't have anything else to do but go, so I left my apartment and walked down the street. I felt nervous as I approached Sweet Tooth's and found myself drumming my fingers against my thighs as I walked to calm my nerves. It didn't really help. When I got there, I didn't see him, so I plopped down at a table to wait. It was one of those self-serve yogurt places where you pay by weight, and I could have served myself if I'd wanted, but I thought that might be rude. So, I waited.

The longer I waited, the more my nerves went out of control until I thought I could feel my pulse jumping in my neck. I had never really hung out with a guy one-on-one before. I was glad the yogurt place was cold or I would have been sweating, too. Finally, through the large glass windows that took up the front of the building, I saw him walking up. He wore an orange muscle tee with the original Jaws movie poster picture on it, khaki shorts, and black high-top Converse sneakers. I noticed several tattoos that I hadn't really been able to see in the nightclub, a half-sleeve on his left arm that looked like an ocean scene and a cluster of tattoos on his right leg. I took it all in, the warm brown color of his eyes, the slight stubble on his face, and his suntanned skin. Mhmm, he wasn't bad on the eyes. His eyes met mine almost as soon as he walked through the door, and he smiled.

I saw a couple young girls walk out half a second later and noticed when they turned and gawked at him, whispering to each other giddily. Apparently, I wasn't the only one who thought he was handsome.

"Hi," he said, coming up to my table.

"Hi, yourself," I said, standing up and awkwardly adjusting my purse on my shoulder, though it didn't need adjusting.

We got our yogurt and I found that talking with him came relatively easily. "So what do you like to do with your free time?" he asked as he piled an excessive amount of cookies into his yogurt.

Recently? Hanging with witches and doing spells, I thought. "Um, I like to read, I play a few instruments..." It had been awhile since I had picked up either a book or instrument for longer than two minutes, but he didn't have to know that.

"Oh, really? What instruments?"

"Oh, you know," I said noncommittally. "Just the instruments everyone else plays in school. Nothing extraordinary."

"Like what?" he pressed.

"Piano, violin, drums... I mostly played those in

school, but in the past few years I've only really played the guitar. I'm the only person in my family that plays music, besides my little cousin recently."

"That's pretty impressive! I don't think I know anyone who can play that many instruments."

"I'm not really amazing at any of them, just know some of the basics," I said, not wanting to mislead him. "I actually haven't played anything consistently in the past couple of months. But music has been a big part of my life, overall."

"Mine too," he exclaimed. "I'm actually in a band, and we've played at a few local bars. Maybe you'd like to come to a show sometime. Heck, maybe we could jam together sometime."

"Er...maybe," I said. I hadn't played in front of people in awhile, and the thought made me nervous.

"Just for the hell of it. You don't have to say yes, just maybe sometime in the future," he said.

Does that mean he wants to see me again? I wondered. "So, what do you like to do in *your* free time?" I asked.

"I am in a band, like I said. I play the bass. I play soccer, also coach soccer, bike, surf..."

"Geez, you do it all," I said.

"Maybe, but I didn't say I do any of them well—except soccer," he said. "Soccer I'm actually good at."

When we were done with our frozen yogurt, we walked in some shops, where we pointed out things we liked and tried to figure out each other's furniture preferences. I pointed out my apartment above Simon's Pizza to him, and he said he lived on the much more sketchy side of town. When we got tired of looking around, we went out to dinner at a Mexican restaurant and got margaritas. By then it was getting late, but we decided to hit one bar before calling it a night. He had to go to work early, he said. Besides being a soccer coach and playing in a band, he also managed a bicycle shop. I liked that he seemed to have many talents and hobbies.

He recommended we go to TJ's, a popular little dive bar on upper King, and I liked him even more for suggesting it, because the bar was one of my favorites. When we walked in, I noticed the place was uncharacteristically dead, even for a Wednesday. With College of Charleston classes just starting back up, I would have guessed it would be swarming with students. After he ordered a beer and I ordered a vodka tonic, I started noticing a strange vibe. I peered over my shoulder toward the large windows to look outside, though I don't know what possessed me to do so. Right off the bat, I noticed a bearded young man smoking a cigarette. He put out his cigarette, reached for the door to come inside, then paused. Unexpectedly, he turned slightly to his right and continued down the sidewalk. I blinked, feeling even more that there was something off about the vibe in the bar, when Jonah interrupted my thoughts.

"I had a lot of fun with you today, Cara," he said, eying me as he took a sip of his beer.

"Me too," I said. "It's been a really good day." It had been an overall great day, actually. As it was coming to an end, we were getting tipsy, and I found myself wishing he could stay out longer.

"I really want to see you again," he said, suddenly leaning closer and touching the small of my back. My back tingled where his skin touched me through my shirt and when I turned to face him, his face was only inches from mine. When I didn't pull away, he kissed me. I tried to kiss back, but his mouth pressed hard against mine, and I felt the pressure of teeth through his lips. It wasn't all bad, but it was a little too forceful for a first kiss. I pulled away, thinking that if we did that again, we'd have to work on it.

"I'm sorry," he muttered. "Was it okay that I kissed you?"

I tried to smile reassuringly as I looked up at him. "Yes, it's fine—" I said, words faltering as I caught sight of someone staring from a booth across the bar. My eyes widened as I realized it was Caymnaburus. *What was he doing here?* I hadn't expected to see him for a very long time, if ever, but there he was! Where Jonah and I sat at the bar, we were almost directly facing him, and behind a pair of dark sunglasses, I was sure a pair of strange, red eyes stared at me. He still looked so wonderful that he seemed otherworldly. Then of course, he was otherworldly, wasn't he? He didn't fit this dark, dingy bar. I felt my heart beating increasingly more wildly in my chest at the sight of him.

"What?" Jonah asked.

I dropped my gaze down, staring into my vodka tonic. "Nothing, I just recognized someone."

"That guy that's mean mugging us in the booth?" he asked.

"Don't look!" I hissed, shooting him a look of disapproval. I hated to admit it, even to myself, but since I'd just seen Caymn, Jonah didn't appear half as good-looking as he had before. I pushed that thought away. It didn't matter that Caymn was practically perfect and Jonah wasn't. *Looks are not the most important thing.*

"Who is he, an ex-boyfriend?" Jonah asked, nudging me.

"Oh, definitely not." As soon as it came out, I knew that my tone implied that there was definitely something between us. If not romance, something. Jonah's interest wasn't subdued.

"So...what is he?" he pressed.

I jumped at that, misunderstanding his question. When I realized that he wasn't questioning Caymn's species, just asking how I knew him, I relaxed slightly. But how could I explain even that? *Oh, just someone who kidnapped one of my friends?* That could hardly go over well. I couldn't quite think of a good explanation. "He...he used to come into the bar I work at."

Jonah stared at me and after a few seconds of silence, I realized he expected me to continue. "He, um, he flirted with me, kind of. I got the impression he was interested, but I, uh...wasn't." I was lying through my teeth and I was so bad at it. But considering the last time I'd seen Caymn at the bar, it wasn't a *complete* lie. Caymn had acted nice and flirty, I had been extremely frightened and unfriendly, he'd asked about Liz, and he'd left. But saying I hadn't been interested was definitely bogus. Not to mention, I was leaving a lot out.

"Well, I really don't like the look he's giving you," Jonah said. I glanced at Caymn. Jonah was right, Caymn did look a little pissy, though he had finally looked away. Why was here, anyway? I was almost sure he was here to watch me, maybe had even been following me. But why? And why would he be so obvious? He had wanted me to see him, I was sure of that, but I couldn't figure out the answer to that either.

"It makes me want to go over there and say something to him," Jonah went on. I could only imagine if he went marching up to Caymn, trying to defend my honor something. I would be so embarrassed. I was starting to feel a lot more sober and a lot less attracted to Jonah by the minute.

"Oh, please don't," I murmured.

Jonah looked back at me and after studying my face, nodded. "All right, I won't say anything, but I at least want to walk you home." He looked determined.

"Um, sure," I said, not liking his possessive tone. "That's fine, I guess." It'd have to be fine, because I didn't want to walk home by myself. When I glanced at Caymn again, I took in his aggressive posture and the way the muscle in his cheek moved as he clenched and unclenched his jaw. *What was he doing here?* I wondered again. *And why did he look so pissed off?* The only reason I could come up with was that he must still be angry that I had tried to bring Liz back, but if anyone had the right to be pissed off, I thought it was me. I imagined myself strutting over to his table and demanding to know why he was there and what he wanted from me. Just the thought made me feel a ridiculous mix of giddiness and downright fear. I wasn't brave or stupid enough to confront a demon, especially him. I sighed, feeling the effects of my happy bubble being burst. I had been feeling so carefree a little bit ago, but seeing Caymn had changed all that.

After our first and only round of drinks, Jonah and I paid our tabs—I made a point to pay separately—and headed for the door. When Jonah slipped a hand around my waist, I knew it was for Caymn to see, and I involuntarily stiffened. Realizing I didn't want Jonah's arm around me, not under these circumstances at least, I shrugged out from underneath it when we were around the corner of the building. I sensed his dejection at my distance and settled for hand-holding, though I'm not sure why I bothered. After a minute, even that felt too uncomfortable, and I slipped my hand out of his. Though we tried to continue small talk on the way, I couldn't stay focused, and the conversations kept ending awkwardly. It had been a really nice day and there was no sense in letting Caymn ruin it, but ah, I couldn't help myself from being distracted.

When we finally came to the door next to Simon's Pizza, I turned to him. "This is it," I said, trying to smile warmly at him.

He seemed a little unsure of how to say bye, making that two of us. "Till next time?" he said, offering to give me a hug.

"Till next time," I agreed, falling into his embrace. If I hadn't seen Caymn and I didn't have a lingering suspicion that he was still be nearby, I might have kissed Jonah again, but it was probably for the best. "Bye for now, Jonah."

"Bye," he said as he walked back the way we'd come. He glanced back once to smile and wave at me, and I waved back before sneaking into the walkway to my apartment. As I walked up to my apartment door and unlocked it, I couldn't help think that even though it had been a wonderful time, I was pretty sure this wasn't what I should feel like after going on a first date with someone. At least, not if I was going to have a second date. Wasn't my heart supposed to be pounding out of my chest? Sure, I had been nervous before meeting him, but I wasn't feeling giggly, excited, or smitten. In fact, I was very distracted, and most of my thoughts centered around someone else...though I wasn't sure what my feelings should be toward Caymn, either.

I dropped my purse by the door and walked straight into my bedroom, where I plopped down on my bed. I grabbed my laptop, setting it into my lap, and hit the power button that brought it to life. I had forgotten to look up that word on the internet, but seeing Caymn had made me remember it. I clicked on the internet icon and started typing in the search engine box.

Suddenly, I sensed something and froze. The atmosphere of the room seemed to change, and I felt the odd sensation of eyes on me. I looked into the room and wondered, *Did it just get darker in here?* Then I saw something. Over by the window, someone was materializing in my bedroom! My body stiffened in fear as the shape of a person came floating before me, as hazy and dim as a person's shadow.

"Get out of my room," I whispered, hardly able to speak. That had been the first command to come to my head, but it did no good and the shape appeared more tangible with every second that passed. *How dare you come into my room!* I thought. A little bit of anger came in and replaced my fear, and that gave me the courage to speak loudly. "In the name of the Spirit, I banish you back to darkness!" I commanded, raising my finger to draw a pentacle in the air. And immediately, it was gone. I sat there for a moment, staring into the room, waiting. My heart was racing in my chest, and I could feel my pulse all the way up to where it pounded my head. After a minute or two of utter silence, I started breathing a little easier and looked back at my computer.

Nephion, I typed into the box and clicked *Search*. The websites that popped up seemed completely random and at the top, the search engine asked: *Are you looking for nephron?*

"No," I grumbled as I cleared my search. I decided to go a different route. *Half demon*, I typed. Right off the bat, I found a description.

"CAMBION /ˈkæmbiən/: In medieval legend, a cambion is a half-human offspring of a demon and a human. Though there have been tales of the succubus being able to bear children, a cambion is most often depicted as the offspring of an incubus, a demon in male form, and a human woman. In some Viking lore, the child is born deformed and/or susceptible to supernatural influences, because the conception was unnatural."

The article continued, making references to books, more legends, and even characters in some present-day movies. I was surprised to find that even Shakespeare had written about a half demon in a play called *The Tempest,* where a deformed beast is born of a witch and a devil. But there was still no link between *half demon* and this word *nephion*, though I thought they sounded a little similar. I scrolled down through the page and some links caught my eye, one in particular. *Nephilim. That sounded similar to nephion, right?* I clicked and was brought to another article.

"The NEPHILIM /ˈnɛfiˌlɪm/ were the offspring of the "sons of God" and the "daughters of men" according to Genesis; and giants who inhabited the earth according to Numbers. A number of early sources refer to the "sons of God" as Angels. Some Christian apologists shared this opinion, explicitly interpreting this to mean that angelic beings mated with humans, and the term has become especially commonplace in modern-day Christian commentaries."

As far as I knew, demons were *fallen* angels, so even though I hadn't found the word *nephion*, perhaps I was headed in the right direction. I had read enough for now, I decided, slamming my laptop shut and lying back in my bed.

I was dizzy with information, and none of it was at all comforting. I had gone through a short period of time where I'd felt like I was just having fun, finally being noticed by people, and enjoying playing with a little magic. When I was doing silly little spells under the sun with Tansy and Darlene, it was easy to forget about the underlying issues at hand. I was starting to feel scared for myself, because I could stop practicing magic, but that didn't mean life was going to go back to normal. Demons weren't going to start ignoring me just because I wished them to. There seemed to be no chance of living a normal life now and on top of that, I didn't feel like I had any support from my family. I hadn't talked to Jessie, Mom, or Bruce in several days, and even if Jessie hadn't said anything to them, I still wasn't brave enough to talk to my parents. Darlene and Tansy wanted me to save people, when I needed to be saved myself! And what did the demons want with me? Whatever it was, I knew it wasn't going to be something I'd be willing to give them.

I felt like praying for some reason, and not to the god and goddess that Darlene and Tansy worshipped. I had a sudden urge to ask God for help, the god my mom prayed to. It was probably because I'd seen her turn to God so many times when things were bad. Before I could think of words to pray, I felt something in the air again. I paused, waiting for someone to start appearing in my room again. No one came.

Suddenly a noise rang out, like the sound of a fingernail tapping on glass. *Clink clink clink.* I stood and went toward the window, thinking the noise could be moths beating themselves against the glass. The sound came again, not from the window but from the other direction, and I whirled around. I studied every object, trying to sense movement. Then I saw it. A small glimmer of purple light shone through the trash bag where I had stuffed all of Darlene's magical instruments. *What the hell?*

$\mathcal{S}$ixteen

When I opened the trash bag and started rummaging around for the source of the light, the tapping came again. It sounded louder and more impatient this time. *What could that noise be coming from?*

When I set aside some of the books, purple light shone brightly, and I found the source. Previously just a murky black square of glass, the scrying mirror now glowed purple. When something seemed to tap from within the glass, white flashed across it like tiny lightning bolts.

"H-hello? Is someone there?"

Nothing for a moment.

Then a face appeared and I gasped, almost dropping the piece of glass. The woman's face was just barely visible in the dark purple-tinted mirror, her head framed in blackness. She looked strange, with eyes and teeth shining very faintly green in her otherwise purple face. It appeared as if she was under a black light. "Cara!" she said, with a voice that sounded as if under water.

I studied the face harder. "Liz?"

"Yes, I am Elizabeth Black!"

That seemed a little strange, but I was too caught off guard to give it much thought. "What is going on?" I asked. "Someone just tried to come into my room, and now you're calling me through a piece of glass—"

"Cara, there is no time! It's Caymnaburus! He is coming for you! You must trust me!"

"Okay," I managed to say before she started spouting directions at me. "Trace this symbol," she said, and a piece of paper with a symbol drawn on it replaced her face. It was a pentagram, sort of, with a lot of complicated swirls and lines going through it. I followed her instructions and traced over all the lines with my finger. *Why was Caymn coming for me? Had he been waiting for me to be alone, so he could appear in my room?* "Now place your left hand over it!" she commanded.

I obeyed and as soon as I did, the glass burst with bright purple-tinted light. As I felt my ears close and the air pressure begin to change, the mirror slipped through my hands. I prepared myself to hear glass shatter, but before it could hit the ground, I was kicked in the stomach by an invisible force and flew back into darkness. I struggled to think as my body seemed to be dragged along by the threads that connected me to my soul. And my soul was being dragged by, what? Was I riding the universal force? I didn't know. I couldn't see a thing in the infinite blackness. Except for some little white dots… were those stars or a trick of my eyes? This time entering the Barathrum, I was a little less panicked and found I could think rather clearly.

When the slightly painful pull on my insides began to loosen, I was on my two feet again. My vision came and I was dumbfounded by what I saw. Everything was the same, yet different. The palaces, mansions, and towers of all different types of architecture were basked in a faint purple glow instead of red. Their doorways and windows glowed a rainbow of colors: orange, green, blue, and pink. I hadn't realized the landscape had hills, but now I could just see rolling hills for miles, decorated with bright colors. The moon, if that's what it was, shone on the city like the world's largest black light. I was in awe.

"Cara," a whispered voice came out of the darkness, and I jumped and spun around. Liz was there, hardly visible in her dark cloak with the hood pulled up high on her head. She looked eerie standing there with her face hardly visible, like the grim reaper poised to take my soul.

"What is going on, Liz?" I whispered back. "Why am I here?"

She came closer and when she pulled down her hood, the purple light shone faintly on her face. Her dark hair came tumbling out, so black that it seemed to be empty space. I realized she looked the part, down to the slight bump on the bridge of her nose, yet something was off. Had she always been that tall? She appeared taller than me, even as she hunched over slightly, her arms hanging in front of her, fingers spread like claws. When she stepped closer the whites of her eyes were very visible and glowing faintly green, her irises like deep black pits. I found myself taking a step back.

She paused, and her eyes shifted anxiously till they settled on a hill in the distance. "We must go to the largest palace on the top of the highest hill," she told me, pointing with one long finger. Her voice was feminine, but it didn't sound right. Too high-pitched to be Liz's sultry voice. "The Queen will know how to keep us safe."

All I knew was that something was definitely wrong with my friend, and I definitely didn't want to meet a demon queen. I needed to figure out how to say no in the most delicate way possible, especially if this wasn't my friend at all. Before I could even try to figure out what to say to get myself out of this situation, something stopped me. Someone was singing. When I stopped to listen, the voice became clearer, louder. It was a woman's voice, but it was so beautiful and wonderful that I almost wondered if it were really an instrument. *A harp? A violin? A flute?* It was all of them, all molded into one voice. Liz's face was suddenly angled to hear it also. The voice seemed to travel down the hill and wrap around me, soothing me. Her words were unclear, but she somehow promised me warmth, safety, love—whatever I could possibly want—all with her voice.

I didn't argue with it. I just started moving one foot in front of the other toward the largest palace on top of the highest hill. I was hardly aware that Liz walked alongside me. Without making the conscious decision to dance, I was swaying with every step, moving with the ups and downs of the voice. It pulsed into my body, through my veins, up to my brain, completely taking me over. I didn't have to think about it, worry about it, worry about *anything*. She would take care of me. She would give me infinite riches and beauty if I would only ask.

I was vaguely aware that demons were coming out of their holes, coming to dance alongside us. They were all similar in height, all of them tall, and for the first time in my life I was the shortest one in a crowd. They all seemed human in some ways, but at the same time, not. They were all strange and beautiful, but some appeared animalistic with horns, scales, tales, or hooves. Some seemed alien with glowing smooth skin, pointed facial features, and ethereal eyes. Some had interesting tribal-like tattoos that seemed to highlight their best, most appealing attributes. Different features glowed under the purple moon, one demon's hair shining neon green, another one's eyes shining pink, and so on—no two demons alike. The whole city, maybe the whole world, was part of this huge black light party. Our bodies moved in unison, with fluid motion.

I was lost in the voice. I reveled in the high and danced in a sea of colors for who knows how long. Up hills, down hills, around bends, we danced. The farther we went, the more crowded it became until we were a swarm of bees going into a hive, and still none of us slowed, bumped against each other, or missed a single step in our dance. I hardly noticed when I danced right into a superstructure, the largest of all the buildings I had seen yet.

"When the voice sings to you and draws you in, you must stop yourself." The words came into my head and I mentally waved them away. What did those words mean? What did that have to do with me? That was something from my former life. Only one thing mattered now. Her voice mattered. All else was useless. Pointless.

Darlene's words in my head persisted. "...It is going to be a trap. When the voice sings to you and draws you in, you must stop yourself. It will be hard to resist, achingly strong, but you must say no and turn away...." I could almost visualize Darlene in front of me as her warning rang clear in my head and my dance began to slow. I glanced at the dancers around me. Liz, or the figure that had been Liz, appeared darker, an almost black figure with no light except eyes and teeth glowing green where they should have been white. Swirling black horns had sprouted and she was naked, her cloak having been discarded on the path.

"...say no and turn away," the voice in my head persisted. *Turn away where?* I wondered. The demon behind me nudged me a little and I heard a rumble in its throat as it stirred from its trance.

Panic struck me as I became aware of my surroundings, and all I could think was *RUN!* So the way I came, I went. I started running against the flow of demons, trying to dodge them as best as I could. I just grazed the first one, barely avoiding hitting it straight on before it danced unknowingly out of my way. It blinked, its frightening black eyes focusing on me for a second, just before returning to its dance. The second demon I hit a little harder and it snarled, gnashing its shark-like mouth full of fangs at my face before going back to its trance-like state as if it had never happened. This happened a third time, a fourth time, and then a fifth time. I tried to walk slower and do my own little dance around them, but it was no use. They would suddenly jump forward and almost slam into me, and I would have to dodge between two hands. I gasped, fearing that eventually I would hit one of them too hard and it would completely come out of its trance.

I was getting tired, and when I started to lose hope that I would ever escape the endless ocean of beasts, I came to a break in the tide, some kind of end to the waves of demons. I ran toward the empty space, relieved to see a hallway just past one last assembly line of entranced dancers. When I darted between the two very last demons, I sped up and ran as fast as I could. I could see nothing in front of me, but I kept running, stretching one hand out in case I might slam into the end of the tunnel. I could hear the loud slaps my feet made on the floor, echoing too loudly, and I made myself slow. I wasn't sure if I was going the right way, but I wasn't willing to turn back. When I glanced behind me, I thought I could see something glowing at the mouth of the tunnel. I wasn't sure what it was, but it didn't appear that the demons were dancing by anymore. The glowing dots looked too still, and I hoped they weren't eyes.

I ran into a door head first, despite my efforts not to, and cursed myself. Under different circumstances, I would have laughed at myself, but as it was, I chewed on my fingernails nervously and looked behind me again. The glowing dots were still unmoving at the other end of the hallway, and my heart was racing like crazy. I was a hundred percent sure this was not the way I had come in, but I could not turn back now. The door didn't have a handle, which seemed like a bad sign, but because there was nowhere else to go, I pushed it open. I slowly walked through the doorway, feeling something strange pass through me, like cold slime moving through my insides. Then everything went completely dark. I had thought it couldn't get any darker before, but I realized I was wrong. I turned my head back once more to see if I could see the dancing hoard or even the dots that looked like eyes, but I could see nothing. I could no longer hear them, or sense anyone nearby, for that matter. I could still hear the singing voice, though it sounded more distant and somehow ominous. The spell on me was broken. For morbid curiosity's sake, maybe, I stretched my arm back toward the way I'd come. To my surprise, I felt something cold and smooth. It wasn't the door I'd opened, but a wall as hard and unmoving as a wall of marble. I hadn't really planned on going back, but the fact that I couldn't, even if I wanted to, was unnerving.

I realized I was gasping for air, and I tried to quiet myself while my vitals returned to sort-of normal. I took a deep, steadying breath, and a weird smell invaded my nostrils. I could almost taste it on the air. Something metallic and tangy. There were other smells too, but only the first seemed faintly familiar and somehow crucial. *Maybe old copper pipes?* I guessed. I wasn't sure what it was, but I told myself to keep walking forward.

My eyes were adjusting to some unseen light in the room, but I couldn't make anything out for certain. I took a few steps, holding my hands out in front of me to prevent hitting anything head-on again. I brushed my hands against something, and before I could even consciously think of what it was, I recoiled from it and made a little scream. My voice echoed loudly and continuously as I realized that what I had felt might have been human skin. I could hear a sound like rope groaning and twisting, coming from above my head.

"Hello?" I whispered. "Is someone in here?" I heard nothing, except the rope groaning as something seemed to sway in front of me. A horrible feeling rose up in my gut. With some effort, I gathered enough courage to reach out to touch the mysterious object again. I poked it with one finger and it felt warm and fleshy, as I had expected. My eyes were adjusting now, and I could see that there was definitely something hanging in front of me.

I thought I heard a muffled noise, like the quietest moan or an escaping of breath from above my head. I looked up, willing my eyes to focus on what was in front of me. Maybe my brain didn't want to process what my eyes were seeing, but I suddenly knew that it had to be a person. I couldn't make sense of it and I didn't want to. I could feel a scream rising in my throat, threatening to make its way out of my mouth, but I clasped my hand to cover it. I started running in another direction, wanting to put as much distance between me and this person as possible, but before I could pick up speed, I slammed into another hanging person. I jerked back, hitting another, and I could see the body I'd slammed into rocking back and forth.

These poor people appeared to be hanging by their wrists with ropes, and I wasn't sure if they were alive or not. How long could someone live being hung by their wrists? Their lungs would collapse and they would suffocate, right? They must be dead. If that wasn't enough to kill a person, cords were coming from their bodies as well, going from their limbs and mouths to a hole through the floor. I screamed against my palm, not able to help myself. I crouched on the floor below their feet, unable to help the whimpers that escaped my mouth. I would get out of here if I had to crawl out underneath them. I hardly noticed that the singing had stopped as I crawled on the floor, avoiding black cords. It was easier than avoiding bodies.

This is worse than being surrounded by demons, I thought.

As soon as that thought came, I heard a loud noise and I felt my heart sink in despair. How could it get any worse? At first it sounded like something was scrabbling above me. I imagined a huge cockroach crawling on the ceiling, and then the sound seemed to multiply, coming from above, behind, in front, *everywhere!* I couldn't move. I didn't know what direction to go.

Fearing I was about to reach the end of my life, I found myself suddenly praying. "Please, God. Please save me. Please, please, please. I'll do anything." And unexpectedly, light came from somewhere and I could see just a little better. Before I could thank God for the light or pray again, the source of the noise became visible. Demons, more menacing than a pack of wild dogs, encircled me.

I scrambled in my pockets, looking for my chalk to make a circle. Once again, it wasn't there, but far away in my purse, maybe a million leagues away. They hadn't pounced on me yet, but they circled around me, both on the ground and the ceiling. Some of the bodies were getting bumped into and a few of them started swinging back and forth, and seeing that made my stomach knot up in horror. I could see the black cords coming from them weren't black cords at all, but tubes as red as... blood. As soon as I thought it, I knew that it had to be blood. Only a few tubes weren't red; one in particular I noticed that was going into a woman's mouth was filled with a light brown liquid. What were they doing to these people? Were they sustaining them, while continuously taking their blood? *I will not throw up, I will not throw up.*

"Please, God, save me," I found myself whispering again. The light became brighter and it was now hindering my sight, shining in my face. From the sudden shrieks and hisses, I knew it must have been shining in their eyes as well. The light seemed to be coming from below me. I sneaked a downward glance and was surprised to see that the cross necklace dangling from my neck was bright, like a beacon of light. Of course, there was a downside to the light. I could see my enemies' faces around me like a hundred rabid beasts, ready to rip my throat out at the first chance.

"A blessed cross," one hissed and spat. Others whispered in languages foreign to me.

I started praying more fervently, for my safety, for the strangers that hung around me, for their families, for my family, anything I could think of. All the while, the cross shone brighter and brighter.

I heard unearthly screams and scrambling around at first, but then one of the demons yelled at the rest. It wasn't in English, but it commanded everyone's attention, like the speech before battle. As I prayed, they collected themselves, though it seemed painful for them to do so. They started chanting something, first sounding weak and pained, then becoming more forceful, more powerful. To my surprise and despair, my cross began to dim. I wasn't sure if it took a few seconds or closer to an hour, but it felt like it went on forever, me praying and them chanting. My cross continued to dim until I could no longer see the demons at all and the light was only faintly illuminating around me. Their voices chanted in unison, sounding more and more triumphant, sensing their nearing victory.

And then the light was gone. The chants were replaced with the sound of so many demons rushing on me, their claws clicking on the marble floors. I felt hands on me and before I could scream, my head was slammed on the hard, concrete-like floor. An explosion of stars crossed my vision, and then I saw and heard nothing.

Seventeen

"She might have a concussion. You can't put her in a sleep stasis," said a feminine voice.

"Why not?" a male voice demanded.

"Because she may slip into a coma and never wake up!" said the woman.

My head throbbed with pain and my vision swam when I glanced at the ceiling above me. I closed my eyes again, concentrating on not throwing up. My head continued to spin, and I let out a low groan.

"Listen to her! She's in pain," the male voice argued. "We must put her under a sleep stasis. Give her the pain elixir, sleep potion, and the healing spell. Give her all of it!" I heard clinking of class bottles.

"No," the woman insisted. "Trust me. She just needs the pain elixir and the healing spell."

Liz was suddenly above me. The real Liz this time, I was sure, though she swam in my vision. "Cara, drink this. It will make the pain go away." She put a gold cup—or maybe it's called a goblet—in front of my face. A male voice was grumbling somewhere out of my line of sight. She tipped something into my mouth, and I drank. It tasted bitter and tickled as it went down my throat, but the sudden relief was welcome.

"A lot quicker than Tylenol, right?" she said, and wiggled her eyebrows up and down.

I felt so much better, but I was too tired and relieved to even speak. "Cara?" Liz looked concerned, but I couldn't muster up the energy to make a reply, and I drifted back into the darkness.

When I woke up a second time, I was disoriented. My eyes focused on a cozy, yet very hideous burgundy blanket that was wrapped tightly around me. I tried to sit up and escape the burgundy cocoon, and the sudden movement had me reeling. I took it very slowly after that, edging myself up little by little onto the pillows behind me. I was still clothed in the same white tank top and cut-off shorts, but they had been severely stained with red dust and sweat. The shorts might've been salvageable, but the dusty red and white shirt had a 6-inch tear that I didn't remember receiving. I warily took in my surroundings. The room was dark, except for the dimly lit center which seemed to be under a dim spotlight, though I saw no candles or overhead lighting. It was as if the light swam in a tight circle around an island counter. *Magic?* I wondered.

The room looked like a cross between a kitchen and a science lab. The island counter, if that's what it could be called, was a glass-top counter with four compartments displaying all sorts of spell ingredients. At least, that's what I assumed they were, since Darlene's spell shelf contained many of the same dried plants. On top of the glass counter was a copper mixing bowl with pink smoke billowing out of it. A potion, maybe? To the left, in the area that was less illuminated, I saw a counter and past that, an old stove—one of those large bulky pieces of iron where you put wood in its chamber to heat up the iron on top. *What a strange room*, I thought. On the other side of the room I faintly saw a large black door, similar to the gothic doors I'd seen in Caymn's entryway the last time I'd come to this further world.

I threw the blanket off finally and swung my legs over the edge of the bed, gathering up courage to explore my rescuer's dwelling. Or was it my *captor's dwelling*? I saw unexpected movement in my peripheral vision, and suddenly Caymn stepped into the light. I froze like a deer in headlights, foolishly wanting to hide under the blankets and play dead. *How long had he been standing in the shadows, watching me?* I wondered. He was as gorgeous as ever in a white billowy shirt, almost knee-length green jacket made tight with a belt, black pants, and tall black boots. All he needed was a pirate hat and a sword and he'd be a green Captain Hook. Not sure how anyone could make that sexy, but he did. I found a little comfort in being confronted by him and not a completely unfamiliar demon, but not very much.

"Hello," he said, smiling and looking as innocent as ever, green eyes shining with humor. No doubt he enjoyed startling me just a bit.

"Hello," I said warily. He seemed awfully cheerful, considering that the last two times I'd seen him, he had been fuming.

"I have some more pain elixir for you if you're in need of it." He motioned a hand to the pot of billowing pink smoke.

"I'm fine," I said quickly, though in truth, my head was beginning to throb. "What time is it?" I asked abruptly.

"You've only slept for about an hour," he said. "It's about nine a.m. on Thursday, according to your time."

So much had happened since the night before. I had been on my first sort-of date, had my first kiss, been transported to this world, danced most of the night with demons, and apparently escaped the demons. I was in Caymn's house, or so I was guessing, but I couldn't exactly remember how I had gotten here. The last thing I remembered was being surrounded by demons with all of those hanging bodies. My stomach clenched and I struggled to push the images of bodies and tubes of blood from my mind.

"You were lucky I saved you when I did," he said, looking into the pink smoke wafting from the pot as he stirred the contents with a spoon. "The queen was trying to hide you from me, I think. If I would have been a few seconds later, it might've been too late."

I thought about the cross and how my prayers had given me a few extra minutes of safety when apparently I had needed it. *Had my prayers been answered?* I wondered. I grabbed the cross and looked down at it, now just a blob of silver-tinted metal. It had melted.

"You have no reason to be scared anymore. You're safe," he continued. I looked up, but he was looking away from me, still stirring the contents of the pot. I *was* afraid, and I wondered if he could feel my fear. The thought that he could be sensing my fear just made me more afraid, and I tried to calm myself. There was something about him that scared me, other than him being a demon. The sight of him made me feel things that I didn't want to admit to, even to myself, and sent my heart beating at a faster pace. *He is just really nice to look at*, I thought. *That's all it is.*

"What is it that you want with me?" I said sharply, and I almost surprised myself with my ferocity.

"Nothing!" he exclaimed, and dropped his spoon, making a dull clank as wood rang against copper. He was silent for a moment, evidently at a loss of what to say or do with his hands. Finally, he said, "I wish you would stop being afraid of me. I would never harm you." But the look on his face was frustrated and not at all convincing.

"For some reason I have a hard time believing that," I spat. I wanted to sound brave or angry, but I was betting I sounded more like a scared child.

"Do you not realize I saved you? I'm doing everything in my power to keep you alive!" he yelled, running a hand through his hair in exasperation.

I was quiet for a second as I considered that. He must have saved me from those demons, but that wouldn't make me forget everything else he'd done. "But you also put a curse on me, you stalked me, you stole my friend, and last time I came here, you rushed toward me like you might tear me to pieces!" My words choked out toward the end in fear at the memory. I remembered the fiery look in his eyes as he'd all but charged toward me. He had looked so... deadly. I hadn't meant for my voice to come out like that. *Stop it, Cara*, I silently cursed myself, embarrassed.

He looked away and spoke surprisingly softly. "I had the suspicion that you were a nephion the first time I saw you. But when I came into the front entry and I saw you here, my first thought was that you had been brought here as someone's familiar and that..." He seemed to struggle with his thoughts before looking at me with a fierce look in his green eyes. "...angered me. I was going to find your host and rip his head right off his shoulders."

I gulped, wondering if he could rip heads off shoulders.

"I don't know why I went to grab you," he continued. "I either planned on shaking you till you told me who he was, so I could try to buy you from him—somehow—or killing him if I had no other choice!"

"I'm not a servant, and you can't buy me like you bought Liz," I snapped.

"That's not what I meant," he said, sounding frustrated.

"Well, what do you mean?"

He grumbled. "I'm just trying to tell you that when I saw you here, I was angry. But not at you. I just had a strange impulse to protect you." He glanced at me under his thick lashes, then nervously looked down to smooth his jacket. "Obviously, when you disappeared on your own, I knew better. You could get to and from with your own power and you didn't need my help."

It really hadn't been all my own magic, but Tansy and Darlene's summoning spell that had dragged me back to my side of the universe, but I wasn't going to willingly say so. Not right then, anyway.

"When I first saw you at the bar," he continued. "I thought you were the most beautiful person I'd ever seen... even with the yellow stain on your blouse." I remembered the mustard stain on my shirt when I'd met him and I burst into laughter, not able to contain the giddiness and slight embarrassment at the memory. His mouth curved in a half smile for just a moment before his face smoothed out again. "And when you saw my eyes, well... I had my suspicions that you weren't completely human."

I should have been more focused on the part where he said I wasn't completely human, but all I could think was: *He thinks I'm the most beautiful person he's ever seen?* A few people had called me pretty when they were trying to be nice, but no one had ever called me the most beautiful person they'd ever seen. Those words together were reserved for people like Liz and Jessie, with bright eyes and tan skin. They were never reserved for me, the complete opposite of those things. The whole thing seemed absolutely ridiculous, but it still made my pulse hammer and my breathing irregular. I suddenly felt like my heart was swelling in my chest. It was painful, yet wonderful. I almost wished that he didn't make me feel this way. It made things very confusing.

"How is it that your eyes are green now when they were red before?" *And very inhuman*, I thought.

He looked toward me and our eyes met. "I believe that when we are on your side of the universe, you can see them because you have some sort of advantage there. Here, you see what everyone else sees."

"Oh," I said.

"I hate to admit it, but when I went to the queen of the third city and told her I was almost certain that I'd seen a real nephion, I..."

"Wait, I'm not following. What exactly is the *third* city? How many cities are there?"

He stared off at nothing, maybe seeing things that I couldn't fathom. "I am not supposed to tell you this, but I'm already doomed," he said, laughing softly, though the sound held little humor. His eyes were suddenly on mine again, very intense in their gaze. "There are seven cities, one for every deadly sin. We are in the third city, Urbem Avaritia, the City of Greed."

When I had no questions, he continued.

"A demon only has one job: to corrupt and negatively influence humans. For example, for the demons in the first city, City of Wrath, their job is to influence humans to be angry, unforgiving, hateful, murderous, and anything to do with wrath. The demons that are best at fulfilling their tasks become favored by the queen of their city. The more favored demon you are, the more familiars you're allowed to have—"

"So, how many familiars do you have?" I interjected.

"Just one. But the third city is different from all the others. Our queen, Deamavarus, is greedy, which is fitting seeing as we are in the greedy city. She keeps almost all the familiars to herself."

"The people hanging..." I said to clarify.

"Yes. She has hundreds of them. She doesn't need them to be functional beings to do her bidding. All the demons in this city do that for her, hoping to gain another familiar and obtain more power. A familiar's blood is our power. All she needs is more familiars than anyone else and she remains the most powerful—"

"Wait, wait," I said, holding up a hand. "How is blood your power?"

"I thought Elizabeth explained to you that I give her what she wants in exchange for her blood."

"No, she didn't tell me that," I said, starting to feel queasy again. She had been explaining that she had everything she'd wanted, and I'd wondered what the catch was. I had suspected it might be more than just running little errands. "So what do you do...drink it?"

"Oh no, demons don't drink blood," he said, then reconsidered. "Except the gluttonous demons in the sixth city. Their queen and *those demons* drink their familiars' blood," he said with some disdain. "Demons have been around for a long time—those that don't drink blood, and the small portion that do—but the former queen of gluttony is the reason for the more-recent tales of blood-sucking demons. She was insatiable, and a few of her sycophants started drinking blood on your side of the universe, flaunting their powers while also revealing our weaknesses. She possessed some influential people in fourteenth, fifteenth, and sixteenth centuries. You may know of at least a few of the humans she possessed—Vlad III of the house Drăculeşti?"

That name sounded familiar, but I couldn't place it. Finally, I shook my head.

"You may know him has Vlad Dracul?"

"Do you mean Dracula?" I gaped at him.

"Not Dracula from the gothic horror novel, but the one who *inspired* that novel. Vlad Dracul—or Vlad the Impaler as he has been called—was possessed by a gluttonous demon, as were many others in the few hundred years that preceded him. Countess Elizabeth Báthory is another infamous ruler who was possessed by the same demon queen."

I was familiar with Elizabeth Báthory, also known as the Bloody Countess, who, according to the stories, bathed in the blood of young girls to sustain her youth. I gaped in wonderment as I listened to this dark side of our human history that few people, or maybe none, knew about.

"Technology is too advanced to be so careless these days. That queen and her demons were put to an end..." He shook his head, as if clearing his mind of memories I couldn't begin to imagine. "If demons could do whatever they wanted at any given moment, there would be pandemonium and death all around your world. The leaders, our queens, are in charge of keeping the demons in check. Can you guess who is in charge of keeping the queens in check?"

"The devil?" I guessed.

"That is your name for him," he said.

"What is your name for him?" I asked.

"He has many names, but we most often call him Diabulus," he whispered, glancing around the empty room as if making sure no one heard him. "If he were close enough, saying his name could draw attention to you, so you should never say it aloud," he warned. "As I was saying, he only allows there to be a certain number of kidnapped humans in any of our cities. Demons have to ask permission of their queen before stealing any humans on earth and using them as familiars. Usually, the only time this happens in our city is when a demon's familiar dies. Because our queen already has so many familiars, we are at our max limit. We can't have more than one, except a very select few of her favorite demons." He wrinkled his nose suddenly, probably thinking of someone in particular.

"If the devil is in charge, couldn't he tell the queen to share?" It seemed like it would be a better scenario for everyone. The demons would have more familiars and the familiars would actually be able to live their natural lives *awake*. Still, I felt a little ridiculous for asking it. Why would I expect the devil to be fair?

"That's been brought up to him several times, but the current arrangement benefits him, so we are not allowed to address it anymore. Because we are greedy and unhappy with what we have here, we more easily instill greed on earth, which is our purpose. So, in a way, we fulfill our jobs better because of it."

"This is crazy," I said. "But I still don't get why blood gives power, or whatever it was you were saying."

"You see, it invokes our curses and enhances our abilities," he said, and as he spoke, he moved his hand over his face as if wiping hair out of his eyes. When I saw his face again, it looked different. I jumped and gave a surprised gasp when I realized I was looking into my own face. His dark, curly black hair was still in place, but he was wearing my own black eyes, high cheekbones, and thinner lips. I wouldn't say my lips are thin, but his are borderline sultry. It was very strange and slightly unsettling, looking at my face on his body like that, but I was amazed. I stared at him with a child's fascination at seeing a magic trick. I was imagining what life would be like if I had that kind of power. I could look like anyone I wanted. Though I had become a little more comfortable with my appearance lately, the deeply rooted desire to have sparkly blue eyes and tanned skin still bubbled up from within. I could be beautiful—no, positively striking—if I had his power. I could go anywhere. I could look like anyone.

Then he moved his hand back and even quicker than it had appeared, my face was gone. "All of our curses call for some sort of human blood—a virgin's blood, blood of a young male, and so on. That is why we have our blood market. To trade."

My amazement with his abilities suddenly ebbed, because even if I could obtain those abilities, human blood was not something I was willing to trade. Maybe I'd shed my own blood if the situation was right, but never would I sacrifice someone else. I remembered that I shouldn't be deluding myself into thinking this was some sort of magical paradise where all your dreams can come true, as Liz was doing. No, it was all games and illusions. But even as I thought that, a small part of me was still enraptured like a child listening to a wonderful fairytale. That little part of me wanted to be a part of this world somehow. I could hardly believe he was telling me all of these stories and demon secrets.

"I can't believe I'm telling you this," he said, echoing my thoughts.

A sudden movement on the far wall stole our attention and stopped our conversation. I hadn't noticed until that point, but the far back wall was dark and slick like black marble, while the other walls were a simple white. White symbols were appearing on the dark wall as if some invisible person was drawing on it. It was like one large scrying wall! Caymn watched, his eyes becoming wide.

"What is that? What is happening?" I asked.

He didn't say anything for awhile, just watched the

symbols being drawn. One large symbol appeared in the middle, larger than all the rest. I couldn't make any sense of it, but it reminded me of my little scrying mirror, probably broken on my floor at home.

When the symbols stopped appearing, we stayed in silence for a long time, me sitting on the bed and him standing by the door. "I should have known this would happen," he finally whispered, too shocked or scared to raise his voice, I think.

"What?" I whispered back.

"It's my death warrant."

"Your death warrant?" I repeated stupidly, and wished that I hadn't pressed it.

He looked toward me, green eyes haunted. "Don't you see? The queen wanted you and I stole you right from her grasp!" he exclaimed with a sudden burst of emotion, sinking to the floor. "Any demon who captures you or me will receive ten familiars. If someone can get us both, they will receive twenty familiars. Every demon in the city will be waiting outside my doors until I have to come out."

"What does she want with *me?*" I asked, startled.

"You're a nephion!" he said, as if that explained everything. It didn't, and when I just stared at him, he went on. "Nephions are never tolerated, because you have the best of both demon and human traits. You possess power and have shape changing abilities, like a demon, but you don't need someone else's blood to do it. You are partially immune to demon tricks and curses, as I'm sure you've realized. You aren't affected by crosses, churches, or any such religious items. You share our weaknesses, but at a much smaller degree. You might be allergic to the sun, silver, and in some cases nephions are allergic to salt, but none those are likely to kill you. I could be stripped of my blood earrings..." he said, pulling some of his black hair back to expose a large blood vial earring dangling from his ear. It was similar to the ones I'd seen at the market that Liz had been trying to buy, though I had assumed they were jewels. "...And I would have no power, no abilities. I'd be as helpless as any human against other demons. You have enough human and demon blood in you, that you are almost unstoppable. *Almost*. That is why she wants you...to put an end to you."

I was speechless for a moment as I tried to wrap my mind around all this information. I imagined myself changing my shape and having the body and face I'd always wished for. It was possible without blood of another human! I wasn't sure what I felt, but my heart lurched into high speed. Even if I could somehow obtain these abilities, maybe I wouldn't live long enough to enjoy them. Suddenly a thought occurred to me and I asked, "Why did you save me if you knew this could happen to you?"

He looked guilty as he softly spoke. "It was my fault you were in danger. Trying to receive favor with the queen, I told her what I thought you were. She told me to keep an eye on you, so that was why I put a curse of observance over you. When you took the curse off, I tried to go find you, thinking I was going to find your dead body. I couldn't believe that you would have been able to lift it or even sense it. I searched your city, looking for police lights, but couldn't find you."

"I was in Johns Island, about thirty minutes away."

"I looked for you in all the surrounding areas until the sunlight sent me home," he said. I imagined him searching for me all night, and my heart swelled in my chest again. "I should have found you, so the only thing I can figure is that you were hidden from me, though I don't know who would have done so..."

I thought of the demon in the woods and wondered if he had somehow shielded us from notice. Was there such a thing as a protective circle within a protective circle? Or had Tansy's circle been shield enough? I almost thought about asking, but he continued, ending the train of thought.

"I went to tell the queen you were dead, but while I waited to get my audience, I heard a lesser demon saying that he had come across you while watching one of his little witches. Apparently, he had been assigned to watch your friend for the past decade and he had come across you by accident. It was the strangest coincidence. He watched you and the witch in the woods, lifting curses, and had seen the greater demon. It was almost enough proof that *that* demon was your father and you were truly a nephion..."

"*That* demon is my father?" I said, horrified. The image of a pale-skinned man with glowing red eyes floated up into my vision and I shuddered. I remembered the way his voice had felt like nails sliding along the inside of my skull. He had known about my fear of snakes and had transformed into—I couldn't even think about it, it had been too horrifying. He was evil down to his very core. I had felt it. How could I be a piece of *that*?

"I can't see how it could be anyone else," he said, shrugging. "Demons don't exactly help one another. There would be no reason for that demon to have hidden you, unless it was for his own benefit. Since no one would order him to hide a nephion, it must have been to cover his own tail."

"But who is he?" I asked.

"No one knows. Since he never mentioned his name and the lesser demon didn't recognize his forms, he could be just about anyone."

I shook my head as if trying to stop the thought of this demon being my father from settling in my brain. I would not accept it. "And the lesser demon is Herman—*that little black cat*?" I asked in disbelief.

"I don't know this name, *Herman*," he said, making the name sound almost hilarious. "But the demon is a worthless creature that can only turn himself into small animals. His name is Vermis, and he's one of the lowest and most despised demons. He has no familiars and will do anything to get one. He spends his free time spying and ratting out the other demons."

I hadn't even guessed that the ugly black cat could've been anything other than just a cat! It made me wonder how many demons I could have possibly come across in my lifetime in both human and animal form.

"When I thought you must be dead and then I found you weren't..." He looked at me, and I couldn't read the expression in his eyes. "I realized then that I didn't want you to be discovered. I ran in there, exclaimed that you weren't a nephion, that it was all just a huge mistake. But the queen dismissed me, saying that I had failed her, and that someone else would take up the job. I tried to warn you in your dreams over and over, but you always pushed me out. Finally, I got to you, but by then it was too late."

I thought about the dream and wondered if our kiss had been real, in any sort of way, or if that part was just a simple dream conjured up in my head. I was too embarrassed to ask, just in case it was the latter. I considered all that he had said, and if he was trying to manipulate me, he was doing a damn good job of it. I was beginning believe him and was getting even more confused about my feelings. This was a demon, right? The very essence of evil, *right?* Then why did I feel like he wasn't evil? Why did my chest ache when I looked at him? That, I knew the answer to, but I wouldn't let myself give into those feelings, or so I told myself.

"You tried to come into my room after you saw me with Jonah," I said, changing the subject. "What were you trying to accomplish?"

"No! I didn't come into your room after I saw you with *Jonah*," Caymn said, making his name sound like it made his mouth bitter. "After I realized it was too late for you to go unnoticed, I tried to follow you so that maybe I could prevent whatever the queen planned for you. I've followed you, but I've never gone into your room *physically*. Not then, not ever."

I didn't miss that he added "physically" in there. He had seen my room through my dreams, at the very least, and maybe many more times in some kind of paranormal-demon way. "So who tried to come into my room?" I asked.

"I bet that was Crassus, the queen's head servant and my replacement in watching you. What did he do?"

"Nothing, really. He started materializing right in front of me, so I sort of... banished him."

Caymn smiled. "This is part of the reason why they want to destroy you. You hold power over them."

"They still got me, so I must not have that much power," I grumbled. "They pretended to be Liz."

"Yes, well, that doesn't surprise me. You know now that you can't trust anyone or anything here."

"Not even you?" I asked.

He shuffled his feet in front of him, looking guilty and uncomfortable. "Obviously not. It's my fault this is happening now."

"It's not your fault," I said, surprising myself. Maybe I should have been mad at him for telling his queen about me and turning my life into this crazy mess, but I couldn't make myself feel mad. Knowing all that I knew—even that he was a blood stealing demon, that he had probably done countless bad things—I was starting to believe he wasn't evil. What I really wanted to do was wrap my arms around him and reassure him that I didn't blame him. I wouldn't do that, though. I wasn't brave enough to let my feelings really show, even if I thought I could be certain of him.

He glanced at me and then looked away, avoiding my eyes. "How can you say that? If it weren't for my interfering, you'd still be in your world, enjoying your life."

"I wasn't enjoying my life," I admitted.

"You weren't?" he asked, somehow looking sullen and hopeful at the same time.

"Well, I was lonely and hidden from everyone's notice before you put a curse on me. If I hadn't noticed your curse and gotten rid of it, I would still have all those other ones. Under all of those curses, my life wasn't really much of a life."

"Oh," he said, and I thought I could sense embarrassment and disappointment in that one word. I realized I didn't want him to feel that way. It was so strange how this demon seemed sensitive, so unlike what a demon should probably be. I wanted to tell him that no one had ever made me feel like he did, but I couldn't. Part of me wondered if this was all just a trick, and the other part of me wanted to *be with him*, whatever that meant.

"What will it take for you to stop fearing me?" he

asked, his voice filled with an infinite amount of sadness that I couldn't understand. I didn't really have an answer. He'd tried to save my life, maybe had saved my life several times, and I still was having trouble trusting him. *Why?*

He sighed, looking away.

"I'm…" I made an effort to explain. "I'm very confused about my feelings when I'm around you. I don't think I'm actually afraid of *you*, exactly." *Oh god, please stop talking!* I screamed internally.

"You're afraid of your feelings for me," he finished for me. I couldn't admit to it, but I wouldn't go as far as denying it either. I desperately wanted to make myself invisible, but I settled with avoiding his gaze. I could almost feel a change of energy in the room, and I finally peeked over at him. He was biting back a smile. "You don't need to be afraid of your feelings for me."

"I don't?" I asked uncertainly.

"No, because I feel the same way. I've been drawn to you since I first saw you. As much as I knew I should stay away, I didn't want to."

I knew that it was true for me, too, and it made butterflies flutter in my stomach to hear him say so. How many times had I searched for him in a crowd? How many times had I looked around, hoping to suddenly see him there? I was drawn to him like he was drawn to me. I had never expected the first person I'd fall for to be perfect, but I'd definitely expected things to be a lot less complicated and for him to be a lot more *human*. But was I even human? Was I being prejudiced? I was getting tired of thinking and fighting with myself.

It was hard to say the words I felt, so instead of talking, I crawled off the bed and went to sit near him on the floor to show my acceptance of him. He seemed surprised when I sat next to him, so close that our arms grazed each other. Electricity radiated from where my elbow touched his arm. His skin was surprisingly warm, or maybe that was just my blood warming my body as my heart sped up.

"I'm glad you didn't stay away," I whispered, not

brave enough to raise my voice in case it came out unsteadily. Not sure of what else to say, I fell silent and glanced away. I was so horrible at this.

Suddenly he was lightly seizing my chin with his fingers and moving my face to meet his. He was so perfect that it seemed both hard to look at him and impossible to look away. My heart was hammering so loud, I could hardly hear above it.

"You're so beautiful," he said. My heart melted in my chest and I couldn't resist anymore. I didn't want to resist anymore. When he pounced on my lips, I let him. When he kissed me, it almost seemed familiar and like we were picking up from where my dream had left off, but this was better. At first the kisses were soft and I relished each one. My lips burned with his touch, like I was being consumed by fire. Or was it burning electricity? The feeling filled me, making it impossible to think of anything anymore, and finally my worries and reservations about him slipped into distant memory. As the kisses continued, I felt more and more eager. Every kiss acted as a drug, making me crave him more. I felt a need so strong that my body began to ache with it, like I had been starved my whole life. He seemed to feel my same need, moving his hands to hold me and press me harder to him, like he couldn't get close enough to me.

When he began running his hands all over my body almost frantically, I gasped into his mouth, thrilled with the feeling of him touching me. I thought I should maybe tell him to slow down, to stop, that we were going too fast, but the truth was I didn't want to stop.

I started pulling off his jacket, breaking away from his lips for just a second to get his white shirt over his head. My breath caught in my throat as I took in his naked chest. His shoulders were broad, pecs were sculpted, and all of his abs were visible. He was slim, but had ideal muscle definition. He was *perfect,* like a dark-haired god. I ran my hands along his abs and up to his chest, lost in my admiration of him. In turn, he went to take my shirt off and I let him, surprisingly not feeling as shy or embarrassed as I thought I might.

Someone this gorgeous shouldn't want me. I almost expected to hear my phone ring or a door slam and to be suddenly awakened from this dream. I wanted him like I'd never wanted anything before. I wanted this to happen.

"You're perfect," he said, his eyes roving over me, approving, before he pulled me close again. As we stared into each other's eyes, I noticed how green his were against his pale skin and I remembered they weren't real.

"I want to see your real eyes," I said, my voice coming out hushed.

"What?" He was surprised. "But these are the eyes I've had for..."

"I don't care," I cut him off and placed a fingertip on his lips to silence him. "Give me your real eyes."

I grabbed his face, pulling him into me for another kiss. I wrapped my arms around his neck, holding him tightly as our mouths moved against each other's. Suddenly he was lifting me up off the ground and I met his new strange eyes with mine. From so close, I could see that they had a thin line of black around the iris, intensifying their redness. The rectangular pupils were just how I remembered, and though they were almost as startling as they had been the first time, I wasn't frightened. He seemed to judge the look in my eyes, appeared to be satisfied with whatever he saw there, and kissed me again.

"Are you sure you want this?" he asked, pulling away just enough to speak.

At that moment, I wanted it. I needed it. I was tired of fighting myself, and I didn't care what the consequences might be, if there were any. I was ready for this, and I wanted it to be him. "Yes."

Eighteen

When I woke up, I didn't open my eyes right away. I hardly remembered falling asleep, but I knew exactly where I was and what I had done. What *we* had done. *Oh god, why had I let that happen?* Who was I trying to kid—I had instigated it!

It wasn't that I necessarily wanted to wait for marriage, but I had hoped my first would at least be my boyfriend. Someone whom I loved and who loved me back. What was this—a one-night stand? That was hardly what I wanted for my first time.

I didn't consider myself a slut now, but I was starting to wonder if I would've been if men had started noticing me earlier. I had gone on a date, sort of, when was it—last night? Twenty-four hours ago? And now I'd lost my virginity to someone other than who I had gone on a date with! I hardly even knew this person that I'd shared this very intimate act with. I was definitely physically attracted to Caymn. Yes, *insanely attracted*, but that's all it was, right? I didn't really know him, so how could it be anything but physical? I took a deep, steadying breath. Everything was going to be fine. I was just going to act like this never happened.

The bed shifted as someone sat next to me, and I felt fingertips lightly brush my arm. "Hey pretty, are you awake?" It was Caymn, as I'd suspected.

I pulled my arm away slowly, trying to escape the electric current his fingertips gave me so I could think clearly. I pretended to just be waking up, blinking as if my eyes needed focusing. "Hi," I mumbled, trying to look happy to see him, but I know I failed at it. "How long have I been asleep?"

He set his hand awkwardly down to the bed where my arm had been, definitely aware of how I'd rejected his touch. He looked good in the same pants he had been wearing earlier and same fluffy pirate shirt, hanging open to reveal some of his splendid chest. His eyes were still odd, and the red of them looked shocking against his pale skin. I found that I couldn't look into those red eyes, and not because I was scared of them. It was what we had done when he'd revealed his red eyes that made me uncomfortable. "Most of the day. It's about eight o' clock p.m. your time."

It was Thursday, and I was supposed to be working. *Shit.* I hoped I wasn't going to lose my job.

"I forgot to make sure you were fed this morning. Are you hungry?"

My ears nearly perked up at the mention of food. "Yes, I'm starving," I said, and my stomach growled as if agreeing.

The corners of his mouth lifted in a sort of half smile. "Okay. Well, Liz is making food for the both of you in her chambers. Put this on, and I'll show you where she is."

He held out a small folded pile of clothes and I grabbed it, shyly hiding my nakedness by keeping the blanket over my breasts. He sat up and turned away to give me privacy, and began putting away his pots and organizing his books. I half expected him to do a *Mary Poppins* "a spoonful of sugar" jig and magically put everything away, but he straightened up like any normal person would. I brought the clothes underneath the covers and inspected them. The slouchy black t-shirt looked like it was more his size than mine, and he'd also given me a pair of small, white cotton shorts. The outfit was comfortable and sexy in an I-just-slept-over-at-a-man's sort of way, and it would do just fine for now. "Did you pick this out?" I asked as I rolled off the bed.

"Yes," he said simply, his back toward me now as he put the last of his books onto the counter. I couldn't understand his mood, but he seemed withdrawn.

"Well, I like it," I said, trying to be amiable. My stomach growled loudly again, begging for my attention.

He sighed, sounding oddly frustrated. "Let's go take you to Liz."

"You could just point me in the direction. I'm sure I could find it."

"No, you couldn't," he said as he led me out of the room.

He was right. I would have never been able to get there on my own. We went through the black door and instead of it opening into a hallway like I expected, it was a room the size of a closet with no doors except the one we'd come in. I was sure it had to be a closet! He shut the door behind us, closing us inside.

I felt like I was Cara in Wonderland. Where was the little "drink me" bottle and "eat me" cake so we could shrink to just the right size to fit through a mouse hole? "How—?" I started.

"You'll see," he said. I noticed the square scrying mirror hanging on the door when he took a piece of chalk from his shirt pocket and started writing on the black glass. It was a complicated sketch of symbols that was as foreign to me as Japanese or advanced math equations. When he was satisfied with his diagram and put his chalk away, the symbols started glowing red, brighter and brighter, till they were just...*gone!*

He knocked on the door suddenly and I was so caught off guard, I jumped.

"Jason, could you get the door?" I heard Liz yell from inside, and I know my eyes were bulging. It was like a magical elevator! But who was Jason?

The door opened and a man stood in the entryway, holding it wide for us to step through. His skin was the most beautiful shade of bronze that only Native Americans are blessed to have. His brown eyes were the color of maple syrup, just a few shades darker than his warm russet-colored skin. He was stunningly handsome, though still not as handsome as Caymn, in my opinion. "Welcome, please come in!" He seemed familiar, and I wondered for a moment where I'd seen him. Could it be Liz's husband? His name was Jason, wasn't it? Though he looked different with his black hair tied back in a bun, he definitely had to be the same man as I'd seen in a picture! *How was this possible?*

When Caymn ushered me forward, I walked past this mystery man into the room and was astounded again when I saw how large the room was. It was a white, spacious living room with TV, coffee table, white couch, baby grand piano, and a large chandelier hanging. And it was more than just a room; it had other rooms attached! I could see a formal dining room to the right and another opening that led into a kitchen. A bathroom was located in the left corner of the living room, and I saw stairs leading to a second floor. I could see windows pointing outside with real light shining in, the last bit of light before the end of a sunset, faintly pink. I could even hear birds chirping! It was like I had just walked into a house in our world, and I could hardly believe that the closet-like elevator could've led us here.

I turned to Caymn, who half-smiled at my shocked expression. "I'll see you after your dinner," he said softly. When he shut the door and blocked my view of him, the black door turned into a burgundy wood front door with a window of stained glass like you might see in any nice American home. Through the frosted stained glass I could see a front yard, a large tree, the street, and even a mailbox, all under a darkening sky.

How on earth was this possible?

"Let me take you to the kitchen," Jason chirped. "Liz is cooking a really good meal tonight. Homemade fried chicken, macaroni, green bean casserole, and chocolate lava cake for dessert." I followed him, my mouth hanging open stupidly. The kitchen he led me into wasn't as modern or expensive as Liz's kitchen in Charleston, but it was homey. There were no stainless steel appliances, or anything in cool colors for that matter; only warm shades of off-white and caramel. I liked it. I imagined Liz smoking a pack of cigarettes while drinking out of a liquor bottle in her old kitchen, but running around like Suzy Homemaker? Never. But there she was, doing the whole bit, with an apron on and everything. It was a completely different side of Liz than I'd ever seen, but here it looked right.

"It's crazy, right?" she said, positively beaming. All I could do was shake my head. I was speechless. "Some things don't work, like the TV," she continued, waving her hand in the direction of the living room. "But it makes me feel like home just having it there."

"But...this isn't your home in Charleston," I said.

"Oh no, of course not. That house was nice and all, but this is my *home*. This was the house that Jason and I shared outside of New York City."

I was baffled. "How did you get the house here?"

"Well, it's not actually *here*," she said, opening the oven to inspect the cooking food, then closing it back. "It's a copy. It's a mix of my memories, Caymn's magic, and how things work in the Barathrum. The rules of space and time don't apply the same way here. Well, maybe time works the same, but I'm not sure, so don't hold me to that."

"So Caymn's house must be huge if it can fit your old house inside of it and who knows what else!"

"Well, I think it works like this. The outer walls of Caymn's mansion are just an outer shell. Every demon's home is a large shell. The only thing that's real in his home is that first entry room you walked into."

I nodded, remembering it from the first time I had been here.

"Demons don't really love to be out in the red-light hours, so they avoid it. If a demon wants to have tea and chat with another demon, they can just transport into their front entries. So that space is real, but when you get to that next door, there's nothing real, exactly. If there are demons waiting for us to leave to ambush us, they might be crawling all over that front room." That made me shiver, but she continued. "If they could get that next door open, there would be nothing but open, empty space. They have absolutely no way of getting in here unless they know the exact symbol sequences. No one knows that. Not even I know how to get in and out of here on my own. It's like we're in some alternate universe working on Caymn's brain and magic."

"That doesn't frighten you?" I asked. "That you could never get out on your own? That you could be stuck in here forever?"

"No, not really. He promised that I could live my old life, never look older than twenty-nine, and I could see my old husband. He gave me all of that. All I have to do is prick my finger and get blood drawn every couple of days and run a few errands here and there. It's more than worth it."

I glanced over at her husband, still standing in the doorway of the kitchen, looking a little unnaturally still and spaced-out. "How exactly is it that you get to see your husband?" I asked. He looked at me then and smiled and I smiled back, politeness ruling over.

"Caymn made him, too. He's kind of like this place, only mostly functioning. He can't say anything that will surprise me, because he runs on my memories of him. But he's enough the same that I can pretend he's real when I'm alone."

My stomach growled loudly, but I ignored it. Caymn's magic abilities were amazing, but could living in imagination-land be good for Liz? At some point, you have to live real life, right? I couldn't relate to losing a husband, so maybe I had no room to make judgments, but I felt like her having her dead husband back was very wrong.

"Let's eat," she said suddenly. "Honey, will you please play the piano for me and my friend Cara?"

"Of course, babe. Just let me know if you need anything."

He disappeared through the doorway, going back into the living room. Finally, Liz pulled out a tray of wonderful looking chicken strips and two different glass casserole dishes covered with tin foil. The wonderful aroma wafted in my face, and my mouth instantly filled with saliva. I was starved.

"You can sit over there at the bar, or we can sit in the formal dining room, if you'd like." I looked at the bar, a high counter overlooking the kitchen with three tall chairs pushed up against it.

"I'll sit over here, that's fine," I said, walking around to sit at the bar.

"We also have chocolate lava cake, and I'll start a pot of coffee," she added. "Or we could have wine or—?"

"Oh my god, coffee," I said quickly, cutting her off. I tried to think of how long it had been since I'd gotten my afternoon coffee, but I was too hungry to think.

She laughed lightly at that and took the foil off the casserole dishes. The lovely sounds of the piano being expertly played drifted from the living room, and I sighed happily. When she put the delicious-looking food on the bar in front of me and handed me my plate and fork, I filled my plate with more food than was probably polite. She made a plate for herself also, but she seemed more entertained at the sight of me shoveling food into my mouth than hungry herself.

"So are you really starving to death, or does sex work up this much of an appetite for you?" she asked.

I gasped, causing food to go down the wrong hole, which sent me into a coughing fit. I dropped my fork which landed on my plate with a loud clang. *How did you know?* I wanted to ask, but instead I kept coughing.

"Are you okay?" she asked, beginning to look

concerned. "Your face is turning red."

I continued to cough, but was able to nod in response. Finally, I could speak. "Did he tell you?" I croaked.

"No, but he didn't have to. While you were sleeping he came to tell me that you were feeling better and that you were definitely recovered from your concussion. Then I noticed there was a certain bounce to his step and he couldn't stop smiling." She cocked her head at me, too much interest lighting up her gray eyes.

I was embarrassed and I covered my face, hoping to suddenly become invisible.

"And then you come in here wearing what looks to be a men's t-shirt and briefs..."

"They're shorts, not briefs," I interrupted, but checked down to make sure. Yes, just cotton shorts.

"Well, I was guessing. But now I know. So...tell me."

"Tell you what?" I asked, bewildered.

"You were a virgin, right? Did you like it?"

I slumped in my chair. I was no longer a virgin, which suddenly made me feel a little sad. Also embarrassed. And confused. "I don't know."

"You don't know?"

"Well..." I tried to explain. "For whatever reason, I'm so drawn to him that I can't control myself. I knew I should stop, that we were going way too fast, but I just couldn't seem to care. Everything was so amazing, I couldn't make him stop..."

"So, it was amazing?" she asked, smiling.

"Yes. Well, when I woke up, it suddenly felt not-so-amazing. Now it's just...awkward." Then a thought occurred to me. "Do you think he could have put a spell over me to seduce me? And then when I slept, I sort of slept it off?"

"Oh, Cara, no," she said, shaking her head. "If there are spells like that, I don't think he would put that over you. I don't know everything about him, but I've spent a month here with him, and he is *crazy* about you. Did you know that he's been harassing me with questions about you almost every day since I've been here?"

"No, I didn't know that," I said. "What kind of questions?"

"Oh god, everything. Most of them I don't know the answers to, but he's asked me, 'What's Cara's favorite color? What does she like in men?' Basically, he's tried to get everything out of me that I could possibly know about you. He's completely love struck, I think."

That made my stomach flutter. "So, you think there is *no* chance he put some sort of spell on me?"

"No way. I think what you're experiencing is something totally normal when you're in love."

Ha, in love?

"When I met Jason, I knew that I wanted to be with him almost instantly. There was this insane attraction that was so extreme, I hardly knew how to stay away. We moved really fast, also, and it was like I couldn't control myself. If you feel that attracted to him, don't run away from it. But that's just what I think."

I couldn't run away if I wanted to. I was literally trapped in his house! I thought about what she said for awhile in silence. I had crazy thoughts when I looked at him— like I *needed* him to be mine. The feelings were so intense and sort of irrational, that they were hard to deal with. If I weren't trapped in this alternate universe, I would have run for the hills by now to escape these feelings. I'd never felt so torn and confused in my whole life. I didn't feel that way about Jonah, I realized. Jonah was cute, nice, funny, sweet, and probably exactly what my parents would consider a perfect match for me. They probably wouldn't be wrong about that, either! He seemed like the kind of guy I *should* date. But when I looked at Caymn, any attraction I had toward Jonah was squashed. No one else existed, for that matter. Was it more than just physical attraction? I shouldn't let physical attraction be the ruling factor, but maybe Caymn and I had something more than that. There was this connection that was more than just sexual. *Was this what it was like to have good chemistry with someone?* I wondered. *Maybe.*

"Do you think you love him?" Liz suddenly asked.

"Not love," I said. "Lust, yes. I am in lust with him."

"That's it though? Just lust?" she pressed.

I sighed, suddenly feeling tired. This subject was exhausting, and my brain was hurting from the internal battle. "I don't know," I said, hoping she'd drop it. Thankfully, she did.

$\mathcal{N}$ineteen

I cradled my cup of coffee in my hands and sniffed it appreciatively. The red mug spread warmth through my fingers and steam hovered over the black liquid. I was so glad they had coffee in Barathrum. *Thank god for small miracles,* I thought.

I wondered what Caymn and Liz were doing exactly, but when I glanced at Caymn, who was meticulously measuring ingredients and mixing some sort of curse with all of his concentration, it didn't seem like the right time to ask. Liz worked alongside him, asking an educated question from time to time and the way they easily moved around each other, I could see that this was a frequent occurrence.

I brought the cup of coffee to my mouth and instantly regretted it, wincing as the hot liquid rolled over my tongue. I swallowed quickly and hissed to myself, glancing at both of them from across the island counter. They were too

preoccupied to notice me, which was probably for the best, because when I looked at Caymn, I was sure a look of longing showed plain on my face. I had never been very good at hiding my thoughts. If he still had feelings toward me, he was good at hiding them. Even when we had gotten back in the closet-like elevator and stood only inches apart, he hadn't closed the small distance to touch me. We had just stood there, my heart racing in my chest so hard that I wondered if even he could hear it. I had glanced at him from the corner of my eye, but he seemed distant as he worked the magical elevator. So close, yet so far away. *Was he over me now that he had already had me?* I wondered with a sudden pang of sadness.

For something—anything else—to look at, I watched symbols being sketched on the black mirrored wall. The wall had been going crazy, being filled with endless amounts of symbols since we'd come back to this room, and I felt almost at peace when I watched it. It was like a complicated math problem being worked that I couldn't understand and wasn't drawn to try, a distraction that I welcomed.

For the tenth time or so, the wall became dark as if someone had wiped the slate clean to start again. But as I waited for it to start up again, nothing appeared. I frowned at it for a moment before finally looking back toward the two other people in the room.

Caymn's face had been stuck in a worried frown since he'd picked us up from Liz's "house" and brought us back to his spell room. When I looked at him now, his forehead was wrinkled and his brows pinched, lips pressing tightly together. I imagined what it would be like to slide up behind him, put my arms around him, and feel the line of his body against mine. I could make that worried frown disappear, I was sure of it. I liked that idea better than watching Liz stand so close to him while I stood on the other side of the counter. A couple of hours before, I'd thought I wanted to go home, but seeing him again had made me want to stay longer. I could almost imagine myself with him in this place forever, as long as we could make countless rooms and countless beds together. Oh, what we could do in those beds... As soon as I thought that, I felt heat creep up into my face.

Gah, what the hell is wrong with me? I thought as I guzzled coffee from my cup. I couldn't think any clear thoughts around him. I felt everything, every irrational thought as if it were on loud speaker. I had never experienced such a rollercoaster of emotions in my life. One thing I knew for certain was we weren't going to stay here much longer, whether I liked the idea or not. Though no one had explained to me what was going on, I got the sense that we were pressed for time.

Caymn rubbed his forehead, staring down at his soupy green mix, and I could feel the stress emanating from him. "I'm going to need a handful of *achillea millefolium*," he murmured to Liz, then got very quiet again. I could almost see his wheels turning, though I couldn't imagine what he was thinking so hard about.

"Which one is that?" Liz asked, sifting through bottles, and they made pretty tinkling noises as they tapped against one another.

"It's also known as the devil's nettle," he said, distracted with something else, and finally added, "but it should be labeled *achilleos*."

"Ah!" she exclaimed when she finally spotted the bottle. "We only have a *tiny* bit left. Should I use it?" she asked, suddenly frowning.

"No," he said, and his own frown deepened. "But this curse has to be made, so yes." He made a frustrated sound and rested his weight on both of his hands on top of the counter, letting his head droop. It was not the time for questions, so Liz and I quietly waited. "We only have two weeks to execute a plan," he finally said. "But it wouldn't be wise to stay here for even that long."

"Why only two weeks?" I piped in, not able to wait in silence anymore.

When he looked at me, his body went rigid, and I wondered if he had forgotten I was there. I didn't think it was possible, but his brow furrowed and frown deepened even more. He didn't say anything, just gave me a look that I didn't quite understand.

Liz broke the silence. "We will run out of food in about two weeks…" She let her words trail off as she looked to Caymn for conformation.

Caymn's eyes didn't leave mine, that strange expression filled with fear and sadness still on his face. There was something more in it though… regret? Did he regret having been with me? I couldn't be sure. After a moment, he finally spoke. "Yes, we will run out of food in two weeks. If circumstances were different, we *could* work magic to make food, but we need to utilize what we have for an escape."

"If we tried to stay here and dipped into the spell supplies to make food, we'd eventually run out," Liz informed me. "The two of us would eventually starve, and then Caymn would starve."

"I wouldn't exactly starve," Caymn corrected. "Hypothetically, without blood to impel my curses, I would be starved from my power. My rooms would shrink until I would be forced out. In comparison to the other demons outside, I would be powerless, and they could tear me to pieces. We need to make use of every bit of our provisions to get the both of you out of here and to safety. I won't let anyone starve." As he said that, he seemed to make up his mind about the spell he was mixing and added, "We will use the last bit of the devil's nettle."

Without question or hesitation, Liz opened the bottle labeled *achilleos* and dumped its contents into a small stone bowl. I don't know what I expected devil's nettle to be, but I was kind of surprised to see that it was just a bundle of dried white flowers. She began to crush and grind the dried flowers expertly with a mortar and pestle.

"So what's our plan of escape?" I asked.

"The two of you will have to escape under a disguise curse that we're creating right now. I will send you both to your side of the universe during daylight hours and from there, you must travel as far from your homes as possible before nightfall. The other demons might sense you leaving here, but they won't be able to follow you—not during the daylight. They will come looking for you when the sun sets, but as long as you go far, far from your homes, they won't find you under the charms."

"Will they be anything like the curses I was already under?" I asked, and I hoped they wouldn't be.

"Well, yes," he said. "Now that I think about it, it may be one of the same exact curses you've been under, with an additional disguise curse. You will look like someone completely different than you are now. They won't find you." He said that like it was supposed to be reassuring. It wasn't.

I thought about what that would mean—looking like someone else. Now that that was an option, maybe I didn't want to look like anyone but myself! But my appearance was the least of my worries. He was telling me I'd be living in hiding. For how long? Forever? I hadn't led a very exciting life until recently, but it was *my* life. I honestly didn't want to go back to being unnoticed like I had been under those curses for so many years. Now he was expecting me to go under curses-of-hiding again? And start over a whole new life? I would lose my cute little apartment on King Street, my job, all my possessions, and most importantly: my family! Living the rest of my life in hiding wouldn't be *living*… it would be just *surviving*. I didn't think I could do this. There had to be another way.

Liz's crushing the flowers came to a sudden halt as if she'd just realized something. "What about you?" she asked him.

I had been so absorbed with thoughts of myself, I hadn't even thought of what Caymn was going to do. He didn't say anything as he took the bowl of crushed plant from her and dumped it into the soupy green mix. "What about you?" she repeated, this time her words lashing out at him.

I stared at him expectantly, but he wouldn't meet either of our gazes. "This is the end of the road for me."

Liz and I spoke up simultaneously.

"End of the road?" I exclaimed.

"What the hell does that mean?" Liz yelled.

Caymn glanced up almost nervously, like he was a mouse being cornered by two tabby cats. "Neither of you understand. There is no way for me to escape. Even if I were to escape this fortress unscathed, I can't go with you in daylight. It is impossible! And where am I to hide from the queen?"

I was too shocked to speak.

"You can go to one of the other cities!" Liz exclaimed. I nodded, thinking it sounded like a good idea. "You can hide there! You can disguise yourself, and you can start over! You can take me with you!"

Take you with him? I was startled to hear that.

He laughed, but the laugh held little humor. "I am a demon from the City of Greed. This has been my set place for my whole existence, as the other demons in other cities have been in theirs. Demons don't move from city to city like human people. If a new demon appears in town, do you think they won't ask me who I am and why I'm there? Where do you think I can go without being noticed?"

Liz pushed herself off the counter, accidentally pushing the stone bowl across the glass so that it made a screeching sound that pierced my ears. Her breath started coming in quick, panicked gasps. "We had a deal!"

"If I'm not alive, I unfortunately can't keep my part of the bargain," he said. "It's regrettable."

Her hands went out like they were going to touch his chest, but she reconsidered, clasping her hands together in a pleading gesture instead. "Please, please don't send me back! I can't go back!" she begged, sounding as if she may be on the edge of hysteria.

He was still frowning, but instead of looking anxious or stressed, his face was full of pity. "I have no other choice, Elizabeth. You must go back to your former world."

"No!" she screamed, and the word came out choked as she launched herself at him, eyes brimming with unshed tears. She clung frantically to his shirt. "You can't send me back! I can't go back to my old life after this! I can't handle his death again, *PLEASE!*" The tears rolled onto her cheeks as she stared at him with desperate, pleading eyes.

He sighed and reached his arms out in a gesture of sympathy. "Elizabeth, I am sorry, but this is how it is. I wouldn't have shown you what you could have if I ever thought it would end this way. You have to believe me that I never wished to cheat you. As it is, you need to hold it together."

A sob broke from her lips and she made an effort to choke it back. "Please, just leave me here in the Barathrum. Please," she begged quietly in an effort to hold her emotions in check. "One of the other demons could take me, and maybe I could still have him. Please." By her devastated expression, I had a feeling she knew what his answer would be.

I felt irritation rise in me at her crying, and not just because she was hanging all over Caymn in the process, though that didn't help my mood. I was irritated because Caymn had said he didn't think he was going to make it out of this alive, and her main concern was keeping her imaginary life intact. It was extremely selfish of her, but I tried to squash my irritation and remember that I had no idea what she had been through in her past. I didn't understand what it was like to truly be in love with someone and lose him forever. Not that I was in love with Caymn, but maybe soon I would understand that more than I'd like to.

"You would not be safe if I left you with another demon. No one else would honor a deal you made with me," Caymn said. "I promise, your best option is to go back."

She violently pushed away from him and began crying uncontrollably, her whole body shaking with her sobs. Caymn looked at me, and I could tell that he didn't know what to do. Though I was annoyed, I went to her. I walked around the counter and wrapped my arms around her shoulders. She fell into me immediately, crying into my shoulder, hardly able to hold herself up in her absolute despair. I tried to pat her back reassuringly and think of something to say, but I had no words. Saying everything was

going to be okay seemed like an insult, because she was obviously not okay. Even if she and I could make it out of this alive, she may never feel okay. I was trying very hard to be understanding.

"Liz is right," I said suddenly. "There has to be another way."

"There isn't," Caymn said simply.

Liz pulled away from me, her crying disintegrating into little whimpers and jumpy movements as she tried to hold it in. I watched as she went to the bed in the corner of the room and collapsed onto it.

"I'm not going to run away and live my life in hiding," I said. "I won't leave you here to die, either! We are going to kill her." I almost couldn't believe I'd said it after the words came out. Cara Hansen, killer of demons? Ha! I had never killed anything bigger than a mosquito.

"Kill who? The queen?!" Caymn burst out laughing, but it was a dark laugh that I didn't like.

"Yes," Liz whispered. She sounded strangely distant. "We could kill the queen." Neither Caymn nor I could resist glancing at her. She lay on the bed, a dull expression on her face as she stared upwards at nothing, hair falling over the side of the bed like a black waterfall. Though her body was intact, I thought I was witnessing a part of her die. I couldn't understand the intensity of her anguish and where it stemmed from. Was this all just because Caymn had promised her an imitation of her old life and he couldn't deliver? I felt bad for her. *Really*, I did! But I hoped that soon she would pull herself out of her despair and be strong. We needed to figure out a way for the three of us to survive.

"It's either her or us, right?" I said, meeting Caymn's red eyes. I was hyper aware of his nearness and how easy it would be to close the distance between us.

"Yes, but..." He stopped as if to consider it. "It's just not possible. You saw all those familiars she has at her disposal. Even if we could take away the blood jewels she wears, those familiars give her the power of a hundred demons."

The power of a hundred demons. That sent a shiver running down my spine. We were in way over our heads, but when I looked at Caymn and he looked at me, I couldn't accept that he should stay behind while we ran to find safety. Whether I was sure I loved him or not, he had saved me when doing so meant signing his death warrant. I wouldn't run away. I *couldn't* run away. Then a thought came to me. "Well, what if we could free the familiars? Could you send them back to earth...then kill the queen?"

By his expression, I saw that he was mulling it over. "I believe I could free them, and that would put her at a disadvantage, but why send them back to earth? Why not give them to the other demons? That might satisfy them enough to forget about her reward or any allegiance to her."

"Because those humans have already missed out on so much of their lives. It's only right to set them free. I can't stop the demons from continuing to steal humans, but if there is any chance we can free those people, I want to do it."

"I need to think about this," he said, going back to mix his curse while giving me a sideways glance. "You think a lot differently than I do, you know...that could be a good thing or a bad thing."

I could see how that could be a good thing, because maybe we could fill the holes in each other's strategies. "How could that be a bad thing?" I asked.

"I've always done whatever keeps me alive, sometimes at the risk of others. Your sympathy for others could shorten your lifespan... maybe all of our life spans."

"Having sympathy for others is not a weakness," I snapped in defense. "And that's not true. You've saved my life at the risk of your own life. And you are willing to stay behind to make Liz and me safe," I argued.

"True," he said. "But now you want me to risk your lives for a chance at keeping mine a little longer by trying to kill our queen. If I agree to this, which I'm considering, that would be very selfish of me."

"You think it's likely that we won't make it?" I asked, absentmindedly chewing a fingernail.

"Yes! In fact, if we don't figure out how to distract the demons outside, we will most certainly die."

My heart sank in my chest a little bit at the mention of the demons outside. I had forgotten about them. He must have felt bad, because he suddenly tried to reassure me. "If we can distract them, our chances are greater at surviving. If I can get to the human familiars and free them, our chances become even greater. If we can confuse her long enough to get her blood jewels off, we will be *golden*," he said, one side of his mouth perking up in a crooked smile. He looked off at nothing for a moment, and I thought he might be imagining a victory.

"Okay," I said. "We will figure out the details, but we are doing this, one way or another."

When he looked at me, any remnants of his smile vanished. "Promise me something, both of you," he said, glancing at Liz, who still stared emptily at the ceiling. "If she kills me and you two are still alive, you will invoke the curses I give you and escape."

I really didn't want to believe that was going to happen, but I agreed.

"Fine," Liz agreed, but the way she said it, I wasn't positive she wholly meant it. I noticed she hadn't said much of anything since her outburst, and she looked very closed off. She never wanted to leave this place, and I hoped she wasn't plotting some plan of her own that would hinder us.

For the next hour or so, Caymn added powders and a few things that suspiciously looked like pieces of some creature's organs into the green mix, turning it into an ugly brown sludge. Liz had fallen asleep, and she lay huddled in the fetal position, arms wrapped around the burgundy blanket. She looked grief-stricken, even in sleep.

I watched as Caymn separated the mix into two different bowls, putting one aside for later. He then proceeded to ask me questions. "What color would you like your eyes to be?"

I sighed loudly. If we ended up using these spells, that would mean that Caymn hadn't survived our first plan and Liz and I would be on the run. I didn't even want to consider that a possibility or assist him in this spell. But, then again, if it did come to that, I might not want someone else picking out what I may look like for the rest of my life. I didn't even like other people picking out my clothes.

"I don't really care. Green, I guess," I said, before I had consciously decided. As soon as I said it, I was almost surprised at myself for not choosing blue, the color I'd always wanted them to be. Red eyes would remind me of Caymn, but I knew I wouldn't be allowed to have those. Green seemed like the next best thing. *If I live and he doesn't, I should have to be reminded of him,* I thought, then tried to push those thoughts away.

"Green," he said quietly, grabbing a handful of a dried plant from a jar, dark green with the same color flower buds. He looked up to meet my gaze for a second and the way he paused, I think he suddenly realized I had purposely chosen his eye color. Maybe he wanted to ask why I had chosen that color, or maybe he knew. Either way, he didn't ask and I was thankful, because I didn't want to explain it aloud. I wasn't sure if I could even explain it to myself. He looked back down finally, smashing and grinding the green plant with a mortar and pestle like Liz had done, his hands moving with more speed and skill than humanly possible. When he was satisfied with the crushed plant, he tipped it into the bowl with the rest of the spell contents.

"Hair color?" he asked.

"If I can change shape like demons can, why are you creating this spell for me? Why can't you just show me how to change?" I absentmindedly rubbed my cheek, remembering how sharp it had been when my face had changed only a few days ago. I vaguely wondered what I had looked like in my sister's eyes at that moment.

"Because I don't have enough time to teach you. Even if you were a quick learner, it takes practice to keep a new shape once you're in it. I can't send you back if there's any chance you would be bouncing between forms without control."

"Oh," I said. That made sense.

"So, what hair color?"

I had never really wanted a different hair color. I had dyed my hair a few times to experiment with it, but it had been too hard to get back to my natural hair, so I'd stopped doing it. Besides my fingernails, it was the only other physical trait I was happy with.

"You can keep it blond, but I think we should darken it a little bit," he said when seeing my hesitation. "I don't want you to be recognized, and the lighter blond makes you stand out a little too much."

Me, stand out? I thought doubtfully, still not very accustomed to people taking notice of me. I wasn't sure what he was so worried about. If the curse of concealment was anything like the one previously on me, no one would be taking a second glance at me even if I had a horn growing out of my head. "Okay, that's fine," I shrugged.

He took the tiniest pinch of a yellow powder and then another pinch of brown spice and added them to the pot. "What do you think about curly hair?" he asked.

"Sure," I said noncommittally. That didn't sound like a bad change, considering my shoulder-length hair had never been able to take a curl before.

"I'm just going to make slight changes now. It will be so minimal that you won't look completely unfamiliar to yourself, but you'll be different enough that no one would recognize you." He glanced up at me, a bare hint of a smile playing on his mouth. "I have to concentrate very hard, because if I did anything out of order, you might end up with something terribly wrong, like green skin instead of green eyes."

"Got it," I said, and pretended to zip my lips and throw away an invisible key. After that, he didn't ask me any more questions, just kept on adding the smallest bits of random things to his mixture. After a long while, he seemed satisfied with the curse and put a cover over the top. "Now we just have to let that set for a few hours, so the plants are thoroughly soaked," he said. His red eyes flicked to me, and I felt my pulse quicken. We were silent as we stared at each other until I finally had to break my gaze. Now that we had nothing to do to hold our attention, I was suddenly nervous.

"I want to show you something," he said.

"Okay..." I said, unintentionally sounding wary.

He walked around the counter and passed by me with just a few inches between us, and my skin prickled at his nearness. When I turned to follow him with my gaze, I saw that he went straight to the closet-like elevator and left the door open for me. I quickly glanced at Liz, huddled into herself in sleep.

"She'll be fine. She knows how to get to her chambers."

That made me feel a little better, and I went to stand by him in the closet. He closed the door, the task making his arm very close to mine. I almost grabbed his arm, which would have been a strange gesture, but I desperately wanted to close the distance between us. I wanted to stop this awkwardness, but I wasn't sure how to.

"I need to get where you're at," he said.

I looked at him and realized I was standing where he needed to be to work the elevator. "Oh," I exclaimed and took a long step backward so that I stood in a corner. All I wanted was to be near him, but I was acting like a skittish mouse.

He moved to the scrying mirror and began his sketch of symbols, the chalk screeching as it was dragged across glass. Like before, when he was done, the symbols glowed red and then disappeared. I thought I could hear birds chirping, and I gave Caymn a questioning look when he peered over his shoulder at me. He smiled as he opened the door, more interested in seeing my reaction rather than what was on the other side of the door. Warm sunlight poured into the closet, and I was momentarily blinded.

Twenty

As my eyes adjusted, I noticed the sounds of animal calls and a scent that I had never smelled before. It was the scent of all things that smelled good in the world, yet wasn't overpowering. Flowers, ripe fruit, lemons, rainwater, and moss. It somehow relaxed and soothed all my stress before my eyes even finished adjusting. I edged closer to the opening and saw so much greenery and ...*life*.

I couldn't keep my mouth from falling open as I looked through the doorway. This wasn't a room or a house...it was a whole other world before us! When I stepped into the grass beyond the closet, I saw trees, many different kinds, intertwined and making a canopy above us. The floor was thick with grass and flowers, and the trees were covered with moss and wrapped in vines. Fruit hung from some of the trees, ripe and delicious-looking, all hanging within arm's length. Everything was as green and alive as poems of spring speak of, but never is it a reality. Not like this.

Caymn walked up next to me. "Do you like it?" he asked hopefully.

"I love it," I said, and I meant it. *How could I not?* When I glanced back toward the closet, maybe curious at how it might look from this world, I saw that it had disappeared. All I could see were trees and flowers going on forever, encasing us like a secret garden.

"This is just the half of it," he said, sounding happy with my reaction. "Take off your shoes."

I did as he said, and I was surprised at how soft the grass was underneath my feet. He took my hand suddenly and it felt like an electric current burst from his fingers into mine, making my heart lurch into a faster pace. We hadn't touched since he had woken me, and I had almost forgotten how his touch had the craziest effect on me. Without saying another word, he started leading me through the jungle, if that's the right word for it.

"Later, I'll show you a waterfall that's not too far away from here," he said, glancing back at me. "Right now I want to show you something else." I noticed the sound of water trickling down rocks, like a small steady stream nearby. Monkeys called to each other from the trees, howling and carrying on, though I never saw one.

He led me to a huge tree—not tall, but immensely fat. Its large, thick branches hung so low to the ground that even an inexperienced climber could scale the tree. He took me around the trunk, and we had to duck underneath a low, thick branch to get to the other side. I touched the tree with my free left hand, and the bark felt softer and smoother than bark should feel; like velvet. Everything was so unearthly beautiful, I could hardly contain the utter joy welling inside me. "Where are we going?" I asked, not able to detain my curiosity for another moment.

"Right here," he answered, abruptly opening a hidden door in the tree trunk. My eyes must have been as big as saucers, because when he looked at me, he laughed. It was a happy, effortless sound. I loved the way his eyes, red as they were, lit up with his smile, all of his stress forgotten for a moment. My heart was suddenly aching in the best kind of way.

"Let's go inside," he said softly. He slipped his hand out of mine, moving it to rest at my lower back, and he gently ushered me inside. It was dark when he closed the door behind us and when I paused, his body gently bumped against my back. My heart lurched at his close proximity. "Keep going," he coaxed.

My eyes adjusted slowly and though it took a lot of effort to move away from his body against mine, I trudged forward. Only a dim glow from above illuminated a spiral staircase in front of me, wrapping along the inside of the tree to a second level. I started walking up the stairs and he stayed very close behind me, never breaking our physical contact. We walked into a cozy, circular room with a low, rounded ceiling. Candlelight danced and illuminated a white bed that took up half of the floor space, thick with blankets and pillows. A wooden table with two chairs just big enough for two people to sit comfortably filled the rest of the floor space. Two windows on either side of the room made it so that whether you were having coffee at the table or lying down on the bed, you could see the beautiful view outside. Last, but not least, there was a small wood-fireplace tucked in the wall, wood already ablaze and sizzling in its chamber. Though small, the space was not claustrophobic to me. It was the coziest, loveliest place, like it had been conjured up from my dreams. I could hear the sounds of trickling water, chirping of birds, and other exotic animal noises, like a lullaby to lull us to sleep. I felt completely safe and at peace.

"Sit down on one of the chairs," he said, and I was too enraptured with this place to care that he had ordered me like he often did Liz. I sat in the farthest chair from the door, and he managed to sit next to me without ever taking a hand off me. It was like he couldn't bear to let go of me now that he was touching me again, and I'd be lying if I said I didn't like it.

From where I sat in front of the window, it looked as if the green canopy went on for miles. A small flock of white birds suddenly erupted from a tree and flew through branches as if they were dancing. "This is gorgeous," I breathed, not wanting to disturb the peace.

"Everyone needs a safe place," he said casually, rubbing his hand across my knee. "It's similar to a garden where I've lived before. It's the only place I've ever walked in sunlight, so I recreated it...but I altered it to have this room in this tree."

"You used to be able to walk in the sunlight?" I asked, my brain working sluggishly in my sudden sleepiness.

"Yes, before we were sent here, to the Barathrum," he shrugged. He removed his hand from my leg before putting it right back, like he thought better of it. "Anyway, do you want some coffee? Some food, maybe?" He seemed uncomfortable and distracted, like he didn't like the direction in which this conversation was going.

I was getting hungry, but I didn't want to be distracted. "Yes, but will you tell me about it?"

"Tell you about what, the food? Let's see what we have..." he said, and his eyes became vacant.

"No!" I exclaimed. "About before the Barathrum."

He didn't answer, and for a moment, I wondered what was happening to him. He was as still as if he'd been frozen, and even his hand didn't move against my leg when I tried to adjust my position. Suddenly he blinked and his hand softened. And then there were two cups of black coffee on the table before us, along with cream, sugar, a couple oranges, and a plate of French macarons.

"Sorry, I had to glance into the kitchen. I hope you like these cookies. Most of our food is just what Elizabeth prefers."

I did like macarons, and I stared in amazement at how he'd been able to magically retrieve them. Then I remembered my question and realized he was trying to distract me. I would not let him succeed. "So, tell me about things before the Barathrum," I said, snatching a green macaron and popping the entire thing into my mouth. If you've never had a macaron, they have a crisp outer shell and when you bite through that, they're soft and chewy inside. This one was sweet with buttercream filling. I closed my eyes for a moment in appreciation, savoring its flavor.

He let go of my leg again and when I opened my eyes, he was frowning at me. He looked away to add sugar and cream to his coffee.

"It's so weird to me that you drink coffee," I said suddenly, taking a sip of the warm, black liquid from my own mug.

"I don't know why," he said. "It's been around for almost six hundred years. I've been drinking it for four."

"Four years?" I asked, assuming that's what he meant.

"Four *hundred*," he clarified, looking at me with incredulous eyes.

"Oh," I said, then gulped. I almost asked if he was serious, but I knew he had to be. I tried to process four hundred years. My own great grandmother was alive on Bruce's side and almost a hundred years old. I could hardly imagine living that long and had a harder time imagining what it'd be like to live that times four. "How old are you, by the way?" I asked, feigning indifference. Part of me didn't want to know, afraid of what the answer might be.

"You're asking me how old I am, but you look like you just tasted something sour," he commented.

"Will you just tell me?" I grumbled. Might as well get it over with and get past it.

He pressed his lips tightly together and stared at me, trying to read my expression. "I have been in the Barathrum for...almost ten thousand years."

"Wow!" I said, shaking my head and trying to process that. I couldn't do it. Only a million questions filled my mind, but I finally settled on one. "How are you so...normal?" I realized that question was too vague and I tried again. "How do you speak normally and act like someone closer to thirty years old, not...not..." I stammered.

"Not ten thousand?" he said. "Well, I have learned the ways of the earthly world from my familiars, for one. In recent years, I've spent more time with them than my own kind. They have been my one link to the times, and when I'm not on this side of the universe with my familiars, I'm on your side…influencing."

"Influencing, right," I said sarcastically, not sure what I felt about him being so old. I didn't know how I felt about dating someone twice my age, let alone someone about *four hundred* times my age! When I looked at him and absorbed his face—that all-that-is-man squared jaw line, those full lips, and that mass of dark, wavy hair—it was almost shameful how easily I could overlook his age. I sighed, trying to dismiss my inner argument for a later time.

"You seem angry," he stated simply, grabbing an orange and rolling it closer to him.

"I'm not angry," I said. "Just surprised and a little confused-feeling." Suddenly, I remembered that we had gotten way off subject, which had probably been his plan all along. I popped another macaron in my mouth before I asked, "So, why won't you tell me?" I mumbled around my food in a very unladylike way.

He had started peeling an orange with one hand while keeping the other hand on my leg, which was impressive. He paused to frown at me again, further confirming my suspicion that he had been trying to sidetrack me. "We're not supposed to talk about these things with humans," he said, ripping off a large piece of orange peel.

"But you said yourself that I'm not human. I'm a nephion," I said, smiling triumphantly at him.

He looked very seriously at his orange as he contemplated telling me the story. He grumbled finally, and I couldn't help my smile as I sensed my victory. "I'll tell you what I can, but I can't tell you certain specifics. There are things we aren't permitted to talk about, this being one of them. Going against our queen is one thing, but betraying our master and demon-kind is…*unforgivable*."

"Okay," I said, releasing my smile. "I won't tell

anyone," I added.

He sighed, pushing aside the orange as if he'd lost his appetite, and began. "In the beginning of time as we know it, there was a place where humans and..." he stopped, trying to find the right word. "Spiritual creatures," he said finally, "lived together."

"Do you mean demons?" I asked.

"Not exactly..." He squinted his eyes toward the green paradise outside the window, and I wondered if he was trying to remember. "I don't think there was ever an English word for it, but 'spiritual creatures' is the closest I can think of that fits."

"Angels?" I asked, trying to be helpful.

His red eyes met mine. "No," he said, shaking his head once. "So, humans and spiritual creatures were living together in a world where we could live in harmony. Here—"

"So you were never an angel?" I asked, cutting him off. I had heard that demons were once angels, and I wanted to get the story completely clear if this was the only time I'd ever hear it.

"No, not exactly," he said. "I'll explain all that, but just listen. I was a *spiritual creature*. This place was a garden..."

"The garden of Eden!" I exclaimed, and he gave me a look that resembled a glare. "Sorry, I'll stop," I said, embarrassed. I just couldn't help my rising excitement.

"Ask your questions at the end," he said. "And if you interrupt me one more time, you can just forget about it."

"Fine," I answered, and took another sip of my coffee, hardly letting my eyes leave his face. The coffee tasted wonderful and I almost said so, but I didn't dare interrupt again.

"There were many spiritual creatures, because we weren't designed to procreate, or that was what we thought. Humans, on the other hand, were born to procreate, so it started that there were only two, a man and a woman. There was only one rule, which I'm sure you can guess?" He paused, allowing me to fill in.

"I know this. Not to eat the fruit of knowledge of good and evil," I announced proudly.

"Wrong," he smirked. "It was that we weren't allowed to lie down with the physical creatures, and they were not to lie down with us."

"Oh," I said, my eyes widening at this new bit of information.

"I don't know exactly how it was later translated into fruit, but that's not important. *So, back to what happened...*"

I almost couldn't contain my excitement when he said that. He didn't say, "so back to the story," but "so back to what happened." I was getting to hear about the beginning of the world from a demon's perspective. Even though I hadn't thought much of it before, it was only because I figured I'd never actually know what was true. I could only imagine how many people would kill to be in my position, and it made me jittery.

"The spiritual creatures had a leader—a favorite, if you will—and he was the most beautiful one of all. He had the most wonderful voice of any of the created beings. In the beginning, he would sing every day, and we would all stop to listen to him. It wasn't like anything you've ever heard before. Imagine a song that's moved you down to your soul so much, you could cry. Imagine that times a million. A voice like that could literally control you. He now gives a fraction of his gift to his queens to control us, and being controlled can feel liberating, but most times it just feels like being stripped of free will. The human woman, like all the other creatures in the garden, would go to see him as he sang. Every day was perfect paradise until *the* day. I remember the sky fell and darkened to black, a color that we'd never seen before, at least not in the sky. Our Maker's voice rang out and we all knew the sins that had been made. The human woman had lain with our leader, the spiritual creature of song, whom she had fallen in love with and who had fallen in love with her. The human man, seeing that the woman was unharmed and the Maker hadn't punished her, lay down with a spiritual being as well.

"The spiritual creatures that had sinned were cursed with ugly appearances, would never again see or feel the sun on their skin, and would not be able to use their abilities unless they partook of human blood. At that time, we loved the humans immensely—essentially lived to entertain them and care for them—and couldn't imagine harming them under any circumstances. Though the human woman loved the spiritual creature of song even in his horrifying form, she was not allowed to follow him into the world with no sun. The human man repented, and after the human woman begged for mercy for the creature of song, she eventually learned there would be none and repented as well. They were shunned from the world where physical and spiritual intertwined so freely together and sent to another world, your Earth, where they would be alone with only animals to keep them company.

"We were left in the garden, our human friends and our singer gone. Within a day, we were arguing. Some said that it wasn't fair, that the creature of song and the human woman shouldn't be able to fall in love if they weren't allowed to be together. Others said that it was not our place to tell the Maker what was fair and what was not. We began to resent each other, and some of us screamed in anger at the sky. Three days passed and the Maker spoke out again. By the end of the day, more than half of us were cursed and sent to be with the two others who had been cursed. We only could see the humans through a sort of veil in the universe after that, and we were so horrible to look upon, we didn't want them to see us anyway. The other spiritual beings, the ones who didn't dare to question the Maker, were brought to his own place to live in his presence. They were rewarded for their loyalty and remained beautiful, even moreso because of their time spent in the Maker's presence, making them reflect his radiance—or so they brag about. *Those* are angels. Something I've never been, though we were once the same thing. Common misconception."

Caymn suddenly fell quiet and his eyes were distant, staring out the window. The green canopy was now getting darker, and I realized night was coming, though I was pretty certain it was morning at home. Though I was interested in his story, I was getting sleepy, which had become normal for me to feel about this time. Fireflies were coming to life, and we could see the river snaking through the trees like a silver ribbon. It would be really nice to sleep when it was dark outside, and I craved it suddenly.

"What happened after that?" I whispered, determined not to fall asleep.

"As far as we know, the garden was locked forever, not to be seen again. The human woman had a child, the first Nephilim, and she was the most magnificent creature I ever saw…"

"Nephilim," I said, recognizing the word I'd read on my internet search. "What is the difference between Nephilim and nephion?"

"Nephilim's original meaning comes from the Hebrew word: nephal, meaning *the fallen*. In the Greek language, the name used for the Nephilim was gigas, meaning *earth-born*, and later, mistranslated into gigantes, meaning *giants*. Though some were giants," he explained. "If you say Nephilim, you could be referring to either half demon, half angel, or both. If you are specifically speaking of half demons, you would say nephion. Half angels, nephraim."

"There are such a thing as half angels?" I exclaimed. "Could I actually be one of those instead?"

"There *was* such a thing," he said. "But I assure you, you are a nephion. I could tell you about the differences between them, but that requires me to tell you a whole other story and a very long one at that. Let me finish this one."

I propped up my head with my hand and sighed, feeling sleepiness start to overwhelm me. "What was she like—the first Nephilim girl?" I asked.

"She wasn't exactly nephion or nephraim, because she was conceived before her father was cursed. Her name was Lilith, and though her name has lived on in legend, unfortunately her story has been twisted tremendously. Human legend says that she was Adam's first wife, and a demon, but in truth she was the daughter of Diabulus and Eve, a small child with fair hair and violet eyes. The one thing that made her especially different from all other Nephilim in later years was that she aged very slowly. Though she lived to be almost a thousand years, she never appeared older than twelve years. She enraptured everyone, human and non-human, because she was as innocent and delicate as young humans are with the power and strength beyond any mortal body. We demons especially wanted to watch her use the abilities that we'd once possessed. Our powers became so minimal that we almost forgot what they'd felt like, but when we watched her, we remembered.

"Anyway, so when we were separated from the humans, they could no longer see us, but we could see them through a sort of veil between our universes. Here we call it Limbus, *the in-between*. After a time, we learned that we could influence the humans a small amount by whispering to them. Even Lilith could not see us, though sometimes she seemed to sense us. We stayed in our new world for a time, building shack-like homes, and trying to live with our new life. We became increasingly angry, the singer the angriest of us all. He plotted to kill the Maker and swore an oath to spoil everything he'd created. Some of his closest companions would go with him into the veil between our worlds and influence the humans, day in and day out. One day the singer and his closest comrades came back, and they were in their former beautiful appearances, their hands dripping with blood. They gloated about influencing one human son to kill his brother and then gathering the dead son's blood, taking their power back. We all stared at them in horror, and at the same time felt horribly envious. Their power lasted only three days, but the overwhelming desire was planted in all of us. The time eventually came where we all had a taste of our abilities and were able to look like our former selves again. We became monsters, desperate for blood and desperate to destroy everything that the Maker had created."

He was silent for awhile after that.

"I'm guessing there was a lot of chaos and blood

being spilled before rules were finally set in," I said quietly.

He nodded, eyes looking distant and sad. "You couldn't imagine."

We sat in silence for a while longer, me trying to be patient as I waited for him to tell me more. "What happened next?" I finally urged. Patience is not my strong suit.

"I'd rather not tell you the rest of the story tonight," he said decidedly.

"Not even just the rest of Lilith's story?" I asked, grasping at straws.

He shook his head at me. "I'd rather not end on a gruesome note right before you go to sleep. Plus, I think I've betrayed my kind enough for one night."

So Lilith's story had a gruesome end, I thought glumly. I didn't want to hear a horrific ending, not tonight at least, so I let it go. Instead of pressing more out of him, I spat out a passing thought. "Are they really your kind, though?" I asked, doubtfully. In my mind, he was nothing like the malevolent beings I'd learned about in my occasional Sunday school visits growing up. He might not exactly be an angel— and I wondered at all the horrible things he might have done throughout his years—but he wasn't evil. In my opinion, talking about old history shouldn't be considered betraying his kind, especially when they were waiting out there, plotting to capture and kill him.

"Yes, they are my kind," he said, eyes gleaming and catching the light of the candles between us. "I am foolish in my attempts to make you forget what I am."

I rolled my eyes at the drama in that one statement, and he glared back at me. I was no longer afraid of him, not because I doubted his ability to hurt me, but because I knew he wouldn't. The demons outside that wanted to hurt us were the things that I was afraid of. I looked out the window and realized I could easily forget our problems outside and even my whole other life at home. Even at night, the scent and sounds of paradise soothed me into carefree bliss. If Liz had been here too, I could understand why she didn't want to go home.

He grumbled. "Only a week ago you wanted to save Elizabeth from me, and you were right in doing so!" he exclaimed, sounding exasperated. "I have tricked you now into believing I am something I am not. I want to show you what I am—what is real—but I'm afraid you would be disgusted with who I really am."

The angst in his voice made me look back at him. He was more beautiful than anything or anyone I had ever seen, but that wasn't why I loved being near him. "It's not just what you look like that makes me like you," I said truthfully. "It's not this place or all the things you can do. You scared me at first..."

"You should be scared still," he grumbled, glancing away.

"And I still am, some of the time!" I said forcefully, drawing his face back to mine. "But I am drawn to you. I can't help myself from being so attracted to you, and not just physically. It's like trying to separate two magnets. I hate being away from you." As I said this, I knew it was true. His age, what he was, and even what *I* was didn't matter to me. They were just the extra details, and though hard to process, they didn't change how I felt.

"I think a moth being attracted to a flame is a better analogy," he said. "And what the flame eventually does to the moth, I'm afraid I may do to you."

"We may be more equal than you think," I argued. "It's because I exist that you're in danger right now. There is a price on your head because of me, for crying out loud!"

"And it's because I couldn't keep my mouth shut that there is a price on *your* head," he countered.

"See?" I said, feeling satisfied with myself. "We are more like magnets."

"Maybe we are not a moth and a flame," he agreed, still sullen. "Maybe we are like two flames."

Maybe he was right. I sat quietly for a moment, then spoke again. "I know being with you may not end up perfect," I said, then recanted. "Or it may not be exactly what it seems, but being with you in this short time has been the most amazing thing that's happened in my life. If for some reason we don't make it out alive, I want us to enjoy this time together." I was surprised with how easily I could talk about my feelings after such a short amount of time.

"I understand—and I agree," he added.

I smiled, and his returning smile was gorgeous. "I don't want to worry about anything except our plans to…" It was hard for me to say *kill the queen*, but that's what I thought. Ugh, how was I supposed to help kill someone when I couldn't even comfortably say the words?

"Yes," he agreed, finally relaxing. "I just don't want to hurt you like I seem to have hurt Elizabeth. I promised her more than I could deliver, and I'd hate to do the same to you." He took swig of coffee and added, "I worry that you might finally realize I'm a monster."

"You're not a monster," I said, resisting the urge to roll my eyes at him again.

"I *am* a monster," he argued, leaning in close enough for me to feel his moist breath on my neck. Against my will, my breath caught in my throat. "No more questions now," he whispered. Suddenly he wrapped his arms around me and with a quick, effortless movement, he pulled me onto the nearby bed. The bed was as soft as it could be, like falling into a marshmallow, and the blankets were filled with down feathers.

And just because he said *no more questions*, I stubbornly wanted to ask another. "Just one more," I said greedily, pulling back enough to get a good look at his face. I didn't give him an opportunity to say no. "So if demons were born around the same time as humans, does that mean earth is only ten thousand years old? I thought it was like four point five billion years old or something…" I let the words hang.

He sighed in exasperation, but answered my question. "Our two species are both about ten thousand years old, but there were other worlds and creatures made prior to us, including the Earth and the Barathrum. Most people that read the current Bible believe that the earth was created in seven 24-hour days, which is another misinterpretation. The original biblical text was written in languages that contained fewer words than modern English, which means that the words in those languages had more than one meaning. The Hebrew word for "day" has three literal translations, one of those being an unspecified period of time. Like saying *the day of the dinosaurs*, for example. We were born, and in a short amount of time separated to our different worlds. Worlds that had been created long before us. So, in a way, both biblical and scientific views have their truths."

My brain was about to explode with all the information he was freely giving me now. What else did I not understand about my world that Caymn could just explain away?

"You're getting tired," he commented. Maybe my brain was too full with new information to think anymore and it was past my bedtime, but I had my suspicions that he had given me decaf coffee.

"Not very," I lied, but my body betrayed me as I suddenly had the uncontrollable urge to yawn.

He propped himself on an elbow and smiled down at me, a fond look in his crimson eyes. In that one unguarded look, I thought I could tell that he might love me, and I felt my heart swell at the thought. I snuggled into his chest and we lay there for a moment, too lazy to get into the covers. The sounds of the jungle outside drifted in as we lay quiet. A light, unobtrusive rain started as if on cue—and maybe it was—to lull me to sleep. He moved away from me for a second and before I could protest, he pulled a blanket from somewhere to lay on top of us. I sighed, feeling more relaxed and at peace then I had ever felt in my entire life. He ran his fingers through my hair and as the minutes passed, I drifted into sleep.

I can't be sure, but I thought I heard him whisper, "I think I'm finally content," and he kissed me gently once more.

Twenty One

When I awoke and reached an arm out to touch Caymn, the sheets were empty. I opened my eyes and sure enough, I was alone in the circular room inside the tree. Light from the windows illuminated the room and when I peeked outside, it looked as if it were early morning. As wonderful as you would think waking up in this paradise would be, I was disoriented and my body clock felt off. It had been a long while since I'd woken with the sun. I also hadn't expected to wake up by myself. I sighed, missing my own bed, my guitar, and no one wanting to kill me.

As I looked out at the trees, I realized the jungle seemed different than it had been before. It had felt like a whole other world last night, immense in its size and filled with magic. It was still beautiful, but it was lacking something. It felt smaller and less vibrant, I decided.

It was when I rolled out of bed that I caught a whiff of freshly brewed coffee and breakfast. Caymn had evidently laid out a mouthwatering display of food as I slept: bacon, eggs, sausage, fruit, and biscuits. On a lone plate sat a note that read, *Planning and scheming our escape, lover. Be back soon.* Though we should have been conserving food and he had vastly overdone it, I couldn't help but smile at his effort. I helped myself to coffee and a plate of grub while my mind buzzed with thoughts about the previous night and what was to come in the next few weeks. My mind eventually drifted to thoughts of my unknown father. Caymn had said that the demon in the woods was my father, but I had my doubts. It wasn't just that I didn't want him to be my father, though that might've been playing a part. Something about the demon in the woods seemed familiar, but for whatever reason, I felt a strange certainty that Caymn was wrong.

I sighed, suddenly tired of being alone with my thoughts. I downed the rest of my coffee and decided to venture out. I took on the stairs that circled inside the tree trunk and opened the door that led into the green utopia. When I stepped barefoot into the grass, I noted that it felt harder than it had the previous day. It felt almost like plastic blades underneath my feet, uncomfortably tickling and scratching with every step I made. I walked through the trees in the direction I thought I remembered the magic elevator being. I walked farther than I remembered walking, but still I continued, believing that I'd eventually hit a wall and by finding that, find the door. I didn't even think about what I would do when I actually found the door, because I certainly couldn't operate the magic elevator. As I went on, I was surprised to see that the trees began to appear pixilated. I blinked slowly, thinking it was a trick of my eyes. As I touched the trunk of a strange tree with bumpy pink fruit, I noted that its bark felt like little sharp blocks as I would imagine a tree made out of Legos would be.

I wondered if I should continue when I heard my name being called from behind me. Before I turned to meet the person calling my name, the tree softened underneath my fingertips. I ran my fingers along the tree in wonderment when I heard my name again. I turned to see Caymn walking toward me as the world seemed to come back to life. I watched as the greenish glow I'd seen previously stretched behind him, expanding throughout the jungle. The smell of flowers, fruit, and moss hit me like a tidal wave. I heard a monkey howl somewhere in the distance, and an orange bird suddenly flittered between us. I had known that his world didn't work like our Earth did, but now I was wondering if it was like a pop-up book on a large scale. When Caymn left one section of his home, everything in that area apparently became less detailed, while wherever he was flourished.

"How are you this morning?" he asked, stopping at arm's length.

"I'm good," I said, tucking a few strands of hair behind my ear and noting how greasy it was. I had seen half a dozen bathrooms since I'd been here, but I had not seen an actual shower. I *desperately* needed a shower.

"I trust your breakfast was to your liking."

"Very much," I said, smiling at him.

"Sorry about you waking up alone," he said, grabbing my hand and tracing my knuckles with his thumb. "There is just so much to plan and do in such a short amount of time. I could hardly lay there without getting some of it done. I hoped I would be back before you woke up."

"It's okay," I shrugged. "The no sleeping and no eating is something I'm going to have to get used to."

He blinked at me. "I eat and sleep. Just not as often or as long." He pulled me to him abruptly, pressing his body against mine. "Stop being so far away from me. I can't bear it."

I smiled into his chest and let out a happy sigh. "Hey, is there a shower somewhere? I'm overdue…"

"Yes, I'll show you where you can get cleaned up," he said happily. "Come with me." He tugged me back in the direction of the tree house, holding me close to him. Though it was awkward walking so closely to each other, it was nice, and we laughed at our clumsiness when we nearly stumbled.

The grass and moss that seemed to be at war with one another to cover the ground were both soft underneath my bare feet. The sun shone through the trees in some spots, creating natural spotlights. Flowers blossomed everywhere and a few hummingbirds flitted from flower to flower, cheerfully drinking nectar.

"This place is like heaven," I whispered, as if I spoke too loud it might disrupt the magic.

"With you here, it is," he whispered back, flashing me a smile and giving me a quick kiss on the lips.

I noticed the sound of water trickling before we came to the opening of trees. The source of the sound was a small waterfall that slid off a low ledge into a lagoon, making a natural shower. The shallow pool of water was about twenty feet wide and greenish-blue, partially mirroring the blue morning sky.

"Wow," I said under my breath. It was like a Hawaiian postcard brought to life, water glittering as it reflected the sun.

"It's not technically a shower, but I thought you might like it more," he said, biting his lip in a very seductive way before playfully wiggling his eyebrows. I laughed, him and this magnificent place making me overjoyed. I wrapped my arms around him and he pressed his lips against mine. We hardly managed to get our clothes off before tumbling into the warm, bath-like water.

I was further disoriented when we returned to Liz's home, expecting to enter a sun-lit living room, but seeing a starless black night through the windows instead. Liz lay curled up on her white couch under the soft glow of a lamp, a murder mystery novel in one hand, glass of wine in the other. She took in our appearances, noting both of our wet hair, and smirked. "Well, there you guys are," she mumbled.

Caymn held the door open for me, gesturing for me to go inside, and I did. When he didn't follow me in, I turned to look at him curiously. "I have more curses to make that need my full concentration," he said. "You girls keep each other company for the night." Then he shut the door behind me.

"Don't you feel like a child being dropped off at daycare?" Liz asked, eyes focused on her book again. I did, but before I mustered a reply she added, "Welcome to my world."

I plopped down on the opposite side of the couch and pulled a dusty pink and cream quilt from the back rail to lay over myself, then grabbed a magazine from the coffee table. Liz and I sat in comfortable silence for a long while before she casually asked me where in the world I wanted to escape to if Plan A fell through. We fantasized together about a few different countries, but the more we discussed it, the more evident it became to me that neither of us was committed to running.

Not surprisingly, we ended up at the kitchen bar with a bottle of red wine later on that night, and I did not refrain from drinking my share. When there was a long stretch of silence, my mind drifted to Liz's outburst the previous day, and I said, "I'm sorry if I ruined things for you here, Liz." She tried to shake her head and dismiss my apology, but I wouldn't let her stop me from saying what I needed to say. "I know you want to stay here. If it weren't for me, you wouldn't be involved in the dangerous situation you've been put in, and there would be no reason for you to be sent back."

She let out a weary sigh. "I'm not mad at you, Cara. If anything, I'm disappointed in myself, and I'm starting to wish I had never come here," she said, surprising me. "I would've done anything to be with my husband again, but now with the possibility that I might be sent back *and* never be allowed to see my family again, it all seems kind of hopeless. I wonder if I traded one month of illusions for a life without family and any possibility of finding true happiness again. My best option seems to be to stay here, though the pull of this place has gone away."

That just made me feel worse. "If I hadn't interfered..."

"Cara, stop!" Liz said, a warning in her gray eyes. "You couldn't have prevented things from turning out this way. It's not your fault that Caymn drew attention to you, but I would rather he'd chosen to save you from the queen at the last minute than not at all." She reached out a hand for me to grasp and I did, tightly holding her hand in mine. "If I'm stuck in this mess with anyone, I'm glad it's you," she added.

"Me too," I agreed, relieved that she didn't hate me or hold me responsible.

We were just finishing our third glasses of wine when we both noticed movement, and Liz grabbed what I had thought at first was a photo frame. "Caymn says to meet him in the spell room," she said, reading the scrying mirror.

When we returned to the windowless spell room, Caymn stood at his work station, removing the cover from the curse we had been working on the previous day. I watched as he added a few drops of red liquid with a glass dropper and stifled a shudder when I realized it was probably Liz's blood. As soon as the last drop fell and submerged into the liquid, the curse swirled and mixed on its own, pulsing like some sort of living thing. It hissed and smoked, the majority of it evaporating into the air. I edged away from it, not wanting to breathe it in or have it on my skin.

"What's happening to it?" I asked, almost having to yell to be heard over the hissing. I turned to look at Liz and was surprised to find she'd slipped out without my notice.

"It's concentrating itself. It means the curse is finished," Caymn replied, just as loud.

I watched as almost the whole bowl of liquid evaporated into the air. I expected it to have some sort of stench that would make me gag or at least let me know that I was breathing it in, but I never smelled a thing. Then it gurgled, as if making one last hoorah, and stopped producing steam.

"Let's see how it works," he said quietly, turning around to go through his cabinets. He went through a stash of jewelry for a moment before finding an earring that suited him: a simple gold fishhook-clasp earring with a glass bauble dangling as decoration. He carefully unscrewed the tiny glass bauble from the clasp, and with a syringe, sucked up what was left of the mix, now a condensed brown-black goop, and gently inserted it into the bauble. It filled the small ball almost all the way to the top and when he screwed the fishhook-clasp back on, it looked like an ordinary earring with a dangling dark brown gem. It was kind of pretty, and I made an *ooh* sound of appreciation.

"Try her on," Caymn said, and I wondered if he meant the earring or the new person I was about to wear. He gently handed me the piece of jewelry and when his fingertips lightly brushed my palm, I felt my pulse quicken. When was that going to stop happening? When I slipped on the cursed earring, a sensation buzzed through me, similar to when I reached for the universal force, but not quite. I felt like the universal force went along with my own will, but this felt the other way around. I felt a slimy pressure on my skin as the curse forced its way onto me, and for a brief moment I felt claustrophobic.

Caymn held up a mirror that he'd pulled from a drawer, and I was suddenly looking at a new face. He had said that he was only making minimal changes and I would still recognize myself, but he couldn't have been more wrong. Every single part of me had been altered, and a complete stranger stared back at me. My whole face was slimmer, pushing my eyes closer together and making all my facial features narrower. My shoulder-length hair was a mass of tight curls and had turned the color of warm honey that wasn't far off from my naturally ash-blond hair. The eyes were pretty, not bright green like I had expected them to be, but a dark muted green. They weren't so dramatic that they'd be shocking to a passing stranger, which I guess was the point. Nothing was very shocking about this new me. I was cute, but not striking.

"I like her," I said, nodding at my reflection, surprised again when her movements matched my own. I had never seen my reflection so…not me.

"Good, I'm glad you like it," he said, taking a step closer to me.

I started to say something and he stopped me, putting his fingers gently on my mouth and taking a quick, almost frightened glance toward the slick black wall behind me. "*Shhh!*" he hissed.

I glanced at the black wall, too, but I wasn't sure what we were looking for. He stared at the mirror for a moment longer, then muttered, "I thought I felt something." Finally, he seemed to dismiss whatever he'd thought he'd felt and reached out to me, clasping my hands and pulling me close.

"I don't want to further discourage you, but I'm wondering if we should give up on our plans," he said very seriously.

"Why?" I exclaimed, instantly frustrated enough to try to yank my hands away. He only held my hands tighter.

"I never fully changed my mind from my original plan, though I like to entertain thoughts about yours, trust me," he said. "I want to kill Deamavarus and spend our nights in your bedroom and spend our days hidden inside my walls. But it won't happen. We can win a battle against a queen, but we can't win the war." He was saying that the devil, or Diabulus as the demons called him, would be after us next, and those were hopeless odds. His words filled me with despair, and against my will, my eyes prickled with unshed tears. I looked down at our hands and though his were much bigger than mine, they fit together so perfectly. Something as noncommittal as holding hands should not make my heart race like it did.

Tap, tap, tap! A sound like a fingernail tapping on glass startled me and I darted behind Caymn like a scared little girl before I had another clear thought. Purple light flashed on the black scrying wall, lighting up the entire room before it darkened again.

"Hide!" He snarled, pushing me toward the closet that worked as an elevator. "Someone is finally contacting me."

I wanted to ask questions, but he all but threw me into the closet and slammed the door behind me. I defiantly cracked the door open, and though I couldn't see much through the door gap, I could see the scrying wall and the faint reflection of the room in it. I could see Caymn's figure, just barely, and I could hear the sounds of copper clanging against glass as he hid some of the curse utensils from view.

"Who is it? What do you want?" Caymn snapped, his voice hostile enough to make me feel a tremor of fear.

A thin, dark figure floated into the glass almost as if he were in the room and I was seeing the reflection of him. His eyes shone faintly green where they should've been white, further accentuating the deep inkiness of his irises. His face showed no resemblance to a human: horns curled up out of a long goat-like head and skin resembling the color and texture of shiny black leather. He had an ugly smile, lipless with too many pointed teeth, glowing green like the whites of his eyes. Though his body was all man, his face was a horrifying combination of goat and shark. I was almost positive that it was the same demon that had pretended to be Liz.

"Caymnaburus!" the beast exclaimed in a horrible, raspy voice that matched his terrifying appearance. I thought his black eyes were opened too wide before I realized he didn't have eyelids. I involuntarily shivered.

"Crassus," Caymn countered, disdain evident in his voice.

"You look awfully pretty," Crassus said through a throaty laugh. "I bet your little bastard mutt hasn't even seen you in your true form. I don't doubt she would be repulsed at the sight of you."

"What do you want?" Caymn said through a growl.

The black figure straightened, suddenly becoming all-business. "I'm delivering a message from Queen Deamavarus." When Caymn didn't respond, he continued. "Turn her in, Caymnaburus! No one else needs to get involved. Just turn her in and the Queen might forget your crimes."

Caymn belted out a laugh. "And if I don't?"

The black figure smirked. "You already know we will eventually get to you, Caymnaburus, but the longer you make us wait, the longer we will draw out your punishment."

There was silence on Caymn's end and I watched as the smile widened on Crassus's face, his too many virescent fangs showing. "If you do not bring the girl in a day's time, I hear she has a pretty sister..." He let those words hang for dramatic effect, and the mention of my sister made my blood go cold. I clasped a hand over my mouth to prevent from gasping. "You know what we could do to her."

Anger rose in me, but for the first time in a while it sent no vibrations within my skin. I did feel a pressure, though, as if my body was pushing against the curse that covered me, wanting to break free of this new face I had. I had an almost uncontrollable urge to stomp out and try to strangle this Crassus for even mentioning my sister. But you can't strangle a reflection on black glass. I clutched my hands into fists, trying very hard to stay still and not do anything brash.

"Her sister is nothing to me," Caymn said coldly. I ground my teeth together. *Whose side is he on, anyway?* I thought, before deciding he probably had to say that.

"Not to you, maybe," Crassus agreed, cold eyes darting around the room as if looking for me. When I thought his eyes were starting toward the closet, I stepped away from the crack to avoid being seen. "You can't hide her forever, Caymnaburus. Your best option is to give her to us. Let's not spill too much innocent blood unnecessarily."

"What confuses me, Crassus, is why you haven't reported me to *His* princes or generals," Caymn said. There was silence for a moment before Caymn continued. "They could summon me and *make* me turn her over, but they haven't. Why?" I had no idea what he was talking about, and I peeked through the door gap to watch them again.

"The queen likes to deal with things herself! She doesn't need Diabulus or anyone else to fix her problems for her!" Crassus snarled.

"She hasn't reported me because she wants Cara for herself, is that it?" Caymn fired back.

"I don't need to answer your foolish questions!" Crassus hissed, then proceeded to spit out what I imagined were curse words in Latin. "Bring her in a day's time, or I'll skin her whole family alive, starting with the pretty sister! Time is ticking."

Skin my whole family alive? How dare he! I suddenly couldn't think through a red haze as my anger took over. I charged out of the closet with my head screaming thoughts about kicking some ugly demon ass. I wasn't sure what I planned on doing exactly, but I obviously wasn't thinking straight. This curse Caymn had created for me made it especially hard to think clearly, making me feel as if I was confined to skin that had suddenly become too tight. As I stomped out, I heard a crackling sound really close to my right ear, but I was too enraged to take notice.

Caymn was talking. "Cara, you can come—," he said, voice faltering as he saw me. "—out."

The scrying wall had returned to just empty black glass. Crassus was already gone. Either due to the curse that felt as if it were slowly smothering me, the red wine, or my built-up anger, I couldn't form words. My whole body shook, and my teeth were clenched hard enough to give me a headache. Hate toward this demon coursed through me, permanently making its residence inside me. I would not let him hurt my family. But what could I do to stop it? At the moment, all I could think was *kill him*. If he wanted to hurt me, fine. But if he was planning on hurting my family, he would be sorry he'd ever crossed me! I wasn't sure how to kill him or the queen, but I was set on it more than ever.

"You know there's absolutely no chance that I'm going to go back to my side of the universe, right?" I finally spoke, my voice shaking in anger.

He shook his head and I noticed that his eyes were too wide as they stared at me. He blindly grabbed the mirror again and held it up for me to see. I gasped when I caught sight of my own reflection. I had the partial face of this curly-haired girl that came with the cursed earring, but my cheeks had become inhumanly sharp and my eyes were...

"Violet," he whispered in astonishment. "You have violet eyes."

They looked more lilac to me, violet suggesting a deeper and darker shade of purple than they were. These were very pale purple eyes. The tightness in my body ebbed as amazement replaced the anger I felt. My cheeks suddenly deflated and my eyes became the dark eyes I was most familiar with. "What does it mean?" I whispered back.

"It makes me think your father must've had violet eyes before the change and black eyes after. It doesn't necessarily mean anything for certain, but it could rule a lot of demons out."

"Do you know any specific demons that used to have violet eyes that have black eyes now?" I asked him, feeling hopeful.

"I don't know if I can remember every demon's name, let alone their original eye color and what they have now, unfortunately—have you been drinking?" he asked abruptly, sniffing the air around me.

"Yes," I admitted. "Some wine."

"You should probably avoid alcohol from now on, at least when you're in the public eye. It seems that alcohol mixed with anger brings out your more demonic side."

My more demonic side? I shook my head, remembering the real issue. "We are not going back on our plan," I concluded. "I'll give myself up before I risk my family," I said, my voice cracking, hardly able to contain the hatred that filled me. I could not let my family suffer for me.

"I know," Caymn admitted, wrapping his arms around me. I stiffened at first, this not being a good time for anyone to touch me, but I took a few deep breaths and let myself relax in his arms. "They did this on purpose, because they want us to come to them," he said, his breath on my forehead. "The queen must be growing impatient, but that she hasn't reported me to Diabulus says something." He peered into my eyes as he reached to remove the earring from my ear. I let him take it out, and I let out a relieved sigh as the weight I hadn't realized I was holding fell away. I touched my hair absentmindedly, feeling its smooth, straight texture. I was myself again. Good.

"Now let's see if I can salvage this curse you broke," he said, inspecting the earring while keeping an arm firmly around my waist. His voice was one of reverence, like he was almost glad I had broken his curse.

I peered over his shoulder and saw the visible crack in the glass bauble. "You think it's fixable?" I murmured.

"Oh yeah," he said decidedly. "It shouldn't be problem."

"So, what does it mean that they haven't told Diabulus about me?" I asked, getting back to the topic I more cared about.

"The queen is supposed to be his one confidant that he can trust in this city. That she could be hiding something like this from him suggests that she's going rogue. What she should be doing is going before the demon council, for lack of a better word, and having them summon me and deal with me personally. I wasn't sure, but now I'm starting to believe that Diabulus doesn't even know you exist, nor will he ever. Not if I have anything to do with it," he said, speaking determinedly. "If he knew that she was hiding information from him, he would kill her."

"Well, let's tell him!" I exclaimed, only thinking that her death couldn't come soon enough.

"We can't, because then we'd have to tell him *you* exist. Her hiding that information could get *her* killed, but telling Diabulus you exist would get *you* killed. And me."

"So is this good news or..." I let the words hang.

"Not great, but better," he said, sounding too calm, too relieved. I couldn't feel his relief until I knew that my family would be safe. "Now that I have a clue as to what Deamavarus is doing, I may be able to successfully predict her moves."

"So you think there's a better chance of us winning

against her?" I asked, feeling hope slowly stir in me again.

"Well, not really," he admitted. "But the best part is, no one may know you're a nephion except a very few demons. The other demons in the city probably think I stole an extra familiar and I'm being punished for it. If we kill her and Crassus, no one will know it was us. The city will become chaotic and we may get away with it. I might go on trial when the new queen arises, but I can promise that I didn't steal an extra familiar and since this is true, I won't be punished."

"But won't all those demons testify against you?" I asked.

"Even if I wanted to, I could not lie in the devil's court. I wouldn't tell the whole truth, but as long as I can say that I didn't do what I'm accused of, my case will be dropped. This might not be as big of a risk as I first thought. Diabulus may never know about you." He ran his fingers through my hair, tucking a few loose strands behind my ear. "About us."

"We just have to execute a plan in a day's time," I said, trying to stay hopeful. Whether we failed or succeeded, as long as it was in a day's time, my family wouldn't have to suffer the consequences. Either the queen would be dead or she would have what she wanted... *me*. "Why would they even give us a day?" I wondered.

"Maybe because it's about to be sunrise where you live and they can't steal any of your family members till night. Or they may need time to prepare as well as we do," he said, the hopefulness in his voice lilting just a bit. He kissed me gently, then drew away just enough to whisper, "I won't give you up so easily."

Twenty Two

The next morning, and just a few hours short of our twenty-four hour deadline, we shuffled from Caymn's living quarters into his dimly lit entry. When I inhaled, a bitter taste in the air immediately threatened to choke me, and when I coughed, I felt no relief. I realized then that I wasn't sensing it by way of smell or taste, but with some unnamed sense. Remnants of dark magic and negative energy lingered in the atmosphere like an invisible cloud, giving me the impression that the air itself was fiercely angry with us. Even if you couldn't literally feel leftover hostility in the air, the absolute destruction of the room hinted at it. To my relief, the entry was uninhabited, though that seemed a little odd. No escorts to ensure our arrival? *She must really believe that Caymn would give me up for a better chance at survival*, I decided.

When Caymn opened the door to go outside, a

strange light invaded my eyes, blinding me. My first thought was that it was some kind of curse and I stumbled backwards, shielding my face. "Cara, what are you doing?" Liz hissed. I cracked my eyes open and saw my two companions standing on the threshold, staring at me with confused expressions from under their dark hoods that matched mine. I finally realized that both red sun and purple moon were out together, making everything I perceived difficult to focus on. I didn't bother explaining and waved them forward. Caymn walked out first, his dark gray cloak billowing behind him, and Liz and I trailed after him.

To any spy, we would hopefully look like a group of familiars on our way to sell our blood at the blood market, wearing our robes of different shades of gray to indicate the level of sins we'd committed on earth. I kept my eyes down for the most part, frightened that I might catch the gaze of a curious demon lingering after the previous night's mischief. When I did glance up, I was reminded of 3D movies and how they looked when you glanced above your 3D glasses. I saw double, and it made me disoriented.

When I glanced at Liz next to me to see how she was faring on our long walk uphill, I was surprised to see my face and hair inside her hood. Though I had known about the curse Caymn had made to make her look like my twin, the sight was no less startling. It had been probably my least favorite part of Caymn's plan, because even if it would confuse the queen for a moment, I didn't like the idea of Liz being my decoy. Of course, she had been willing to do it, and they'd both ignored my qualms. My second-least favorite part of his plan was that he intended to kill the queen with a dagger. *A freaking dagger!* It was a magnificent-looking weapon, I have to admit, with a handle made of gold, a blade made of glass containing salt and a *sun spell*, and a silver tip to better pierce demon skin. It was a special blade, Caymn had tried to reassure me, dropped during a battle against angels. But I knew that if you could wield a sword, you could have it taken away. I had expected a much more devious plan from a ten thousand-year-old demon, but he was in the mindset of an ancient demon-soldier, a side of him I was just learning existed. His whole plan was too simple, but when I had said that, he'd argued that the more complicated the plan was, the more likely it was for something to go wrong. Unfortunately, I hadn't had any better ideas.

My legs trembled from the effort it took to walk so far uphill, and just when I was beginning to think I couldn't take another step, Caymn's pace finally slowed. When I peered up from under my hood, we were at a huge door with so many details, it looked more like a shrine or a statue on the side of a huge marble structure, rather than a door. Shiny golden hands were molded into it, reaching out and upwards as if in warning. *Come no further!* they seemed to say. In between the hands, golden spikes and nails jutted out. The only features that let you know it was a door and not some random gold monstrosity were two large circular medieval handles held by a set of gold hands and a thin crack down its center.

Caymn grabbed me by my shoulders and abruptly pulled me to him. "I'll see you soon," he said, but I didn't miss the uncertainty in his voice. His lips met mine and he kissed me fervidly. "Oh, and I forgot to tell you: absolutely *no praying.*"

"O-okay," I stammered uncertainly.

He kissed me one last time, preventing any questions I had from leaving my lips. "Stay here and wait for the signal," he whispered. He seemed to vanish in a cloud of red dust as he bolted.

"Why no praying?" I muttered to Liz after a moment. I was certain prayers had helped me against the demons before.

"It's not necessarily crosses and rosaries that demons are afraid of," Liz informed me. "It's prayers from a believer that calls to their enemies."

"Angels?" I asked.

"Yeah," she answered. "Angels might answer *your* call, but they will not help someone like me, and they certainly won't spare Caymn."

I wondered why she thought they'd answer my prayers and not hers, but I decided it wasn't the best time to have a religious discussion. I hadn't realized how out in the open we would be, and my courage was starting to dwindle. The moon was gone and the red sun was higher in the sky now, casting a bright and angry light over everything. We were so high above the rest of the city, I could see palaces and towers going on for miles below us. I imagined demons could see us as well, and their eyesight would be far better than mine if they happened to peer this way. If not demons, their human familiars would surely notice us. My pulse was pounding so hard in my head, it was giving me a headache.

Though only minutes ticked by, I felt as if we stood there forever, waiting for someone to spot us. Our plan depended on Caymn being able to release the familiars, but even he wasn't sure he could get to them. Our hope was that the queen would keep their door open for her own quick and easy access and that she wouldn't dream of us taking them. It seemed unlikely to me that she would be stupid enough to *not* keep something so important and necessary to her under lock and key. "You'd be surprised what people will let slip when they believe they have infinite power and control," Caymn had said.

I glanced at Liz, who looked like my long-lost identical twin, staring intently down at the colossal black ring on her finger. It was a scrying mirrored ring similar to one Caymn was wearing so we would be able to communicate. In silence, we waited.

The altitude shifted and though Liz kept her eyes on the ring, her wide-eyed expression told me she'd felt it, too. I felt static electricity lift my hair and when I looked back toward the red city, I saw little grains of sand slowly drifting upwards. A boom suddenly sounded from within the queen's palace and both my hair and the floating grains of sand fell. "What was that?" I asked.

"I have no fucking idea," was Liz's reply.

Then we heard the signal. A couple quiet taps came from within the black ring, sending little white lightning bolts flashing along its dark face. "Go, go!" I hissed at her. She grabbed for a huge handle and in an instant my hands were on it too, pulling it with her. The process of opening the heavy door took maybe one or two seconds, but it seemed to take too long, and I could feel adrenaline coursing through me. Then Liz was just running through the door and I counted down the seconds. I was supposed to go after her in *100...99...98...97...96...95...* I silently counted down.

"Cara!" Liz hissed, and I lost count. "There's no one here!"

No one there? Caymn had said she would be on her throne, which was supposed to be through this door! "Just-Just stay there for a moment," I stammered, not sure of what we were supposed to do now. Then a thought occurred to me and I sucked in a scared breath. Had we heard the signal wrong? Had it been two taps or three? I could have sworn it had been two taps, the signal that we were supposed to wait for, but I hadn't really been paying enough attention! I hadn't expected anything but *two taps*. I should have known that things were going way too easily!

"Liz, come back out here," I hissed.

There was no answer. *Shit.* I stood there for a moment, fiddling the two different cursed earrings in my pocket, one for sending me home and the other to disguise me. I wasn't sure what to do! If I was smart and wanted to live, I would activate the curses and escape. I knew that's what Caymn would tell me to do. He had been very clear when he'd said, only about fifteen times, "If anything goes wrong—anything at all—*run*." I'd have a better chance at survival if I ran, but I wouldn't be able to live with myself if I abandoned Liz and Caymn. I couldn't just leave them behind. How would I ever know they'd made it out?

I stepped through the open doors and the red light was suddenly less severe. If the door had been ridiculous, the room behind it was nonsensical. It was huge and open, everything brilliantly shining. Large golden pillars that looked as if they were made from yellow diamonds ran along each side of the room. The floor shone brilliantly like pure yellow gold and precious jewels. The ceiling was rounded and detailed, like that of a cathedral, golden figures molded into it. Instead of angels or baby cherubs like you might expect, there were life-sized horned beasts doing malevolent things, and I didn't want to look at them too closely. My eyes were drawn to the golden stairs that rose high like a pointed pyramid to hold an empty throne. Images were molded into each golden step, reminding me of Egyptian wall paintings that told their histories. The throne looked like a larger than life shrine where she would be at the very top. Her throne room made a statement: *I am not queen, I am god.* The room was so outrageously gaudy and the throne was so high above that if I hadn't already known, I would've assumed then that she was very greedy and proud. But none of that surprised me. The strange thing was that the room was completely empty. No queen, no Caymn, and no Liz.

I noticed two doors, one on each side of the pyramid. *Maybe they're in there*, I thought as I took a few cautious steps toward the door to the right, the one closer to me. The red light was choked out by glittery golden light with every step I took.

Suddenly I felt something on the back of my neck and I paused. It came and went so fast, I wasn't sure if I'd imagined it, but it felt like little worms crawling along my neck to the back of my skull. I touched the back of my head, moving my fingers through my hair, and felt nothing out of the ordinary. *Strange.* I tried to shake off my unease and took a few more steps.

Something white like wisps of hair flashed on my line of vision and a sound rang out, bouncing against the walls. I turned quickly and nothing was there, but the noise remained, echoing. Laughing? A laughing child? *No*, I suddenly realized. *Crying.*

Before I could produce any coherent thoughts, the room around me disappeared and I was in a dark hallway, the only light coming from the room at the end of the hall. I stared wide-eyed at my surroundings and placed a hand on the wall to make sure it was real, or at least tangible. I knew it couldn't be real, but the wall felt authentic and gave no way under my palm. It was the house from my childhood. As I stood in silence, I heard voices as they drifted from my parents' open bedroom. As I walked toward the open door, I thought this felt like a distant memory or a very bad dream that I was on the verge of remembering.

"Hello?" I asked, knocking on the doorframe. When I realized that the speaking voice was female, I called out uncertainly, "Mom?"

I vaguely knew that I was still in the throne room, but my perceived surroundings seemed so real that I couldn't stop myself from going along with the illusion. I felt that I should be stopping whatever was happening, and the more I acknowledged what I saw, the more real it became. Suddenly I heard a bloodcurdling scream that pierced my ears and made my heart stop. Even worse than the scream was the complete silence that followed and stretched on after it. My blood felt cold in my veins. I stood in the hallway for quite some time, trying to collect my thoughts, when I heard someone crying. It only took a second to realize the sound was coming from my old bedroom. I slowly turned to face the closed door that seemed unnaturally ominous, wondering if I should go in there. I could hear the soft, sad cries coming from the behind the door, and though I didn't want to go in there, it seemed that for some reason I had to.

I opened the door to my old bedroom and it was just how I remembered it. In the dim light and dark shadows brought on by my *My Little Pony* nightlight, I could see my old Barbie house, my small pink guitar, and a few of my other toys. I froze when I saw the younger version of myself lying in the small bed, blankets pulled up to cover most of her face except for her wide, panicked eyes. The little me seemed so frightened that she was holding her breath, but it wasn't me she was afraid of. I turned to see what she was looking at, though something in my head already knew what it was and screamed *don't look!* I couldn't stop myself from looking up into the opposite corner where it was so dark. Something was there. I sucked in a scared breath of air as I saw the black figure huddled in the corner where the ceiling met the wall. Its body was as black as empty space, as if even light was afraid to touch it. Light touched his eyes though, and not only touched it, but reflected it. Bright, large, and yellow. *Snake eyes*.

My breath started coming in quick, panicked gasps. The lid I'd so successfully closed over my memories was suddenly opened and all that I had suppressed spilled out. This wasn't the first time he'd come. He'd come many times. The days were good, filled with happy memories, but the nights? *Hopeless terror.* When the visits stopped, he was only gone long enough for the anxiety to subside, and he always came back. To watch her. To scare her. *Bad dreams*, everyone had said. *Just night terrors*.

Something in me wanted to protect this small version of myself, and instead of uncontrollable fear, I felt some anger. Anger was good. It gave me strength, even in the presence of my deepest fear. "Get out of here!" I screamed at it. It didn't look at me, and when I looked back toward the child version of myself again, she didn't seem to notice me either. Then the creature was coming closer to her, and I had no choice but to step back. Though part of me wanted to strike it, I couldn't. Not because my fists would probably be useless against it, but because my bravery was choked out by fear. It radiated through me like I was still there in that bed. It was coming toward the small version of me, and I couldn't do anything about it but scream, "Don't! Leave her alone!"

I grabbed the pink guitar, and in a sudden fit of rage I threw it at the creature. I was a horrible aim and I missed, the guitar splintering and making a loud *bong* sound as it struck the wall. I might as well have done nothing, because no one noticed my tantrum. When I looked at the little girl version of myself again, she was no longer a child in her bed, but a baby in her crib. The demon leapt onto the edge of the crib and perched itself, staring down with those huge, yellow snake eyes. I stopped yelling and I didn't move to throw anything else. I think the truth was, I just became too scared to move.

He began whispering ugly, guttural words, waving

his clawed fingers over the infant's head. Dark black smoke emerged from his fingertips, snaking its way down, and I looked away. Whether this had really happened in my past or not, though I was pretty sure it had, I didn't need to relive it now. I knew now where my fear of snakes had stemmed from. It had never been snakes, but the memory of those eyes that I had worked so hard to shove deep into my unconscious.

I wanted to be far away from this nightmare. *This is not really happening,* I reminded myself. As soon as I remembered that something more crucial was happening, everything seemed to flicker. I caught a glimpse of a golden wall, like a sudden flash of light. Then I was back in my old, dark bedroom.

I looked toward the demon perched on the crib again. "This isn't real," I whispered.

And finally, the demon noticed me and turned its horned-head to face me, yellow eyes staring. I was shaking all over and I hated that. But it wasn't real and it couldn't hurt me! The beast didn't move toward me, but a deep laughter came from him, loud and booming. I slapped my hands against my ears and screamed at him, "This isn't real! This isn't real! This isn't real!" Everything began to flicker again, quicker and more frequently. Light flashed before me and for a few seconds I was caught between a dim-lit bedroom and a golden throne room.

I kept screaming till finally it was just me and the yellow gold room. I gasped, placing my hand over my heart and trying to catch my breath. I realized then that someone was *still* laughing. It wasn't the same horrible, guttural voice of a monster, but a melodious sound like wind chimes. And then I saw her.

She was incredibly beautiful and small on her large throne, her feet just barely touching the floor. She looked younger than I'd pictured her being, like she might even be as young as fourteen. Her eyes were innocently wide and yellow, like polished citrine crystals in her soft, angelic face. Her hair was impossibly thick and long, going all the way to the floor in smooth waves of gold. Her appearance told me that she was harmless, but I wasn't fooled, at least not completely. On that beautiful head was an intricate and heavy-looking headdress of gold with red, sparkling jewels. There were hundreds, maybe thousands, of ruby-like jewels clustered on her crown and cascading down her hair like dripping blood. I knew without a doubt that the jewels actually *were* blood, many little vials of it.

Her light, innocent laughter finally came to end, but the smile and shine of her eyes stayed as she stared down at me from her golden pinnacle. Her gentle, sing-song voice rang out. "So this is the *real* Cara Hansen," she said, acknowledging me and admitting she had figured out Liz's disguise in the same breath. "The girl who can even woo the hearts of demons." She chuckled at that.

"Where is Liz?" I demanded.

I glimpsed the barest hint of movement to my left, and when I looked more intently, I saw a little droplet of blood on the golden floor. I looked toward the ceiling, thinking I might see something, but it looked just as it had before, the ugly golden statues in the same positions of sex and killing. I was almost afraid that I'd see Liz up there, dangling off one of the statues, and I was very glad I didn't.

"She isn't up there," the little queen said, and when I glanced back at the droplet of blood, it was gone. Was something happening in this room that I couldn't see?

She stepped off of her throne, little glass vials tinkling against each other musically. I wanted to be far, far away from here, but I couldn't move.

Run! I thought I heard Caymnaburus shout inside my head, his voice sounding so clear and sudden that I almost wondered if I'd really heard it. It couldn't be real, I decided, and even if it were, I wouldn't leave without him and Liz.

"Do you want to go back home?" the queen asked, tilting her head and sending large gold earrings encrusted with ruby red vials swinging. "Would you like to be with your family again, with Liz, and still have your precious Caymnaburus?"

I *did* want that, but I had a feeling she wouldn't give me that. At least, not the real thing. She could lock me up in a cell or hang me by my wrists, where I would think I was living with my family, Liz, and Caymn. That, I didn't want. I had a feeling she wouldn't even give me that, though, but a much darker cell where I would live in a world of fear.

"No," I said through clenched teeth.

"No?" she seemed genuinely surprised. "Why not?" She was trying to figure me out, but I wouldn't help her. All she could do was find my fears, but she wouldn't get further inside my head. I didn't answer. I wouldn't give her any ammo to use against me. I had to figure out some sort of new plan.

"You want your family and Liz *without* Caymnaburus, is that it? That is understandable, seeing that he betrayed you," she said, decidedly.

I stared at her, unmoved. Caymn had already told me that he had been the one to tell her about me. She moved down the stairs, her thick hair like bright gold moving behind her, and for the first time I saw what she was wearing. She was topless with perfect, ample breasts that many women went under the knife trying to achieve. It really ruined the image of innocence and youth. Low on her hips, just above her pelvis, she wore a golden skirt cascaded in blood jewels.

"Deamavarus!" I heard Caymn's voice as clear as day from behind me and I jumped, then silently cursed myself. I could sense someone running up behind me and I wanted to look, but I forced myself to stare at her, not trusting her with my back. Caymn ran into my line of vision and crossed to the bottom of the stairs in front of me. My heart ached at the very sight of him. Suddenly Crassus was there, whispering in her ear like the snake he was. I was confused until I realized that it wasn't really Crassus, nor was this really Caymn, but a snippet in time she was trying to show me.

"Forgive me, your majesty, for any interruption," Caymn said, bowing low at the waist, then rising. "But I believe I found a nephion whilst on my mission to lure my familiar."

Crassus gasped dramatically. "Kill it!" he shouted.

"No!" the queen said, looking down at Caymn. "Don't let her get away! Place a curse of observance on her."

Caymn gave one quick nod and suddenly he and Crassus froze as if she'd hit pause. "Do you believe me now? Or do you want to see more?" she said to me from the middle of her pyramid.

I didn't answer. If I could somehow rip those blood vials off of her, she wouldn't be able to perform any more mind tricks on me. If I could trick her into thinking that I was on her side, that I'd comply, maybe she'd get close enough. I had never been a good liar, though.

"Fine, I shall show you more," she said.

Before I could figure out what she meant, Caymn and Crassus moved. "I have done as you commanded," Caymn exclaimed. "I've placed a curse on her."

"What curse?" she asked him.

"The curse of the watchful eye."

"Excellent. Now seduce her."

Seduce me?

"Seduce her, my lady?" Caymn asked.

"Conjure up some kind of plan to get her to trust you. Use your best schemes and advances. Then bring her here!"

"Yes, my lady," Caymn said. Then both Caymn and Crassus were gone and it was just she and I.

"I asked him to bring you, and here we are," she said, smiling at me triumphantly. "And where is he?"

Caymn had told me not to believe anything that happened in this room, but was that to save his own ass? Had he betrayed me? Against my will, my heart slowly sank in my chest as I started to question everything. Was this true? Had she told him to seduce me and bring me here, and that's what he had done? Though a seed of doubt was planted, I told myself I wouldn't believe it. I could question Caymn's motives later, but not now.

"That you were able to come out of the spell that brought you here the first time was quite amazing," she said.

"I thought for sure that you would dance right up to my arms and give me what I wanted."

"What is it that you want?" I asked.

She laughed, high and melodious. "Why of course, I want your blood!"

Of course, I thought. Deep down I must have already known that. If human blood conveyed power, in theory, my blood would equal *more* power.

Suddenly the door to the right of the pyramid swung open and Caymn stood in the doorway. *Finally!* My heart leapt in my chest again at the sight of him. I wanted to run into his arms and have us do this together, whatever it was we could do against her, but I didn't dare move toward him. I didn't know if this was the real Caymn or not. Hell, I didn't know if Caymn was really on my side anymore! Every time I felt like I was getting close to figuring something out, she did something else to distract and confuse me.

Caymn was wearing the same hooded cloak he had been wearing earlier, but instead of red goat-slitted eyes I'd come to know him with, his were green. His smile was uncharacteristically mischievous as he walked up the stairs to her instead of coming to me. I tried to tell myself that maybe this wasn't real, but my heart felt like it was breaking with every step he took toward her and away from me. When he was close enough to her, he stepped behind her and wrapped one arm around her, moving a hand to one of her breasts. I waited for him to thrust the knife he'd brought with him through her back and out her chest, but he didn't. He just stood there. Anger rose inside me, and I wished more than anything that I could tear that smug smile right off her pretty face!

When Caymn's green eyes met mine, my heart ached and my stomach twisted painfully. I found myself saying, "This isn't real."

The little queen jumped at that. "What do you mean this isn't real? This is real!" she snapped, childlike face suddenly losing its roundness and sharpening into something else.

I think I had meant to say "This *can't* be real," because I didn't want it to be real, but the way she had snapped made me pause. She had made her first mistake. She had shown me some fear of her own. Fear that I might know what she was attempting. Fear that I might break her spell again.

I took a deep breath and reached for the universal force, something I should have done from the get-go. It seemed to come from somewhere else here than it did on my side of the universe, coming from above instead of beneath me, but I found it and pulled. I drew it into myself, winding it through me and closing the imaginary door, locking it inside. Using it, I pushed out to fill the room and to shield myself. "This isn't real," I said, a smile playing on my lips as I felt power surge through me.

She laughed her melodious laugh, feigning her ease.

Then Caymn spoke. "Cara, I'm sorry, but you don't have what I want," he said, nuzzling her neck. Seeing them so close to one another made me want to throw up, but I didn't lose my nerve. Deamavarus was trying to distract me again, but I would not let her succeed. If it was the real Caymn, he would either have his usual red eyes or he would know to switch back to them. But he didn't, because *she* didn't know I preferred his real eyes. Maybe I was grasping at straws, but this was what I told myself.

Laughter burst from my lips. "I know he isn't the real Caymn!" I exclaimed, not able to help the mad laughter that suddenly erupted from me. They both stared at me, smiling back like idiots when they should have looked puzzled and asked what the hell was wrong with me. She was working very hard to maintain her façade, but she was failing. I pushed farther out with the universal force till I felt it touch something solid.

"Cara," she said coolly. "I'll give you anything you want. I'll give you your old life back..."

"This isn't real!" I shouted, my voice echoing against the walls, followed by my insane laughter. I pushed the universal force as hard as I could, sending its power out into the room. I couldn't physically see the bubble that encircled me, but I could feel it and taste her power on my tongue when it touched my own. When I acknowledged that I didn't believe her tricks, her power seemed to fall back in fear, but only for a second—and then she regained her strength. I saw the room flicker and change for just a moment. For a tiny instant, I could see two lumps on the floor to my left and my right. I was breaking her hold on me.

She didn't look panicked, but stayed smiling. *Could she be afraid of me?* I wondered, thinking I could sense her fear. "Cara, I'll give you Caymn if you want him. I'll let you live your 'happily ever after,' as you say…"

"I don't want anything you can give me!" I growled, but she didn't seem to hear me.

"…I'll give you money. Beauty. I'll give it all to you! All you have to do is…"

"Get out of my head!" I screamed. As I pushed the universal force against her power, everything flickered again, changing. I wasn't sure what the two lumps on the floor were, but I saw them reappear and disappear again. What happened to her and Caymn then was even more startling! They were suddenly gone and then back again. *They weren't even physically there!* I had expected that maybe Caymn was a trick, but I never expected that I'd been yelling at a complete mirage. So where was she?

Her voice was coming out more high pitched. "…give me some of your blood!"

Whispers erupted from either side of my ears, one voice sounding like Liz's and the other like Caymn's: "Let her have your blood, let her have your blood." I had the urge to swat at my ears, but I didn't do anything that would take my focus away from the universal force.

"Give me some of your blood, and I will let you go in peace. You three may be on your way! *All I want is a little bit of blood!*"

She was trying to distract me again, and it was working. Maybe I could give her some blood, and maybe she *would* let us go in peace. But she might not be capable of keeping her word, and I was certain that I was just inches away from breaking her power over me.

Little did I know, she was standing right behind me, tall and black, claws extended over my head as they worked their illusions.

Twenty Three

"*Get out!*" I screamed, pushing the universal force as hard as I possibly could one last time. It exploded from me and the metaphysical claws embedded in my skull slipped away. I saw the room as it was at last. It was gold and gem filled, but it didn't look radiant as it had been, and I saw the two lumps clearly for the first time. Where I had seen the droplet of blood to my left, Liz lay face down and unmoving. The spell that had made her look like me had been stripped away and her mass of black hair was matted with congealing blood.

Caymn was to my right, or at least I thought it was he. Almost nothing about him looked the same. Instead of having the soft wavy locks I'd come to know him with, he had two yellow horns protruding from the top of his bald head. Where his skin had been flawlessly smooth before, it looked to be the scaled skin of a lizard, mostly ivory, but becoming yellow at his clawed hands. I recognized his facial features, but half of his face was a black, bloody mask, his jaw hanging crookedly, and one eye either gone or hidden in blood. His visible eye was red and goat-slitted like I remembered, fluttering in an effort to stay open.

Seeing my friends so brutally beaten made me feel a flurry of strong emotions. I wanted to run to Caymn, but before I made my first step in his direction, a hand covered my mouth, thin, yet impossibly hard and muscled.

"Such a waste for such strong blood to be in such a useless body," she whispered in my ear as she snaked her other arm around me, pinning my arms to my sides with an iron-like grasp. "I'll make better use of your blood than you ever could, I promise."

I bit into her hand, but it was too hard, like armored steel, and didn't give way like skin is supposed to. Pain radiated through my teeth and jaw like I had just tried to bite a steel pipe. I screamed loudly in frustration, kicking as hard as humanly possible and trying desperately to escape her grip. I looked at Caymn once more, despair starting to take over, but when I saw his red eye open, wider than ever, my kicking slowed. I watched his jaw move as he tried to say something. It moved in a way it shouldn't, not because he wasn't human, but because it was nearly broken off. He coughed and black blood spurted out onto the floor. He was going to die, and it was up to me to save us, but I didn't know what to do!

I don't know what he had been trying to say, but a thought suddenly occurred to me. I couldn't fight her with my human abilities alone. I couldn't expect to win against her by kicking my little girl legs at her. I had already used the universal force to push her illusions away. I wasn't sure what I could do with the universal power, but it had already helped me once.

She was talking to me, but I wasn't listening, just pulling the universal power into myself. Without thinking about it, I silently asked God to give me as much of the universe's power as he would allow me to have. I realized too late that I wasn't supposed to pray, but there was nothing I could do to take it back, nor did I want to. Like someone had turned on a faucet that before had just been steadily dripping, I no longer had to pull on the universal force, and it poured into me. I felt more of it than I ever had before, my skin feeling as if it sparked and popped with electricity. She must have realized I wasn't listening, because suddenly she violently shook me. I shut the metaphysical door, locking the force inside myself before I could lose any of it. At the edge of my vision I could see her face peering over my shoulder, black and slick. Pain radiated through my scalp when she yanked my head down by my hair, forcing me to look at my friends and away from her face. "Look at your friends," she hissed in my ear, her voice losing its melodic edge. I looked at them and Caymn's red eye staring at me drew my attention. He was making horrible, gurgling noises and I couldn't tell if he was trying to speak or if he was choking on his own saliva and blood. It crushed me to see him in so much pain, though I didn't dare look away. Even in this form, his true form, I loved him. Yes, I was sure now. I loved him.

"Promise me your blood, and they will walk away from this," she said, lowering her hand from my mouth to my throat so I could speak a little easier.

"Promise you my blood?" I snarled, and the depth of my voice that boomed off the walls startled me, though I wouldn't let that surprise make me lose my forcefulness. "Why don't you just take it if you want it so badly?"

She seemed even more surprised than I was at the change in my voice and when she peered down at my face, her grip suddenly loosened. I didn't need more of an invitation. I tore one of my arms away and quickly raked fingernails I didn't know I had down her cheek. She hissed, releasing me so suddenly that I almost fell backwards. I caught myself, but I wasn't fast enough and before I could get away from her, she had recovered and wrapped those vice-like arms around me again. This time she got one arm tightly around my neck as well as replacing the hold around my body, pinning my arms down again. It felt like metal bars were wrapped around me, impossibly strong.

"Fighting will do no good here. Now promise me your blood."

I breathed heavily against her tight hold on my throat. "Why should I?" I breathed.

"Because if you don't, your friends will die here and you'll become my blood slave anyway."

I already knew that, but what I didn't know was why it was so important to get my permission! I doubted she'd give me a straight or truthful answer, but I needed extra time to think. "Why do you want permission?" I growled.

She laughed, nuzzling herself against me like I had seen Caymn do to her just a few moments ago. "Because the blood is tainted when I take it by force."

This wasn't taking it by force?

"You have two choices," she said, tightening her grip on my neck and giving me another little shake. My head was starting to hurt from the blood not being able to pass very easily through my neck, and my air supply was slowly becoming limited. "Sell yourself to me for the lives of your friends. Deny me, and your friends will die here."

Sell myself to her? It suddenly occurred to me that she wanted me to sell my *soul* to her! I had never really been much of a Christian, as in I had never gone to church unless for Easter or Christmas Eve when my parents asked me to, but I *did* believe in God. Could I sell my soul to her, so that Caymn and Liz could live? I looked at Caymn and I saw that his useful eye was staring at me, wide and scared. Not scared for himself, I realized. Scared for me.

I would not sell my soul to her. I would not live for eternity on the chain of Satan's mistress, living my life in my own personal hell until I was sent to the real one. Still, I couldn't let my lover and my best friend die here. As I bounced between two impossible choices, anger toward her built up inside me. The universal force pulsed through me like waves of hot electricity, angrily waiting to be released.

"Never!" I screamed, and with a newfound strength,

I flung her arms off of me. I twirled around, so much cosmic energy pumping through me that I felt like I was floating on air. I don't know what I'd imagined her face to look like, but I was almost struck with horror at the sight. The face that met mine was unlike any face I'd ever seen; thin with skin as black as tar, no undertones of brown or yellow as some human people have. No, she wasn't human or like anything living I'd ever seen. Her skin had gray and green undertones, like dark skin of the rotting dead. Her eyes were spheres of white, murky and filmy, making the appearance of death complete. Where her nose should've been, there was only flat wrinkled skin. Her mouth was lipless and small in comparison to her head, but equipped with too many teeth, long and pointed. Her large head was bald, tall black horns twisting through the blood vial headdress she wore. Her whole body was a mass of black, saggy skin, breasts hanging like deflated water balloons. From her elbows down to her clawed fingers, her arms were like a lizard's, firmly muscled and scaled. Faster than humanly possible, those clawed hands were suddenly around my neck, pushing me up off the ground.

I reached out to her, to push myself off of her maybe, or to hold myself up so I wasn't strangled. My arms shouldn't have been long enough to grab her, but they were. I hardly noticed in my angry frenzy that took over, but my arms were pale white down to my fingertips. My skin had always looked pale, but this was different. My arms were inhumanly smooth without hair, pores, or wrinkles. White and hard like the arms of a carved statue. My knuckles were larger, too, and my fingernails were thin and long like little knives, very unlike the chewed-up human fingernails I'd had. When I grabbed her shoulders to brace myself, my fingernails dug into black flesh. I used my feet to kick her in the stomach and catapult myself off her, tearing through black skin as I flew backwards. I tumbled through the air and with a strange liquid movement, I found myself on my feet. When I faced her, one of her hands was on her shoulder, black blood oozing through her lizard fingers, and her other arm was wrapped around her stomach. With some effort, she straightened.

I launched myself toward her, too one-track minded to feel even a glimmer of fear. She braced herself, for all the good it did her. I smacked into her chest with my open palms, sending her several yards into the door. She slammed against it, blood vials popping and oozing human blood, and the door cracked open behind her. Before I could take a step in her direction again, an ugly gray hand slid from between the crack. I hesitated as a black arm shot through the opening, then another one. The queen's sudden smile was triumphant as the golden door was opened wide. The demons basked in the red light of the strange sun, making them look especially sinister in that long stretch of time. I could only guess how many there were. *Hundreds? Thousands?*

They started swarming in. There was no other way to describe it. They poured in like bugs, too fast for me to understand their movements, hiding their queen behind their masses. I walked slowly backwards, fear squashing what little bit of confidence I had. The door closed and before it could be opened again, a demon unexpectedly pulled down a crossbar, barricading the door, and I heard screams of protest from outside. I was trapped, but at least I only faced a limited number of demons. Fifty of them, maybe. Still, too many for my comfort by at least fifty. They drifted around me, sliding against the walls and blocking all doors. I spun in circles, catching glimpses of ugly faces staring at me. I saw that Liz's head was turned to one side now, gray eyes opened wide. From what I could see, an oozy cut across her hairline had made a stream of blood that pooled on the floor, and I hoped that that was the worst of her injuries. Caymn's one visible eye glanced around the room and he tried to move himself up without much success. *At least they're alive*, I thought. *For now.*

When the demons had formed a perfect circle around me and my friends, they came to a halt. I hated to have any demons at my back, but there was no way around that, so I faced where the front door had been and where the demons were at their thickest. "Seize her!" I heard

Deamavarus scream from somewhere within the crowd, her high-pitched voice piercing my ears. No one moved to seize me, but some stared wide-eyed and others glanced at one another, their strange eyes making it impossible for me to read their expressions.

"What are you doing?" she screamed, and I thought I could see some movement in the crowd. "No!" she screamed in defiance. There was more movement as she was pushed into the open circle in front of me. She pushed back, trying to hide amongst them. "No! Get her! I am *YOUR QUEEN!*" She made one final piercing scream at them and pushed, but they shut her into the open space like they were playing a dangerous game of red rover. We were trapped in this circle together, and though I wasn't happy about that either, at least they hadn't moved to kill me. *Yet.* Deamavarus faced me, murky eyes filled with hatred.

A demon took a careful step out of the crowd toward me. It was a horrible-looking creature with a sickeningly-gray skin tone, huge curling horns like a ram, and yellow goat-slitted eyes. "We felt your power wash over the city," he said, voice surprisingly smooth and welcoming, reminding me of a radio host. "It pushed her power away for as far as we could see." They could see my power? That was interesting.

"I can feel the power now," one demon said, squirming like that pleased him. A humming sound rose up as the demons murmured to one another. "A new queen," several voices whispered, echoing through the room.

"Crassus!" screamed Deamavarus. "Crassus! Where is Crassus?"

The grayish demon, evidently the spokesperson for the others, looked at her and smiled a hideous grin that revealed too many black pointed teeth. "Crassus has gone to hide in a hole. No doubt, he too awaits his own demise."

"Kill the queen!" an unseen demon screamed. The phrase was repeated and whispered throughout the room.

"To become our queen, we would ask that you kill the old one," said the yellow-eyed spokesperson, looking toward me again.

"You want me to be your queen?" I asked, dumbfounded.

There was more murmuring and nodding of heads.

"Wait!" Deamavarus screamed. "She can't be the queen..." She wanted to say what I was, but she paused. I could see in her face that she was contemplating revealing my identity, but then she would lose any chance to have me and my blood. Maybe she thought if she could disable me, she could have me. But if I killed her, her effort would all have been for nothing. Then again, I was just a weak half-human. The chances were probably in her favor.

"We already know she's not from the Third City!" another demon yelled, misunderstanding.

"And we don't care!" another hissed.

Deamavarus glared at me. I looked toward Caymn lying on the floor, hoping for some sort of help. He had managed to turn himself over on his side and though he was healing at a quick rate—*thank God!*—it was not quick enough to be of any help. He shook his head at me. "Don't," he said through his offset jaw.

Don't? This was my only chance to get out of this! To kill her was what we'd come for! And he was shaking his head no? Demons encircled him suddenly, blocking him from my view. I took a step to stop them, but they didn't hurt him, just pulled him into their masses, preventing him from further assisting me.

Suddenly Deamavarus slammed into me, claws spread and going for my jugular. I was fast to react, faster than I would've thought I could be, and swatted her arms away with a flick of my hand. With my other hand I grabbed her neck and squeezed. Nothing about the feel of her skin felt normal. It felt like iron. Iron that within seconds was bending and cracking underneath my fingers.

"No," she choked out. I forced her down, pushing her to the ground as she tried to pry my fingers from her throat without success. I sat on top of her, pinning her arms down with my legs. I saw a look of pure panic and surprise in her wide, filmy eyes. I had her completely immobilized. "She's a..." I gripped tighter, squeezing the words back down her throat. Her neck seemed to tear underneath my white fingers, oozing slick, black blood. She squirmed, but it did no good. I wasn't sure how this was possible, but I didn't question it, just kept pushing her harder into the ground. I pushed with all my might and began to slip forward on top of her, almost pushing her head from the rest of her body like I was going to pop it off. I doubt that would've worked, but it didn't matter, because then everything unexpectedly changed.

I heard a little pop of glass breaking, hardly audible, and at the same moment the universal force escaped me. It seemed to gush out of my mouth, unseen and unheard, but the lack of power made me feel like I had just exhaled my last breath. As her power took the place of mine, I found myself staring down at a young, doll-like girl with flowing golden hair and citrine eyes. There was no blood visible on her slender neck, and I could no longer feel the warm stickiness I had felt seconds prior. The room shone bright around me and the figures that surrounded me were not ugly creatures, but beautiful, almost heavenly, beings.

With a sudden chokehold on my neck, I was flung onto the hard ground so hard that spots exploded across my vision. For a split second, unable to move, I saw the golden ceiling above me, and then her face filled my vision. I tried to turn my head, to search for Caymn, but her grasp on my throat was immovable. I hadn't caught my bearings yet, but still, she continued to press down on my neck, squeezing the life out of me as I had done to her. "Doesn't feel good, does it?" she snarled.

What had just happened? I wondered, trying to think through the fog of my brain. I could feel something wet and oddly slimy on my hip and I realized that one of the cursed earrings Caymn had given me had broken and the contents were spilled onto my skin. It didn't really matter what I looked like now, but if I could have seen myself, I was sure I would have had curly golden hair and dark green eyes. The problem was that the curse that changed me physically also shielded me from my abilities. The spots were growing in my vision, blocking her out. *Stay awake!* I told myself. *You have to make it out of this!* I desperately tried to pry her fingers off my throat with one hand and rub the wet, slimy spot on my robe with my other hand, but I was only successful at moving it around on my skin. After what seemed like an eternity, I realized that she wasn't going to release the pressure on my throat. As I looked into her too-wide golden eyes, I saw the unrestrained excitement in them. Then I remembered the other cursed earring in my pocket, the one designed to send me home. When I found it through my robe, I slammed my fist against it, hoping to break it onto my skin like the other one. Pain radiated from my side as I slammed my fist down, but I struck the earring a second time, a third. Finally, on the fourth, I felt the glass break. My ears popped and I felt the familiar swift kick to the stomach. Any air that had been in my lungs whooshed out, and I expected to fall into the familiar darkness that came when traveling between universes. A few agonizing seconds passed and as I stared up at the golden-haired queen, I wondered, *Why isn't it working?* I desperately tried to breathe, but nothing would come into my lungs.

She leaned in close, all of her weight on my throat. "I'll make sure you won't escape this time," she whispered for only me to hear. When she pulled back, her eyes glowed gold. I wasn't sure how, but she was blocking the curse from taking me away. *I'm going to die*, I realized.

My impending death was my only thought after that. I thrashed against her, kicking my legs as hard as I could. I furiously tried to dig on her face or pull her fingers from my neck. It did no good. She kept her face easily out of my way, and the fingers that compressed my airway were secure. I began to stop feeling the pain in my throat and only felt panic swallowing me alive. Then all I could manage were pathetic kicks and pushes. It seemed like a bad dream; when you try so hard to get away, but you can only move at turtle-speed. It was about to be over. I heard a deafening roar of pure anger, so pain-filled that even in my state, it pierced me. Caymn, I knew. I began to feel nothing and darkness filled my vision.

Twenty Four

I gasped and leaped upright, causing dark spots to cross my vision again. Something pushed against my chest and when I frantically pushed back, it reminded me of a seatbelt. That couldn't be right, could it? I blinked, trying to focus and make sense of shapes behind the blinding light that invaded my eyesight.

"Cara?" I turned my head toward the voice so quickly that it was painful. I blinked a few more times and Darlene, sitting in a driver's seat next to me, came faintly into view. I slumped back in my seat, too relieved to respond. I was not dead. I couldn't believe it. The sudden burst of energy I had upon waking was gone and I sank into a state of semi-consciousness.

"We didn't even know if it was you at first," I heard her say. "We thought for sure we had summoned someone else by accident." I almost couldn't hear her over the ringing in my ears.

I laid my head against the window, warm from the sun, and closed my eyes. "I want to go home," I whispered hoarsely. I almost couldn't believe the pain just whispering caused me, and I silently vowed never to speak again.

I must have fallen asleep then, because something Darlene said woke me. The first thing that my eyes focused on through the window was my family, standing at a hospital's drop-off area. I saw Bruce's hopeful face twist into an expression of horror as the station wagon pulled up next to them. My mom was crying and nearly launched herself for my door handle before the car even came to a complete stop. As soon my seatbelt was off, I was in her arms. "Baby, what happened to—?" Sobs burst from her mouth, suspending her words. When sobs erupted from my own mouth, I felt excruciating pain in my throat, and I immediately tried to suppress the sounds from escaping.

Bruce exchanged some words with Darlene, thanking her, and when I turned to look at them, I saw Tansy slide into the passenger seat. I hadn't even realized she had been in the backseat.

"Here, we brought you some shoes," my mom said, pulling some flip-flops out of her purse and putting them down for me to slip into. I hadn't even realized I was barefoot and when I looked down, I saw that either Tansy or Darlene had replaced my robe with an oversized sweatshirt and mesh basketball shorts. I slipped into the flip-flops slowly, my mother's arms steadying me. "We're going inside," she snapped at my step-father when it became evident that he wanted to talk longer. When I was ushered inside the cool lobby, Jessie in tow, a numbness came over me. I didn't even attempt to conjure up a story, not able to grasp a clear thought in the fog of my brain. When the nurses at the front desk saw me, they sprang into action, something I wasn't familiar with when going to the doctors. One nurse began asking my mother questions while another nurse called someone on the desk phone and I caught the words, "patient coming toward ICU." Before I knew it, someone had a wheelchair for me to sit in and I was being rolled into a hallway. Everything felt like a blur, like I wasn't even in my own body, but I vaguely remember going through several big double doors as my mom and Jessie stayed close behind. The next thing I remember is being in a bed with no memory of getting into it. A doctor walked in with two other nurses in tow. As he asked me questions, one nurse checked my vitals while the other nurse stood behind him and tapped at a hand-held machine, evidently logging the answers to his questions.

"Do you have any neck pain?" he asked.

"Yes," I rasped.

"Difficulty breathing?"

"Yes."

"Difficulty swallowing?" "Pain with swallowing?" "Lightheadedness?" "Voice changes?" "Headache?" "Loss of memory?"

Yes, yes, yes.

"Vomiting?"

"No," I said.

"Yes," my mother interjected. I stared at her in confusion. "At least that's what the woman that found her said," she added.

All answers were yes, except when he asked about loss of control of urine and bowels, which thankfully hadn't happened. The doctor gently inspected my neck, then started talking aloud to the nurse behind him as she tapped at her handheld machine. "I'm already seeing a significant amount of redness and swelling around the neck area. Subconjunctival hemorrhage in the right eye and some redness in the left eye, though not as severe as the right. Some petechiae on her cheeks, eyelids, forehead. Bleeding from the ears and nose..."

The way he described my face was alarming, even to me, as much pain as I was in. I touched my nose and just as he'd said, I found something dried and flakey there.

"Ms. Hansen?" the doctor said and I met his gentle,

brown eyes. "We are going to do some X-rays and an MRI to make sure you there is no serious damage done to your neck, lungs, and brain—that sort of thing. But I have a few more questions for you, okay?"

"Okay," I whispered hoarsely.

"Do you know who did this to you?"

I wanted to tell the truth, but even in the fog of my brain, I knew that I shouldn't. I swallowed to buy myself some time and I winced at the pain that caused. "I-I don't know," I said.

"You don't know who they were or you don't remember anything?"

"I don't remember," I lied.

My mom cut into the conversation. "She was found in the woods like that—" She made an effort to suppress a sob. "Passed out and barely breathing."

Bruce was led in by a nurse then, and my mom was further occupied with getting him up to speed as the doctor continued to ask me questions. He asked me so many questions—if I knew it had been one or two hands, if I knew the length of time I was strangled, if they had said anything to me while strangling me, and on, and on. I desperately wished I could tell this nice doctor everything, but I couldn't, so I answered as vaguely as possible so as not to give away my lie.

"Two more questions," he assured me. "What did you think was going to happen to you?"

"I thought I was gonna die," I admitted.

"And why do you think they stopped strangling you?"

Tansy or Darlene must've saved me. But how? Had Darlene gotten another one of her premonitions? However they had known I was in trouble, I owed them my life and I would be eternally indebted to them. "I don't know," I croaked.

When I woke up the next morning, I felt surprisingly

like myself. Thanks to some sort of pain medication they kept inserting through an IV, I had had a wonderful night's sleep and the scraping pain I had felt with every breath felt like a mild sore throat now. The previous day had been the worst day of my life, and if the beating hadn't been enough, I had endured a countless number of questions and tests. My mom had become hysterical when they'd asked me about performing a rape test, but she'd calmed down a little when I assured them it wasn't necessary. I think at that moment the doctor knew I was lying about not remembering anything, but I wasn't as concerned about keeping my lie believable to him as much as keeping my mother consoled.

As I blinked to focus my sleepy eyes, I saw my sister and mom sitting on either side of me, eyes glued on the TV near the ceiling, unaware that I was awake. I went to say something—good morning, maybe—when the newscaster speaking excitedly on TV caught my attention as well.

"...sixty missing people and counting in the United States so far. We are still unsure where these people have been, but there is already wide speculation that the mysterious reappearances could be *alien related!* One of these persons that has reappeared is said to have been missing for thirty-five years! People are coming in from all different areas of the country claiming they've seen someone appear out of thin air! Others are coming in saying that they have missed months, years, even decades from their lives! These individuals appear to have nothing in common except that they seem to have been held indoors for an extended period, and many appear to have incisions in their skin as if they had been studied..."

Caymn, I thought, feeling relief sink in. He had done it! If everything else had gone wrong, he at least had saved those people, and I had been partially responsible. Only a day had gone by since I'd seen him, and only a short portion of that I had been awake, but I missed him terribly. I desperately hoped he had made it out all right. *What if he didn't make it out at all?* The thought suddenly occurred to me along with a crippling surge of panic.

"Hey, you're awake," Jessie exclaimed.

My mom turned with a smile, but it fell when her eyes met my battered face. "Hey, how are you feeling?" she soothed, rubbing my foot from above the covers.

I took a few deep breaths, trying to calm myself. "Fine," I said. "Ready to go home."

"Something crazy is going on out there," Jessie interrupted, glancing back at the TV. "It's on almost every channel."

Mom ignored her, still focused on me. "I brought my makeup incase you wanted to freshen up," she said, pulling her floral makeup bag from her purse.

I did want to put on makeup. For one, I hadn't worn makeup in days, and it was part of my routine that made me feel normal. I was ready to get back some of my normalcy. I reached my hands out for the bag, but when she handed me a mirror, I wasn't prepared for what I saw. My whole face was swollen, especially underneath my eyes, and angry red dots decorated my cheeks where blood vessels had broken. The whites of my eyes were alarmingly red, the left one being bloodshot, but the right one having a subconjunctival hemorrhage, causing bright-red coloration to the entire eye. There were bruised reddish-purple marks scattered across my neck like a necklace and scratches from my own fingernails when I had tried to get my assailant off of me. I'd expected to have some cuts and bruises, but I hadn't anticipated it to be this bad. This face that had to be my own was just as alien to me as the disguise Caymn had made for me just a couple days before.

"You still don't remember who did this, honey?" my mother asked eagerly. I couldn't blame her for asking me over and over. I was her daughter, and she wanted to put the bastard that had done this to me behind bars. I wished it could be that easy; that I could name the person who did this to me and they could be locked away.

"No, Mom," I lied again.

"Could it have been that young man, Jonah?" she asked.

I shot a glance toward Jessie, wondering what she might have told them. She made a face and shook her head, implying that she hadn't been the one to tell them. "No," I said, looking back at my mom. "How did you even know about him?"

"We went through your phone," my mom said, unabashed. "When we went to your apartment and saw broken glass on the floor and your cell phone on the bed, we knew something bad had happened. We had to see if we could find any clues to where'd you gone. Your last text message had been to a boy you had gone on a date with on Wednesday, so we contacted him first."

"It wasn't a date! We were just hanging out," I retorted. I couldn't really be irritated that they had snooped through my phone, because it had been for good reason. Still, I'd never planned on telling them about Jonah or having Jessie find out I'd hung out with him. "What did he tell you?" I asked.

"He said that he had walked you home on Wednesday, but he remembered another man staring at you while you were out. He went as far as saying that the way this other man looked at you startled him! He sounded so sincerely concerned about a possibility of you being missing, we believed he was telling the truth and thought you had been kidnapped by the person he described. It made me think of when you said one of your regulars at Angel Oak might've kidnapped one of the waitresses, and we assumed the worst! We were about to call the police when we got a call from a woman saying she'd found you in her backyard." My mother's expression changed from one of calm reason to one of suspicion as she remembered something. "This woman pretended to not know who you were, but you had her number saved onto your phone."

I just stared, not sure how to explain any of this. I had always been very honest with them, because until recently I'd never had anything to hide. By the look she gave me, I could see that she wondered how many times I'd lied to her before.

"I want to know the truth, Cara," she insisted. "I want to know what you're hiding from me."

"Tell me what you're hiding from me, Mom," I shot back. "Like who my father is, for starters!"

Her expression was a mix of anger and confusion. "Excuse me?" she shook her head as if not able to make sense of my question. "I've already told you everything I know about him. What does this have to do with him?" She gave an uncomfortable glance toward Jessie, like she hated to talk about my father in front of her. I hated when she did that. She never necessarily treated me like the dirty secret, but at times like this, I felt like one.

I glared at her, not sure if I should accept the answer she gave me. There was something more that she wasn't telling me. "It has everything to do with him," I said. *Let her chew on that*, I thought bitterly. A few seconds of anger-filled silence passed between us and I began to consider apologizing, but a few raps on the door stopped me. The doctor from the day before walked in, smile very white against his tanned skin. "Hello, Ms. Hansen, how are you feeling this morning?"

"Fine," I grumbled, not feeling as cheery as I had upon waking.

Mom muttered to Jessie to press the mute button on the TV so she could better be involved in the conversation, and Jessie reluctantly did as she was told.

"Looks like we can release you very soon, but first I wanted to ask you a few more questions," the doctor said.

I stifled an exasperated sigh. "Okay," I said tightly.

"You do not remember anything from the past few days, correct?" he asked.

"Correct."

"Amnesia is fairly common with patients who have suffered from trauma like you've experienced, but that you can't remember several days is definitely abnormal," he said.

I had almost ached to tell this doctor everything the day before, but I was starting to get aggravated with the continuous questions. "Are you saying I'm lying?" I asked, letting my irritation show.

My mother balked at my rudeness, but the doctor didn't even blink. "No, I'm not saying you're lying," he said, though his expression hinted otherwise. "But strange things are happening, and a lot of missing persons have come forth without any memory of their time..." He groped for a word and finally said, "away."

There was complete silence for a whole five seconds. "Are you saying she could be one of these...these..." My mom glanced toward the muted TV with newfound revelation before looking back toward the doctor.

"Alien abducted people?" Jessie filled in, eyes bulging in shock.

"Uh, well," he winced. "I don't know if I would say they've been abducted by aliens, but whatever happened to them, yes, I think it's possible she could be one of them, and I'd like to do some further testing..."

I wondered if I should be impressed with him for associating me with the strange events or if he was just hoping that one of his patients would be one of these interesting reappearances. Regardless of how he'd put a small piece of the puzzle together, I had no intention to help him sort it out.

"Well, if you think she should do further tests, we'd be happy to oblige..." My mom began.

"No, no, *no*!" I started saying, my voice getting more high pitched with every no. Everyone looked toward me and stared, my mother looking slightly horrified. "I am *not* going through any more tests and I am *not* answering any more questions." I didn't care what this doctor thought of me or that my mom was embarrassed, because they hadn't been the ones to endure the countless questions *after* being nearly strangled to death. And I *had* been nearly strangled to death. There was no question about it.

Though my doctor didn't look happy about it, he had to accept my answer. "All right, well, a nurse will be in shortly to release you."

When he left, there was an awkward silence that

dragged on and I felt my mother's eyes on me, hoping that I would give her some answers. I sifted through the makeup bag for something else to look at, determined not to feel guilty. I could imagine the anxiety she felt when she'd realized I was missing, but telling her what had happened wouldn't do anyone any good. Unless my mom knew a lot more than she was admitting, she would think her daughter had gone off her rocker. Even if I could get her to believe that I'd been meeting with witches and abducted by demons, it would probably do her more harm than good.

As I emptied a bottle of concealer onto my face, Jessie exclaimed, "Missing Charleston local reappears?" and un-muted the TV.

"That's right, Paul," said a news reporter standing in front of an old brick house. "One of these mysterious reappearances has happened in our own city of Charleston. Behind me is the home of Amaryllis Cleary, who has reportedly been missing for six years! Here we have Amaryllis's neighbor and friend..." The camera pulled back enough to show a crying woman, relieved to have her neighbor and friend returned home safe.

"Oh my god," I muttered, not expecting this turn of events. In the back of my mind, I had known she had been snatched up by demons, but I hadn't considered that she could have been in Deamavarus's human meat locker.

"Do you know her?" Jessie asked, glancing at me before returning her gaze to the TV.

"Not personally, but I know *of* her," I admitted. Darlene had known from the first time meeting me that I would save hundreds of "lost souls," as she'd called them. I might not get any recognition for it, but that didn't matter to me. I smiled at my reflection as I spread the concealer on my splotchy skin, feeling better of myself despite my current unattractive appearance.

Twenty Five

A nurse was not in shortly like the doctor had promised, and I wasn't released for three long hours. It was seven o' clock in the evening when I was finally pushed through the hospital doors in a wheelchair, which fortunately was just a hospital rule and a precaution, not a necessity. Jessie offered to take me to my apartment to gather up some of my clothes for the next few days while our mother went ahead of us to get dinner started at their house. I had been all but ordered to stay with family until I got better, and I didn't pitch an argument. I didn't want to be alone for any length of time and I would have invited myself to stay if they hadn't. I thanked the male nurse after he helped me get into Jessie's Toyota 4Runner, and after I put on my seatbelt, went to fiddle with the radio as she slid into the driver's seat.

Every station she had saved to her shortcuts was

playing talk radio, and when I started scanning through the unsaved ones, most of them had talking as well. When I found that they were all talking about the alien abduction story, I finally left it at one. The story had become national news now, and people had reappeared on every continent. I was surprised by how much of a disruption the freeing of the familiars was causing, only because I hadn't had much time to dwell on it on the other side. I had only wanted to save people, but it finally occurred to me that the aftermath might cause serious consequences, especially for Caymn. Demons weren't supposed to stir the pot, and he was changing human history! I wished I could talk to Caymn to know that he was okay. He hadn't been able to save me, but I had to believe that he had been able to save himself. Anything else was just too painful to think about.

"Cara, I just wanted to say that I'm sorry," Jessie spat out. She glanced at me before returning her eyes to the road, gripping the steering wheel hard enough to make her knuckles white. "I know I've been really hard to get along with lately. And I know I've gone on and on about how hard marriage is, but Scott's the reason why I've been so short-tempered. I can't take him, Cara. I am this close to leaving him." She held up two fingers to indicate that she was *very* close to leaving him.

"Are things really that bad?" I asked. *How much could their relationship have changed in a little over a month?* I wondered. Then again, I knew better than most how much a month could change your life.

"Worse," she groaned. "Cara, he talks about other girls almost every other minute."

"What!" I exclaimed.

"And he's been talking about you most often these past few weeks. It's driving me crazy."

"Me?" I said doubtfully. "What does he say?"

"Well, when he got drunk one night, he said he wanted to have a threesome with you."

"What!" I exclaimed again. "Jessie... that's so... *disgusting.*" I wasn't even sure how to respond that. I almost couldn't believe that this was Scott we were talking about. Polite Southern-boy, Scott! Then again, I remembered the not-so-subtle look he'd given me over Jessie's shoulder when we'd gone to dinner at Kendall's.

"It used to be little comments like 'so-and-so looks nice,' but since we've been married, he's ogled other girls right in front of me, not even trying to hide it. My self esteem is taking hit after hit."

"I'm so sorry, Jessie," I said.

"No, no, I'm so sorry! Ever since we thought you were missing, and then when I saw you at the hospital…" She shook her head as if to clear an image from her thoughts. "I've felt so horrible! I realized I could have lost you, and the last few times I've seen you, I treated you like dirt! I've just been so angry and mean, but now I realize that you're not the person I should be angry with. Will you forgive me for treating you so horribly?"

"Yes," I said automatically. "Of course."

"Good," she said. "And if you want to tell me anything, you know that you can, right? I know there are things going on and if you're not ready to talk about them, that's fine, but just know that you can." The way she said it, I knew she meant it and that I wouldn't get any more pressure from her. Still, I didn't want to tell her anything before I'd had a chance to think things through. Thankfully, she became distracted with parallel parking into a small loading spot and was too occupied with the task to continue the conversation.

"You're not going to want to leave your car here unattended," I told her. "I'll just go pack some overnight stuff and be right out."

She was poised to take her keys out of the ignition, but after squinting at the loading only sign, slumped back into her seat. "You're probably right," she sighed.

"I'll be quick," I promised as I leaped out of her car. The jarring pain that shot up my spine as my feet landed on pavement made me remember my near-death experience just the day before and reminded me that I still needed to take it easy. It took a moment for the pain to subside, but when it did, I opened the green door off the sidewalk and took the stairs slowly up to my apartment. When I swung open my door and flicked the switch that lit up the entry, I thought it looked oddly barren. I focused on the brightened space and finally noticed that Amber's coat rack was missing and my coats were neatly folded into a pile in the corner. I walked into the kitchen, and though her table and chairs were still in the far corner of the room, we were missing the majority of our dishes, cooking utensils, and all of our refrigerator magnets—all of them belonging to Amber. Then I noticed the note taped to the refrigerator.

Cara, I have moved out.
I will be sending the landlord a monthly check until our lease is up. I won't be back and you'll find my key on top of the fridge.
-Amber

I read it a second time, expecting to find some sort of explanation as to why she would've moved out, but there was none. Amber had always been very short and to the point with me, but this was especially vague.

"Cara." I heard my name from right behind me and I jumped, spinning around and throwing myself against the refrigerator. An explosion of pain came from where I slammed my hip against the refrigerator handle, and I was certain that was going to leave a bruise. I put my hand on my chest and tried to catch my breath, already knowing who the voice belonged to before I saw that heart-achingly beautiful man standing in front of me. I hadn't realized that the sun had set, but it obviously had if he were here. We both stared wide-eyed for half a second before he rushed toward me and I fell into his arms. He made an effort not to slam into me, and when his lips met mine, they were more tender and sweeter than I remembered. After he pulled away from my lips, it was only so he could press his forehead against mine and sigh heavily with relief.

"You scared me to death," I breathed, and I wasn't

sure if I meant just a second ago or when I hadn't been sure if he was okay. *Both*, I decided.

"I'm so glad you're okay," he said, mirroring my thoughts and pulling enough away to gently touch underneath my right eye where it was swollen. "Or alive, I should say."

"You too," I said, trying to smile.

He put his hand down and with a sudden sense of purpose, grabbed my arm and started leading me to my bedroom. "There's no time for discussion. Crassus is looking for you and he's coming here, I'm almost sure of it. Get into your bed and pretend that you're sleeping." Then he was putting me into my bed, fully clothed and shoes still on.

"Okay," I started as he pulled the covers over me. "But my sister..."

"Shhh," he hissed, then cocked his head as if listening to things I couldn't perceive. When he looked toward me again, his red eyes burned bright with intensity, making every surrounding color dull in comparison. "Sleep," he ordered as he backed into my closet.

Though I was dying to ask questions or do anything but lie down, I rested my head on my pillow and closed my eyes. I silently prayed that my sister wouldn't walk in on whatever shit storm was about to happen. If I made her wait too long, that's what *would* happen. A change in the air that was neither wind nor smell stopped my train of thought. I felt a chill all the way to my bones, and the air I breathed in and out became thin and lacking in oxygen. I desperately wanted to open my eyes and see what was possibly looming over me, but I didn't dare disobey Caymn. A disturbingly wet and slimy sound disrupted the silence, and before I could stop myself, I was opening my eyes.

When you see death for the first time, the memory of it is permanently ingrained in your brain. It's nothing like watching an actor pretend to die on TV or accidentally hitting an opossum with your car, though that's jarring enough. I'm talking about staring into someone's eyes as the light behind them is replaced with a cold, dead stare. One second, alive.

The next second, not. It helped—only slightly—that his hand grasped a knife that he'd probably intended to plunge into me. This knowledge would help my conscience, but it wouldn't make the memory any less prominent.

Caymn stood right behind this figure that had to be Crassus, though he didn't look like the part man, part shark, and part goat I had seen him as before. He was beautiful like the angel he had been intended to be, but something silver protruded from his throat in a way that at first didn't make sense to me. When the sickeningly wet and slimy sound continued, I finally understood that the source of the gruesome noise was the silver-tipped dagger that was being yanked back and forth. The blade moved obscenely through Crassus's throat until Caymn grabbed the hair of his victim and yanked the blade out one side. A black spray went across my walls and though I thought I should be screaming, nothing came from my mouth. With another swipe of the blade accompanied by another nauseating wet sound, Crassus's head and body separated, the latter falling and slumping to the floor by my bed.

Caymn's face didn't look like the face I was familiar with, and I was frightened by a light that flashed within his eyes. I'd seen my debatably-alcoholic uncle's eyes shine similarly to that when he had his first beer after a week of being on antibiotics that he couldn't drink with. Pure ecstasy was what I saw for just a flicker in time as Caymn held someone else's head before me, almost like a prize. Then he sighed and the somehow glorious, yet disturbing moment was gone. I closed my eyes to block out the image of black blood and gore, but it seemed to be etched on the inside of my closed eyelids. My stomach heaved and a horrible retching sound escaped me. I all but leapt over the body and ran to my small trashcan on the other side of my bedroom as my stomach heaved again. I heard a sort-of sizzling noise, and when I glanced up over the trashcan to see the gory scene in the middle of my room, I was horrified again. Gray smoke poured from the body, and it withered and wriggled obscenely as if it were burning in fast motion. It was slowly disappearing while the head still stayed the same, frozen in a mask of ugly horror. Caymn pulled the red vial earring from its ear and with a sudden explosion of smoke, the head began to shrivel as well. I heaved a third time and in a rush, I lost my lunch. I threw up continuously in my trashcan for a minute and before I was done, Caymn was pulling my hair up and rubbing my back. I flinched away from his touch at first, but remembered that Crassus had come with the intent to kill or capture me, and I relaxed against his palm. I was grateful to have been saved and to have the demon that had threatened to kill my family dead, but I was also in shock.

I heard the front door slam and my sister yell my name, followed by her deliberate stomps toward my bedroom. When she opened the bedroom door, I heaved again, but nothing came. "Oh my god, Cara, are you okay?" She didn't give me a moment answer, but barked out a question at Caymn. "Who are you?" she demanded to know.

"I'm her boyfriend," he said, surprising me.

I looked around the room and was stunned to see it empty and without a body in the middle of it. The spray of black blood on the wall was gone. There was absolutely no evidence of the death that had just happened, though I felt there should be. As deeply as the vision was ingrained on my brain, there should always be physical evidence of it. I heaved one last time, and it hurt. My medication was wearing off.

When I glanced between my sister and boyfriend, I noticed their very rigid stances. For a moment, I thought Jessie could see his eyes like I could, but then I recognized her expression and realized they were having some sort of showdown for my protection. I ignored them then and slumped to the ground in exhaustion next to my trashcan of vomit. Finally, Jessie looked concerned. "This must be some sort of side effect from your painkillers. Just sit down and I'll gather your stuff together," she said, then glanced at Caymn. "Maybe you should leave."

"I'm not leaving," he said.

"No one is leaving," I agreed. "Jessie, my duffel is underneath my bed." She wrinkled her nose at me, but went to retrieve my duffel bag.

Caymn crouched down so that he was almost at eye-level. "Do you want to lay on your bed instead of the floor?" he asked.

That was where I had just watched someone get beheaded. "No!" I exclaimed a little too loudly. Jessie glanced at me and I cleared my throat. Oh god, how clearing my throat hurt. The painkillers were definitely wearing off. "No, I'll just sit in the kitchen." Caymn helped me get to my feet and I sat down at the table just outside my bedroom. "Will you go get my toothbrush and makeup bag from my bathroom, please?" I asked him.

He went to my bathroom to collect my things and in only three minutes flat, they had me all packed up and ready to go.

"I thought you didn't like me anymore," Caymn said after I locked the apartment back up and we were walking down the metal stairs.

"What?" I asked.

"Well, you hadn't answered my phone calls in days, and I was starting to wonder if you were over me."

I realized he was trying to convince Jessie that he also hadn't seen me in the last few days. His attempt to dissuade her was pointless, because I knew my family, her included, and they would believe whatever the easiest conclusion to make was. Jonah had described Caymn to my parents, so when they saw him, they would instantly recognize him. They would believe that Caymn had been my secret boyfriend and when I'd gone to hang out with Jonah, he'd gone into a jealous rage and beaten me to a pulp. Bringing Caymn to my parents' house was a bad idea, but I also didn't want to be away from him again.

"I'm glad you're okay," he said sincerely and wrapped one arm around me. "I promise, I'll never let anything happen to you again," he whispered in my ear. Our eyes met from inches apart and I felt my heart ache in my chest.

Jessie cleared her throat noisily, and with some

effort, I tore my gaze away from him. She stood expectantly by her car, waiting for me to get in, and I could tell by the look on her face that Caymn was not welcome.

"I'll take Cara and we'll meet you," Caymn announced, looking down at a car key and pressing a button. I heard an engine start from across the street and glanced up to see a shiny, black luxury car. Where had he gotten *that*?

Jessie looked like she had just swallowed a bug, but I tried to smile reassuringly at her. "Jessie, it's fine," I assured her. "I'll see you in a little while."

She sighed in defeat and went to her driver's-side door. I would have told Caymn that tonight was not the best night to meet my parents, but I couldn't find it in me to tell him so. He grabbed my hand and led me across the street to the shiny black Cadillac, only releasing me so that he could open the door for me. I smiled at him as I slid in and when he walked leisurely around the front of the car, Jessie sped by us, engine roaring. I sighed when he plopped down next to me, feeling all my tension melting away. "I can't believe you are here with me," I admitted.

"If I'm being honest, neither can I," he said, laughing softly. "But I'm glad I am."

"Me too," I agreed. He glanced around us and pulled out of the parking space, following the direction my sister had been going. "So whose car is this?"

"It's Elizabeth's," he said casually.

I had been so worried about what had happened to Caymn, I had almost forgotten about Liz, and I felt a pang of guilt for that. "Where is she? Is she okay?" I blurted.

"Yeah, she's fine," he said. "She's back in my home."

"Tell me everything that happened after you left me and Liz," I demanded.

"All right," he started. "After I left you to free the familiars, I had no trouble getting inside and freeing them one by one, but it was taking too long and every time one left, the shift in energy made too much noise. I started getting anxious that the queen would hear and that it was taking too long, so I worked very hard to send all the humans at once. As soon as

I sent them, the energy shifted so much that I was sure she knew I was there—"

"I think I felt it," I murmured, thinking of when the sand had suddenly drifted upwards and fallen, along with the loud boom.

He nodded. "I ran toward her main hall, hoping beyond all hope that she hadn't realized where the shift had come from, and as I gave Liz the signal on my scrying ring, I was suddenly in darkness." He licked his lips and let out a shaky breath. "She had wormed her way into my head and I was...lost in fear."

I wondered what kind of horrible fears a ten thousand-year-old demon would have, but I didn't ask and he didn't inform me.

"I was completely unaware of what was happening to you and Liz. Then, it seemed that out of nowhere I was free from the darkness, and there you were...fighting her and *winning*."

I huffed at that.

"Laugh if you want, but it was amazing," he said.

I could've said the same thing about him and his ability to free so many familiars at once. Surely the average demon wouldn't be able to accomplish that. We were silent for a few moments and finally I asked, "What happened after I left?"

"After you disappeared, everything all but went into chaos. In everyone else's mind, there should have been no way for you to get out of the queen's grip or the circle she put you in. Even I hadn't known you'd be able to get away, and I just stood there, horrified that you had almost died and I hadn't been able to help you." He glanced at me and I could see the guilt and anger on his face. "The demons that had piled on top of me to stop me from intervening, let go, and everyone erupted into conversation. *How had you been able to do that? Who were you?* That's when Deamavarus snuck back into her chambers, and when everyone realized she was gone, they turned to me and started asking *me* questions. I was so relieved that it took me a while to learn to breathe again, let alone speak, and before I could answer them, they started putting words into my mouth. They were convinced that you were a demon from another city sent by Diabulus to destroy the queen. They're all but in love with you." He snaked his hand around the center console and I took it, intertwining his fingers with mine.

"In love with me?" I asked, bewildered.

"They saw you in your demonic form, and you were...*beautiful*," he said that as if he were in awe. "You're always beautiful," he corrected himself and smiled at me before returning his eyes to the road. "But you looked like us in our true form. Our original form before the curse. We try to look like what we did, but never fully succeed at it."

"So I have a second form," I said, trying to process that. "That's what I've been turning into?"

"I don't know what random changes you've experienced since your curses were lifted, but what I saw in that room was like...there's no word for it. A shining silver goddess, or something."

A shining silver goddess? I thought, wanting to laugh at how ridiculous that sounded.

"They've all but forgotten about my supposed crime. They just think I'm some lucky fool that got caught in the crossfire somehow. They hardly think I'm worthy to have anything to do with you." He pulled my hand to his mouth to kiss it. "Which is true," he added.

"That's not true," I laughed. We caught eyes again and smiled shyly at each other. My heart felt full when I looked at him and in this moment, I was the happiest I'd ever been. I was on my way to my parents' house for dinner, I was safe and alive, and so was he.

"So then..." he said, continuing his recollection of the last twenty-four hours. "In all the chaos, I slipped away with Elizabeth. When I opened the door to leave the queen's palace, some tried to stop me, but then they were more interested in what was happening inside, which was nothing more than a discussion at that point, so it was easy to elude them. I slipped back into my house, left Elizabeth, and went to find you. By the time I did, you were fast asleep in a hospital bed."

That made me want to look at him. "You saw me in the hospital?" I asked.

"I found you with my ability to see into your world, but when I found you, I needed to see you...to touch you. I made myself to look like one of your nurses and went into your hospital room."

"You did?" I exclaimed, staring wide-eyed at him. "Why didn't you wake me or something? The whole day I kept on trying to tell myself that you were okay, but I was going insane!"

"I'm sorry, but I couldn't exactly tell you with your family around," he shrugged. "I just pretended to be checking on you for a few minutes, and when it started getting awkward between me and your parents, I left and slipped back into Limbus."

I didn't want to accept that there was no way he could have tipped me off, but when I tried to think of scenarios in my head, I couldn't think of any. If I would have woken up with a demon-eyed nurse standing above me, I would have put my arms around him and probably kissed him. That would have been hard to explain to my parents, and the thought almost made me laugh.

"I think I'm about to be in the middle of a demon rebellion. They're convincing themselves that the queen is a public enemy, but truth is that Diabulus never sent you to overthrow our queen. I can try to stay out of it for as long as possible, but eventually Diabulus's attention is going to be drawn, if it isn't already, and he'll get to the bottom of it. "

"And then he'll know it was us," I said when the realization struck me. I felt a surge of panic. "*We* are at the bottom of it."

"I know, but don't worry," he said firmly, tearing his eyes away from the road to give me a hard, determined stare. "I will not let you into harm's way again. I will do everything right this time. I am going to protect you." I wasn't sure how he was going to do that, but I tried to relax into the leather seat.

"The queen has no familiars at this point, and her only faithful servant, Crassus, is dead. I knew he was going to come back to her with his tail between his legs and that she would tell him that if he wanted back into her good graces, he'd have to snatch you. Even if Diabulus didn't send you to kill the queen, I think soon he will be taking care of her."

And then taking care of us, I thought glumly.

We hit a red light and slowed into a stop. "Hey, it's going to be okay," he tried to reassure me. His lips found mine and he wrapped his arms around me, drawing me into him. The light flashed green and the car behind us started honking before we finally drew away from each other and he stepped on the gas. We laughed at ourselves and I held onto him tightly as we drove over the connector, the long bridge overlooking the Charleston Harbor. The full moon was out, shining over the water and it was so beautiful, I didn't even notice the stink of the marsh. I was in love, and my heart felt as if it were filled to the brim.

"You know what?" I said suddenly. "I'm so glad Liz didn't sell her soul to Deamavarus or something. I was afraid that she might've even asked to be taken captive. She was so set on having her old life intact..."

"Oh, I'm sure it wasn't for lack of trying!" Caymn exclaimed. "But you can't sell what you don't have."

I leaned away to get a good look at his face. "What do you mean by that?"

"She already sold her soul when I adopted her as my familiar," he said, casually shrugging a shoulder.

I could hardly find my voice. "She sold her soul to you?" I breathed.

"No," he said, raising an eyebrow as if to say I should already know this. "She sold it to Diabulus. That is part of my job—collecting souls for him."

"I thought you said your job was to influence people to be greedy," I said in disbelief.

"That's a big part of it. Influencing humans to sin brings us closer to obtaining their souls, which is the *ultimate* goal."

I couldn't get enough air in my lungs and my heart felt as if it were sinking to an impossible low. It suddenly occurred to me that when Liz had had her breakdown, it wasn't because she just selfishly wanted to keep her fake life intact. She hadn't been crying because her fake life was coming to an end. She had been crying because she must've realized she'd lost her soul for nothing. *"We had a deal!"* she had screamed.

In the tree house, he had warned me, hadn't he? *"I'm afraid you would be disgusted with who I really am."* I had so easily brushed off his warnings. I looked at him then, red eyes shining bright when we passed under a streetlight, and I was finally afraid.

If you enjoyed
The Devil in her Heart,
look for upcoming books in
the series

meet the author

Photo © Jenica Prescott

Elle Charles was born in Santa Maria, California and currently resides in a small town in South Carolina with her husband and three small dogs.

For updates on upcoming novels: facebook.com/authorellecharles